Odd Birds

Other work by Severo Perez

. . .and the earth did not swallow him, a film adapted from the novel by
Tomas Rivera

Willa Brown & the Challengers, a novel

Speaking of Cats, a play

Soldierboy, a play

A NOVEL

Odd Birds

SEVERO PEREZ

TCU
Press

FORT WORTH, TEXAS

Library of Congress Control Number:2019943496

TCU Box 298300
Fort Worth, Texas 76129
817.257.7822
www.prs.tcu.edu

To order books: 1.800.826.8911

Cover and Text Design by Preston Thomas

for Judith

CHAPTER 1

San Antonio, Texas, Presa Street Bridge, 1961

Seventy-year-old Cosimo Infante Cano dreamed rarely these days. Forty-four years ago, after the Great War, nightmares recalled panicked flashes of enemy-held villages, his own death or capture imminent. He would awaken startled, perspiring, and grasping at the sheets.

On a Monday morning in April 1961, that same nightmarish anxiety revisited him. This wasn't Verdun, 1916. Stranded far from his apartment in Paris and his house in Cuba, nearly penniless, his luggage stolen, Cosimo stood alone on a bridge spanning the banks of a winding canal in a distant American city. He was terrifyingly wide awake.

What had happened? Five weeks ago he and his longtime lover and companion, Sara Hunter, were in Paris preparing for their temporary move to San Antonio, Texas. Because of family business responsibilities, Sara had flown ahead. Cosimo followed by ship and train to this cultural backwater. Feeling queasy, he grasped the bridge railing for support.

Approaching the Presa Street Bridge, fifty-two-year-old Ruthann Medlin nearly stumbled into the stranger in a Panama hat who was partly blocking the narrow walkway.

Stepping sideways to pass, she paused, her attention focused on the man's dark skin. The man didn't belong here. He wore a peasant shirt, cross-stitched with green and red geometric flowers across the chest. On his shoulder hung a weathered leather courier bag. A slender black cane drew her eyes to his legs. The man's beachcomber pants didn't cover his calves. He wore no socks, and the red espadrilles were secured with ribbons to his mahogany ankles. She inhaled audibly. Only women modeled espadrilles in the magazines she read.

Sensing a presence, Cosimo Cano glanced in her direction. A stout woman in a tweed suit clutching her purse to her chest squinted back at him. Caught staring, Ruthann turned abruptly and quick-stepped toward the Presa Street entrance of the San Antonio Public Library. She entered the chain-link gate at the rear of a 1930s Moderne building, featuring floor-to-ceiling arched windows on the first and second floors. Ruthann climbed the six steps to the loading dock and the employee's entrance before glancing back.

The man remained on the bridge, gazing at who knows what. She dismissed him as a passing phenomenon, like the blue heron that appeared by the river the previous year. He'd be gone by noon.

"Odd bird," she said to herself.

Before Ruthann could retrieve the library's key in her purse, Virgil, the black custodian, opened the door for her.

"Good morning, Miss Medlin."

"Morning, Virgil." The custodian's crisply ironed, gray twill workman's uniform reassured Ruthann. He closed the door behind her.

"Keep an eye on that vagrant on the bridge," she said.

Virgil reopened the door and made a survey of the street and bridge. He didn't see a vagrant.

"If outside agitators have their way, that sunbaked creature could end up looking for a comfortable chair to sleep in, quite likely in my department. Virgil, surely, cooler heads and good colored people will recognize that keeping with their own is better for everyone."

Virgil didn't reply. On hearing the door close, the odd bird from the bridge disappeared from Ruthann's thoughts.

"Miss Medlin?" Virgil motioned for her to stop. "Doctor Samuels wants you to see him before you do anything else."

"Thank you, Virgil. Do you know what his nibs wants?"

"No ma'am," responded Virgil. "Not a clue."

The library's second-story rear windows looked out from above the loading dock. Dr. Edwin Samuels, director of the library, stood in his office gazing at the bridge and what he could see of the river. A six-car parking lot, the river's retaining walls, and a six-foot chain-link fence hid the river's landscaped walkways directly behind the library. Only the occasional cypress trees rose above the wall. He could see the Presa Street Bridge and a glimpse of the river down the next block.

Samuels suppressed a guilty laugh on seeing Ruthann Medlin bolt from the man in the Panama hat as if she'd been startled by a rattlesnake.

He waited at the window until three sharp knocks at the door straightened his spine. Ruthann leaned into the room. "Virgil said you wanted to see me?"

"Leave the door open. Have a seat." Samuels looked at the clock. "I have a few things I want to go over with you."

"Like?" she asked. Ruthann appeared every inch a librarian in her tweed suit, reading glasses on a gold chain, and sensible shoes. She focused her eyes on him.

Samuels's boyish face and prematurely grey hair placed him anywhere between thirty-five and fifty years old. Ruthann noted his solid maroon bow tie and his blue and white striped dress shirt.

"*Who dresses like that?*" she whispered to herself.

Samuels didn't return her stare.

"Ruthann, the library board has approved new policy, and I'm implementing changes as of today for new staff and on May 8 for all patrons."

"New staff? What new staff? What kind of weasel things are you up to? Why didn't I learn of this before?"

"Please, Ruthann, you're being insubordinate. Don't make this more difficult than it has to be."

"How did Mayor Forester vote? I saw him this weekend and he didn't say a word."

"Your uncle's vote made it unanimous. Ruthann, since I'm aware of your sentiments, I've asked the board to allow me to tell you their decision myself. The city can't use taxpayers' money for legal fees to deny taxpayers their city services. Last summer lunch counters in all the downtown businesses integrated. The swimming pools were opened to all, with no problems. This summer the main library and branches will be open to all qualified residents. The board has set the date for Monday, May 8. I want every librarian, assistant, and page to know this is happening, and I expect everyone to comply with policy."

"They're going to regret this." Ruthann's face reddened.

"Ruthann, you don't have a say in this. What I want to know is will you comply with the new policies, or no? What's it going to be?"

"I don't believe the coloreds have a right to use this library. They have their own." Ruthann cocked her head, affirming her point.

"I'm not going to debate this with you," Samuels snapped. "It's been settled. What will it be? Yes, or no?"

"Don't you dare raise your voice to me." Ruthann stood. "I can get you fired. I've been here from the opening of this building. I've seen directors come and go."

"I don't want to fight with you. And yes, perhaps you could have gotten me fired if I hadn't gotten a contract. The mayor and the board want me to operate the library as a resource for the community—the whole community."

"What about the position of head librarian? I have seniority."

"I haven't decided. As of this moment all positions remain as they are. Jane Jenkins is still the head of the children's room. Ilene Fischer is the reference, nonfiction, and special collections librarian. You're still the head of the art and music department, and still in charge of training and supervising the pages. And the new hires start today."

"Today? No! There's been a big screw-up. The names at the top of my list have not been informed they were hired."

"That's because they weren't hired."

"You saw their applications. They're all qualified."

"The library board agreed with me that all new hires must be selected from the top scores on the general aptitude test given by the Texas Employment Commission. Starting this week and next, we're going to have busloads of patrons coming from the military bases. I'm bringing in extra help. These young people are smart, and more importantly, they've demonstrated to me they know how to use a library."

"I never had to take a test! We've run this library just fine before you got your sorry butt installed here."

"I'll make a note of that remark. I know your tenure goes back to the opening of this building, but today a librarian needs a degree in library science. Ruthann, the new hires I told you about will be reporting at 9:00 a.m. Perhaps you should prepare."

"I'll give your changes a try." Ruthann stared back.

"Ruthann, this is not a tryout. This is library policy."

She grabbed her purse *"They're going to regret this,"* Ruthann muttered as she left the room.

"What was that?" called Samuels.

"I said, I'm getting on this."

CHAPTER 2

On the Presa Street Bridge, Cosimo Infante Cano stared at the canal's landscaping below. Despite his heightened emotional state, this wasn't a nightmare. On the contrary, the day was bright, the temperature twenty degrees Celsius. The air retained the rusty scent of morning dew.

Sara had written to him about this view, a river sanctuary hidden from the bustling city at street level. At river level, a short twenty meters from the stairs, was a bench carved from native limestone. He assumed it was there she wrote asking him to come to Texas. The walkways, abutments, walls, and a pedestrian bridge were carved from the same beige limestone. At intervals cypress trees fourteen meters tall shaded the river and paths. Crape myrtle trees, dark asparagus ferns, and elephant ear plants filled in the planters. The river made an s-curve, ducked under a bridge a block away, and disappeared behind the office buildings to the right.

Cosimo needed to think, and Sara's bench below seemed appropriate enough. Before he could take a step, a young man wearing a white shirt and tie dashed across Presa Street, jogged down the steps, and sat on Sara's bench. Dropping a lunch bag by his side, he glanced absently at his watch. It didn't appear he wanted to know the time, rather how much longer he had to wait.

Cosimo reached into the courier bag and brought out an oversized pocket watch. He flipped open the case and the first twelve bars of Erik Satie's *Gnossienne No. 1* chimed. The time was 8:35 a.m. Cosimo closed the watch; the music stopped. He turned the watch and studied the sun face embossed on the back. Its mechanically animated eyes searched back and forth as if surveying this unfamiliar locale.

"It appears it may be just you and me, old friend." The watch had been a gift from Sara, and one of its charms was how the sun's expression changed subtly depending on the time of day or light source. Cosimo returned it to his bag.

The young man sitting on Sara's bench opened his lunch bag, tore a crust of bread from a sandwich, and tossed it several feet into the canal. He stood and watched the bread drift toward the bridge bobbing and jiggling, appearing alive.

Cosimo stepped toward the railing. A cloud of silvery, iridescent fish, darting and biting, kept the bread crust animated. A larger fish splashed the surface, and took the bread crumb in one bite.

In the shadows of the bridge, a couple kissed passionately. They must have thought they were out of the public's view. Cosimo stepped back from the railing. *Life goes on*, he thought. And as for a pensive moment by the river below, his spot on the bridge would have to do.

Five Weeks Before

Cosimo and Sara Hunter bid *au revoir* to their friends and assured them the move to Texas was temporary, two years at most, after which they would return to Paris where they retained a *pied-à-terre*.

As far as he could recollect, Sara had done everything correctly. She booked him first class on the *Queen Mary* sailing from Cherbourg and arriving in New York six days later. The concierge at the Roosevelt Hotel in New York greeted him like a celebrity, something Sara undoubtedly set into motion with a substantial tip, and partly as a playful prank to welcome him to the United States of America. She left instructions with the concierge for in-city transportation and train tickets for the rest of the journey. That first night, he called Sara from the hotel around 10:00 p.m. eastern time. The phone rang and rang until the operator ended the call. "I don't think there's anybody home. Try again later."

Later was not going to be possible. With the delays at customs, and keeping track of his luggage, he'd been on his feet all day.

The next morning, he continued to Chicago's Union Station on the 20th Century Limited. There he was directed to change platforms to board his connecting train. He stepped away from the car to call a porter. In those few seconds, the larger of his two suitcases disappeared. In a panic, he and the porter searched and . . . nothing.

His street clothes and address book were in the stolen suitcase. He had cash in a money belt. His passports, tickets, wallet, watch, and several of Sara's letters were in his courier bag. The thief left Cosimo's Panama hat, cane, and a small suitcase with the casual clothes he intended to wear in the privacy of the sleeping car. He considered checking into a hotel but sensed that his luggage was gone for good. He had the essentials needed to survive until he reached San Antonio.

Filing the lost luggage report took longer than expected, forcing him to hustle to make the Texas Eagle. Settling into his tiny train compartment, he remembered that with all the chaos he missed the opportunity to call Sara. "You damn fool," he muttered to himself. "That was your own fault. You know better."

In St. Louis the telephone operator told him storms had knocked down phone lines in Central Texas. Reboarding the train, he observed that the black passengers had moved to segregated cars. Cosimo decided to stay with his accommodations. A woman passenger in the dining car called over the conductor and nodded toward Cosimo. The conductor whispered loudly enough so those nearby could hear, "I think he's Mexican."

As the Texas Eagle pushed south, he saw the separate, but certainly not equivalent, white and black water fountains and toilet facilities. He called Sara from Little Rock, again no answer. In Dallas he began to think he had a wrong phone number. That confounded him. Sara never made mistakes like that.

The Texas Eagle pulled into the Missouri Pacific Station in San Antonio on a Thursday afternoon. He expected Sara to be waiting for him. She wasn't. He called; still no answer.

The vast faux Moorish hall of the Missouri Pacific Station emptied, and in his peasant shirt and beachcomber pants he became a curiosity to the depot employees. After two hours, he took a taxi to the address she'd placed in his wallet. The cab pulled into the driveway of a three-story red brick Tudor mansion in the well-to-do enclave of Monte Vista.

Carrying Cosimo's luggage to the door, the cabbie looked at the large house and at Cosimo. "You sure this is the correct address?"

"Of that, I am certain," Cosimo insisted.

"I'll wait out by the street," said the driver. "If this is your house, give me a wave."

This was definitely Sara's place. He recognized the wrought iron and glass door she had commissioned from sculptor Diego Giacometti, brother of Alberto Giacometti. A gift for her mother, she had it shipped and installed several years before. The house felt unoccupied, even with the lights on.

After three knocks with his knuckles, he lifted his cane and rapped with the back of the handle. A pale woman in a dowdy bathrobe and slippers peeked out from behind the glass and iron door.

"I am expected," Cosimo announced. "This is Sara Hunter's address, correct?"

"No, well . . . I can't . . . Wait here. I'll get someone who can help you." The woman retreated into the house. In the light of the setting sun, Cosimo scanned the neighborhood. Stately residences were set back from the street with driveways curving to the front entrances. Sara's address had a carriage house and servant's quarters. Broad manicured lawns and oak trees defined the entire block.

A gaunt gray-skinned man with a pencil-thin moustache and a cigarette in his hand opened the door. His pink watery eyes looked down at the stranger on the portico.

"Can I help you?"

"Where is Sara Hunter? I am her guest," Cosimo demanded.

"Hold on a minute there. I don't know anybody by that name. We're only here to make the property look lived in until it sells.

"Where is Sara Hunter, the owner? I know this is her house."

"The owner? I think she's dead."

"No, you are mistaken. Sara's mother died last year. This is her daughter's house, Sara Hunter, the daughter."

"Look, we're hired by the real estate brokers. We take care of properties when the owners die all of a sudden." He took a drag off his cigarette and exhaled into the air away from Cosimo.

"There must be a mistake. I know this is her house."

"I'm sorry. I don't know more than that. I assume the owner is dead and buried. Otherwise we'd be staying somewheres else. That's how I work."

"How long have you been staying here?"

"Two and a half weeks, about . . . " he said, tapping the ash from his cigarette into a planter.

"Dead?" Cosimo knees wobbled. A deep sob shook his body. His vision blurred. He shut his eyes and forced himself to concentrate. "This has to be a mistake. Who knows where she is? Someone must know I was coming."

"I wouldn't know. It's a hell of a thing to tell you. Honestly, I don't know jack shit. I could be wrong."

"Wrong? This is lunacy." Cosimo shouted, his voice breaking. "How can I find out where she is? We are moving here together from France."

"You'll have to ask the family."

"How do I contact them?"

"I suppose, call the brokers."

"And how do I contact these brokers?" he demanded.

"There're some cards here on the table by the door. Here, have more than one." The man handed him several business cards.

"I need a room for the night," Cosimo said, desperate to get off his feet.

"We're not allowed to let anyone other than the real estate people inside. I'll call you a cab and he'll find you something."

"Thank you. There is one waiting for me."

The taxi driver took him to the Bluebonnet Hotel on East Travis St., where he noted many of the guests were black.

The following morning, Cosimo asked the head bellman to call him a taxi to the immigration office.

"No need," answered the bellman. "We're right close. Go down St. Mary's Street to Houston Street; take a right to Alamo Plaza, about six blocks. It's Good Friday before Easter Sunday, though. Most of the stores and offices are gonna close at noon, if they open at all."

Cosimo felt apprehensive about making his way around an unfamiliar city. The bellman handed him a rudimentary map of downtown San Antonio. He followed the bellman's directions. Houston Street with the numerous well-appointed store fronts and the occasional Art Deco building conveyed a sense of successful Americana. Arriving at Alamo

Plaza, he couldn't miss the block-wide, five-story Beaux Arts Post Office and Federal Building, with brass gates and columns rising above the first floor. Inside, the post office was to the left, and the federal offices to the right. He took the stairs to the second floor. The male receptionist at the Immigration and Naturalization Service desk examined his passport. "You only just arrived. You have thirty days before you have to check in. Today isn't the best day—"

"I must speak to someone," Cosimo interrupted. "It is urgent."

"Sir, I'm sorry, today is—"

"I beg you. I must speak to someone, now."

The clerk closed Cosimo's two passports. "I'll hold on to these. Go back out in the hall and go to Room 203."

Two other men were in Room 203, a smaller waiting area likely used for test taking or filling out forms. Cosimo exchanged nods with a middle-aged businessman in a suit. The man sized up Cosimo's clothing.

"*Que pais?*" he asked.

"*Francia,*" replied Cosimo.

The man grimaced. "*Como?*"

"*Naci en Cuba, ciudadano francés.*"

"Humm . . . " the man grunted. "*Argentino.*"

The third man either pretended or actually slept.

"He's alive," the businessman commented. "His chest is moving." He laughed and gave the sleeping man's chair a shove with his foot. "Are you dead?" he chuckled. The man waved his arm as if to say, go away.

"Are you recently arrived?" asked the Argentine businessman.

"Arrived yesterday." Cosimo didn't feel inclined to say more.

Two hours passed. The building had gone silent except for the occasional distant opening and slamming of doors.

About 11:15 a.m., the receptionist entered. "This is terrible. I'm so sorry. I expected Mr. Carmichael to come in this morning. Obviously, he didn't. The INS office has closed for the rest of the day. I apologize."

The third man stirred, fingering dried tears from his eyes.

The clerk returned the men's passports, matching each photo to the recipient. "The earliest anyone can see you is Monday morning, 9:00 a.m. Again. I apologize." He turned to leave the room.

"Is there no one who can tell me what happened to one of the citizens of this city?" Cosimo called after him.

"Mr. Cano, I'm sorry. All state and city offices are closed for the weekend. The post office will be open tomorrow." The clerk ushered the three men out of the office, locking the door.

"Then, I need a place to stay. Something for a day or two, not too expensive. My luggage was stolen."

"Let's stop at the front desk. There's a list of low-cost housing options."

Outside the Federal Building, all shops had shuttered. What appeared to be a Spanish-era ruin stretched out on the left and a tall monument loomed across the street. Too dazed to take in the sights, he trudged back the way he came to North Saint Mary's Street, to the YMCA, and registered. He called the broker's number from a bank of three pay phones in the lobby. The phone went unanswered. Hungry, he found a Chinese restaurant open nearby.

Except for the dormitory, the YMCA's recreational facilities were closed. In the darkened lobby, a single light illuminated the front desk where a young man sat working on a school assignment. Cosimo's room consisted of a cot, a small dresser, and a door. He showered and used the toilets in a common area.

Lying on the cot, he wondered if the American racial divide was the reason Sara kept his coming to Texas a secret. If her relatives were as reactionary as she portrayed them, that might explain things, except that wasn't like Sara. The questions circled back on themselves, over and over. Was she or wasn't she dead? Had she abandoned him? The thoughts kept repeating, keeping sleep at bay.

On Saturday morning as Cosimo crossed the bustling YMCA's lobby, boys playing ping pong and billiards paused to look at the old man in beachcomber pants and espadrilles. From the pay phone, he called the broker's number and asked to speak with a representative of the Sara Hunter property. He left the phone number for the YMCA's front desk.

At Alamo Plaza, the stores were open. He had a pancake breakfast at Sommers Drug Store across the street from the Post Office and Federal Building. Entering the post office, he paused to study the Depression-era murals on the ceiling. The painting technique was realistic in the grand American style, similar to work by Thomas Hart Benton, except stilted rather than fluid. The main hall was tiled in beige marble with impressive Italianate chandeliers. Cosimo approached one of the Italian brass tables with glass tops and pens on chains. He wrote five letters on stationery he'd taken from the Bluebonnet Hotel: one to the concierge at his address in Paris, two to friends in France, another to a friend in Venice, Italy, and a letter to the French Consulate in Houston, Texas. He knew his own address on *Rue Delambre, 14 Arrondissement,* Montparnasse, but without his address book he could only guess at the street names and numbers for his friends. He bought the appropriate number of stamps and posted the letters air mail.

Exiting the post office, Cosimo paused at the top of the stairs. Alamo Plaza stretched out before him. He read on a plaque that the restored ruin of the Spanish-era Mission San Antonio de Valero was the site of the Battle of the Alamo in 1836. It spanned most of the eastern boundary of the plaza. Directly across the street stood an eighteen-meter-high cenotaph to the fallen of the battle. Two hundred meters south was a bandstand with a green copper roof, surrounded by Spanish red oaks.

Completing the perimeter of Alamo Plaza were the city's foremost commercial, civic, and medical establishments: Joske's Department Store, the Menger Hotel, the Medical Arts Building, Thom McAn Shoes, among others. Window displays were decked out in full Easter fashion with imitation rabbits, baby chicks, colored eggs, pale violet and yellow crepe paper streamers. Not that it made any difference to him; nowhere could Cosimo find the blacks and purples of the crucifixion and resurrection. He had dinner at a Mexican restaurant on the river level. The food was forgettable and a trifle expensive.

On Easter Sunday, the shops and businesses were closed. Cosimo forced himself to walk the city. Using the bellman's crude map with key points of interest, he calculated shorter routes to the post office. He ate Chinese again and found the movie houses open. At the Josephine Theatre, a film entitled *Room at the Top* was on the marquee. It starred an acquaintance of Sara's, the actress Simone Signoret. The story of a doomed love affair depressed him too much. He returned to the YMCA after twenty minutes.

Looking at the map, he saw how the river looped through the city, and found where the river passed behind the public library. That's where she sat to write him letters. He needed to see it for himself. He would do it in the morning.

✧ ✧ ✧

That is how Cosimo found himself standing on the Presa Street Bridge looking at the young man feeding the fish. A sharp cry of "No!" startled Cosimo from his thoughts. A slender young woman ran out from the shadows of the bridge and sprinted up the stairs. She took a step onto the bridge and stopped two meters from Cosimo. Her teary hazel eyes searched the surroundings. With her long hair, light dress, bare legs, and sandals, the young woman looked like a student he might see in Paris. She turned abruptly and walked in the direction of the library's gate. The man following her up the stairs appeared to be twenty years older. His closely trimmed hair hinted he was possibly a military officer in civilian clothes.

Nearing the library's gate, the older man caught the girl by the arm. She wrestled her arm free and kept her eyes on the ground as he appeared to plead his case.

The young man who had been tossing breadcrumbs to the fish charged up the stairs in three lopes. He noticed Cosimo but continued to the library's gate. The girl broke away from the older man, took the young man's arm, and gave him a peck on his cheek as if they were acquainted. On reaching the top of the loading dock stairs, she glanced back. The older man had gone.

Cosimo left the Presa Street Bridge and made his way to the INS office. What struck him as curious was that on Saturday the window displays at Joske's Department Store had been filled with Easter trappings. Now, Easter Monday, the displays had been replaced with summer dresses and picnic tableaus. Looking back across the plaza from the vantage of the cenotaph to the fallen heroes, he felt the weight of his enormous mistake in coming to Texas.

CHAPTER 3

Ruthann's three new charges waited in the conference room. Maddie Parker, the young woman from the bridge, stood when Ruthann entered, one hand on her hip, her feet in ballet's third position. Oscar Buscoso, the young man who tossed breadcrumbs to the minnows, stood next; and the third, Richard Krabb, a skinny, pale-skinned young man with a shaggy ducktail, remained seated.

Ruthann cocked her head disapprovingly at Richard's unironed shirt buttoned to the collar and long sleeves buttoned at the wrists.

"Sit," she ordered. "Is this the director's idea of our new staff? A gypsy, a hobo, and a shoe salesman . . . more odd birds."

Ruthann pointed at Maddie's bare legs and handmade sandals exposing her unpainted toenails. "Missy, you will wear proper shoes with stockings. And no, to whatever those things are on your feet."

"Can I wear flats with Peds?"

"Stockings or hose above your knees."

Ruthann noted that Maddie's interests listed dance and drama. "You'll be working in the children's department on the first floor."

"Richard Krabb, that's some name." The pale twenty-year old with the sunken chest straightened. In Ruthann's opinion, his scruffy Hushpuppy shoes and unruly hair made his future at the library tenuous.

"Richard, you say that your field of interest is music composition. I believe you'll have something in common with the fiction department. You might consider an iron for your clothing."

"They're clean," replied Richard quickly.

"Yes, well, iron them, and get a haircut."

Lifting her chin, she turned to the third hire dressed in white dress shirt, tie, dark trousers, and polished shoes.

"Mr. Oscar Buscoso, are you a shop clerk here to sell me something? Why are you here?"

Oscar appeared surprised by the obvious question. "Keep books in order, and other duties, I assume."

"You assume. A slow one!" Ruthann rolled her eyes. "You, my slow genius, will be working in the art and music department where I can keep an eye on you."

The three spent the next hour in the conference room listening to Ruthann read the library's rules and codes of behavior. On the long lists of "no's" was an entire section on sex. Richard pretended to wake up.

"No one is allowed into the second and third floor stacks alone. Anyone wanting to use the private collections must have research credentials from a university, or special permission from the director. Restrooms are for one person at a time." As Ruthann read, Richard crossed his eyes and held his crotch as if he had to pee. Maddie choked back a laugh.

"Something funny?" Ruthann looked up from her notes.

Maddie shook her head. Richard snickered loud enough to have Ruthann glance at him.

"No fraternization with other pages and library employees. No kissing, hugging, or handholding in the building by patrons or library employees."

She put down her text. "Books with photos and artwork displaying nudity are censored from the public. If anyone asks why the pages have been removed, tell them to speak to me. I represent the Decency Council."

"Censored?" Richard sat up.

"Does that mean all female nudes are censored?" asked Maddie. "How do you do that?"

"The offensive images are cut out of the books, male nudes, as well," Ruthann replied.

"But, isn't that destroying public property?" asked Oscar.

Ruthann flashed Oscar a dagger eye. "Nothing is destroyed. The obscene pages are carefully excised, cataloged, and placed in special collections."

Ruthann closed her notes and added, "Besides your duties in your departments, you will take turns at the front desk issuing library cards, giving directions, checking out books, and naturally, reshelving books. Finally, there is no smoking in the building. All food leftovers must be disposed of away from the premises. Sign the form I'm giving you stating that you've listened to this lecture and will comply with all library rules."

She slid the forms across the table. "Sign them in ink. You may take a break now and report to your assigned departments in fifteen minutes." Ruthann collected the forms. "We wouldn't have the likes of you working here if it wasn't for the Kennedy administration."

"Kennedy has only been president since January," said Oscar. "We took the placement test last year before the election. How could Kennedy have anything to do with us getting hired?"

Ruthann assessed the moment. These three new hires were unacceptable. With that she picked up her folder and left the room.

"I should have kept my mouth shut," admitted Oscar.

Maddie pulled Oscar aside and said privately, "Don't make anything of that kiss I gave you. I was trying to get rid of that guy I was with."

Oscar shrugged. "Sure. Okay."

CHAPTER 4

Cosimo entered the expansive quiet of the post office lobby. Seeing no queue, he hastened to the nearest window, retrieved his passport, and held it up for the clerk to read.

"I posted five letters on Saturday. Can you tell me if they went out?"

The clerk brought out a box with three letters on stationery Cosimo had taken from the Bluebonnet Hotel. They were stamped, "Insufficient Address."

"Sorry, Mister Cano. The post office needs more than a name and a city."

"These are famous people. Everyone knows them."

"There's nothing I can do about it. Without complete addresses the mail is going to be sent back," said the clerk.

"I sent five letters. One had an address, and the one to the French Consulate in Houston, Texas, did not."

"There's only one French Consulate in Houston. It'll get there." The clerk admired the envelopes before handing them back to Cosimo. "You have outstanding penmanship. If I could write like that, I'd never use a typewriter. Every letter I wrote would look like the Declaration of Independence."

The clerk leaned out to check the queue. No one waited their turn at the window.

"Are you all right?" asked the clerk. "You look lost."

"No, I am not lost. I am stranded in the city until I can contact friends for help. My address book and clothing were stolen."

"The consulate should be able to help you with that."

"My problem is that my belongings are here. It may take weeks before I can return to my domicile."

The clerk, a sympathetic young man maybe in his mid-thirties, smiled. "One of your letters will make it. I know the feeling of waiting. Right now, I'd settle for an official manila envelope from the Texas State Bar."

"What is that?"

"My bar exam results."

"Have you been to law school?"

"Five years of night classes at St. Mary's University. I graduated in December and took the exam in February. The test results come out in late May or early June."

The clerk's name tag read, Francisco Orozco. "Best of luck, Mr. Orozco."

"Call me Francisco. I gave the test my best shot, but they say night school graduates take it an average of three times before they pass."

"To achieve an average of three, a fair percentage must pass the test the first time," Cosimo said.

"I hope so." Francisco had the slender face of his European fathers, the dark eyes, straight black hair and swarthy complexion of his Indian mothers. He sported a neatly trimmed moustache that made him appear older. A mestizo, Cosimo concluded. His own lineage was just as American, only heavier on the indigenous swarthiness.

"Tell me, Francisco. Where can I find a good *papelería,* you know, where they sell paper and envelopes."

"Envelopes you can buy across the street at Sommers Drug Store. But for stationery, fine paper goods, you'll find it at Clegg's Engineering and Architectural Supplies. It's at the corner of Travis Street and Broadway. They carry everything, art supplies, surveying telescopes, slide rules. One of my favorite shops."

"Thank you." Cosimo dropped the returned letters into his bag and proceeded to the second floor and the immigration office.

The polished terrazzo floors, Italianate chandeliers, and brass handrails reminded him that the stone steps at the entrance to his local Cuban post office were worn concave from centuries of foot traffic.

A half dozen petitioners along with relatives and children registered for interviews at the immigration office. Cosimo took his place in the queue and after registering, joined the others in the three rows of wooden chairs under a sign reading, "Wait here until your name is called." It had taken considerable courage to come. In his courier bag he had a letter he hoped would save him.

Panic radiated through his chest. Cosimo took a deep breath and closed his eyes. What was he going to do about Sara's family? He had called the real estate brokers twice and left messages to contact him through the YMCA front desk. And what was he to do without his address book? Normally, he could have ticked off several solutions to any predicament. Now, he felt fatigued and brain blocked. Sara would have known what to do.

"Cosimo Infante Cano." A voice snapped Cosimo back to the room. A short, balding man in his fifties held up a folder in his direction and beckoned with his head.

Ernest Carmichael's small office had a desk and two chairs. He plopped Cosimo's file in front of him.

"Mister Cano, sorry we sent you home on Friday. What can I do for you today?"

Cosimo removed his hat revealing his white hair touching his shoulders. "Well, I am attempting to reclaim some of my property so I may return to France." He spoke in precise accented English.

"What property, and why do you want to return to France? You've applied for residency in the United States."

"I have been told my friend, Sara Hunter, is dead. I have no proof. She could be alive. Our intention was to live here for one or two years, until she finished her business dealings. However, if she is dead, and apparently there is no provision for me, I have no reason to remain in the United States. However, two trunks were shipped separately, with my clothes and art supplies. Sara is . . . was . . . also holding a substantial amount of money for me. If you could call the family on my behalf. "

"There's nothing we can do here at INS. You have to speak to an attorney. Perhaps if you check with the Cuban Refugee office down the hall. They have resources we don't have and vouchers for housing. You must declare yourself a refugee at risk of arrest or assassination if you return to Cuba, and—"

"I am not at risk. I am not a refugee," Cosino replied.

"Well then, you must make contact with the family. Your stay is good for six months. Getting anything done legally could take longer."

"I entrusted forty-five thousand dollars to Sara Hunter to keep for me until I arrived."

"That's a hell of a lot of money. How well did you know this woman? Have you considered she may have absconded with your forty-five thousand dollars?"

"What? No, absolutely not. No!" Cosimo gasped for air. "No, I've known this woman for fourteen years. No, no, no."

"I believe you."

"I was saying I have money, yet I am housed at the YMCA in a room as small as a matchbox. I bathe and take care of my biological needs in a common area with strangers. I do not have to live like that. If I have access to my things, I can return to France. Please, I have a letter I can show you that tells you all I say is true." Cosimo opened his satchel.

"Put those away, Mr. Cano. By law, I can't look at your letters because I am not an attorney, and even if I were, I cannot advise you on legal matters. You have a French passport. Have you appealed to the French consulate in Houston?"

"I sent a letter on Saturday. These are the French. It could take weeks before they help me. I cannot wait; I must help myself. For that I need my things and my money."

"There's nothing the INS can do for you. The city has a decent public library. There are newspapers from around the United States. There are research books that might help you find your friends. Do you know when Sara Hunter died?"

"About March 16."

"Go to the library. In the art and music department there is a reading room with recent newspapers. They should have her obituary. Check the *San Antonio Light*, and the *Express and News* March 17, 18, 19, even the next several days."

Carmichael's comment about Sara absconding with his money infuriated him. Sara was clearly gone. That was the only reason she hadn't answered his phone calls or met him at the train station. Larceny? The idea was ludicrous.

CHAPTER 5

Without having made plans in advance, Maddie, Richard, and Oscar ended up taking a few minutes of their fifteen-minute break by the river below the Presa Street Bridge. Richard lit a Pall Mall cigarette and held out the pack. Finding no takers, he put the pack back in his shirt pocket and stretched out on a stone bench. Maddie walked toward the bridge. She'd seen something curious there earlier, and now she couldn't recall what it was. Oscar walked along the bank searching the surface. Five minutes passed and no one said a word. Finally, Oscar motioned for Maddie to look in the water. A silvery minnow with a large iridescent dorsal fin swam close to the surface.

"Jeez, look at that," Maddie whispered. "Is it a tropical fish?"

"No, it's native, a sailfin molly, *poecilia latipinna*."

Richard looked up. "Damn, did you just use the Latin name for a local fish?"

"It's pretty common. That's the male."

"Well, Mr. *poe-cilia la-ti-pinna*," Maddie spoke to the fish. "May I call you Po? I feel we already know each other. How are the little *latipinnas*?"

"It's time," said Richard jumping to his feet. He clapped Oscar on the shoulder. "I wanted the job in the art and music collection. Now, I'm glad it ain't me, and I'm sorry for you."

Maddie elbowed Oscar, "Ruthann Medlin is going to keep an eye on you."

"Yeah, my luck," he mumbled.

Oscar followed Maddie up the stairs, his eyes on her lithe hips and well-toned calves. The girls he knew from school dressed altogether differently, either in dresses with petticoats, penny loafers and bobby socks, or straight skirts and pointed flats. At the top of the stairs, Maddie turned and smiled. She'd caught him looking at her legs. Oscar flashed an embarrassed grin.

Oscar's first day as library page felt like parochial school. Ruthann Medlin paced behind him as the nuns did on a test day. His frustrating first-timer mistakes gave her pleasure. She allowed him to waste twenty minutes pulling books and stacking them on a table attempting to justify shelf space before she let him know that the sequence continued in the next aisle.

"That's a mistake you'll never make again," Ruthann gloated.

"Thank you," he answered, silently furious and humiliated. He needed the job. At the last place he worked he made fifty cents an hour. This paid ninety cents and accommodated his class schedule. He envied his new coworkers in the other departments.

Ruthann took the moment of victory back to her desk, opened her calendar, and penned a note.

Standing at the entrance to her department was Cosimo, the odd bird from the bridge. She shut her calendar, rose, and marched toward him, waving her arms as if she were shooing crows. "Boy, or whoever you are, is there something you need in this library?" She stared at his hat.

Cosimo didn't react to the use of "boy." However, he recognized that the locals had a custom of men removing their hats when indoors. He took off the hat, and Ruthann took a step back. Cosimo's longish hair and prominent aquiline nose reminded her of a raptor, an eagle.

"I was told I could use the library," Cosimo said.

"You can't be here," Ruthann insisted. "Call Dr. Samuels, right now!" She shouted loud enough to be heard at the front desk. "And you, sir, boy, either leave . . . or you stand right there." Cosimo didn't move.

Holding a stack of books, Oscar watched the confrontation unfold. The other patrons in the room pretended not to notice.

Ruthann turned to Oscar, "Don't stand there gawking. Get about your work."

Within a half a minute, Dr. Samuels entered and went straight to Cosimo. "I'm Doctor Edwin Samuels, the library's director. How can I help you, sir?"

"I was told this was a free public library. I came to use the services while I am in town." Cosimo glanced around the room. His beachcomber pants, red espadrilles, and Panama hat were not the only issue.

"The library is free," Dr. Samuels said. "However, there are restrictions on its use. We'll need a local address, and I have to verify your identification and status. How long do you plan to be in San Antonio?"

"Are you asking me for my papers? I have passports right here."

"I need to know if you'll bring our books back," Samuels replied, lightheartedly. "How long do you intend to be in town?"

"I've been here since last Thursday. And for the time being, my stay is indefinite."

Samuels opened the passport to the page with Cosimo's photo and leafed through the numerous entry and exit stamps from different countries. He thought for a moment before handing back the passport. "Welcome to the library. Please fill out an application with your local address and we'll issue you a library card."

"So, you are the library director and border agent?" Cosimo ribbed impishly.

Samuels blushed. "Just bring our books back, sir. San Antonio has five military bases within thirty-five miles of here. People get shipped out, and our books go with them."

As Samuels turned to leave, Ruthann tugged at his arm. "He's a *nigra*," she whispered. "How can you let him use the library? We don't open *for them* yet."

Samuels pulled away from her grip. "The gentleman is a guest in our country, with dual citizenship in France and Cuba."

"Look at him, he's black as coal," she said loud enough to be heard around the room.

"Miss Medlin," Samuels lowered his voice so only Ruthann could hear, "Please restrain yourself. We're in a delicate situation."

"What if the N-A-A-C-P goons set him up to this?" she hissed, pronouncing each letter. "Call the police."

"There are no 'N double-A CP' goons. Ruthann, it's been decided we will open to all people who fulfill the basic requirements for residency. Please, as of May 8 we are a racially integrated facility. And I'm not calling the police."

Cosimo found the periodical reading room. The *New York Times, Christian Science Monitor, Dallas Morning News, Austin American, San Antonio Light,* and *Express and News* were mounted on dowels and hung from racks. The March 17 through the 19 issues were no longer on dowels.

Cosimo approached Oscar. "Would you still have March 17, 18, and 19 of the San Antonio newspapers?"

Oscar put down the book he was shelving. "Yes, sir. Have a seat and I'll get them for you." Oscar glanced in the direction of Ruthann and entered a walk-in alcove. Cosimo could see stacks of newspapers. Oscar appeared to know where the issues were located.

"Just leave them on the table when you're through." Oscar said, returning to shelving books.

Cosimo found the same obituary, word for word, in the March 19 issues of the two San Antonio papers. Under the banner of the Porter Loring Funeral Home, both identified Sara Hunter as a forty-six-year-old college professor, translator, and heir to Hunter Enterprises. Victim of auto accident on March 16, she leaves three cousins and an aunt. There was no mention of a funeral, a memorial, her years in France, nothing about himself, or whether she was buried or cremated. The confirmation of her death didn't make him any sadder than he already felt. It only confirmed what he knew: Sara never would have abandoned him.

He wasn't ready to return to the YMCA. He scanned the display of popular periodicals. There were three to six months of back issues of *Punch,* a British humor magazine. There were recent issues of *Saturday Evening Post, Time, Life, Look, Harper's Bazaar,* and a two-week-old issue of the English version of *Der Spiegel.* There was nothing in French or Spanish. One magazine caught his attention. *Filmmaker's Forum* had the familiar face of a well-known director. "The French *Nouvelle Vague*" read the caption.

He carried the magazine to the overstuffed leather chairs in the corner.

Seeing Cosimo pass her desk, Ruthann huffed, "I don't care where he was born. He's one for certain."

Cosimo placed his courier bag, hat, and cane on the floor out of the way of foot traffic.

Sara had met with that very same *New Wave* filmmaker in Paris to discuss her translation of an American pulp mystery novel. The coincidence of finding this man's face on a magazine cover here in Texas elicited a laugh more pained than mirthful.

He recalled the young director asking Sara, "What insights did you come away with when you translated the novel?"

Sara's eyes brightened when she was about to kid someone. "The author's characters are pale Edward Hopper creatures living in bleak hotel rooms. Having sex, not for pleasure mind you, but out of boredom. It's as if they're playing a winless game of tic-tac-toe. They soldier on because there's been a murder. I think it rings true of a certain American angst."

The young director didn't know whether to laugh or take Sara seriously.

"It's a murder mystery with a lot of fucking. Get it?" She laughed.

The memory was too tender. Cosimo wanted to scream, cry. He glanced around the library and took a deep breath.

Turning to the article in *Filmmaker's Forum*, after two sentences of dense academic jargon, he put the magazine down. This was the kind of writing he would hand to Sara and ask, "What is this man trying to say?"

His eyes refused to focus. The trip to the INS office, the confrontation at the library door, and the obit had left him drained. Before he could form another thought, exhaustion swept over him. The magazine slipped from his hands to the floor. He'd fallen asleep.

CHAPTER 6

Paris, France, September 1947

Sara Hunter saw Cosimo the day he arrived in Paris. She assumed correctly by the crates and luggage carried in by the truck driver that he was a new tenant in her building.

He lingered outside the doorway at the *Rue Delambre* address in Montparnasse, taking in the narrow street lined with late-nineteenth-century apartment buildings, hotels, a green grocer, and a familiar bistro.

He wasn't very tall, Sara observed. He wore a dapper two-button black suit and a gray fedora. He strolled toward the newsstand and tobacconist, stopping in front of the day's headline: *British Rule Ends; India and Pakistan Become Nations.* He purchased a copy of *Le Monde* and stared for a moment at the restaurant across the street.

Next door to the apartment building a frail woman at the flower stall struggled with a metal bucket of lavender-colored freesias and set them alongside the pink mums and white peonies. He handed the woman a coin, selected a bouquet of freesias, and strolled into the lobby straight for Charlotte, the ageless white-haired concierge.

Charlotte, in a well-worn apron over her faded dress, signed for the new arrival's belongings. On seeing Cosimo, she dropped the pen and rushed to embrace him. "*O Mon Dieu! Mon Dieu!* Did you come with the truck? I didn't see you."

"*C'est moi.*" He handed her the flowers, and they continued to speak in French. "I took a short walk to the corner, remembering the street." He held up the newspaper. "I have much to catch up on. But look at you, you have not changed one bit."

"You're a sweet liar." Charlotte patted his face. "What do you think of the old neighborhood?"

"Surprised," he replied. "I expected changes, and there are some. The place feels the same, tired, but the same. I can't say that about the train ride from Le Havre to Paris. The devastation, my god!"

Sara didn't have to eavesdrop. They spoke as if she wasn't there.

"We're not back to normal. Perhaps, there will never be a normal," said Charlotte.

"I see the bistro across the street has changed names," Cosimo said. "What happened to the owner?" Cosimo acknowledged Sara with a polite nod.

"He still owns it. The café was a favorite with the Germans. The owner changed the name after the war. *'Les Deux Canards'* was a code name for the local cadre."

Charlotte set the freesias on her desk, lifted a suitcase, and carried it toward the stairs.

"The lift hasn't worked since 1939. I'll have someone bring up your crates."

"The owner of the bistro, was he with the resistance?" Cosimo persisted. He followed Charlotte up the stairs.

"Was he in the resistance?" huffed Charlotte. "Maybe. . . . Until the last few weeks of the occupation, informers were everywhere. To know what he was up to would have been dangerous. As the Germans left the city, collaborators were paraded on *Rue Edgar Quint*, some naked, some with their heads shaved. The bistro owner who had done so much business with the Germans wasn't touched. Who can blame the collaborators, though? The Germans took what they wanted. After the baker was dragged from his shop and executed in the street for refusing to serve the Germans, people got the message."

Sara learned more about the neighborhood in that short exchange than she'd learned in the previous eight months.

Several days later, Sara was standing by her mailbox when Cosimo bounded down the stairs, wearing a peasant shirt, beachcomber pants, and blue espadrilles. He handed Charlotte a large envelope and money for postage. When he cleared the lobby, Sara casually approached Charlotte.

"Who's the new tenant?"

"Mister Cosimo Cano is an artist. Not famous-famous, but famous just the same. He used to visit every year before the war. The last time was eight years ago, he reminded me."

Sara tilted her head to read the recipient's name on Cosimo's envelope. Charlotte turned the envelope away. "Aren't you the nosy little mouse."

"I'm curious. Who's it for?"

Charlotte squinted and held the envelope at arms length. "It's to a Paul Éluard."

"*The* Paul Éluard?" Sara whispered.

"I suppose there could be more than one," chuckled Charlotte.

"And what's with those clothes? *Pajamas?*" Sara raised an eyebrow.

"Miss, I judge he looks quite at ease. Don't you think? It's what he wears when he's working. Outside, it is nearly always coat and tie, and *de rigueur* in the evenings."

That evening, eating dinner at *Les Deux Canards*, Sara recognized the notorious author Georges Bataille greeting Cosimo like an old friend. A few days after, she saw him dining with Paul Éluard and a man and woman she didn't recognize.

As a graduate student at the University of Paris, Sorbonne, Sara knew of Georges Bataille and Paul Éluard as minor figures in the Surrealist writers' movement. Sara hadn't read Bataille's books. He had haters and passionate fans, with the haters in the majority. Sara jotted a note to read his latest book.

Sara found Cosimo intriguing. Maybe it was the way he laughed, or how he appeared at ease with his dinner companions. When a Spanish friend arrived with a guitar, Cosimo removed his jacket, unbuttoned his shirt collar, and performed the *palmas*, the rhythmic clapping that accompanies flamenco. With his salt and pepper hair combed straight back, dark skin, and sharp features, Sara was reminded of a figure from a Mayan codex.

"I know he's fifty-six," said Charlotte. "I saw his passport."

"Does he like . . . women?" Sara asked.

"*Mademoiselle*, what a question. He's much too old for you!" Charlotte lowered her voice. "Are you interested?"

"No, not like that. But, he's interesting. I'd love to talk with him."

"I don't know anything about who he sees. He's widowed, and years ago he had several lovers, all women. You'll meet Leonor Fini. She's already sent him letters, and is famous, too. I don't care for gossip, but the truth is the truth; that woman keeps men like other women have cats." Charlotte shrugged. "There was this one nervy American named Margaret Manheim, a very rich collector. What can I say? She kept coming back. She'll probably show up, too."

"Were there many women?"

"I don't pay attention to those things. Now that I recall though, I believe there were only the two. They were here so frequently it felt like there were many." Charlotte lowered her voice. "I can tell you this. He likes derrieres. You should have seen him this morning when the Lebeq girls pranced off to dance class. He's not obvious, but he didn't miss a thing."

By her own assessment, Sara had a horsey Katherine Hepburn smile, a long torso with graceful breasts, a firm well-formed bum, and thin legs she hid under ankle length skirts. She had her hair cut efficiently short, in the style of nurses in the military, and peered through bifocal wire-rim glasses.

After several weeks of running into each other in the building's lobby and crossing paths at the local markets, Sara calculated when Cosimo would be dining alone at *Les Deux Canards*. She walked into the café, stopped, and smiled as if finding him there was a coincidence. He nodded.

She approached. "I'm alone. May I join you?"

He motioned for this tall angular woman with blue eyes to sit, and signaled for the waiter to bring a bottle of wine.

"*Gauloise?*" she said, retrieving the French cigarette from her purse. She lit one for herself. "What language should we speak? *Francais? Español? Italiano?* English? *Que lengua?* My German is a little shaky, but I'm game."

"I have ordered," he advised her in French.

"I'll have what he's having," she told the waiter. "We're going Dutch, by the way."

The waiter uncorked a bottle and poured two glasses.

"Dutch? What is Dutch?" asked Cosimo.

"We pay for our own meals," she said. "And split the cost of the wine."

"Miss, I have seen you out and about. Tell me, who are you? You speak French very well."

"I'm Sara Hunter from Bastrop, Texas. I have a master's degree in French and Italian literature from Smith College. I taught French at Texas State College for Women to young women who will never speak this wonderful language ever in their lives. I am in Paris finishing my oral exams for my doctorate on mandala symbolism in early French poetry."

"Wait." Cosimo laughed. "Mandala symbolism? In early French poetry? Mandala symbolism?"

"Yes, that's true. And for a living, I translate tawdry American novels into French."

"Now that is a noble and respectable profession."

"Taking trash and turning it into dross, noble?" Sara mocked in English. "Well, that's one hellava thing, ain't it?"

They laughed.

She held up her wine glass. "And if I may ask, what is your business in Paris? I saw you mailed a package."

"Perhaps this may sound pretentious. I am here to have a gallery sell my artwork."

"Why do you say pretentious? It's business."

"Thank you. It is business. In my home, Cuba, people, not all, but some, look at me dubiously when I say I am an artist."

"Well, that's prejudiced and ignorant."

"Not really. In Cuba, most people know me as the man who peddles vegetables," he laughed.

"What gallery is showing your work?"

"*L'Idiote Gallery*. Do you know of it?"

"That's . . . Yes . . . on Avenue Montaigne, it's quite the place. I'm impressed. I hear the owner is, shall I say, eccentric."

"One has to be crazy to be in the gallery business. Truly, Emile, the owner, has his moods and was a patient at Waldau Clinic in Bern for three years. He is my friend, and that is how I can have a gallery like *L'Idiote* show my work. Saying he's eccentric is kind."

"Well, that lets me off the hook."

Cosimo enjoyed Sara's company, particularly how she switched from French to a smart salty English. When they finished dining, each paid their own check.

She leaned close. "I have a cozy little kitchen in my apartment. I hate to eat alone and I love to cook. Tomorrow night at my place at seven. I'll make you a meal and we can continue our conversation. I've enjoyed this very much."

"As did I. I have nothing planned for tomorrow night. Dinner would be agreeable."

"About seven. You know where I live."

The following evening, Sara served a lamb shank with carrots, pearl onions, and herbs, on a bed of couscous.

"How did you acquire lamb? It is not available anywhere!"

"Let me say that Charlotte has a way of getting anything you request." Sara poured more wine. "Were you born in Cuba?" she asked.

Cosimo stabbed a piece of lamb and put it in his mouth. "Que . . . This is splendid," he followed with a sip of wine. "Yes, I was born there. My father was Peruvian, studying agronomy at the University of Havana when he met my mother. After they married, he took charge of her family's commercial farm, growing vegetables for the Havana markets. I inherited the farm in 1925. It's not very exciting, but that's my business."

"And what about your mother?"

"My mother was a talented pianist. She entertained, and we dressed properly for all occasions. There was a great deal of pretension at our house. In truth, we had the house and the farm and not much else. We were not rich, though we dressed as if we were. Mother supported my decision to come to Paris to study art when I was seventeen. If she had known how I survived that first year . . . I slept in doorways. She would have come and dragged me back to Havana in leg irons."

"Besides the gallery, are you working on anything else?"

"I am doing three illustrations for an endeavor my friend Paul Éluard is orchestrating. That was the package you saw me post. He's working with close friends on a conference for world peace. It is going to be an exhibit, a book of poetry and art, and a motion picture."

"World peace?"

"Paul is a pacifist. I have known him since 1916. I can vouch he has a good reason to hate war. He saw the worst of the trenches. For a time,

I evacuated wounded from the Battle of the Somme, until a doctor discovered I knew anatomy and made me an orderly. The war experience changed me. It changed Paul, most certainly. He latest obsession is a book, *Hiroshima*, by an American journalist. He believes that if something is not done, the atomic bomb will be the end of civilization."

Sara swirled her wine and took a long drink. "Cheery thought. And when will we see a result of this art show and/or book/movie?"

"The same question I keep asking. It will happen. When?" Cosimo shrugged. "Paul assures me it will make money for his cause. If not, it was for a good cause."

"Speaking of books, what do you think of Georges Bataille's new book?"

"Ah, you saw me having a cup with Georges."

"And he writes . . . such . . . "

"Yes, I know. Thirty years ago he became infamous for his naughty books. He declared he wanted to shock people out of their complacency. Truth is, Americans were buying his pornography and smuggling it back to their country. His latest book on economic theory, by the way, is not new. He has worked on it for almost twenty years. And, like the works by Jean-Paul Sartre, I find it incomprehensible."

Sara laughed. "No French intellectual would ever admit that."

"That is because I am neither French, nor an intellectual." He held up his empty wine glass; he'd finished eating. "Thank you for the excellent meal."

Sara's cheeks glowed from the wine. She reached out and took his hand, drawing him from the table to the settee. She found his slender fingers with nails trimmed into impeccable crescents particularly sensual. Sara removed her glasses, placed them on the end table, and planted herself on his lap. His scent was different from that of any other man she had been with. Unlike French men, he bathed. After fervent kissing and fondling, she gave him oral sex to orgasm.

He took her by the hand and led her to the bedroom. He kissed the back of her neck and unbuttoned her blouse. Her skirt fell to the floor, leaving white cotton panties with bristles of pubic hair lifting the fabric. Her body quivered involuntarily. He gently guided her onto the bed, removed her panties, knelt, and kissed her vulva. Within three minutes Sara Hunter, at age thirty-two, had her first orgasm brought on by someone other than herself.

CHAPTER 7

San Antonio, 1961

On Thursday morning Cosimo found a message taped to his YMCA door to present himself at the law offices of Bluhorn & Carnahan on the ninth floor in the Alamo National Bank Building at 2:00 p.m. He also received notice that Sunday, April 17, would be his last day at the YMCA.

Cosimo arrived at the appointed hour and presented himself to the receptionist. A well-dressed man in his fifties came forward to greet him.

"Senior partner, Estes Bluhorn," he said, removing his suit jacket and handing it to a secretary without a word. The scent of cologne followed him as he led Cosimo to a small conference room where piles of legal documents covered every surface. Removing a stack of files from a chair, Bluhorn invited Cosimo to sit. Cosimo rested the cane against the chair and placed his hat crown-side down on a stack of files on the table.

Estes Bluhorn exuded the confidence of a man at the top of his profession. The letters "EB" were monogramed on the pocket of his shirt, and his Johnson & Murphy shoes were polished a deep burgundy.

On one wall hung a series of old black and white photos of oil rigs with names and dates scribbled in ink, and on the opposite wall a photo of a man holding a rifle stood next to three dead deer.

"You're here about Sara Hunter? My sincerest condolences."

"I must know. How did this happen?" Cosimo asked. "She was here for no more than a day or two, and she is dead?"

"We believe she was returning from Wimberley where she had a house. She came in on the Austin Highway at dusk. A drunk soldier stationed at Fort Sam blew past a red light going seventy miles an hour and broadsided her car on the driver's side. If it's any consolation, she died instantly. Killed the soldier, too."

"How can that console me? She's gone. Her obituary said nothing."

"It was quite sudden."

"Where did they bury her?"

"She's not buried. She was cremated. The family hasn't decided what to do with her ashes. They may scatter them on the Blanco River, where Miss Hunter scattered her mother's ashes last year."

"Did anyone know I was coming to live with her?"

"Mr. Cano, Miss Hunter's family does not want any communication with you."

Cosimo shifted in the chair and asked, "I have a purpose for contacting the family. I need to access my property and my money. As soon as I have my things, I will go."

Bluhorn shook his head. "We have no evidence she left you money."

"No, you see, my money is part of the immigration application. She had forty-five thousand dollars of mine to hold in trust, until I could start a bank account of my own. I am not indigent."

"*You* gave Sara Hunter *forty-five thousand dollars*? And your address is the YMCA?" Bluhorn asked, incredulously. "That's an enormous amount of money. Miss Hunter was a very wealthy woman. Do you plan to attach her estate?"

"No, I simply want my money and those things that are mine, nothing more."

"Pardon my reservations, but sir, you do not dress like a man of means."

"My suitcase was stolen at the train station in Chicago. I stepped out to find a porter, when I looked back it was gone. I was left with the clothes I have on."

"That's terrible. I'm sorry to hear that." Bluhorn almost sounded sincere.

"Sara Hunter also shipped two large trunks with most of my clothes, my tools, and brushes. I need my things."

"What about the forty-five thousand?"

"Of course, more than anything else, I need that. I accompanied her to the bank where she transferred my funds from *Banque Suisse* to the Alamo National Bank downstairs on Thursday, February 25, 1961. I stood by her side as she did it. Look at her accounts. There must be a record of a deposit on that date."

"Do you have documentation? A trust agreement, or a certificate of transfer from your bank to hers?"

"No, I gave her the money in effective funds."

"Cash?" Bluhorn shook his head. "Forty-five thousand?" Bluhorn feigned a laugh.

"Not cash, a certified cashier's check. My copy of the purchase of the cashier's check is in her files. I have her letter. She mentions the date and the deposit we made together. I have it here." Cosimo reached into his satchel. Bluhorn took the letter, perused it and handed it back.

"It's in French. This isn't a legal document. I don't see any numbers."

"It says she was accepting the money into her account until I set up my own banking account. I can translate it for you word for word."

"The letter doesn't say how much she deposited, does it? It could be ten dollars. Frankly, her family believes you preyed on a vulnerable woman because you were after her fortune."

Cosimo's heart beat faster. "I believe in good faith. I have her letter; you have her bank records. I only want what is mine."

"Unless you have documentation that says as much, we don't have to honor your requests. Legally, you have no rights to her records. You weren't married."

"We were as much as married. We lived together for nine years."

"That's an empty claim without a marriage certificate, or document."

"I will request a photographic copy of my cashier's check from *Banque Suisse* which will have both our signatures. As you know, that could take two or three months. I need money now so I can return to France. And here you can help me. Sara had three paintings of mine she was going to purchase. If I had the paintings, I know where I can sell them."

"You're an artist? Imagine that! And once you get some cash you'll be rip-roaring to skip town. What was she going to pay for these 'works of art'?"

"Fifteen thousand dollars. Of course, not right away, but over time."

"Mighty shit!" Bluhorn coughed. "You think she owes you fifteen thousand dollars, on top of the forty-five she deposited in a bank for you? That's sixty thousand dollars. She certainly had the money, but if you don't have documentation you'll never see a penny. The family is adamant that you don't receive a cent."

"I only want what is mine. You understand that I will get the documentation for my money from *Banque Suisse*. This is not the end regarding my money. For the time being, return my paintings and the trunks and I'll be on my way. There's nothing in those trunks but books, clothes, and art supplies."

"You must understand I cannot release any property without the family's permission. And as of this moment, you have nothing giving you rights to any of her possessions."

"Those are my belongings! It is hard enough that I uprooted my life to come to this American backwater. You tell Sara's cousins and her aunt to return my possessions to me. Tell them I'm not going away until I have my things."

"I'll pass that on. If you can prove legal claim, and have a lawyer, I bill by the hour." With that, Bluhorn stood and opened the door for Cosimo. The meeting was over.

Bluhorn escorted him to the elevator, pressed the down button, and waited. When the door opened, he reached in and pushed the button for the lobby. "You have a good rest of your day," Bluhorn said, as the elevator door closed.

Reeling, Cosimo walked to the Presa Street Bridge, took the stairs to the river level, and sat on what he assumed was Sara's bench. This was madness, he thought. Not one iota of compassion or consideration. He sat there long enough for his head to cool.

CHAPTER 8

osimo had become familiar enough with the river walk to take the short cut it provided from the Presa Street Bridge through the city to Crockett Street, the closest exit to the Post Office and Federal building.

At the immigration office, Eugene Carmichael, seeing Cosimo in the registration queue, waved him into the office. "Did you have any luck getting through to Miss Hunter's family?"

"They're thieves, worse than my friend Sara Hunter described. They've stolen my money, and only you can help me."

"You know what I said last time."

"In that file you have here, there are statements from Sara Hunter attesting that I am not impoverished, and I have a letter proving I gave Sara money. The immigration department must do something,"

Carmichael shook his head. "The immigration office has no juris-diction over the affairs of US citizens," he said. "That's a matter for the police or the courts,"

"I have been advised that I can sue. That is madness. I have no money to retain an attorney. This morning I was told I must move out of the YMCA by Sunday."

"I know. They only house men temporarily. Mr. Cano, I can't help with your legal problems. If it's a place to stay you need, there's a situation in the Mexican part of town where some of our clients and transient workers stay. They're small shotgun houses, I've seen them. They're like cabins. This time of year there are vacancies. They're about eight dollars a month."

Cosimo shook his head. "Mister Carmichael, I cannot stay in this country any longer. I want you to deport me to Cuba. I am a Cuban citizen. From there I can sue for my money."

"Mr. Cano, the United States does not have diplomatic relations with Cuba. I can't deport you."

"What am I to do? Sara Hunter is dead. I have very little money."

"Mister Cano, refugees come into the city, twenty or so a day. Go to the Cuban Refugee Office down the hall, and they'll arrange for a place to stay and a stipend so you can eat."

"Here is the reality. I am not a refugee, Mr. Carmichael. Please. The solution for me is to go home to Cuba. I have property there. I have friends who can help me. My address book was stolen, and the addresses I could recall were so old they were useless." Cosimo leaned back, tired. "Sara had been like my wife. She had the addresses of my friends, and now her relatives won't allow me to see her files. I had become dependent on her. I did not realize how much."

"Mr. Cano, I recommend you accept the special status Cubans have currently. The refugee office is down the hall on the right. Take advantage of it. Your temporary visa allows you to stay six months, and at that point I don't know what we'll do with you. With special status, you're here permanently."

"I don't want to remain permanently. I would leave tomorrow if I could."

"If you can hold out a couple of months, the Castro government is certain to fall and the US will regain normal relations with your country."

"You Americans believe yourselves to be, as a nation, decent and fair, while on the international stage the United States struts like a bully with an atom bomb."

"We're not here to discuss world politics. Here is something you need to think about. Since the fall of the Batista regime, Cuba and the US do not have diplomatic relations. There is no way you can sue for your money from Cuba. Even if Castro falls soon, it could still take three or four years before diplomatic relations are restored. Will you accept refugee status?"

"To apply for status I must swear I am in danger of death or imprisonment in Cuba, and that would be a lie. If I were to seek asylum, it is possible I could never return."

"Hasn't your property been nationalized?"

"I turned my property into a cooperative in 1952. I wanted to spend more time in France, and I negotiated with neighbors who work my farm, to run it as a cooperative, with myself as one of the shareholders. Although I no longer own the property, I can return. Cuba is my birthplace."

"Are you a Communist, Mr. Cano?"

"If I say yes, will you deport me?"

"No, because you have signed your application that all your statements are true. If you are a Communist, you lied on your application. That's a criminal offense."

"How am I supposed to live in this outpost?"

"Outpost? Mister Cano, San Antonio is a vital American city. I think you should be grateful to be here. It's a Spanish mission city."

"Does the city have a ballet? An opera? An art museum?"

"We have Brackenridge Park, a fine zoo, the River Walk, and the McNay Art Museum. I hear it has one of the best Impressionist collections west of the Mississippi."

"Strange you should mention the McNay. I took the bus out there yesterday. It is far away, on the highway to Austin. If that is the best Impressionist collection west of the Mississippi, it is a sad statement about this country. Have you been there?"

"No, I heard of it, never been there."

"That is a shame. You should see it. Any comparison to the Prado or the Louvre would be a ludicrous. It is a tiny private collection in an elegant private home. It would not fill a corner of one room at the Prado. Thirty years ago I met Marion McNay in Paris, though that wasn't her name at the time."

"Were they able to help you?"

"No, Mrs. McNay is dead, and no one there was authorized to help me. Of course, with addresses like the YMCA or General Delivery San Antonio, I do not engender confidence. Look at me. I am dressed like a street urchin."

"Mr. Cano, that has nothing to do with your status."

"And where is the museum located? So far away from the working class of the city, they'll never see it."

"There is no social class here, Mr. Cano. This is the United States!"

"You Americans. Did you know that Pablo Picasso, the most capitalistic and commercialized artist in the world, is a Communist?"

"Mr. Cano, what you're saying is considered political speech. I'm giving you advice that I probably shouldn't. Zip the communist rhetoric, and make the best of it."

"The best of it?" Cosimo pointed at his own chest. "I am not an anarchist, Marxist-Leninist, Trotskyite, Stalinist, or Communist, but I may be a bit of a socialist and a capitalist."

"All right, I have other people waiting. Here's the address of those cabins I mentioned. Mr. Cano, you're a man of the world. Give the city a chance. Talk to people in the refugee community. They might possibly direct you to an attorney. You're right. San Antonio does not have an opera, or a ballet. We do okay without them. Make the best of it."

CHAPTER 9

Paris, 1947

After completing her doctorate, Sara remained in Paris to assist Cosimo with the art opening. Cosimo shipped thirty-two paintings and fifty drawings. He was able to reduce the bulky volume to a manageable and affordable size by removing the canvases from the frames.

Sara appeared at the back room of the *L'Idiote* gallery in dungarees, holding a hammer, and quickly became proficient at assembling the stretcher bars. As the paintings were remounted, she fell in love with every image.

Cosimo bent over canvasses intently applying dabs of paint, repairing dings and scratches from the journey.

"I want them all," she said. "I want to buy the man in the bird costume."

"No, it's for the show."

"What about the man with the mirrors?

"No."

"Why not? Once they're in the gallery, anyone, even I, can buy one."

"Please, don't." He looked up from his work. "I'm selling them because I no longer want to live with them," he confided. "You are the present."

Sara and Cosimo became inseparable. She wanted to know everything about him, where he had lived in Paris. When not working on the show, they took long walks through Parisian neighborhoods, retracing his life, talking about anything and everything. He introduced her to his friends, Georges and Paul, and of course, she'd become well acquainted with Emile, the gallery owner.

Seeing his past through her eyes reminded him she was young enough to be his daughter. As much as he loved her, it pained him that she might move on. He selfishly accepted her lust and returned a tenderness he didn't know he still possessed.

Sara used all her contacts to promote the art show, but when it opened at the *L'Idiote Gallery,* the turnout wasn't the mad success she had anticipated.

"I expected as much," Cosimo consoled. "I have been out of the art scene for nine years."

Sara's efforts weren't wasted. *Le Monde Libertaire,* a small left-wing anarchist weekly, welcomed Cosimo back with a rave review. "Figurative Surrealism has not run out of things to see. Cano's photo-realistic images of men and women going about their lives reveal absurd juxtapositions: In *The Mirror,* oil on canvas, a man watches himself looking in a mirror, watching himself looking in a mirror. In an etching, *The Music Lesson*, a man with eyes closed conducts a chorus of pigeons." Sara translated the review to English and submitted it through one of her clients to the Associated Press wire service. There an anonymous editor more than likely assumed the review came from the better known daily newspaper, *Le Monde.* The translation was forwarded and picked up by *Harper's Bazaar* and several travel publications. Gallery owner Emile Campo was quoted as saying, "It's unbelievable. I didn't realize how many people read *Le Monde Libertaire.*"

Sara knew that Cosimo's plan all along had been to spend six months in France and six in Cuba. For him, those months with her had been an island of sanity, with something he thought he would never experience again: ardent, loving sex.

For Sara, watching him pack killed her. She wanted to beg him to stay. Instead she affectionately, stoically said goodbye and dared not tell him what was in her heart for fear it might terrify him.

Each week she wrote chatty letters about the goings-on in the neighborhood. She allowed herself one sentence to say how she missed him. He replied in a narrative about whatever disasters he confronted in a day, bringing in cassava root, cucumbers, and melons. He enclosed a small drawing of an animal or a quick sketch of one of his compatriots. He ended each letter with how he wished his arms were around her kissing the back of her neck, a gesture that had made her irrationally passionate.

Six months later, on returning to Paris, Cosimo brought a bottle of *ron añejo* for Charlotte, the concierge.

"Thank you, you're a dear to remember me." She drew him close and whispered, "Your friend has been preparing for your return like a sailor's sweetheart. She had her hair cut and colored at a salon, had manicures and pedicures, shaved her legs and armpits in the American style, and trimmed herself down below and purchased condoms."

"How do you know all that?"

"I make her appointments and accept her deliveries."

"You are shameless." Cosimo laughed.

Sara opened her door wearing a tailored Moroccan-indigo silk shirt, taupe slacks. Her hair was perfect as if she only moments before stepped away from the salon.

She suddenly felt awkward. "Do you think my lipstick is too dark, too purple?" Without waiting for an answer she wrapped him in her arms, and put her cheek on his forehead. He felt her tears on his face.

"What is wrong?"

"I was afraid you wouldn't come back to me," she said in English.

"And I was afraid you would come to your senses and realize I am too old for you." She drew him closer.

CHAPTER 10

aving paid for his YMCA room through the week, Cosimo stayed until the last hour, packed his things, and trudged the two miles to the address given to him by Ernest Carmichael, the immigration officer.

His suitcase weighed less than ten pounds. Still, every five minutes he put it down to allow blood to return to his fingers.

The Buena Vista Cabins were obscured from the street by a decaying trellis held upright by thick wisteria vines, and by three-story apartment buildings on either side. The address numbers had become obscured by growth, and if there had been a sign for the Buena Vista Cabins, it was gone. The driveway opened to a courtyard with six shacks, each with a place for a car and a small landing, or porch, as Cosimo heard the locals say. Trees in the yard, like the wisteria at the entrance, shimmered with spring growth. Normally, nature's renewal would have pleased him. Instead what crossed his mind was that he had to come to the United States to become poor and desperate.

A Spanish language radio station chattered in the background, and the scent of grilled onions brought on a stomach spasm and lightheadedness. He hadn't eaten since morning.

A short man with a crooked spine limped from the apartment building to Cosimo's right. The shoe on his left foot had a platform to compensate for a short leg.

"I'm the manager, Pedro 'Pito' Vasquez, *a sus ordenes*," he introduced himself, in Spanish. Pito had a thin face and straight black hair with a streak of white that began at the widow's peak and was combed back.

"Cosimo Cano. I need a place for a short time. At the most, several weeks," Cosimo replied in Spanish. He put down the suitcase and flexed his fingers.

"Don't see too many people like you around here," Pito said, leading Cosimo in the direction of the cabins.

"I'm Cuban," Cosimo replied, lifting his suitcase and following.

"A-hum," grunted Pito, as if being Cuban explained the unusual clothing and red footwear.

Pito switched to English. "The cabins have no kitchens, and I don't allow cooking inside." Pito pointed to a fire pit crudely assembled with large stones and cinder blocks. A steel rack from an old stove served as the grill. "If you have a pot, you can use this to warm up beans." Pito gestured toward the cabins. "If you're here for three weeks, cabin number 4 has a new shower. Plumbers from Monterey put it in. The others need a little work but they're livable. It's eight dollars a week."

"The man at the immigration office said eight dollars a month."

"I don't know where he gets that. We haven't charged eight dollars a month since 1950. The doors don't have locks that work, and there are no phones or televisions, so I'll make it six dollars a week. I'll give you a two-by-four you can wedge against the door when you're inside so you can sleep in peace."

"No locks? What about my belongings during the day? I only have these clothes and I'd like to keep them."

"Nobody here has anything worth stealing." Pito motioned for Cosimo to step outside with him.

"You said your name was Cano? *Señor* Cano, come here for a moment. Look around. There is only one entrance and exit to the cabins. We have at least two women looking out windows at all times. Right now there are even more wanting to know who you are. They're better than those German guard dogs."

As Cosimo glanced in the direction Pito indicated, he saw curtains flick and blinds close.

Pito continued, "The building they live in, that surrounds us, is an old hotel built in 1890. It is now apartments. At one time *gringos* traveling from New Orleans to San Antonio on the Sunset Limited or the

Katy from Dallas stayed here. These cabins were added in 1932 because people wanted to sleep close to their cars. I don't understand *gringos* and their love of cars. I was eight years old. They tore up a bandstand, gardens and paths, tennis courts, and a dance floor to build them. The wisteria trellis and trees are from that time. Now, mostly Mexican families stay here. We're cheap. People stay when they come for weddings or funerals."

"How do you know so much about the place?"

"I was born here. My father ran the hotel kitchen. I own the land between the two apartment buildings, and the cabins."

Reentering the cabin, Cosimo cleared his throat on seeing the stained mattress. "Shame on you. The mattress is not fit for a pig. The dresser is missing a drawer. The bathroom and shower are barely acceptable. What about sheets and a towels?"

"You have to buy them because the guests drive away with them," shrugged Pito.

"I thought you said no one stole."

"My towels and sheets are the exception. It's seventy-five cents for two sheets and one towel. A clean army surplus mattress, that's another dollar-fifty. We can also wash your towels and sheets once a week for fifty cents."

"I was sent here by a representative of your government. I expected accommodations. In France or Cuba someone would have offered me a room in their flat with a meal for less money than I am going to spend on this . . . this shack.

"I prefer to call them cottages." Pito didn't take offense.

"Nonsense. I am not going to steal your sheets and towels." Cosimo raised his voice and pointed his cane toward the bed. "Clean sheets, towels, and a respectably clean mattress are supposed to come with the room."

"All right, don't get your Cuban blood boiling."

"This has nothing to do with where I was born," Cosimo protested.

"*Bueno, viejito... calmate*. This isn't the St. Anthony Hotel. If you keep up with the rent, your last week is on me. Pay now, and I'll get you a new mattress. I'll throw in an army blanket, a pillow, and a pillowcase. Just leave everything when you go, and we'll call it square."

"*Don* Pito, I can do plumbing, electrical, carpentry, and most of all, painting."

"*Señor*, I may look like half a man to you, but I can do all of those things," Pito countered.

"*Don* Pito, I do not mean to insult. You mentioned that the other cabins need work. I own a house and farm in Cuba and I can fix things. Give me three cans of paint and I'll show you what I can do."

"A house and a farm, you say." Pito squinted at Cosimo's shoes. "*Señor*, please don't push my generosity. I need to cheat a little to survive. I don't need competition." Pito laughed.

Cosimo took off his hat and wiped his forehead with his sleeve. "I'm not your competition. Not today, not ever. One day soon, you'll see what I can do and you will pay me."

Pito slapped his leg. "*Cabron*! You've got balls. *Mira viejito*, I'm no fool. I've had more than a few *chuecos* pass through here with their *movidas*. I rent the places and collect the money. That's all I do. And *señor*, you're no spring chicken. I don't see you doing any roofing, which is what I need."

"I'm an old rooster who still knows how to crow." The old man spoke with such conviction, Pito snickered.

"Pay the rent and we're in business." Pito put out his hand.

Cosimo took out his wallet and handed over nine dollars. "I believe that covers everything. Now, please, this is an emergency. Is there someplace I could get something to eat?"

"Everything is closed around here, and you're on foot. I'm sorry."

"Anything, a leftover chicken wing. Anything."

"I don't know. Maybe *Señora* Graciela has a spare taco." Pito stepped out where he could see a certain window. "*Señora* Graciela," he called out. A window shade across the yard flashed open.

"*Don Pito, que se ofrece?*" the woman called back.

"A taco for my new guest," Pito glanced over to Cosimo. "The man is starving."

"Come on over right now, because we watch my show, *Perry Mason*, at seven."

"Thank you," Cosimo replied.

Several men played cards and smoked in what used to be a hotel lobby. A fair-skinned woman with a pleasant face and broad grin stepped out of her apartment and motioned for them to enter and sit at the kitchen table.

"Graciela Vasquez, *señor*."

"Cosimo Cano, I am in your debt."

In the combination living and dining room, pictures of children and family were displayed in the breakfront. The scent of grilled onions had originated here; now, something more ineffably pleasing caused his stomach to gurgle.

The spacious kitchen looked as if long ago food was prepared here for hotel guests; it now was fitted with three domestic stoves with ovens. A second, older woman stood by the sink washing pots. Both women wore flowered print dresses with round collars, and aprons.

"Such a big kitchen," Cosimo commented.

"Graciela owns a restaurant," said Pito, "the Little House Café by the courthouse. They serve breakfast and lunch. She prepares large dishes here."

"Don't stand there. Sit down," Graciela said and pulled out a chair for him. "This is my sister, Emma."

Emma nodded shyly and returned to the sink and the pots.

"Would you like some tea?" asked Graciela.

His stomach growled. "My stomach speaks. What do you have?"

"Lipton."

"I mean, I apologize, I mean what do you have to eat?"

"It's our Sunday supper, home cooking," said Graciela. "It's leftovers. I have maybe two tacos-full of *carne guisada*. I just finished making baked potatoes for the café. I have eggs and a little *pico de gallo*.

She sprinkled flour on a marble surface, took a golf ball-sized hunk of flour dough and plopped it in on the stone. She applied a rolling pin until the dough was seven inches across and about a quarter of an inch thick. Like a magician doing close-up illusions, she levitated the flattened dough with her finger tips and deftly moved it onto a hot griddle.

She took a baked potato and diced it into half-inch squares, tossed the pieces into a frying pan, added a dollop of bacon fat, gave the pan a swirl, and began to roll out a second tortilla. She tossed the second tortilla on the griddle, and turned over the first tortilla.

She reached for an egg and broke the shell with a snap on the pan's lip and poured it over the potatoes, gave everything a stir, and started to roll out a third tortilla. Cosimo felt embarrassed by the effort.

At any moment, Cosimo thought something would catch fire. Graciela flipped the second tortilla, stirred the eggs and potatoes, picked up the first tortilla with her fingers, placed it on a kitchen towel. She ladled a helping of what looked like a thick beef stew onto the tortilla, folded it on a plate, and placed it before him.

He lifted the taco, feeling the warm, supple, freshly-made flat bread. It was the scent that had filled the kitchen: beef tips, cumin, serrano pepper, stewed with caramelized onions and tomato. He bit into the folded bread and thick beef stew and closed his eyes.

"Que *riqueza*." He bit again. "What is this?"

"*Tacos de carne de res*," Graciela placed a second taco on his plate.

"I am not a beggar. I will repay you."

Emma brought a third taco and placed it before him.

"This is *papas con huevo*. It's very simple. It's potato and egg,"

"You have saved my life. These are not corn tortillas." He spoke between bites. "I've been to Mexico City, Veracruz, and Oaxaca numerous times. I have had flat breads before but this is nothing like anything I have encountered. Is this middle eastern bread?"

"*Que? No,*" Emma, the older sister laughed. "*Es harina de trigo*, flour tortillas."

"With skills like this you must be a very rich lady. No wonder you own a restaurant."

Emma laughed again.

Graciela scowled at Emma and nodded for her to get out. "Yes, I'm a *very* rich lady."

The meal had made him pleasantly euphoric. He settled into the clean sheets on his clean mattress. A two by four board was propped against the door. Perhaps it was a breeze through the pecan trees outdoors, or the scent of cumin, that recalled Sara's laughter.

CHAPTER 11

Paris, 1948

Over time, Sara gleaned from overheard conversations between Cosimo and his friends that before the war, he had serial relationships with three women. By 1948, when he was seeing Sara exclusively, he remained friends with all three. One lived in the adjoining *Arrondissement* and was now married to a businessman. She became Sara's nodding acquaintance. The second, Margaret Manheim, lived in Venice, Italy, and corresponded regularly with Cosimo. The third woman, as the concierge had foretold, made her appearance during Cosimo's next stay in Paris. Poised and compact, the forty-two-year-old Leonor Fini, a well-regarded artist, writer, set and costume designer for motion pictures and operas, was one of Cosimo's closest friends.

She dropped her wrap on the settee and kissed Cosimo before turning to recognize Sara. After introductions, as Sara struggled with a cork jammed in the corkscrew, Leonor cozied up to Cosimo.

"I was disappointed I didn't get to see your show when you came to Paris last year. I was on a film with Rossellini. Very raw. It takes place during the war, about a man forced to infiltrate the resistance for the Germans. But, enough of that. I heard good things about your show. How was it for you?"

"Realistically, good, very good, thanks to Sara, here. She translated the review in *Le Monde Libertaire,* and it was reprinted in American magazines. The show did well."

"*Brava.*" She clapped her hands lightly in Sara's direction. "Emile says he wants to exhibit me next year. What do you think? How is he?"

"That's Emile from the gallery," Cosimo said to Sara.

"I know," she mumbled, at last winning the battle with the corkscrew.

"Emile is doing well. If he's putting you in the front room, it will be the right space for your work."

"I think so. By the bye, I hear you had coffee with Georges."

"It seems everyone knows. We reminisced. Well, he did. He talks so fast I only half listen. He's a tormented soul."

"My Georges. He provokes." Leonor laughed. "Have you read Georges Bataille?" she asked Sara.

"Yes," Sara replied, looking up from the wine. Leonor didn't wait for her answer.

"Cosimo, do you still do pen work?" Leonor asked, getting down to business.

"Not for a few years, why?"

"I am doing production design for a play. I want the cover of the program to have an eagle with its wings outspread, in flight." She held her hands out in front of her, fingers open and her thumbs overlapping, approximating the neck and head of an eagle. She flapped her fingers as wings. "In its talons it holds a large heart."

"Literal or cartoon?"

"Literal. It's a heart torn from a thousand kilo tiger."

"Is this a happy, screaming, angry eagle?"

"Simple and heroic! As if created by one line without lifting the pen from the page."

"That's impossible," said Sara.

"Naturally, it's impossible. That's why I've come to Cosimo," said Leonor, accepting a glass of wine.

"I can try right now, if you like. Let me sketch one or two ideas. In pen?" winced Cosimo.

Leonor nodded.

Cosimo excused himself and went into his studio in the next room.

"Do you live together?" asked Leonor, surprised by the open door between their apartments.

"Yes and no. I convinced the neighbor to move, and we now have adjoining apartments, with an open door."

"You convinced a neighbor to move, here in this building? That must have cost." Leonor rubbed her thumb quickly across her index and middle fingers. "What do you do?"

"I translate American pulp novels into French. *Murder Witch*, *Listed Missing*, and *Paper Trail* are mine."

"You translated those? I love them. On the film set, I often have hours on my hands. Your books are a pleasure to read. I don't recall your name as translator."

"The publisher uses a man's name instead of mine to make the books sound macho. Frankly, I don't have a say and don't really care. I'm not translating Faulkner. I enjoy the work. I'm pleased that you know them and like them. It's my excuse for remaining in France, far from my roots, and not having to explain to my family why I'm never going home."

"I know the publisher. He doesn't pay enough to afford this address."

"It's a small apartment."

"Are you Canadian?" Leonor asked in English.

"Eh, No siree." Sara's accent slipped from Canadian dry to a Texas drawl. "Ah'm Sa-ra, Sa-ra Hunter of the Bastrop, Texas, Hunters."

"And what brings you to France?"

"I was working on my doctorate—"

"It's about mandala symbolism in early French poetry," shouted Cosimo from the next room.

"*Quelle erreur*," hooted Leonor. "An academic intellectual? What have you done, Cosimo?"

Cosimo stuck his head in the room. "Very well, thank you. She's my *confidente*. And by the way, she may speak more languages than you. So don't say anything thinking she will not understand." He retreated to his studio.

"Your accents are marvelous! And your French is excellent for an American, and a cowgirl no less."

Sara took an ample swallow of wine and changed the subject. "How did you meet Cosimo?"

"I believe it was 1936, Emile introduced us. Cosimo had this divine show, and I fell madly in love with him. Then he suddenly returned to Cuba, only to show up six months later wanting to pick up where we left off. And I was fool enough to let him do it."

Cosimo reentered the room. "Leonor my love, I was never your one and only. Remember Gregory and Count Dish Rag."

"Count d'Estaing . . . at least, that's what he said his name was." She laughed. "He was so beautiful. And a complete charlatan. How was I supposed to know he wasn't a count?"

"Perhaps, because he was twenty-two, and Count d'Estaing was an eighteenth century French general," teased Cosimo. "You always had more than one lover, and I am sure you still do."

"True . . . true . . . I confess. It's hard to find all the qualities I'm looking for in one man, or woman. One is pretty, another is witty and writes plays, or plays an instrument, and perhaps sings, but it's never all in one. After all, I'm all in one." Cosimo and Leonor laughed. Sara took another swallow of wine.

"Take a look at this," Cosimo handed Leonor a sketch pad.

Sara's mouth opened as she leaned over Leonor's shoulder. A heroic eagle, wings outspread in flight, grasping a heart in its talons, veins and arteries trailing. The drawing apparently was done with the pen never leaving the paper.

"Simple and perfect," Leonor declared and rose to hug Cosimo.

Leonor looked over her shoulder. "Normally, I would take this delicious man to bed, but I can see he is smitten. I'll strike you a deal. You reward him for me, and I'll make sure your name is on your next translation. I know the publisher, and he knows how I feel about the subjugation of women." She laughed.

Sara laughed, too, though through clenched teeth. It took Sara a couple of years before she would leave Leonor and Cosimo alone in the same room. They eventually became friendly, and later, even friends. Sara did the English translations for Leonor's program notes for operas, ballets, and art exhibits, which Leonor typically repaid with a bottle of champagne, or a small case of sterlet caviar.

The other woman from Cosimo's past, Margaret Manheim, the heiress art collector, swept through several times. Instead of feeling competitive, Sara warmed to the six-foot-one eccentric scarecrow draped in elegant clothes.

CHAPTER 12

Cosimo must have finally slept because he woke hungry for *Señora* Graciela's flour tortillas. When he rolled out of bed, a dull soreness in his right arm remained, a memento of yesterday's hike from the YMCA. He had plans for the day. After breakfast he wanted to check in with the post office, then visit the public library. If he could find his friends' addresses, they would certainly help him.

Seeing himself reflected in the bathroom mirror, he sighed and shook his head. He needed to do something about his appearance, and the soles of his espadrilles were fraying.

His stomach urged him to get moving. He took out Sara's watch and placed in on the dresser.

"Today, it will be all business, my friend," he said to the watch.

When opened like a clam shell, the watch had small bumps that allowed it to stand. The sun grinned, its searching eyes reminded Cosimo of a vigilant thief. He closed the watch and wound the crown; with each turn the sun's eyes rolled back as if in pleasure. Cosimo slipped the watch into a leather case and replaced it in his courier bag. He also packed the letters he'd written on the Bluebonnet Hotel's stationery.

The Little House Café sat in the center of a row of unpretentious storefronts a block west of the red sandstone Bexar County courthouse.

Unlike Alamo Plaza and Houston Street with their modern storefronts, this vicinity retained something of the feel of an airy midwestern town. Two storefronts to the south of the Little House Café hung a sign advertising "Kallison's Western Wear." Cowboy hats, boots, riding gear, and saddles dominated the window displays.

The storefront on the north side of the café housed a *botánica*, a shop specializing in herbs for potions and medicinal teas. A hint of copal incense lingered in the air. The window display was a crowded pyramid of religious icons. On the top were framed portraits of Jesus staring agonizingly toward the sky, a crown of bloody thorns on his head. The tier below contained a procession of figurines of Saint Anthony, Saint Teresa, and Saint Martin of Tours on horseback, cutting his cape in half and handing it to a naked beggar. At the base of the pyramid, numerous versions of the Madonna with arms outstretched appeared to bless a sea of silvery votive charms, *milagros,* in the shape of legs, eyes, hearts, heads, hands, farm animals, and trucks.

"Here the cowboys meet *el caribe*, and in between the Little House Café," Cosimo said to himself.

To say the place was unpretentious, Cosimo thought, would be an understatement. The gold leaf lettering of the "Little House Café" had seen better days. The "We're Open" sign rattled and a cluster of small bells jingled when he opened the door. The place had the appearance of a 1930s diner, with the stainless steel backsplash behind the grill and steam table. There were eight stools at the counter and six tables with chairs. Cosimo took a seat at the counter. There were only two customers besides himself.

Graciela recognized him immediately. Her older sister Emma smiled over her shoulder, tossed three strips of bacon on the grill and gave a stir to a mound of hash brown potatoes. They wore tan and brown waitress uniforms.

Graciela's infectious grin made him smile back as she handed him a menu. "*Buenos dias*, can I get you coffee?"

He put aside the menu. "Yes, and I want some of those astonishing white tortillas with perhaps eggs and sausage."

"I'm sorry, *señor,* I don't serve those here. I can make you eggs with bacon and toast."

"No, no, not white bread toast, no. Your tortillas with the potato and eggs, like you made for me last night, or was that a dream?"

Emma at the grill turned, "That's what we eat at home." She smiled shyly and turned back to the grill. She looked very much like her sister, only a bit older and softer.

"We don't serve Mexican food. This is a diner. We serve what people want, eggs any style, bacon, hamburgers, fried chicken, fries, chicken fried steak, and meatloaf on Wednesdays. These are our regular customers. If we change the menu, they won't come back."

"A kitchen is a kitchen. You can cook whatever you want." Cosimo glanced around the room. "This is the breakfast hour and only three customers. You have a gift for cooking."

"A restaurant like the Mexican Manhattan on Houston Street serves tamales and fresh corn tortillas. They have machines and eight workers just in food preparation. They're air-conditioned and are opened at night. I close at 2:00 p.m."

"I've eaten at the Mexican Manhattan. It's traditional food, enchiladas, corn tortillas, rice and beans. It is good but not like yours. They do not have your tortillas. Could you change the menu a little?"

"We can't change because I'm not rich," she snapped.

"Please, did I say something wrong? *Señora Graciela? Lo siento.*"

"*Señor,* I don't remember your name, and normally I don't talk business with strangers, but you've been in my kitchen. You can see I'm not rich. I've worked here for fifteen years, and I ran the place. I bought all the ingredients and supplies, paid the staff, and the taxes. I thought I was buying a successful business. The owner gave me a good price, and I thought I could run it myself, except . . . "

Emma ladled scrambled eggs onto a plate, along with the bacon and hash browns, added toast on a separate plate, and handed them to Graciela.

Graciela grabbed the coffee carafe, took the dish to a waiting customer, and refilled his coffee cup.

"Have you spoken to a lawyer?" Cosimo asked as Graciela returned to the counter.

"Yes," she managed hoarsely. "We're going to have to close. I've lost my savings." She hid her face, turned abruptly, and walked quickly to the pantry.

Emma stepped back from the grill. "The fifteen-thousand-dollar debt, and a five-year lease, the place isn't earning enough to make the payments. We've only owned the business six months, and we're already behind."

Cosimo raised his cane and placed it on the counter. "Emma, *en ese caso, dame huevos estrellados, tosino, y las papitas* with wheat toast."

Emma tossed several strips of bacon on the grill. "Come back tomorrow. I'll make you tortillas," said Emma.

The incident at the Little House Café wasn't the way Cosimo had intended to start his day. Nearing the Post Office and Federal Building, he saw a red 1959 Chevrolet Impala convertible enter Alamo Plaza honking its horn in short blasts. Two men in military fatigues sat atop the back seat like parade dignitaries waving oversized Cuban flags, shouting *"Cuba Libre! Cuba Libre! Cuba Libre!"* On the second time around the plaza, a small crowd gathered cheering in unison, *"Cuba Libre! Cuba Libre!"* They encouraged strangers on the street to join in, and a few, caught up in the moment, did. A local newspaper photographer ran alongside the car, carrying a Speed Graphic news camera. The car stopped directly in front of the Alamo long enough for the photographer to take two shots.

Before they drove off, one of the flag-wavers, a man with light blue eyes and pale skin burned pink by the sun, shook his finger and pointed directly at Cosimo. *"Cubano!"* he shouted. *"Cubano, Cuba Libre! Cuba Libre!"* The swarthy driver sneered when Cosimo didn't join in. He had never seen these men before. How did they know he was Cuban? And what was going on?

He opted to head to the library and found the reading room crowded. The latest newspaper editions were in use. He could read on the *New York Times* front page, "ANTI-CASTRO UNITS LAND IN CUBA; REPORT FIGHTING AT BEACHHEAD."

He didn't have to read more to understand what had happened. He returned to the Federal Building and Post Office and pushed through scores of people filling the hallways. For an instant he caught the attention of agent Carmichael, who signaled, "Don't even bother."

He forgot he had intended to have his letters typed. For the next twenty-four hours he only left the Buena Vista Cabins for his meals at the Little House Café.

The atmosphere in San Antonio didn't feel volatile, not like Madrid in 1936. Nonetheless, the news of the Cuban invasion left him anxious about his public presence. On Wednesday, he took the River Walk shortcut to the post office. Once in the queue, he allowed others to go ahead of him while waiting for Francisco Orozco's window to become available.

The sound of scuffling, shouts, and angry voices exploded from the second floor. Unnerved eyes in the queue looked toward the source. Half the patrons ducked under the cordon and scurried for the nearest exit.

"What's the excitement?" Cosimo asked.

"It's the Cuban invasion." Francisco commented

"The Americans invaded. Is it over?"

"You don't know?"

Cosimo drew a blank. "Yes, the Americans invaded."

"No. not the Americans. *Cuban exiles* landed in Cuba and were defeated and captured. Dramatics? You'd think *Richard the Third* played out right here. Federal marshals had to be brought in so we could open. The marshals are upstairs now keeping a lid on things. This morning a man in the lobby threatened to shoot himself if the Americans didn't bomb Havana."

"What happened?"

"Nothing. He didn't have a gun," chuckled Francisco.

Another round of shouts and shuffles exploded.

"Is it safe?" Cosimo looked toward the uproar.

"It's the Cuban refugee office. It's mostly dramatics."

"They only invaded on Monday, and it has failed?"

"Afraid so," said Francisco.

Cosimo wondered about the men in military fatigues riding in the convertible shouting, "*Cuba Libre, Cuba Libre.*" The episode had felt staged. What irritated him was that he was made part of the charade. Was he supposed to cheer like a partisan fool?

He didn't know Fidel Castro, or anyone in his movement. The rebels were forty, even fifty years his junior. If he were still in Cuba, he could likely have known of them indirectly. Cuba was an island, and if you were born there, attended a university there, and, like himself, ran a business, you got to know who was who. Considering the ineptness of the Batista mobsters, and how quickly gossip spread on the island, it wasn't surprising to him that the rebels had survived and succeeded. As he left the federal building, he even felt relieved that the invasion had failed.

He returned to the Buena Vista Cabins. Frustrated, angry, confused, he threw his hat and cane on the bed. "*Merde, merde, merde, merde,*" he repeated. He placed the watch on the dresser. "I am going insane," he said to the watch. "Look at how we are living! These are not cabins, they are shacks, hovels. I must pull myself together!" he shouted. "If I am going to survive this damned situation, I need to work with my hands. I miss having a painting or a drawing giving me a goal for the day. Without my brushes, every day a part of me feels ground down."

Cosimo sat on the bed. "Several times a day, I think of something I want to tell her, and she is not here."

CHAPTER 13

Paris, 1952

Cosimo considered relocating to Paris and moving in permanently with Sara. In 1952, whether he was ready for it or not, change swept Cuba. The Cuban presidential election was suspended and Fulgencio Batista came to power in a military coup. One of the farm's drivers was shot by a thug from the truck drivers' syndicate. Overnight, he found himself at odds with local toughs aligned with Batista. Cosimo decided it was time to retire from the vegetable business.

He wrote to Sara about the political situation and added, "What do you think about my coming to live with you permanently?"

A week later he received a telegram, "I'm ready! Come!"

The farm had been in the family for at least a hundred and fifty years. After his parents passed, he and his brother had run the place until his brother died. Since then he had operated it as a cooperative; it's what had allowed him the liberty to go to Paris in 1947.

With the 1952 coup in mind, Cosimo paid the local magistrates and signed an agreement so the new cooperative management of the farm would be recognized and approved. As one of the shareholders, he retained the right to return and work for his housing and meals. He added this paragraph because once as a student he had slept in doorways and survived on a single dried fish a day. He always feared it could happen again.

Sara rented a larger apartment and he took a loft in an adjoining building to use as a studio. To commemorate their union, she gave him an oversized pocket-style watch designed by Salvador Dali and had it inscribed, "*Cosimo, Time began with you. Forever Yours, Sara, 1952.*" He gave her a juvenile Amazon green parrot she adored. Because the bird would outlive them both, she named it Proust.

Whatever uncertainties he may have had about the move to France vanished. He didn't miss the twice-a-year hot-blooded reunions. He had the company of the delightful Sara every day. He regretted dithering over the decision. He missed his friend, Paul Éluard, who suffered a fatal heart attack while Cosimo was in Cuba. He muttered to himself more than once, "You fool, why did you wait so long?"

Margaret Manheim and Leonor Fini, hearing of Sara and Cosimo's official cohabitation, descended on Sara with bottles of pinot noir and pressed her about her hold over Cosimo. They stared, a bit envious of the much younger woman.

"It's not like I roped and branded him," said Sara. "I did plot Cosimo's seduction like a military campaign, using psychological, chemical, and biological weapons. I flattered him, I fed him, and I sucked his cock."

Margaret and Leonor roared.

"My dear, who here hasn't done that?" Margaret cackled.

"It's that you made a match when so many others tried," said Leonor.

"I don't know how that happened. Once I had him in my trap, I promptly surrendered," laughed Sara. "The right place at the right time, I suppose. He has always been on his own. He either stayed or left. I had no control over that." Sara lifted her wine glass. "We're an unlikely match. I'm as pale as winter asparagus, and his complexion is cinnamon. Our work schedules are opposites. I begin my day at seven and dive into my translations with small breaks for food and Turkish tobacco with a sprinkle of hashish. My parrot Proust is my only companion. Cosimo doesn't wake until ten. He reads the newspaper, has his lunch, and drinks coffee. He arrives at his studio at two in the afternoon, takes a short nap, and paints until eight in the evening. When he comes home to me, I put Proust to bed, and Cosimo and I get to play."

Over time, and to Cosimo's relief, Leonor and Margaret came to visit with the gregarious Sara, and not him. She could match them joke for joke, drink for drink, and he could drift off to his studio and work.

CHAPTER 14

Saturdays brought students from throughout the city to the main library where the larger reference collections, microfiche, and bound periodicals were kept. All staff, full- and part-time, worked Saturdays.

A bus from Fort Sam Houston stopped on Market Street in front of the library. Army wives, children, and soldiers streamed out the door and headed toward the library.

Inside, Ruthann led Maddie, Oscar, and Richard through the crowd to the reference department.

"Pages consider the research desk the worst job at the library," Ruthann warned. "People will scream at you if you're not fast enough." Behind Ruthann's back, Richard pretended to hang himself with an imaginary noose.

Students desperate for help with assignments crowded three deep around the reference desk. Ilene Fischer waved for them to line up along the wall.

"Please line up. Who's next? First come, first served." Two timid souls moved back, the rest held firm.

"Doctor Samuels asked me to send these three to help you out," Ruthann said.

"Ruthann, stick them in the corner until I can give them instructions. None of your cousins ever, *ever* have library experience." Fischer turned her attention to the patrons. "I'll take the next person."

"These are Samuels's bright new hires," Ruthann insisted.

Ilene took off her reading glasses. "What can you do?" She looked at all three.

"I've done research. I think I can help." Oscar stepped forward. "First come, first served, who's next?"

"I'll take the next one." Maddie followed. She waved for the waiting patrons to queue up.

Seeing that help was on the way, the patrons looked at one another and consensually lined up.

Ilene Fischer noted that Oscar answered questions without searching for the subject in reference books. When asked, what's the deepest part of the ocean, without hesitation he replied, "The Marianas trench, six miles, plus. Check the encyclopedias. *Newsweek* had an article a couple of years ago so check *Readers Guide to Periodical Literature,* 1957 to 59. Next? You're writing a paper about Zebulon Pike? In the card catalog there's at least one biography. Check articles in the historical periodicals, from 1907 to 1909, then *American Historian* to the latest issue, and the encyclopedias. . . . You have to write a report on the *Canterbury Tales* by Monday? Have you read it? No? You'll never finish if you try to read the Middle English. Get the modern English version. It has an introduction that you'll find useful. If it's not on the shelf, go to Nic Tengg's Used Books on Commerce Street and tell him you want a clean fifty-cent paperback version."

Fischer tapped Oscar on the shoulder. "Wait, what's your name?"

"Oscar."

"Tell me, Oscar, how do you know these things?"

"I've used libraries all my life. What should I be doing?"

"What if they needed citations about Chaucer?"

"If they ask for one, I'll direct them to look under English literature criticism, Geoffrey Chaucer; and the *Reader's Guide to Periodical Literature*. Like I told the student, the modern English version of the *Canterbury Tales* has an introduction that's useful for book reports. He said he needed it by Monday. Am I wrong?"

"You're doing fine." Fischer wrote a note to Director Samuels that she wanted Oscar in her department.

Returning to the children's department, Maddie found the room in chaos. The military wives, desperate for adult conversation, had camped out at the child-sized desks and chairs, while their little princes and princesses tore around the book stacks as if they were playing tag in a labyrinth. The children's librarian was nowhere in sight. A toddler waddled toward his mother dangling a book by a single page, ripping the paper. The mom furtively placed the damaged book on a shelf.

"Mothers, children, and patrons," Maddie shouted above the din. "In five minutes I will do the Tiger Lily dance from *Peter Pan*. And afterwards, I'll read a book aloud." Maddie pointed across the room. "Come over here in this corner," she herded the moms and children. "Arrange the chairs in a semicircle."

While she had the moms occupied arranging chairs, she found a pair of scissors, several sheets of 8 ½" x 11" colored card stock, and cellophane tape. Scrounging through storage cabinets, to her surprise she found a tambourine.

"I learned this dance for a production of *Peter Pan* at the San Antonio Little Theatre last fall. The director told us he assisted Jerome Robbins on the road show production." She spoke loudly enough to keep them in their seats as she cut two card stock feathers for an Indian headdress.

"I was only supposed to be an understudy in case someone got sick." She placed the finished headdress on her head.

Maddie kicked away her shoes, peeled off her knee length stockings, and stepped out in bare feet, banging a steady rhythm on her hip with the tambourine.

She cocked her head as if she'd heard a twig snap. "Did you hear that?" She rattled the tambourine softly. "I sense danger." Maddie looked intently into their faces. "I don't know who you are, but I'm Tiger Lily, and I live in Neverland," she lowered her voice. "No one is supposed to know about Neverland. Have you heard of Neverland?" She leaned toward the smaller children." No one moved. She turned to the older children. "Have you heard of Peter Pan?" Several of the older children raised their hands. She asked the moms, "How about you?" The women nodded. "Well, Princess Tiger Lily knows that her friends, Peter Pan, Wendy, and her brothers, are in terrible danger. Tiger Lily is nine years old, as old as some of you." She changed the tambourine's rhythm. "Boom, boom,

boom, boom. A pirate, Captain Hook, is coming, and Tiger Lily has to warn her friends." She hit her butt with the tambourine, and the children squealed with delight. As she established the beat she hummed the melody and danced.

Coming back from an extended cigarette break, Jane Jenkins, the children's librarian, found Maddie in mid-performance.

"Tum, tum, tum tum," called Maddie, performing Tiger Lily's war dance.

Drawn by the clapping and tambourine, dozens of patrons hurried through the lobby following the beat to the children's department. The lithe Maddie riveted Oscar and the soldiers crowding into the room.

The children's librarian ran across the lobby frantically summoning Ruthann.

"I stepped out of the library for five minutes and came back to find this crazy page beating a tambourine and stomping about like a lunatic."

Ruthann stood outside the room with the overflow, craning her neck to get a glimpse of the Maddie spectacle.

Maddie told the story with her body, hands, and eyes.

Entranced, the children laughed and were frightened by Maddie's expressions.

She ended the dance by silencing the tambourine, stopping, and turning away from the audience. She removed the paper head dress, turned back around, and took a bow.

Applause echoed throughout the library. "Now, if anyone needs some help with books," said Maddie, as Ruthann pushed her way through the departing patrons, soldiers, and students. Oscar managed to avoid her and returned to the art and music department.

Maddie reached for the first book on the display shelf and held up *Horton Hears a Who.*

"This is by Dr. Seuss." Several children applauded. "You know the book?" she asked. Two girls held up their hand. "It's my favorite," said one.

"It's one of my favorites, too," replied Maddie. "That makes us book buddies. And everyone here can become a book buddy if you like to read."

Maddie walked closer to the children and their mommies, holding the Dr. Seuss book so everyone could see the illustrations. She paced the reading to keep the children engaged, changing voices to suit the characters. She shrugged when she turned to the torn page.

When she finished the reading, the children and moms surrounded Maddie as if she were a celebrity.

Ruthann signaled for Maddie to join her in the break room.

As Maddie entered the break room, Ruthann jabbed her finger towards the door. "Shut the door," she barked. "What do you think you're doing? Look at your legs! Where are your hose and shoes?"

Maddie held them behind her back. "When I got back to the children's department there was no one in charge. The room was out of control, and the only thing I could think to do was this dance. I improvised and I got them to sit still."

"This isn't a saloon. We don't bare our legs and dance to maintain decorum. People are here to borrow books and read. Did you tear that book?"

"No! I reached out for a book, and that's what my hand landed on."

"You must have torn that book because we do not put damaged books on the shelves."

Dr. Samuels stuck his head into the break room. "All copies of the Barrie books have been checked out, and the mothers want us to show the Disney version of the film in the theater. What should I tell them?" He looked straight at Ruthann.

"I'll order the film. I can show it in the auditorium," she said, as if the idea had been hers.

"Good, and what in heaven's name are 'book buddies'?"

Maddie raised her hand. "I said, if the children like a book, and I like the same book, we can call ourselves book buddies."

"Well, the mothers think it's some kind of club and they want their children to join."

Ruthann shook her head. "The library doesn't have a club named *Book Buddies*."

"I think it's a great idea," said Dr. Samuels. "Let's start Book Buddies and we'll have a special book for them each week. I want to get Jane Jenkins in on this. She should be selecting the books. And they want Miss Parker to read. It seems you did quite a job with *Horton Hears a Who*. Will you do it?" he asked Maddie.

Ruthann bore a hole into Maddie, who nodded but didn't gloat.

"Good," said Samuels. "We'll do it in the theater so Miss Parker can introduce the motion picture. And one last thing, Ruthann, a mother told me her toddler tore the book Miss Parker was reading. She wants to pay for it. Can you take care of that?"

Ruthann returned to the art and music department to find a note from the director assigning Oscar to the reference department. The transfer upset her doubly since the new hires were her domain.

"We never needed tests before, and this place ran pretty darn well," she grumbled. "Mr. Buscoso," she said loud enough for all in the room to hear. "After you finish shelving books, report to the reference department." She crumpled the director's note and tossed it dismissively in the trash.

"Thank you, I'll finish shelving."

Ruthann smiled wanly and waved a faint goodbye without looking at him.

For Ruthann, if it wasn't one irritant, it was another. She saw Cosimo entering her department.

"He's going to fall asleep in that chair," she said to herself.

Cosimo put his belongings on one of the leather chairs and went to the bookcase with the oversized art books. His finger scanned the titles, stopping at one of the titles. Appearing almost in shock he carried the book to the chair.

Ruthann felt the contemptible little man was mocking her as he sat and opened the book.

Cosimo appeared confused. The spine of the book felt floppy. Opening it he found that pages had been removed. A quarter of an inch of the excised page remained to keep the stitching intact.

Cosimo carried the book to the librarian's desk as if he were holding a dead animal. "Your book has been vandalized," he said. "Who would do such a vile act?"

Ruthann didn't blink. "I removed the offensive pages myself."

"What offensive pages?"

"The . . . undressed women."

"You mean, Matisse's nudes?" asked Cosimo.

"The nudes . . . yes . . . the nude human figures censored by the Decency Council."

"Decency? What was indecent? And who are you to decide what is or is not decent?"

"The figures were naked."

"Matisse's women? His dancing women? They are impressions, not real figurative paintings."

"Hardly. They're salacious, and not for our patrons."

"And the pages that were removed, where are they? Can I see them?"

"They've been destroyed."

"Destroyed?" Cosimo couldn't believe the ignorance. "As a librarian you must know that Matisse's paintings are masterpieces in the Louvre, the Prado, and the Metropolitan Museum in New York."

"Here, a committee decides what is decent. This is not a museum. It's a public library. We have our own standards."

"This book is important." He placed the book on her desk.

"All our books are important. That's what we have." Ruthann stood and left the room.

CHAPTER 15

"On Saturday nights vagrants, thieves, and frantic students try to hide in the library until Monday morning." Ruthann Medlin spoke to a handful of pages. "It's illegal. They're trespassing. We call the police. There's a fifty dollar fine, and they go to jail. Search your own department, and when you've checked all the nooks, offices, closets, bathrooms, and carrels, we can go home."

Ten minutes later, Richard spoke for the pages. "All clear."

Ruthann pointed to the exit.

Maddie sprang for the loading dock door, steps ahead of Richard and Oscar. Out the door, down the stairs, they saw her settle into the passenger seat of a canary-yellow Corvette convertible idling outside the library's back gate.

The crew-cut young man in the driver's seat gunned the engine and left a short strip of tire rubber.

"Do you think she's beautiful?" Richard asked.

"Yeah," said Oscar.

"Do you think you have a chance?"

"She must have thought I was cute," Oscar said, good-naturedly. "She kissed me before I knew her name."

"The slut," Richard mocked.

"Lay off. Okay? Man, don't be such a . . . goddamn hick."

"Hey! Lighten up. I'm making sarcastic."

"No, sarcasm is saying the opposite in order to ridicule. As in, 'Do you think Maddie and the Corvette driver make it to the church service?'"

Richard laughed. "You're right. Okay, I'm backing off. That's the exact reason I want to have a beer with you. You talk. Come on. I know a place where we can get a schooner for a dime."

"I'm not twenty-one."

"Neither am I. Let's go, and I apologize. She's beautiful, but neither of us has a chance and you know it."

"I don't have to own a work of art to take pleasure in its beauty."

"Who the hell talks like you?" groaned Richard. "When we get to the bar, just play along with me. When I say show him your driver's license, just do it."

"Sure. Whatever you say," replied Oscar. "When Maddie got back to the children's department this morning, the place was a mess. In less than five minutes, she had all those squirmy kids and their moms fixed on everything she did. I don't have a crush on her. If I did, I wouldn't do anything about it. I'd love her from afar." He grinned, resigned to his luck.

"From afar?" Richard chortled.

"Yes, I'd moon over her for a while, I'd make up an excuse to say something to her at the front desk, or spend a moment alone with her in the break room. And then that would pass, and my next love might be the girl I see on the bus every day."

"You should do jokes for the Steve Allen Show."

"It's funny because it's sadly true."

"Are you for real?"

"Yes, I'm aware that I have exactly thirty-five cents in my pocket, enough for a beer, maybe two, if I'm willing to walk the three miles home. At my last job, I ate peanut butter sandwiches the week before payday. Who has time or money for girls?"

The bar was on corner of a three-story brick hotel, across the street from the Missouri Pacific Railroad Station. The date 1889 was carved into the keystone above the entrance.

"I know this place," said Oscar. "My grandfather would drive by here sometimes on the way to the produce market." He stopped outside the door. "It's seen better days. I remember well-dressed travelers schmoozing inside this bar. Now, look at it. It's a flophouse for transient laborers."

Richard pushed the door open. "If the bar had swinging doors, it could pass for a saloon in a Western movie."

The rancid smell of stale beer, cigarettes, and human sweat gave Oscar the urge to spit. Construction workers sitting at the tables made it clear the clientele had changed.

"Elroy, one last round," a tired voice called.

The men were drained. Salt stains formed around their shirts' armpits and backs. They were done with conversation. This last round was their ticket to sleep.

Behind the bar hung a tobacco-yellowed reproduction of Anheuser Busch's "Custer's Last Stand."

"I don't think the décor has changed in fifty years," commented Oscar.

The bartender gave them a sideways glare, "I know you," he said to Richard. "But this is a new one. Can I see your ID?"

"Yes, sir, he is twenty-one. It's his birthday," Richard indicated Oscar. "I'm buying him a beer."

"Let's see your ID," growled Elroy.

"Show him," urged Richard. "Take out your wallet and show him."

"Eh . . . "

"Show him. Come on."

Oscar took out his wallet and handed the bartender his driver's license. The bartender's blood-shot eyes studied it, turned it, and held it up to the light before handing it back.

"So you are. What'll you have? Plain or frosted glasses?"

"Two drafts, plain glasses." Richard carried the beers to a table by the window where they could see the main entrance to the Missouri Pacific train station across the street.

"I won't be twenty-one until June," Oscar said in a hushed voice.

Richard paused. "At first, I thought the man had bad eyesight, but he never makes a mistake with money."

"Apparently, he covets our precious dimes."

"Yep. And for a dime more he'll serve the beer in a frosted glass. Keeps the beer cold longer."

Oscar took a swallow of beer. "I hear they're going to stop passenger train service across the street."

Richard turned to see out the window. "It's one of my favorite buildings, with that bronze Indian on top. Inside it's like a Moorish palace for travelers."

"It has to be cheaper to ship freight than human beings. People are messy, carry luggage, need food, toilets, and they take up a lot of space. And it must require an army of people, you know, engineers, porters, conductors, cooks, waiters, ticket clerks, and janitors, all on the payroll to provide passenger service. Airline travel is cosmically faster, and a load of lumber doesn't complain when the sun is in its eyes."

Richard laughed. "How did you do that?"

"Do what?

"You tossed off an analysis on railroad trade."

"No, I said, it's cheaper to ship objects than people."

"That's pretty good bullshit!"

"Not bullshit. Speaking of shipping something cosmically faster, the Russians sent a man into space yesterday."

"I heard about it this morning. Did they circle the equator, or the Arctic circle?"

"The *New York Times* said the man traveled 22,000 miles, so not as far south as the equator but close, and two hundred miles above the earth's surface. It took one hour and forty-five minutes, and he lived."

Richard thought for a moment. "Shit, that's like two hundred and ninety miles a minute. That's fucking far out."

"There goes something worth talking about. Out there. There's that man." Oscar pointed outside.

Cosimo walked past the window.

"I've seen that old man several times, dressed just like that," said Oscar.

"What's his story?" Richard strained his neck to see.

"I don't know. Medlin hates him. I know that. Besides looking like Robinson Crusoe's man Friday, he's an outlier. This afternoon he was looking at a book of paintings and he went nuts. He asked her, who was *she* to censor books?"

"What did Medlin say?" Richard leaned back for a last look at the old man.

"She told him that she had removed the pictures of naked women herself, as approved by the Decency Council, not exactly her words, but close."

"Decency Council? The original blue-haired grannies," Richard raised his glass and downed the contents. "Another beer," he called out to Elroy.

"An 'outlier,' 'cosmically?' Where do you get these words?"

Oscar shrugged.

"Maybe the old guy gets off on Matisse's voluptuous women," said Richard.

"There's nothing to see, and it's not that simple. He fell asleep reading a copy of *Filmmaker's Forum* his first day here. He asked for the obit section of the local papers. He appeared incredibly miserable. He speaks with an accent, and he's right. Who is Ruthann Medlin to decide what is decent?"

"You won't be deciding what's decent," teased Richard.

"Ruthann also told him the censored pages had been destroyed, when she told us they were cataloged and filed."

"You like sexy women, but do you like male nudes?"

"I appreciate bodies. I was on the swimming team in high school. Our competition were these guys from Northside High. We weren't in their league. Northside High has an indoor pool, and they train year-round. We trained for a week before the big city meet. The Northside High swimmers won everything. They were tall, broad shoulders, flat stomachs, and smooth muscles. They looked like Greek statues. One guy, Brian something-or-other, even made it to the Rome Olympics last year. The American team got creamed by the Australians, but he went to the Olympics."

"How did you do in your meet?"

"I came in third in the one-hundred-yard breast stroke."

"So, did you see them naked? Did they have little dicks like Greek statues?"

"I didn't fixate on that."

"You brought it up. You like guys."

"I'll tell you what I like. I like girls' waists, small breasts, and you know, their hips where legs become the butt. And a face like Athena."

"Basically, you like slender young men."

"I was describing Donna Matranga, a girl I went to high school with. She played volleyball. I never dated her. I had crush on her . . . from afar. In that cold gym, wearing a T-shirt and shorts, her nipples would poke through her thin size-A bra."

Richard's second beer arrived. "*Bleah!*" he said, raising the glass to his lips. "Let me cleanse my palate of that image. Finish up; the first beer is on me."

CHAPTER 16

Paris

Cosimo kept the Dali Zodiac watch in a dresser drawer and brought it out only after Proust was covered for the night. From the first day the watch's moving eyes became a target for Proust's curious beak.

Two years after Proust entered their lives, a blue-green parakeet flew in through an open window. He had food, water, a warm room, and a willing stooge. Even though Proust was fifteen times larger, Tito, named after the Yugoslav dictator, was the boss. The two birds sat and chatted for hours as in serious conversation.

"They're plotting something," Sara whispered to Cosimo.

"Are you spying on the parrots?" Cosimo looked up from the newspaper.

"Yes, but they only speak in a damned bird patois. The parakeet refuses to learn French."

Sara never made any attempt to teach Proust to speak. On his own, he learned to say, "Zala" for Sara, came closer with "Como" for Cosimo. They found his mispronunciations endearing. Passages from books Sara read out loud, he would repeat. He imitated her laugh and coughed like

Cosimo. He'd call, "Halo, halo," when he saw Charlotte the concierge. Proust was always aware of the activities in the house.

Sometime in 1958, in the moments before dawn, they heard Proust scream, "Zala, Como. Zala, Como." Cosimo turned on the light and found Tito on the floor, gasping. Sara scooped up the parakeet and tried to warm him with her breath and hands. She gave him water with an eyedropper. Tito's eyes clouded.

Observing it all, Proust hopped on the table where they had placed Tito's small body on a newspaper. He tapped the dead parakeet with his foot, then tenderly scratched the top of Tito's head with his beak.

A half hour after Tito was taken from the room, Proust returned to his cheerful imitation of Sara's laughter. Life went on.

CHAPTER 17

Cosimo's daily walk to the Little House Café took him through the city's wholesale produce market. The scent of dried *ancho* peppers, garlic, and onions, drifting from the stalls, even the unmistakable stench of a rotten potato that had fallen behind the bins embraced him. This was a world he knew and understood. Here produce, grains, even live chickens were sold in bulk.

As busy as it appeared at eight in the morning, he knew from experience that the real action took place long before the rest of the city awoke. By eight, work traffic slowed, and merchants had time to wave at the man in the Panama hat.

For entertainment and sale, stalls displayed vegetable curiosities outside their doors. He'd seen misshapen carrots that looked like men's legs with penises, an eggplant with ears and a crooked nose like a prize fighter, and on that day, several five-foot long cucumbers. At the shop specializing in flour, he saw four sacks set aside like the other oddities. They were priced for much less than a larger pile of similarly packaged flour. The flour sacks were made of colorful cotton fabrics suitable for a child's dress or shirt, Cosimo supposed.

"Why is this smaller pile cheaper," Cosimo asked the merchant.

"Those haven't sold. Women hate that shitty pattern. They've been here two days." The pattern featured little yellow ducklings swimming on a blue background.

"The ducks?"

"Yeah, the ducks. All these other sacks inside will be gone by this afternoon, except for those damn things. My son accepted the delivery. I would have sent them back."

"Is it the same flour as those bags?"

"Exactly the same."

"Will they sell?"

"They better sell today, otherwise the mice will piss on them and I'll have to throw them out."

Before he discovered the Little House Café, Cosimo took his meals at the Kress cafeteria, the Mexican Manhattan, and Schilo's German Delicatessen. The food had been fair to good, and not too expensive. Still, the dollars were adding up. He estimated that he if he were stranded for five or six more weeks, at the rate of four dollars a day he wouldn't make it with the cash in his money belt.

Cosimo shuffled into the Little House Café carrying a twenty-pound sack of Pioneer Mills all-purpose wheat flour. He put the sack on the counter and held it upright while he caught his breath.

Emma turned from the grill and laughed. "Look at you. *Harina del Viejo.*"

"*Viejo?*" He took a labored breath. "I admit, I'm old and I brought flour." He coughed. "Calling me *viejo?* Even if true, is not kind."

"I'm not talking about you, silly. It's the picture on the bag, *harina del viejo.*" She pointed at the paper label with a nineteenth-century tintype photo of a bearded old man.

Cosimo lowered himself onto a stool by the counter.

"What are you going to do with it?" Emma asked.

"It's for you." He closed his eyes, took a deep breath, and coughed.

"For me? You shouldn't have." Emma laughed. "Gracie, come out here," she called toward the back of the café.

"What?" Graciela backed out of the pantry and pushed her reading glasses to her forehead. "Emma, get that man water. He's choking."

"Where did you get it?" Emma asked abruptly.

"I didn't steal it," he said, clearing his throat. "I was amazed at the price."

Emma put a glass of water in front of him.

"Thank you." He took a long drink. "I brought flour for the café," he said. "I want you to make flour tortillas and, of course, put some of your specialties inside them. I offer this in what I hope is an acceptable down payment until I can pay my bill, which will be soon."

"You want me to feed you, and you're paying in advance with a sack of all-purpose flour?"

"Actually, four sacks with the little ducks."

"How will they get here?" Graciela asked. "You can't carry sixty pounds of flour."

"I know. I shouldn't have carried this. I thought my offer would be more credible if I had the flour to show you. The rest will come with your next delivery."

"Did they give you a choice of fabrics, or did you choose the ducks?" niggled Emma.

"I find them surreal in their cheeriness." He put palms together as in prayer. "The ducks do not matter. If the flour was packaged in a paper sack, which you would throw away, it would still be a great price."

Graciela looked to Emma. "Why not?" They laughed.

"I have one additional request," he added.

"Okay?" Graciela couldn't help herself, she laughed even more. "This is going to be good."

"I noticed the café is empty from about nine thirty until about eleven."

"Thank you for pointing that out!" Graciela reacted.

"No, *por favor*. I have a skill I learned when I was a young. Let me try it for a few days and we'll see how it works."

"Is this legal? I run a café, I'm not licensed for anything else. What will you do?"

"No money changes hands. No business will be involved. I need a place to draw, and I will only work from 9:30 to 11:00 in the morning. People will find it interesting. Believe me."

Graciela hoisted the sack of flour onto her shoulder. "Four sacks of flour, it's the best offer I've had today. We'll try it for a week and then we'll see." She carried the flour sack to the pantry.

✧ ✧ ✧

Cosimo had been meaning to get to the library and have his letters typed. Not wanting to confront anti-Castro Cubans, he took back streets paralleling the main drag to arrive there.

As Cosimo approached the front desk, Maddie looked up from clearing returned books. She recognized him as the man from the bridge.

"Do you have a public scribe?" he asked, taking out several hand written pages from his courier bag.

"A what?" Maddie looked confused.

"A person who can type letters for me."

"There is. It's to my left, in the reference department."

"How much is it?"

"They'll tell you there."

"I need more help than typing. I'm writing to famous establishments and I don't have their addresses."

"You definitely need the reference department. Ask for Oscar."

He found Oscar in the stacks, shelving books. "A young woman at the front desk said you could help me with this." Cosimo handed Oscar several hand written pages.

"They're in French."

"I need them typed, and I need addresses."

"I don't speak French, and I don't know if there's anyone here who can type this. I'll have to ask. I can try to find your addresses."

"I have a list. Banque Suisse, Charles De Gaulle branch, Paris. The Gallery *L'Idiote* also in Paris, and two friends, individuals, Leonor Fini in Paris, and Margaret Manheim in Venice, Italy. They are both famous."

"The individuals can be hard." Oscar pushed the book cart out of traffic. "Let me see what I can do about addresses. Miss Fischer? Can you please take a look at this?"

Ilene Fischer looked up from her work. She removed white cotton gloves and sleeve protectors and approached the reference desk. She dabbed her nose with a tissue and stuck it in her vest pocket.

"My! That's breath-taking penmanship." She said, taking the paper. "I haven't typed a letter in French for several years. And, understand these are American English typewriters and don't have the French accents. I can put them in by hand afterward, if that's all right. Your letter looks perfectly good. Why do you want it typed?"

"I want it to look businesslike. And I want an exact copy for my records."

"To be clear, your address is General Delivery in San Antonio? You're writing Banque Suisse? For a copy of a check written February 25, 1961, by you, Cosimo Infante Cano in the amount of forty-five thousand dollars?"

"That's correct."

"That's a lot of lettuce." She glanced up.

"Or, cabbage," he deadpanned.

Ilene cracked a smile.

In less than five minutes Oscar returned with addresses for Banque Suisse, Paris, Charles De Gaulle branch, and the gallery.

"I have two addresses for Gallery *L'Idiote*. One on Avenue Montaigne, and the other on Rue Jean Goujon. Do you know which it is?"

"Rue Jean Goujon. It moved there a year ago. On Avenue Montaigne they were within the perfumed proximity of Chanel and Balenciaga. Too expensive for a small gallery specializing in contemporary art."

"I'm narrowing down on Margaret Manheim. Leonor Fini may take me a little longer. Miss Fischer can start on these two."

"How did he do that?" Cosimo asked.

"I actually don't know. He's very quick."

Ilene sandwiched together typing paper, carbon paper, and onionskin paper, tapped them on the desk to align the edges, placed the sandwiched papers into the typewriter carriage, and cranked them into position. She paused. "The carbon's near-fresh and should be good enough. I won't charge you if I have to type your letter again.

"Please, go ahead. I'll pay."

He found the steady tapping comforting. He closed his eyes and imagined Sara at her desk, a dictionary and the thesaurus opened next to her. Her hand-written translations crumpled, littering the floor. Proust on his stand rocking back and forth as if dancing to the rhythm of the typing.

Oscar touched Cosimo's shoulder.

"Mr. Cano, I have an address for a Manheim Museum on the Grand Canal in Venice. Could that be Margaret Manheim?"

"That is her, thank you. Thank you."

Before Ilene started the second letter to Gallery *L'Idiote*, she reviewed the contents. "You are requesting they send you photos of paintings sold to the person, Sara Hunter? And to please send photographs of all documented paperwork? And to urgently contact these two names on your behalf, Margaret Manheim and Leonor Fini?"

"That's correct," he replied.

"I can't find anything on Leonor Fini," said Oscar. "She's not listed in *International Who's Who*. What does she do?"

"She is a famous artist and works as a set designer in cinema and opera."

"I haven't given up. If you can come back at two this afternoon, I'll see what I can find. If I'm not here, I'll leave a note for you at the reference desk. What is your name?"

"Cosimo Infante Cano. Do you wish for me to spell it?"

"I have it. *Cosimo,* as in De Medici, Infante as in Pedro, and C-A-N-O, Cano."

Oscar's glibness reminded Cosimo of critics who loved the sound of their own voice more than they understood art. He regretted even having that thought about someone so eager and naïve.

The librarian's first drafts with the carbon copies came to three dollars and twenty cents. Not a lot of money but a reminder of his dwindling cash.

CHAPTER 18

The following morning, Emma kneaded fresh dough for tortillas and served Cosimo breakfast. In the lull between the breakfast and lunch crowd, he did something he had not done for fifty-two years. As a seventeen-year-old living in Paris, desperate to find a way to feed himself, with nothing more than a folding chair and a sketchpad, he had set up near other artists above the River Seine, and for a franc he would narrate an Aesop's fable and illustrate a key moment from the story. He'd drawn the images so many times, each sketch varied only slightly. Of course, that had been several lifetimes ago.

Sitting at the table in the corner at the Little House Café, he un-wrapped a newly purchased wooden ink pen with a flexible pointed steel nib. He opened a one-ounce bottle of Bombay India ink and dipped the pen. He practiced crosshatch, curved lines. By carefully changing the pressure on the nib, the lines he drew on the page could taper from broad to slender. He drew a mouse's nose and a lion's snout next to it.

"I'm not as dexterous as I was when I was eighteen," he said to Graciela and Emma.

"I didn't say anything," Emma replied.

Here, far away from his artist friends and critics, he felt safe attempting something different. His life's experiences had made him rethink his interpretation of the fables. He felt thrilled and terrified at the prospect of beginning a work of art.

He went to the shelf where Graciela kept the uncirculated menus, selected one, and handled it with his fingertips, as if it were fine drawing paper. He placed the menu on the table, blank side up.

Graciela and Emma were riveted by his every move. He dipped the pen in ink, and where the paper had been white space before, a sad lion with a thorn in its paw appeared.

From the first day, customers lingered with a cup coffee and a piece of pie to watch him draw. By the third day a handful of strangers became regulars and hurried from their office breaks to watch how the drawings were progressing.

"He reminds me of Gustave Doré," a middle-aged man in a tweed blazer said to a woman he'd wanted to meet for weeks. About forty years old, she stood a few inches shorter. He'd seen her once at a bus stop and had no idea where he might see her again.

She turned to him. "Except the line is more whimsical and spare."

"His use of the pen is masterful, and I'm a draftsman. I should know," the man boasted, then felt like an idiot for saying it.

She nodded in an agreement. "His feathered lines make me want to cry. Look how the lion's claws taper at the end, or the whiskers on the scared little mouse make a statement!"

"I know. I know. I'm fascinated. Ah . . . However, I have to get back to work. I'll be coming back tomorrow. My name is John."

"My break is at 10:30. I'm Colleen."

"Tomorrow, then." They nearly said together.

John glanced back as he was about to exit. There she was, the woman he'd wanted to meet for weeks, and at that moment she turned and acknowledged him. He couldn't help grinning as he hurried away.

Cosimo smiled and opened a narrow metal box of Faber-Castell colored pencils.

That evening, back at the Buena Vista Street Cabins, Emma brought Cosimo men's clothing she had washed, ironed, and put on wire hangers. Cosimo appreciated the good intentions. Nothing fit, and he looked even more derelict in the baggy hand-me-downs.

"Tomorrow we go to Solo Serve," Emma said. "Come by the café at four o'clock. I'll take you and show you how to shop. I worked at Solo Serve."

The store reminded Cosimo of shops in Havana crowded with stock, some new, some old, and some peculiar.

"Solo Serve sells stock overruns, seconds, and irregulars from the clothing factories here in town," said Emma. "These linen trousers sell at Macy's in New York for thirty dollars. At Solo Serve they are eight dollars." Emma held up a pair.

"How do you know that?"

"It says so on the tag. It's a stock overrun. There are only so many, and they're a good deal."

Cosimo purchased two. Among the counters stacked with men's shirts, one displayed shirts for nineteen cents each.

"You don't want those." Emma took his arm, leading him away. "They don't have collars. Over here are the Hathaway and Arrow shirts, name brands with the labels removed. Those are antique stock that's been sitting in the warehouse for over forty years, and they put them out with every sale."

"I know they're out of style. Look at how well they are made, and they fit." He slipped one on. "I wore shirts like this in Cuba with celluloid collars."

"You can't find celluloid collars anymore."

"I won't need the collars, and at nineteen cents I can have five shirts for a dollar."

"If that's what you want, okay," said Emma.

The Solo Serve leather shoes were stiff. The only footwear that didn't hurt his feet was a pair of grey knockoff Hushpuppies. To retain a bit of his previous *persona*, he purchased six red workman's bandanas.

Emma washed, lightly starched, and ironed the shirts. The following morning, he put on a clean shirt and pants, tied a red bandana loosely around his neck, and went to the Little House Café for breakfast and his drawing session.

CHAPTER 19

Monday morning, May 8, 8:55 a.m., the library staff assembled in the lobby for a morning briefing. Dr. Samuels paced, stopping to look out through the glass panes at the main doors.

Ruthann, Jane Jenkins, the children's librarian, and Crissy Lamb, the literature librarian, entered last and stood apart from a larger group that included the custodian, Virgil Harper, Ilene Fischer, Maddie, Richard, and several other pages.

Samuels stopped pacing, noting Ruthann and her allies stood apart from the other staff.

"We're going to do business today as if this were any other day," said Samuels. "Nothing is different. Everyone must be treated as any other library patron. Remember, library card applications require a name, a current address, and a phone number if they have one. Our application has a space for the patron's age. As you all know, filling that space for adults is optional. No one should make an issue of it."

"How do we know if they can even read?" Ruthann grumbled.

"Ruthann, it presupposes that if they can fill out an application, they can read."

"What if they just make marks?" She baited him.

"My god! Ruthann!" Samuels raised his voice. "As long as the marks look like a name and address, that's enough. And . . ." He looked at the three librarians. "And of course, as you should know, the library actually has books to help people learn to read."

Maddie and Richard suppressed a laugh. Ruthann glowered at them.

"That doesn't mean I have to have any contact with them. We have our rights, too!" Ruthann spoke for the three.

"That's exactly what this means." Samuels took a deep breath.

"If they have a right to be served, we have a right not to serve them," Ruthann argued.

Samuels turned his back to the rest of the staff and addressed the three in a lowered voice. "No. We've been over this. You, Miss Jenkins, and Miss Lamb do not have a choice in this. The library board has settled the lawsuit, which means we, and that means *you* too, must provide service to all residents. Not complying at this moment will reflect on your future employment."

"Are you threatening us? Morris Forester will hear of this."

"Tell your uncle whatever you want. He voted with the rest of the library board. Please, unlock the doors," he said to Virgil.

Virgil, in his gray twill uniform, unlocked the door.

Most of the regulars and experienced patrons went about their business. A group of ten African American men, women, and children entered and approached the front desk. The men wore suits and ties, the women, dresses and hats, and the children, their Sunday clothes.

Samuels stepped up like a guide about to give a tour. "Welcome. I'm Dr. Samuels, director of the library. Please look around. As most of you know, there are different departments. If you need directions just ask here at the front desk. I expect that all of you, at least the adults, know how to use the card catalog and our reference department. If you have a library card from any of the branch libraries, including the George Washington Carver Branch, we will accept those here."

Ruthann and the children's and literature librarians left the lobby.

Samuels stepped behind the front desk. "Who wants to apply for a library card?" His eyes searched hastily for the applications. He turned to the staff. "Will someone please get our patrons applications for a card?"

None of the white employees moved. Ilene Fischer held a tissue to her eyes and exited, as did most of the pages. Samuels fingered through different forms, not finding the applications.

Maddie stepped in, quickly locating the forms. "Sorry I didn't start right up, college finals, you know." She mimed a yawn and winked at the three adults waiting in line. She held out a box with pencils in all lengths and colors. "Wait, I'm discovering that some of these pencils don't have points. Hand those back, I have plenty of sharp ones."

Ruthann reentered the perimeter of the room and glared.

"Does anyone have any questions?"

"I can't stay long. I have to be at work." said a young woman. "But I'll be back. I love mysteries, you know, like Raymond Chandler."

Maddie took the woman's application, spun a blank library card into the typewriter.

"Connie Childress?"

Connie nodded.

"Have you read *Anatomy of a Murder* by Robert Travers?" asked Maddie.

"You mean like the movie?" asked Connie.

"Yes, like the movie. Which I haven't seen. Over the Christmas holidays I started reading the book on a Saturday afternoon and didn't put it down until 3:00 a.m., Sunday morning." Maddie finished the card and handed it to the young woman.

"I look forward to reading it." Connie filed the card in her wallet.

Maddie tried not to focus on Ruthann's relentless stare.

The next patron could hardly see over the desktop. "I would like an application, please," asked a tiny voice.

Maddie leaned over the desk. "How old are you?" Maddie smiled, surprised by this petite person who spoke so clearly.

"I'm five and a half. May I have an application?"

Maddie pushed a form across the desk. "Get your mommy to help you fill this out. When you return it, I'll issue you a library card."

The child looked into Maddie's eyes. "May I have a pencil, please?"

Maddie placed a sharpened pencil in her small hand.

Ruthann shook her head. Maddie was about to issue a library card to an illiterate. Of course, she was hoping for a better example, but there it was.

The child stood on her toes and wrote slowly, deliberately. When she finished she dropped back on her heels and slid the form back to Maddie.

Maddie chuckled, rolled in a blank library card, and typed the child's name, address, and phone number.

"Childress, Shirley. Is that lady waiting over there related to you?"

"She's my auntie," said the child. "She's waiting for me. She takes me places when my parents work." The child bent down and brought up several books. "I want to check these out."

"How . . . how did you even have time to look for these?" asked Maddie.

"I'm very fast," she replied. Across the room Virgil beamed.

All the library employees had returned to their posts; only Richard remained. He slipped behind Maddie. "I'll check out your books over here," he said, taking the books from the child. "Shirley, you'll have to return them in two weeks." He stamped the books with a return due date.

"If it's all right, I'll be back on Wednesday," she said.

"That's perfectly all right," Richard replied.

Shirley and her aunt gathered the books and left the building.

Richard spoke in Maddie's ear. "I saw what you did."

"Do you think we still have jobs?" Maddie whispered, seeing Ruthann charging in their direction. Ruthann snatched the applications from the desktop.

"Who was that, some kind of circus midget?"

"She's five years old. Wasn't she sweet? She did that all by herself."

"How dare you. There's nothing sweet about this. This whole deal has to be a confidence game."

"Confidence game? That's nuts. What are they going to con? Free library books?"

"What? Did you just call me nuts? I don't take backtalk from the likes of you. I'll have you fired for that."

Maddie took the forms from Ruthann's hands and found the child's application. She read, "Shirley Childress, date of birth, November 6, 1956. That makes her five and a half. She filled out the application herself. Look at that handwriting. It belongs to a very bright child, not some adult."

"She's a damned circus midget!" Ruthann said with finality and turned to leave.

"And if she were a dwarf," Maddie called after Ruthann, "would you deny her a library card for being short?"

Ruthann paused. Unable to think of a retort, her face flushed red, and she stalked away.

An hour later, Richard and Maddie were summoned to the library's conference room. Waiting there were Dr. Samuels and a very tall man in his fifties, in a tailor-made western-styled suit and Stetson hat. Ruthann followed them in and took a seat at the head of the table.

"Maddie Parker and Richard Krabb, take a seat anywhere. This is Morris Forester, president of the library board, and as you may know, mayor of our fair city."

Maddie and Richard nodded.

Forester glanced from Ruthann to the two pages. "I understand there were problems this morning with the first day of integration."

Dr. Samuels's thin neck squirmed in his shirt, "No sir. There were no problems. In fact, everything went smoothly, I thought."

"That's not what I'm being told. I'm talking about the disrespect shown to Ruthann, here. Do you allow underlings to speak insolently to their supervisors?"

"Sir," Richard, his voice wavering, raised his hand.

"*What*!" Forester replied sharply.

"Sir, no one spoke insolently to anyone, and I was there. Maddie wasn't in any manner disrespectful."

Ruthann couldn't contain herself. "She backtalked, contradicted me, and called me nuts. That's what she did. She's a page! She's only been here a short time and she's become a disruptive force."

"No!" Maddie looked at Samuels. "No."

"And Dr. Samuels berated me this morning in front of the entire staff. I was humiliated," Ruthann continued.

Samuels held up his hand. "I'm stopping you right there, Ruthann. If we're going to discuss my actions, policy says we do so in private."

Dr. Samuels stood and opened the door. "Sir, I'm not firing anyone. I am letting these two return to their posts. They don't have to be here."

Samuels closed the door behind them. Maddie continued toward the elevator as Richard dropped to one knee to tie his shoe. He leaned toward the door, straining to hear Samuels's defense.

"I didn't see the exchange between Miss Parker and Ruthann, but those are two outstanding young people. I am not going to fire them."

The mayor's voice thundered throughout the floor.

"I don't give a crap about them. Fire them, don't fire them. I don't care. I got a call from the newspaper today. They asked me if this was going to change policy across the board for the city, with this civil rights violence breaking out all over the South. Do you know how this makes me look to white voters? It makes me look weak on segregation. Soldiers

91

don't vote, Mexicans don't vote, and only a handful of the coloreds vote. White people vote. You don't rile them 'cause that makes them vote for the other guy."

"Sir, we have grants. And you approved them."

"If you hadn't applied for those goddamned grants, we wouldn't have to share our library with Negroes, at least, not in this off-year election."

"Sir, political issues aside, economically, without the grants the library is unsustainable. The joint command of the five military bases has made it clear. Any business that denies services to military personnel or their dependents will be declared off-limits. For us, that means pulling our funding."

"That was President Kennedy's doing. Mixing all the races," chimed in Ruthann.

Samuels shrugged. "Ruthann, you may be right, but for all the wrong reasons."

"See, how he is?" Ruthann said to the mayor.

"Shit . . . yeah, well," The mayor shook his head. "Samuels, I'll tell you what's the right thing to do. If I hear any more complaints about disrespect or humiliation to Ruthann, I don't care what your excuse is, you're out. Got that? You're out."

Richard hastened to catch up with Maddie. The conference room door opened. Dr. Samuels emerged, his face pale. Walking past, he muttered, "Go back to work, and for god's sake, stay out of her way."

CHAPTER 20

Virgil opened the loading dock door and held it as librarians and pages hurried past.

"Are we still on for beer?" Oscar caught up with Richard.

Richard drew Oscar away from the exiting staff. "I asked Maddie to join us."

"What happened to . . . you know?" Oscar whispered.

"It was stupid of me. She changed my mind. Man, she's got nerve. I mean like, she's got backbone, pluck."

"Pluck? Like *Nancy Drew: Detective* pluck?" Oscar smirked. "How'd that happen?"

"Not here, I'll tell you in a bit."

Maddie exited and grinned at seeing the two. "Hi, guys."

"Getting a beer with us?" Oscar asked, delighted by the prospect.

"Sure, after the day we had," indicating Richard and herself. "I can use company and a beer."

"We don't have a Corvette," teased Richard.

"Come on guys, you're not going to hold it against me because I got a ride in a sports car?"

"Not from me," said Richard.

"Oh yeah, not you," grumbled Oscar. "By the way, the bar isn't close."

"Guys, it's a beautiful night. Let's walk and talk." She pushed between them and locked her arms through theirs. "Which way?"

Richard nodded toward the street. Arm-in-arm, half-running, laughing, she dragged them down the stairs. Richard caught a whiff of her hair and Oscar felt her breast press against his arm.

As Richard closed the gate behind them, he saw Ruthann Medlin standing on the loading dock, scowling.

"Let's bug out," he urged.

"Like flies let's flee from the flue," Maddie laughed.

Ruthann couldn't hear what they were saying, but seeing them parading arm-in-arm down Market Street toward the seedy part of town, she couldn't help but conclude that they were laughing at her.

Richard leaned across Maddie to speak to Oscar. "Long story short, this morning, tense situation. First day of integration, no librarian steps forward to support Samuels. Maddie comes forward and saves Samuels's butt."

"Not Fischer?" asked Oscar.

"Nope," said Richard.

"No one did, except Maddie."

"It was embarrassing watching the boss of the library fumbling for an application," said Maddie.

"First day of integration, people got library cards, checked out books, and everyone went about their business. Afterwards, the situation got strange. Ruthann claimed a five-year-old kid was really a circus midget. Maddie told her the idea was *nuts,* then asked Ruthann if she would deny someone a library card because they were short!" Richard laughed. "Ruthann got the red ass. She's the mayor's niece, and Forester threatened to fire Samuels if she isn't treated right."

"Which means if he goes, we go." Maddie shook her head.

"Samuels left the meeting looking like he was going to puke," said Richard. "And I'm afraid this creates a problem for you."

"How's that?" said Oscar.

"You're guilty by association. Ruthann was standing on the loading dock and saw you leaving with us tonight."

"What say, Mr. Oscar?" Maddie asked, impishly.

He shrugged.

"Guess what? This guy wouldn't shut up the last time we got a beer.

And now he's a clam," Richard ragged.

"I've got nothing to say," Oscar said.

"He's had an opinion on everything," continued Richard, "except for this evening. And do you want to know why, *senorita*? Because, you're his perfect woman, see? And he wants to love you from afar."

"Shut up! That's not what I said," growled Oscar.

"He moons after you. He loves your body: your legs, your butt, and has an appreciation for your small breasts. Oh yes, he likes that you're smart." Richard grinned.

She turned to Oscar. "Is that true?" she asked sternly.

Oscar nodded, afraid of other misrepresentations Richard might make.

"That's really sweet, thank you." She drew him closer and kissed his cheek. "Do you think my breasts are small?"

"I never said small. I never said anything about your . . . They're . . . oh, crap, I don't want . . . they're perfect for you. Richard's being a prick."

"Hey!" Richard reacted.

"Asshole," Oscar mouthed behind Maddie's back.

Maddie freed her arms. "Let's get to know each other. Tell me, Richard. What do you want to be when you grow up?" She patted his shoulder like a big sister.

"I'm a music major."

"What instrument?" She asked as if she also played.

"I play piano, which is definitely passé. I do modern composition. This Sunday afternoon I'll perform my latest work at 2:00 p.m. in the basement of Holy Trinity Church. I have a flyer in the break room, and one on the public bulletin in the lobby. Will you come?"

"How is a piano passé?" Maddie wondered aloud.

"Like the harpsichord is a primitive piano, the Theremin or something like it will become the next step in music evolution."

"Is it like John Coltrane?" asked Maddie.

"No, it's abstract, maybe hard to comprehend if you're not accustomed to music that doesn't have a melody, and we don't play on instruments."

"What *do* you play on?" Oscar said.

"You have to hear it. It is part edited recordings, part electronic, static and feedback, and for the lack of a better explanation, part live percussion."

"Anything like John Cage?" asked Maddie.

"You know John Cage?" Richard asked, surprised.

"What I've read in *Dance Magazine*. Cage is Merce Cunningham's musical director. I've never heard his music. The article said he once made an audience listen to four and a half minutes of nothing, while he stared at a piano."

"It wasn't 'nothing.' The audience listened to ambient sound. That's not composing to me. It's an idea, an art performance. Silence is beautiful, but so is noise. My work is a little like experimental John Cage, more like Karlheinz Stockhausen, but very different."

"Stockhausen? Don't know him. How about you?" She turned to Oscar.

"You guys left me at John Cage," admitted Oscar.

"What do you think of jazz, like Miles Davis?" asked Maddie.

"I like Coltrane, Miles, Horace Silver. Lately, I'm listening to Ornette Coleman's *The Shape of Jazz to Come*. I have the album if you want to hear it. It's great, not like anything that I would compose, though."

"What about you, Oscar? What kind of music do you like?" Maddie pressed her forehead into his head.

"I like Nat King Cole, Ray Charles; Mexican music, *mariachis*, and *huapangos*, particularly. Music I've heard all my life. I like the Platters, the Temptations, Chuck Berry, pop stuff."

"And besides *me*," Maddie pushed her hip into his, "what are your passions?"

"Yeah, what are your passions?" echoed Richard.

"I want to write."

"Anything I can read?"

"Yes, this semester the college newspaper published a literary edition. I have a short story and four poems in it."

"Well, I'd like to read them. I'm in the company of a composer and a published author. And . . . I'm? I don't know what the fuck I am."

"You dance. I saw you." Oscar said.

"Yeah, I wanted to do ballet. When I was ten, I saw *The Red Shoes* and thought it would be so cool to die dancing. I took classes for a couple of years, and then we moved and moved again. By the time you're seventeen, if you're not already in a company, you never will be. I want to work in theatre. And guess what? We're one thousand four hundred miles from where I should be."

"You want to be in New York?" asked Oscar.

"There, and at Columbia University, instead of San Antonio Junior

College that I'm forced to attend, though through my own fault, I admit."

"We're all SAC students. It's not the University of Texas. So what?"

"Nothing. I'd just like to be someplace else."

"What does that make us? Nobodies?" asked Richard.

"No, you guys are somebodies. I'm an army brat, as special as gum on your shoe. I've lived in Turkey, Korea, Germany, Virginia. Now, *here*."

"Today you showed everyone you've got the guts of an Amazon," said Richard.

Her shoulders sank. "About today? Shit. I don't know why I did that. I wanted to make the moment right. The director was floundering and I felt sorry for him. And then came Ruthann Medlin. My god, what's with that woman?"

"It was the right thing to do," said Oscar.

"You defied Ruthann Medlin and all the librarians." Richard bowed ceremoniously.

"I was hoping someone else would follow, and you did. That's worth a kiss." She gave Richard a peck on the cheek.

"You've traveled. That's something," said Oscar.

"It doesn't make me special."

"It makes you cosmopolitan," said Oscar. "You don't dress like the girls in any of my classes."

"Cosmopolitan? Hardly, but thank you."

"Look, I've lived here all my life. The farthest I've been from home has been for a week with my family, in the summer at the Triple L Motel on North Beach in Corpus Christi. The smell of the place and the feel of sand in my flip flops make me want to see more than what I see here. In the psychology class I took freshmen year, the instructor asked the class how we saw ourselves, middle class, working class, lower class, or upper class? One pasty clod said he was upper class, but everyone else, including myself, said we were middle class. It's bothered me a bit since that day. My father works as an aircraft radio repairman for the Air Force. My mom does alterations for a local dry cleaner. I felt ashamed to say I'm working class? That bothers me a lot."

"You see what I mean, he just goes off like that." Richard nudged Maddie. "Once he gets on a roll you can't stop him."

"I can understand what Oscar's saying." Maddie nodded. "After twenty years in the Army my father's only a captain, and guess what? I can vouch that he has little or *no* money. He owes two ex-wives back child support. I have stepbrothers I never see. He has no choice, he has to work. He's definitely working class. And me, bouncing from school to school, my grades were crap. They tell us that our permanent record will follow us the rest of our lives. When it's as bad as mine, they're not lying."

"Can't be that bad," said Oscar. "You had to submit a transcript to get this job."

"How do you expect to get into Columbia University?" Richard asked.

"A girl can hope. Good things happen when I've put myself into the trajectory of my dreams."

"Seriously? Has it worked?" asked Oscar.

Maddie cracked a smile. "I keep trying."

"I bet you're one of those types who gets an A-minus and believes you're a failure," said Richard.

They laughed.

Nearing the bar, they passed a dark maroon car parked in the penumbra between the streetlights and darkness. For an instant Maddie caught a glimpse of something inside the car. She was about to mention it, when Richard ran ahead and held the barroom door open for her.

"Across the street the Missouri Pacific train station, and over here cheap beer and atmosphere," said Richard.

"What kind of honky-tonk is this?" Maddie closed her eyes. "Wow, it comes with the scent of farts and aftershave."

"I think it's called Elroy's. That's what they call the bartender." Richard waved to Elroy, who ignored him.

"Here, nostalgia reeks," remarked Oscar.

Three sunbaked good-old-boys sitting at the bar leaned back and leered as Maddie entered.

"Can't be a honky-tonk, there isn't a jukebox." Richard took a seat at the table by the window.

A rangy good-old-boy immediately rose and approached. "Hi, girly, I'm Jake. These are my friends, Slim and Casey." Two men in their late twenties or early thirties joined him. Their tanned faces were shaved, and their fresh haircuts were slicked with Brylcreem. They were likely the source of the flatulence and aftershave cloud.

"We've been waiting for you. Get rid of the Mexican and the wimp and we can party hardy." Jake looked at Oscar and Richard like he could wad them up like a sheet of paper.

Under the table Maddie squeezed Oscar's and Richard's knees.

"We've got forty-eight hours before we report back to the rig, and we've got money and time for fun." The men's arms and knuckles were scarred and scabbed from oil rig work.

"Roustabouts! What an offer! I'm very flattered, gentlemen. You see, I can't do that tonight, as much as that sounds enticing, especially with your roll of cash. I'm on diplomatic duty. No can do. I represent the city of San Antonio, and these are the mayor's guests. I want you to meet John Cage. He's in town for a production of his new symphonic piece. What's it called, John?"

"It's . . . it's called *Air, Water, Earth, Fire, Synchronous,*" Richard mumbled.

"Do you have one of your flyers?" she asked.

"Eh, no."

"Well, they're all over the city. It's too bad since you only have two days. I'm sure the mayor's office would get you tickets for the performance on Sunday afternoon."

She motioned toward Oscar. "And this is Kemal Ataturk, a brilliant young Turkish author. He doesn't speak English. He's on tour to college campuses in the United States. And I'm Ruthann Medlin, Mayor Forester's niece. The train station was one of the sites these gentlemen wanted to see. And as part of the mayor's volunteer welcoming committee, we're here absorbing the atmosphere. Would you like to join us?"

She turned to Oscar. "*Ben mavi bir kalem. Nasılsınız?*"

She squeezed his thigh, Oscar nodded, he hoped convincingly.

"Bullshit," said one of the roughnecks.

"If you don't believe me, look outside. You'll see a plain maroon sedan parked about twenty yards away with a man in the driver's seat facing straight ahead. It's our police escort. They're keeping an eye on our dignitaries."

One of the men went to the doorway, took a look and nodded.

"Would you like to meet him? I have a police whistle."

Jake tossed two dollars on the table. "No need to call the police. We're sorry to bother you, ma'am."

The men exited the bar, glanced toward the maroon sedan and walked in the opposite direction.

Richard exhaled. He'd been holding his breath. "They scared the crap out of me."

"They sure beat it out of here in a hurry. What the hell did you just do?" Oscar cracked. "What did you say to me, and what if they had agreed to join us?"

"You would have had to keep your mouth shut all evening. Under the circumstances, the less you guys said the better. And what I said was, 'I have a yellow pencil, how do you do,' in Turkish."

"See, your cosmopolitan skills saved our ass," said Oscar.

"I didn't see a dark sedan." Richard looked toward the door.

Maddie opened her purse. "When we walked past, I saw the driver staring straight ahead; and there was someone in the car on their knees, apparently giving him a blow job."

"What!" chortled Oscar.

"How did you see that, and we didn't?" Richard went to the door to check for himself.

"Because you were paying attention to me," she laughed.

The bartender came to their table and Maddie handed him her ID. Elroy studied the card.

"Let's pool our cash," offered Richard. "Thirty-three cents apiece buys a pitcher!"

"Not tonight. We don't need that. Our friends bought us two pitchers." Maddie gave the bartender two dollars.

"Can I see that?" Oscar asked Maddie for her ID.

"It says you're twenty-two. And, your name is Eunice Roebock." He handed the ID back.

She replaced it in her wallet. "I have two IDs, one for me and one for her. We're the same height, weight, have the same color eyes. It goes without saying that I drink, and this Maddie person doesn't."

Elroy brought two pitchers and three glasses, deftly placing them on the table without spilling a drop. "You sent away my best customers. If you ever do that again, I'll kick your underage asses out of here." Elroy returned to the bar.

"I told you, he just wanted our precious dimes," Oscar said.

"And I told you I was buying the beer. You guys will have to leave the tip." Maddie took her first sip and grimaced.

Outside the bar a man's faint voice could be heard, "Ahhh. Ah . . . ahhh . . . aaah . . . ooooooooohh shit." A few minutes later, the door swung open. A man entered, his hand shot to the door and held on until he regained stability. His fly was open and his pants sagged below his potbelly.

Maddie laughed, gagged, and snorted beer through her nose. Oscar rolled out of his chair, knelt on the floor laughing. Richard's face reddened, contorted, and froze. He gasped for breath until laughter came.

CHAPTER 21

Paris, 1959—1961

By 1959, Cosimo felt his mastery of his brush and hand were the best they'd ever been. The problem was he'd run out of inspiration. He'd missed two deadlines to deliver new work. Emile Campo, the owner of *L'Idiote Gallery,* reluctantly informed him that his space was going to another artist.

The world around him had become too familiar. He was blind to the things that normally inspired him. He was forgetting things, too, losing track of where he left a book or a favorite brush. Sometimes he'd find himself standing in a room and not remembering why he was there. He continued to go to his studio and spent the day tidying to the point the studio looked more like a painting than his work space.

In April 1960, Charlotte brought an envelope to their door. Normally, mail was placed in their boxes in the lobby.

"You have an international airmail special delivery," said Charlotte. "I assumed it was urgent."

"Thank you, Charlotte." Sara accepted the envelope and closed the door.

"What is it?" asked Cosimo.

"Well, it ain't gonna be good news," she said in English.

Sara opened the envelope and read the letter. When she finished she sat at the dining table across from him. "It's from mother's attorney. Mother's dead."

"I'm sorry, *querida*." Cosimo rose and stood beside her.

She buried her face in his chest.

As her initial grief ebbed, her shoulders relaxed.

"Damn, damn, damn. I'm not ready for this," she said, drying her eyes.

"No one is ready for deaths."

"No, that's not it. I'll be acting CEO of Hunter Enterprises until the board selects someone else. I'm afraid I have to return to Texas."

"You do what you must do. Proust and I will manage," said Cosimo, glancing at the parrot.

Hoping for a quick turnaround to the Hunter business, Sara flew to Texas only to discover that all board meetings and legal proceedings had to be scheduled with time allowed for deliberations. The work of a CEO wasn't foreign to her. She'd grown up at her grandfather's knee. She was a teen when he had a stroke and her mother, as CEO, oversaw the expansion of Hunter Enterprises.

She loved her grandfather and mother, but generally clashed with the money-obsessed cousins and their similarly obsessed spouses and offspring.

"I'm stuck here," she wrote Cosimo. "I may have to remain a couple of years. Please, please, come join me. San Antonio is a hick military town. The river and the Mexicans make this the only place to live in Texas. I'm sitting on the banks of the San Antonio River, behind the public library on a bench made of native limestone. It's a tranquil haven from the wretched business of business. From where I sit, I can see a bridge that appears to be made with an Erector Set right in the middle of the city. I digress. I've inherited a city house in San Antonio and a second house in Wimberley. Until I get all the business done with, we can grow our own food, and you can have a studio. I know you don't want to fly, but please, come," she wrote. "I'll arrange for everything. Please."

Cosimo knew his life options had narrowed. Before all the Texas business materialized, Sara had suggested they take a sabbatical from Paris. He was thinking Beirut or Cairo, but San Antonio, Texas?

His friend Margaret Manheim, with Max Ernst and other artists, had waited out World War II in the Sedona, Arizona, desert. Margaret raved about it being as close to heaven as any place can be on earth. Perhaps San Antonio could give him a similar creative kick. He agreed to join Sara in Texas with the proviso that they lease a smaller apartment in their *Rue Delambre* building where Proust could reside until they returned. It was a ridiculous idea, an apartment for a parrot.

"Anything you want, Babe," she wrote. "I'll make the arrangements for everything."

Sara returned to Paris in February 1961, to help with his immigration papers and arrange shipping of two steamer trunks of his personal belongings. She accompanied him to *Banque Swisse* to transfer funds from his account to her American bank.

He would travel to Texas with two suitcases, the larger one for his street clothing, the smaller with his studio garb and personal items he'd need for the two-week journey.

On the morning she departed for the US, she hurriedly tended to last minute details. "I put in new underwear in your small bag—"

"*Querida*, do you want to put a note around my neck, too? I am not a child on my first boat ride. I have traveled to the United States before."

Sara shook her head. "Don't tease me. I'm doing the best I can. And, dear heart, you were in the United States forty-eight years ago. I hear they drive cars now. I've put four hundred dollars in your new belt, and my address and phone number in your wallet. When you get to New York, call me. I'm always home after 4:00 p.m. central time zone. I don't have servants so if there's no answer, obviously I'm not home."

Sara handed him a typed letter with her signature. "Last night, I remembered there was one last thing I had to do. I wrote you a letter stating that the transfer of the money from your bank to mine is only temporary, until you open your own account. There are also a few mushy lines about how I feel about you. You need to sign it, too."

He signed two copies and returned one to her.

"That makes me feel better," she said, folding the letter into her purse.

Proust rocked back and forth calling, "Zala, Zala." The bird knew this was goodbye.

"Proust, sweetie. I'll be back. I've arranged for Charlotte to spend time with you every day." She kissed his head.

She kissed Cosimo. "I'll be in London for two days to finish some business. In New York you'll stay at the Roosevelt Hotel. I'll leave your train tickets and all the travel details you'll need at the front desk."

Charlotte knocked on the door; Sara's taxi had arrived.

At the curb of *Rue Delambre*, life looked ever so normal. Cars and motor scooters buzzed past. The newsstand's headline read: "Bomb Explosion Kills Mayor of Evian. French Algerian Peace Talks on Hold." *Les Deux Canards* was opening its doors as if waking. The flower stall had set out a tray of fragrant violets. Cosimo selected a bunch, kissed it, and pressed it between Sara's breasts. She mock-frowned. Her hands were full and there was no way she could stop him.

"Thank you for doing this for me," she said.

CHAPTER 22

Pounding on the cabin door startled Cosimo awake. The two-by-four wedged against the doorknob fell aside and the door swung open. Pito stuck his head into the room.

"*Señor* Cano?" he whispered.

"Pito, what the hell? What time is it? I thought that board was there so I could sleep in peace." Cosimo stood and stepped into his trousers.

"It's 1:00 a.m." Pito backed out to the porch. "Can you pay the rent today?"

"The rent's not due until Friday. Can it wait until then?"

Pito's eyes looked down. "*Heh*," he sighed. "*Hombre*, if you can, I need the money now. I gave all my cash to workers to buy tiles. My aunt is dying and I have to catch the bus to Pearsall. I'm her only relative. So, if you can pay two weeks in advance . . . "

"Two weeks?" Cosimo went to the dresser and opened the drawer.

"I'll make it up to you when I get back. I'm sorry about the board. I have a lock for the door, I just haven't gotten around to installing it. I'll fix it. Pearsall is seventy miles up the road. I'll be gone a week."

Cosimo handed Pito twelve dollars. He had sixteen remaining.

"*Gracias*, I'll make it up to you, *Señor* Cano. I promise."

Pito's tired body limped into the darkness.

"*Señor* Pito," Cosimo called after him.

Pito turned.

"My sympathy about your aunt. Considering our mutual financial situations, I know this is a peculiar question. What is the best jewelry store in town?"

"Everybody knows Hertzberg's at the corner of St. Mary's and Houston Streets. There's a big clock in front." He waited, expecting an explanation.

"I have something I might sell," Cosimo replied. He turned off the light and went back to bed.

In the morning Cosimo showered, shaved, brushed his fake Hushpuppies, shouldered his courier bag, and adjusted the bandana around his neck. "My friend, do not take this personally. I am seeking a temporary solution to our problems," he said to the watch before placing it in his courier bag.

He may not have dressed like everyone else, but because Emma washed and ironed his clothes, he no longer felt like a vagrant. He had breakfast at the Little House and fulfilled his morning art performance.

Hertzberg's Jewelry's exterior mimicked the look of an old world shop. A large dark green cast-iron clock stood on the street corner. The shop was painted the same shade of green as the clock, with black semi-gloss trim around the display windows and doorway. Clerks stopped whatever they were doing when he entered.

"I would like to speak to the manager, please," he said to the clerk closest to him.

"Mr. Goodman is on the phone," said the clerk.

Seeing Cosimo, the manager pointed to the phone as if the call was important, then waved with the back of his hand to send him away.

"He's on the telephone I don't know how long—"

"I can see he's engaged," Cosimo interrupted. "I will wait. When he's finished, you can tell him I'm here to see him."

The ruse of appearing too busy didn't work. "I'll have to call you back," Goodman said into the receiver and returned it to the cradle.

Approaching Cosimo, he held out his hand. "I'm Allen Goodman, the manager. How can I be of assistance?"

"Yes, may we speak in your office?"

"We can speak here." Goodman looked about the room, and saw five curious employees.

"I am Cosimo Infante Cano. I am a citizen of both France and Cuba."
He took out his passports and held them open for Goodman to see.

"I am in the city by unfortunate circumstances, which are too long to explain. What is important is that I am who I say I am and have documents to verify my identity. I am here for no more than a few weeks, days maybe. Until then, I have no money to survive and I must make a loan with something that is extremely dear to me, my watch."

"Sir, this isn't a pawn shop. We don't give loans," said Goodman.

Cosimo took out a leather pouch, removed the gold pocket watch and held it out for Goodman to see. The absurd grinning sun's eyes scanned the room.

On the watch's lid, the zodiac symbol for Leo, and the constellation Leo formed the skyscape above the Nemean lion and Heracles locked in battle.

When he opened the watch case, Satie's *Gnossienne No. 1* chimed. Goodman put his two hands together and pressed them to his lips.

On the watch's face, a long second hand swept past the moon cycles, month, day of the month, and day of the week. The hour and second hands pointed at 11:32 a.m. Goodman glanced at the store's indoor clock.

"Your clock is two minutes fast," Cosimo noted.

"It's that way on purpose. The one outside is correct," replied Goodman.

"It's eighteen karat gold, with a thirty-two sapphire movement."

Goodman knew exactly what he was looking at: a limited-edition zodiac watchcase designed by Salvador Dali, with a Piaget movement.

"How do you come by this watch?" he asked, brusquely.

Cosimo turned the watch to see inside the lid, and handed his French passport to Goodman.

"*Cosimo, Time Began With You. Forever Yours, Sara,*" read Goodman.

"I am that Cosimo, and the watch was a gift from Sara Hunter. I was to join her but she died a little over a month ago in an automobile accident. Now I am stranded in this fine city with no money."

Goodman took the watch in his hands. "Meyer, bring your loupe." He beckoned for one of the clerks to approach.

Cosimo continued, "Mind you, I don't believe in any of this astrology part, but it meant a lot to my friend. I was born on August 10, so the zodiac symbol in the front is Leo, and Leo is a sun sign."

Meyer, a short balding man in his sixties, took the watch and put the loupe to his eye. He held his breath and made a long careful inspection, observing the marks and workings of the watch. Looking up, he allowed the loupe to fall into the palm of his hand.

"All the stamps are there," said Meyer. "I believe it's real. I'll have to take it to the bench and have a closer look to make certain. So far, yes."

"This still doesn't make it your property. Do you have a bill of sale, something?" insisted Goodman.

"I have a contact at the immigration office who can tell you who I am, and about my situation. And that this is my watch, as declared in my forms. I told him I was coming to speak to you. Here is his card. You may call him."

"If I call him and he confirms that you are who you say you are, what do you want for this watch?"

"I'd like to make an offer for your consideration. Advance me five hundred dollars, and in sixty days I will buy it back for eight hundred and fifty dollars. You make three hundred and fifty dollars for keeping my watch in your safe. If I cannot make the sixty-day deadline, the watch is yours, and you know the value is over two thousand dollars. I also have the accompanying leather case."

Cosimo looked to Meyer, who shrugged as if to say, "I don't make those decisions."

"I have no intention of losing ownership of this watch," said Cosimo.

"Five hundred, that's a lot of money. And we don't know if it's legally yours," said Goodman.

"Even if it were stolen, which it is not, there would likely be a substantial reward, more than five hundred dollars."

"I'm not a risk taker," admitted Goodman.

"There were only twelve Zodiac watches made in 1928." Cosimo took the watch from Meyer. "Each watch is dedicated to a sign of the Zodiac. On this one, man verses lion, man and nature under the cosmos and the sign for Leo. On the back the sun sees all and grins at the folly around us."

"All that, on one watch," commented Meyers.

"My friend Sara Hunter found the Leo in 1952, the year we moved in together. She had it inscribed as you read."

"I need to think about this," said Goodman. "Meyer, how long will it take you to authenticate the watch?"

Meyer spoke to Cosimo, "Sir, it's not only what I find at the bench here. The timepiece may be one hundred percent authentic. However, before a purchase on anything like this, I have to check the registry for stolen works. I need to know what the eleven others in the series sold for, and what they're going for now. If this were a regular production Piaget, I could tell you what it's worth this minute. I can't with this. It will take at least a week, maybe two, to put an honest value on your watch."

"You will give me a receipt for the watch, signed by two witnesses."

"Actually, we have a form for that. It's a receipt for accepting the watch for appraisal. We do it all the time."

"If you should lose the watch while it's in your possession, you will pay me one thousand eight hundred dollars. My first choice is that I stand by *Señor* Meyer until he finishes his examinations and I take the watch with me."

Meyer grinned. "I can't get over how the sun's eyes move."

"Give the crown two turns," said Cosimo.

Meyer looked at Goodman. Goodman nodded.

The sun's eyes rolled back in its head with each turn. Meyer's face flushed.

"Please open the watch," Cosimo encouraged. "If you open it, on the back and front there are tiny bumps that allow the watch to stand on the mantle or a bedside table," said Cosimo. "It will wake you with Satie's *Gnossienne No. 1*, famous first twelve bars."

Goodman opened the watch as Cosimo suggested and set it on the counter. Visible were the front and back of the case, and the watch face as well.

"How about this as a proposition?" said Goodman. "This watch is a unique work of art. I will not deceive you by telling you otherwise. It is museum worthy. We have nothing in this shop that can match it in design and craftsmanship. I want to put it on display in the window for the public to see. At night it goes into our vault. I will give you a signed receipt and take responsibility for it at nine hundred dollars, if anything should happen to the watch. For this I will pay you fifty dollars a week. In two weeks we will have determined the provenance and authenticity of the watch and know its value. In the meantime, your watch will earn us both money by being on display."

Meyer grinned. "It's a magnificent watch."

"It's not for sale to the public," answered Cosimo. "The value then is not nine hundred dollars. This watch was made for collectors. Make that a hundred dollars a week and a thousand dollars if lost and we have a deal."

"Seventy-five a week, and a thousand," Goodman replied.

"That will do," said Cosimo.

Meyer typed up an agreement that Goodman and Cosimo both signed. "I should be through with the appraisal by Tuesday, two weeks."

"Wind it twelve turns in the morning about 8:00 a.m." Cosimo said as he accepted the cash.

The following morning, Maddie stepped off the bus at St. Mary's and Houston Streets and became one of the first to see the Dali Zodiac watch displayed in Hertzberg's main window. Placed on a black velvet turntable, all sides of the watch were made visible. A framed page from a trade magazine identified *The Leo* as one of the twelve watches in the Salvador Dali-Piaget Zodiac series. Behind the display, a clerk in a dark suit stood sentry.

The lion and male figure locked in combat on the front of the case made Maddie smile, the grinning sun on the back made her laugh.

Maddie caught a brief glimpse of Cosimo inside the shop. He wore a white shirt with no collar and a red bandana, giving him an artistic air, she thought. He turned his head and spoke to someone unseen behind him. She had assumed that the man in the Panama hat was a clever but destitute transient. Now, she couldn't tell. Maddie glanced at the clock outside Hertzberg's. The time matched that on the zodiac watch, 4:41 p.m. She hurried on to work at the library; her three-hour shift began in less than twenty minutes.

CHAPTER 23

M addie and Oscar stepped down into the basement of Trinity
Church, a cavern the size of half a basketball court. Maddie took a
Japanese sandalwood fan from her drawstring purse and snapped it open.

"What is it with you men? You thrive on the fragrance of mildew and
sweat socks." She hid her nose behind the scented fan.

A shallow proscenium stage was built into the front wall, and a back-
board and hoop were mounted on the back wall. Two huge yellow Civil
Defense loudspeakers set twenty feet apart commanded the room. Metal
folding chairs facing different directions surrounded the speakers.

Scuffling noises from behind a four-foot amplifier revealed Richard on
his hands and knees, dragging electrical cords. He scrambled to his feet.

"I know, I know the smell is . . . smelly. I have some incense for that."
He tucked his shirttail into his unbelted Levis. "You came. You may be
the only ones."

"Come here." Richard led them to the proscenium where he had a
folding table with three tape recorders and a four channel mixing board.

"What's this?" She pointed her fan at a second table with a collection
of incongruous objects: door hinges, sticks, a soprano recorder, a short
wave radio, castanets, a rusted tire rim, a jar of nails, one seventeen-inch
Zildjian cymbal, and more.

"Those are the instruments." Richard grinned. "The other part is the sound montage that will come from the tape recorders."

Maddie and Oscar examined the curious instruments.

"A rusted garage door spring?" wondered Maddie.

"That's the Well-Tempered Garage Door Spring," added Oscar.

"You guys look so good." Richard stepped back to admire them.

"Thank you. I tried." Maddie curtsied in her Mexican blouse with flowering rose vines; a Navaho silver and turquoise squash-blossom belt gathered the blouse at the waist. Over her shoulders she draped a deep maroon Mexican *rebozo*.

"And look at you," Richard teased. "In a houndstooth sports jacket, trousers that touch the top of your brown loafers exactly. Oscar doesn't have any money, but he dresses like the kind of man who reads *Playboy*."

"Richard, be nice." Maddie tapped his shoulder with her folded fan. She reached out her arms for a hug. Richard awkwardly accepted.

"We're here to lend some class to your dreary affair," said Oscar.

"I still have a lot to do. My composition adviser is supposed to come. There's a music appreciation class, maybe. I put up a flyer in the library, at the school. And hell, I'm in trouble. My helper backed out. Can you give me a hand?"

"Glad to," volunteered Oscar. "As long as I don't have to get down on the floor like you."

"Cool, whatever we can do," said Maddie. She snapped open the Japanese fan again and held it to her face as she paced the room. "These really smell," she said, stopping by the speakers.

"They're real Civil Defense speakers just like the ones you see at fire stations. They've been stored in chemically-treated crates to prevent rust. Don't stand too close."

She backed away, fanning herself. Folding tables, standing long side vertical, did their best to conceal boxes marked "utensils" and "Christmas decorations."

Richard waved for them to come into a walk-in storage closet and closed the door. He lit a joint, took a drag, and held it out. Maddie's hand met Richard's fingers. She took a long draw, held her breath and passed the joint to Oscar.

"Have you done this before?" she asked Oscar.

"Sure." Oscar had actually never smoked pot. He took a hit and coughed. The joint was passed. His second hit came easier, and maybe he took a third hit. He didn't remember.

Richard lit a long stick of patchouli incense, and re-entered the basement.

"Civil Defense speakers?" asked Oscar. "What if there's a town out there without civil defense protection, and the big *bomb* comes and they die without knowing they were supposed to be terrified?"

"Surplus, I'm told. This audio guy in Pleasanton has maybe six in a warehouse. I got the loan of these."

"Why are all the chairs facing in different directions?" Maddie sat in one of the twenty metal folding chairs.

"The echo acoustics here are terrific. No seat is any better than any other. As the sound waves bounce off the tables, walls and ceiling, you're bathed in sound waves. Each seat is slightly different."

"But wouldn't the sound be different even if the chairs were facing the same direction?" Oscar needled.

"I thought they looked better this way."

"You say this isn't like John Cage?" Maddie asked.

"There's a score, just not for traditional instruments." He placed a score on a music stand. "This will be recorded by the one multidirectional microphone hanging from the steel beams above."

Richard turned on the shortwave radio to a frequency broadcasting a ticking clock. He pressed a button on the four-channel mixing board and the ticking stopped.

"Oscar, there are only a few things to remember. When I give you a thumbs up, you will press record on Wallensak one."

"I hope I can do this. My hand is numb. Wallensak one, thumbs up, record." Oscar closed his eyes. "Wallensak yea-ah." He opened his eyes.

"Are you okay?" Maddie leaned close.

"I'm okay," mumbled Oscar. "Wallensak one, record."

Richard held up two fingers. "On two, press play on Wallensak two, and three fingers press play on Wallensak three. Can you remember that?"

"Two, three got it, press play," said Oscar. "I'll do my best, *herr* conductor."

"Then step back, until . . . I'll show you what to do as we go.

"Maddie, can you introduce the piece?"

"I'll do what I can."

"Tell them my name, Richard Krabb. The title of the work is *Air, Water, Earth, Fire, Synchronous*. Here's a list of introductions. My

Professor, Mel George, a class from SAC, and introduce yourself and Oscar."

As they ran through a brief tech rehearsal, students from the music appreciation class arrived and bonded as an audience of strangers watching the three exotic people preparing for the performance.

Mel George, a thirty-six-year-old professor of music composition, arrived with an entourage of undergraduates.

"Richard, quite a setup," Mel George said. "Are you still pursuing what you told me in conference?"

"It's what we talked about. I want you to meet Madeline Parker and Oscar Buscoso. They're helping out with tech."

Mel George nodded and turned to the class. "Be sure to sign my attendance sheet. To receive class credit, you must stay until the end. As the composition adviser for the music department, it is part of my job to attend events like this. Hopefully it will be good, otherwise consider this this is part of your educational experience." He turned to Richard. "Well, we're all looking forward to this performance. A premiere."

The students formed a line to sign the attendance form.

Mel George made one of the students relinquish a chair in the center of the room, where he believed he could observe and hear all.

Ten minutes after two p.m., Richard nodded to Oscar to stand by the Wallensaks and pointed at Maddie to introduce the piece.

Maddie waved her open fan, gesturing to those still standing to fill in the empty seats. "It's time to start. Welcome, everyone. Sit anywhere. Please, everyone sit. I am told that the audio experience is different, depending where you face. There is no one seat better than another." She waited until all had settled.

"Think of it as your own personal performance. Welcome, Professor Mel George and the music appreciation class. Over here we have Oscar Buscoso, who will do things beyond my capacity to either explain or comprehend." Oscar nodded and kept his focus on the buttons in front of him. She waited for the light laughter to subside, "And I am Maddie Parker. This evening you will hear," she glanced at the paper, "*Air, Water, Earth, Fire, Synchronous* by Richard Krabb. Be prepared for something different and challenging. Would you like to add anything, Richard?"

"No, let's start."

"Then here is, *Air, Water, Earth, Fire, Synchronous* by Richard Krabb."

Richard emphatically gave Oscar the thumbs up. He paused, held up two, then three fingers. Oscar stiffly completed his tasks. Relieved, he stepped back.

Richard flipped a switch on the mixing board and the sound of a ticking clock echoed in the room.

A man's radio voice announced over the ticking: *"At the tone, WWV Greenwich Mean Time will be fourteen hours . . . and twelve minutes . . . exactly . . . beeep . . . "* The ticking clock faded.

What sounded like thousands of tiny hands applauding evolved into a breeze blowing through a forest of broad-leafed trees. Birds chirped, insects buzzed. Richard took a drumstick and began a rhythm on wooden boxes. The audience seemed pleased until Richard took the garage door spring and whacked it with a hammer. A resounding *spoing, spoing* reverberated, followed by a squeak from a rusty hinge, causing most in the audience to cringe. At the mixing board he faded out the sound of the cottonwoods and turned up a track of ocean waves. He began to tap the cymbals with his fingernails.

The sound of distant surf was overwhelmed by a wave crashing nearby. Foam hissed as the wave retreated, the distant surf remained. Richard handed Maddie a long stick and indicated for her to turn it upside down. Maddie turned it, and was surprised to hear the stick produce the gentle ticking of rain.

He struck the garage spring again. The sound waves felt palpable on the skin. Half the audience covered their ears.

Richard signaled for Oscar to take over the mixing board. He showed him four tracks and indicated up and down as a conductor might gesture for soft or loud.

At ten minutes into the performance, several students caught Mel George's attention.

"Please, enough," a young woman mouthed. "Give us credit for staying this long," she whispered.

George rolled his eye, shrugged, nodded. "Yes, yes . . . go," he muttered. The clutch of students nodded, got up and left. The remaining students not part of the walkout glanced around. They, too, stood and deserted.

On the track dogs barked, people chatted, and traffic noises mixed with the rumble of thunder. Richard used a wooden soprano recorder to create a trilling accompaniment a little like Bach, and then not.

Richard handed Maddie drumsticks and pointed to the wooden boxes. He indicated a slow beat as the sound of rolling thunder caused the empty folding chairs to vibrate and move on the concrete floor. He began to repeat the skin-crawling sounds from the large rusty hinge. The rumble of thunder diminished. A man's voice, tinny and distance intoned, "Trinity ready, Countdown, nine, eight, seven, six, five, four, three, two, one." A sustained explosion followed. Richard motioned for Oscar to join him as all three beat rhythms on the wooden boxes and cymbals. Richard blew a police whistle in panicky spurts. Like a symphony conductor he motioned for Oscar and Maddie to bring it way down, and then out.

An atomic explosion evolved into an electronic hiss. Richard finished his composition by pouring a jar of nails slowly over the cymbals. When the last nail fell and the resonant echo dimmed into silence, a man's voice announced, *"At the tone . . . WWV Greenwich Mean Time . . . will be fourteen hours . . . forty-one minutes . . . and thirty seconds . . . beeep."* Richard raised his arms. The composition was over.

Maddie exhaled, "That was incredible!"

"Wow, man," said Oscar. "Big, wow. That was air, water, earth, and fire."

Richard didn't know what to think. His audience, except for his professor, Mel George, had abandoned him. He wasn't ready to accept his friends' cheery praise.

"That was very interesting." Mel George stood. "I don't usually criticize a student's work. In this case, I can't help myself. It's not my cup of tea," he said. "But if you get me a copy of the tape, I'll send it to the department head." He looked at his watch.

"Absolutely," Richard replied.

As the door closed behind Mel George, Richard blurted, "If the department head likes the tape, it means a letter of introduction to a composition lab at the Curtis Institute."

"Well, break a fuckin' leg." Maddie held up a fist.

"I was impressed. I felt it. Really, best of luck. Hey, I've got to be someplace," said Oscar. "It was great, Richard. I'll see you on Saturday."

"You're going? I want to celebrate. I thought we could get some beer," said Richard.

"Can't. Family obligations," Oscar begged off. "It's mom's birthday. I want her to see me looking like this so she knows I'm not a total screwup.

Did you think this get-up was for you? I'm getting supper and leftovers for a week."

Maddie hugged Oscar goodbye. "You look good."

"See you guys." He took the stairs two at a time.

"Weren't you two together?" Richard rewound the reel-to-reel recording tapes.

"No, we met at the bus corner," answered Maddie.

Richard made notations with a fountain pen on the back of the flat reel-to-reel tape boxes.

"Do you have to put away all this stuff today?"

"No, I have the basement until Wednesday." He put the tape boxes in a briefcase.

"Great, let's do it. Do you want a beer tonight, or not?" Maddie opened her fan.

"I do."

"Then what? You're usually ready to toast Oscar's vocabulary."

"We're the three musketeers. Without Oscar . . ."

"Tonight we do without Athos," said Maddie.

"Which are you?" asked Richard.

"I'm Aramis, naturally. That makes you Porthos. Are we going?"

"Sure, I have to get the lights. Stand by the door."

"Wait. Do you have another joint?" He nodded. "Well, light it up."

Richard dug in his shirt pocket. A Zippo lighter blazed the joint to life.

Maddie toked deep. "You were very brave to do this." She managed to say all that while holding her breath.

"What do you mean?"

She exhaled. "You were out there . . . and you pulled it off. It took planning and creative energy. It was truly cool. I'm still feeling it. Really."

"I don't know," griped Richard. "Nobody said anything. They wouldn't look me in the face."

"The performance wasn't for them. Did you see them? They were staring at us like we were the aberrations." She took his hand. "It was for you, me, and Oscar. It's for whoever hears your composition in the future and understands."

He pulled back his hand. "I've got to turn off the lights. Go stand by the stairs." He snapped off all power to his amplifier and speakers. Turning off the lights left him to feel his way back in the darkness. Reaching the stairs, Maddie stood in his way.

She drew Richard close for a kiss, slipped her tongue in his mouth, and fluttered an invitation. For a moment she closed her eyes and breathed his scent. Richard pulled away.

"Wow. I apologize. It should have been obvious," said Maddie. "You're not turned on by me."

"What? I am."

"I can tell. It doesn't make any difference to me. I still like you. In fact, this makes everything a lot easier. Am I your first? It's like you didn't expect tongue. You've never kissed a girl before. Have you?"

"Sure, lots of times. Let's get a beer."

"Do you like Oscar more than me? You can tell me."

Richard stumbled as he backed into the stairs. "Nooo! That's crazy. Stop making up shit. Okay?"

She touched his face as if he were a child and gave him a push with her fingertips to turn and go up the stairs.

CHAPTER 24

A yellow Corvette idled outside the library's back gate, partly blocking the employee exit. The crew-cut fellow who gave Maddie a ride before reclined in the front seat, his left hand dangling above the steering wheel. Staff hurrying to make their buses had to sidestep along the fence to get past the car.

Maddie said goodnight to Virgil and stepped out onto the loading dock. "Shit," she muttered the instant she saw the car.

Squeezing past the gate, she approached the car on the street side. "Toby, what the hell are you doing here?"

Freshly showered and splashed with aftershave, he leaned back. "I'm here to pick you up and take you to dinner. Hungry?"

"Don't you have anything better to do than drive around in a car you can't use on city streets?

"You're right. What say I drive us to the Gray Moss Inn for a steak dinner? You know, out in the Hill Country. We'll go for a real ride, thirty miles in twenty minutes."

"Go away. I'm not interested." She turned and walked back to the gate.

"I owe you a good dinner." Toby, tall and muscular, stepped out of the car. "You said you had a good time."

"Goodbye Toby."

He blocked her path. "I've been busy. I'm free tonight, darlin', come on." Toby lowered his voice "We did the deed. You said you liked it? Come with me. I'm hungry. How about you?" He took her arm.

"Don't touch me." She pulled her arm away. "Go back to your apartment and leave me the hell alone."

"Why are you being such a tease? You liked it."

Maddie looked about to see if anyone was near. "Tease?" she said in a hoarse whisper, "I told you what you wanted to hear so you'd stop hurting me. You got your jollies off. Now leave me alone."

"Come on, get in the car. We can work this out." Toby took Maddie by the arm and pulled her toward the passenger's seat.

"You're hurting me," Maddie struggled. "Get it through your thick skull. No!" she screamed.

Coming out the door, Oscar heard Maddie's cry.

"Hey, you," he yelled, running down the stairs. Maddie pulled free and Oscar stepped between them.

Toby put a large hand on Oscar's chest. "You thinking she would rather go out with you?"

"Probably not, but she clearly doesn't want to go with you." Oscar had no idea what he was doing. This guy was a giant.

"Get the fuck out of my way." Toby gave Oscar a hard shove and pushed him down on his butt between the car and the gate.

"Hey, ow," grunted Oscar.

"You want more?" Toby raised a fist.

"Toby! *Stop it! Stop it!*" shouted Maddie. "Mister Harper, call the police." She called out to the loading dock.

A half-dozen library employees now watched from inside the library's gate.

Oscar struggled to his feet, and Toby shoved him down harder.

Maddie knelt next to Oscar. "Toby, that's aggravated assault and a crime. Take your fucking car and get out of here before the police arrive. I am not going anywhere with you. And don't ever come here again."

Toby surveyed the scene through half-closed eyes. Virgil held up a telephone on the loading dock, and onlookers stood nearby.

"Fucking bitch." Red-faced, Toby avoided eye contact with the witnesses, stalked to the car, climbed in, put the car in gear, gunned the engine, and sped away.

"I'm so sorry." Maddie helped Oscar to his feet. "I'm sorry. I'm sorry."

Oscar waved at the onlookers. "I'm okay." He slapped the dirt off the back of his trousers and winced.

"Are you sure?" Maddie flicked off dust from his shirt.

"That was stupid of me."

"Which way to your bus?" asked Maddie.

Oscar pointed. "By Walgreen's." The pain in his butt caused him to step delicately. Turning the corner from Presa Street and out of the view of the library, Maddie took his arm and drew him closer.

"You want a beer?"

"Yeah, I'd like that a lot. I think that son of a bitch cracked my coccyx."

"I'd kiss it and make it well, but not here."

"Oh . . . Don't say that. It hurts to laugh," moaned Oscar.

"How about this?" Maddie stopped, her lean body pressed against his. She kissed him, her tongue flicked his tongue. Oscar kissed her back, his tongue caressing hers. Her perfume reminded him of a fragrant white peach. Her lips tasted of it, too.

Maddie felt his arousal. "You're a great kisser. I'm not going to fuck you."

"Since I wasn't asking, that's good to know."

"You were my Galahad tonight. Thank you." She kissed him on the cheek.

They walked several blocks before he could think of what to say. "Do you know how confusing that is? You kiss me and then tell me you don't want . . . to have sex with me? I didn't expect a reward, nor am I asking for one. You probably would have done better without me."

"If you hadn't stepped in, I likely would have gotten the same bruising as you, or worse."

They entered Elroy's bar and took the booth by the window. Maddie held up two fingers. Elroy acknowledged with a nod.

A sharp pain straightened Oscar's spine when he sat. "Shit, that hurts. What do you see in a jerk like that? Is it the car?"

"Don't analyze me. I like you a lot, but I know if I fuck you, I'll end up hating you."

"Hating me?" Oscar laughed. "Wow, make me feel like a piece of crap."

"No. I'm just saying it's best we don't go getting serious."

"True! I don't have a lot of experience, and I'll probably disappoint, also true. Here's the thing. Richard, the asshole, told you about my fantasies. Except that they weren't about you, well, not entirely. Just because you're, you know, gorgeous doesn't mean you're what I'm looking for."

"Thank you, I think. What did you just say?"

"Heaven forbid we do anything serious. I certainly wouldn't want you to hate me."

"Now you're making fun of me," she protested.

"Look, I'm just a toad without a car."

"Now, you're fishing for compliments. You're good-looking. You have kind eyes, nice lips, kissable face, and probably have lots of girlfriends."

"Kissing girlfriends, a few, yes. And not that often, either. I don't make moves on girls because I simply can't afford them."

"You must have had sex with one of them?"

"Sex? Look, this talk is getting too weird. Why are we talking about this?"

"Why not?"

"Well, to start, I asked you about why you would go out with a guy like that."

"I don't defend dating him. I had to go out with him to find out he was a jerk. His family is rich. Besides the car and good looks, there's nothing else there. Let's not talk about him. So, you've gotten to second base, right?"

"You certainly get to the point. I dated a girl I worked with. When we parked, I made a clumsy attempt to touch her breast. She stopped, looked me straight on, and said she was 'willing.' I froze. I felt that if I even touched a nipple I'd owe her big time. And sex? I'd be in debt to her the rest of my life."

Maddie laughed. "You're hilarious, I mean, you've never, ever?"

"Never ever. Scout's honor." He held up the three-finger Boy Scout hand sign.

Maddie laughed. She looked out the window and forgot whatever she was about to say. "Look! There's that man. I saw him at Hertzberg's in town."

"That's Mr. Cano. His address is the downtown YMCA," said Oscar.

"This is pretty far from the YMCA."

"It's a free country. He can be wherever he wants," said Oscar.

"This has nothing to do with freedom. People who walk with a cane like that don't walk any farther than they have to. That's what my grandmother said, and she had arthritis in her knee. She walked just like that. Finish your beer. Let's go see where he's going."

"You mean, now?"

"Yeah, let's go." Her eyes flashed.

They chugged their beers. Elroy looked over and saw that they'd left two quarters for two ten-cent beers.

Cosimo was more than a long block away. Walking as briskly as Oscar's tailbone allowed, they followed him for a quarter of a mile. When he turned a corner, they lost him. If he'd gone into one of the nearby houses or apartment buildings, there was no way to tell which, and there was no one on the street to ask.

"We narrowed him down to this neighborhood," Maddie said, turning back.

"Why do you want to know where the old man lives?"

"I don't want to know where he lives, as much as I want to know who he is. I saw him on Wednesday at the jewelry store on Houston Street. He was looking at this incredible watch. You've got to see it. It's Salvador Dali meets the cosmos. My first impression was that he was a clever European. He dresses like an eccentric. Now, I'm not so sure what he is."

"He knows about art. He had Fischer type letters for him," said Oscar.

"What were they about?"

"He wrote to a bank for information about money, and to an art gallery. He asked me to find some addresses, and to look up the 1913 New York Armory exhibit of modern art. I found several articles in periodicals, and there's one book in special collections. The Armory show was kind of a big deal, Duchamp, Matisse, Picasso, Leger, Munch . . . and Edward Hopper. Can you imagine? All we know of modern art began there."

Oscar paused before taking the steps up to Houston Street. "Em, before we part for the evening, I have a question. If we're not going to have . . . you know . . . sex, can we kiss?"

"I thought you were talking about modern art," she smiled slyly. "I can do that."

CHAPTER 25

Cosimo awoke rested for the first time since he'd arrived in Texas. He didn't have the money he wanted or needed, but he'd soon establish that his watch could finance his return to at least Cuba, if not France. And for the time being, even his meals were assured.

Later that morning, as he prepared for his drawing session, Cosimo asked Graciela if he could hang his drawings on the wall.

"I don't know anything about art," Graciela admitted. "But I like the fox and the sour grapes. It reminds me of my financial mess. I'm that fox."

He hung *The Mouse and the Lion*, *The Fox and the Sour Grapes*, and *The Ant and the Grasshopper* around the café.

Cosimo did his drawings with no talk or explanation. As soon as he arrived, the tables filled quickly. After taking a table, some customers ate their tacos standing, looking at the drawings on the walls, or watching the progress of the latest fable. John and Colleen entered and joined with several regulars. Colleen carried a copy of Aesop's Fables she'd borrowed from the library.

Most drawings were done in one sitting, but *The Ant and the Grasshopper* took four days to complete. The pictorial flowed from the grasshopper's youth and the abundance of food on the top left corner. In between, the grasshopper played, found a mate, danced, and loafed; all along the ant went about his tasks, gathering and storing food. On the bottom right of the drawing, the grasshopper died and the ant carried away his remains. The ant died, as well.

"At least, the grasshopper led a full life. The poor ant toils until he drops," commented Colleen.

The customers started a tip jar, which Cosimo turned over to Graciela and Emma when he finished his drawing session each day.

"Don't you need this?" asked Emma.

"I am not doing this for the money. Keep it, spend it, or share it."

"The man, John, who comes with the woman, Colleen, he wants to buy *The Ant and the Grasshopper*," said Emma. "He offered fifty dollars."

"They're not for sale. I will change the drawings every few days to keep the customers looking at something new. Just make sure no one walks off with them."

"John said he could go higher. He really wants to impress that lady."

Cosimo shook his head, and left the café for the day.

From the first day, customers seeing Cosimo eating the freshly made flour tortillas filled with potato and egg for breakfast asked if they could have the same. Over the first week, the clientele went from less than five a day to over twenty customers hungry for flour tortilla tacos.

"I need a sign for tacos," Emma told Cosimo. "I have to repeat everything two or three times."

Cosimo took one of the unused menus and set it on his drawing board. "Tell me what you can prepare and I'll make a sign that's right there in front of everyone.

Cosimo made a list as Emma and Graciela dictated their taco menu. Emma wanted to add more items.

"Any more items and it will be too hard to read," said Cosimo.

"We can make a taco out of anything," laughed Emma.

Cosimo hand lettered the menu. At Clegg's Engineering and Architectural Supplies, he had the menu mounted on strong poster board, and had the entire menu laminated. He also purchased a black cardboard portfolio to keep his collection of drawings flat.

He returned to the café and hung the menu above the grill where all could see.

All Flour Tortilla Tacos 60¢
Carne de Puerco
Bean and Cheese
Carne de Res
Picadillo
Lengua
Potato and Egg
Eggs and Bacon
Eggs and Chorizo
Tripas (on Thursdays)
Taco Plate (2 Tacos, Rice and Beans), $1.45
We'll make a taco from anything.

Graciela needed extra help. She paid women from the apartment building to get tested and apply for health permits required for working in food preparation. By the end of the third week, when Cosimo exited the Little House Café at 11:00 a.m., people were queued beyond the *botanica* next door waiting for a table.

CHAPTER 26

Cosimo returned to Hertzberg's street corner and found two dozen docile souls waiting for the bus so trapped in routine that the store displays were invisible to them.

Tapping his cane on the pavement, he pretended to inspect the Dali Zodiac watch, and asked no one in particular, "Did you see this amazing time piece? It's quite amusing."

Cosimo stepped back. A mother holding a three-month old sleeping baby took a few steps to see, and laughed as the sun's face came into view. She was joined by several others waiting for the bus.

"It must be worth a fortune," Cosimo whispered. "And look, it's exactly the same time as the Hertzberg clock. I don't have my glasses. Who designed this work of art?" asked Cosimo.

A heavy-set woman read, "It says it was designed by Salvador Dali."

"Is he famous?" Cosimo asked.

"I think so," she said.

"Yes, he's very famous," a man's voice said behind him.

He didn't push it more than that. He walked away and didn't look back as other bus riders who'd overheard the exchange came to take a look. The grinning sun with its searching eyes nearly always drew a laugh. Each day for a week he repeated the routine at different hours so as not to encounter the same bus riders.

Inside the store, Allen Goodman, Hertzberg's manager, noted that the people looking at the Dali watch continued to browse the other window displays as well. On payday Friday, impulse buying spiked. A line of Hokosai-inspired costume jewelry, brooches, and pendants with bamboo leaves made of jade sold out by close of business Saturday.

Cosimo returned again to Hertzberg's on Tuesday, the day Meyer said he would have his appraisal complete.

"Mr. Cano, please come in. Can I get you coffee, something to drink?" asked Goodman.

"No, thank you. That's very kind of you to offer," said Cosimo.

"Well, I'm so glad you're here. I'd like to keep the watch in the window for another two weeks, and of course for another seventy-five dollars a week."

"Certainly, Mr. Goodman," Cosimo replied, not really surprised. "Have you been able to determine the value of my watch?"

Goodman looked out on the floor, "Meyer, please come here."

Aware the other clerks were watching him, Meyer stepped forward.

"Mr. Cano, a pleasure to see you again." Meyer extended his hand. His eyes telegraphed an eagerness to tell what he'd learned. He brought out a notepad from his suit coat pocket. The sales clerks inched closer. Goodman stared until one excused himself and returned to his post by the front door.

"The watch is an authentic Salvador Dali, Piaget Zodiac." Meyer stopped to see how Cosimo reacted, who nodded, accepting what he already knew. "It's a magnificent timepiece, Mister Cano. This is a work by incredible talents, geniuses. Not only the clever design, and the music mechanism, but the works! I have peered into thousands of watches, and I can say I am in awe."

Cosimo assumed Meyer's presentation had had some rehearsal, noting that Goodman didn't flinch.

"As to what it is worth, one in this series sold at auction in Zurich in 1958 for eight thousand dollars. If we were to buy this from you, we could only offer you a fourth of that." Meyer stepped to the counter and retrieved an envelope. "For insurance purposes, I take photographs of valuables people bring us for appraisal. That way we all know what the insured item looks like. I took photos of your watch and here are your copies." He handed Cosimo an eight by ten-inch envelope.

"In Zurich," asked Cosimo. "Who was the buyer, Homer Schuster or Otto Whitt?" He opened the envelope.

"Anonymous." shrugged Meyer. "The buyer could have been anywhere in the world."

Cosimo slid the photos out of the envelope. "What did you use to photograph this?"

"A Leica M3, using Kodak fine-grain black and white film. I used extension bellows to do macro photos of the production stamps. The camera is mounted on a copy stand and I compensate for parallax."

"Very good." Cosimo slipped the photographs back in the envelope. "The auction was three years ago, and for Zurich that is not a lot of money. The dollar is strong at the moment to the Deutsche Mark, so between four thousand and eleven thousand. Let me think about it," said Cosimo.

"Take all the time you want. You have two more weeks," said Goodman. "Of course, you understand that an auction price doesn't reflect the real value of anything. It tells us how much that particular bidder was willing to pay for something he desired," said Goodman, still negotiating.

"Naturally," Cosimo replied.

"Are you friends with Salvador Dali?" Meyer asked. It was a question everyone else in the room wanted to know.

"I know him," Cosimo lied without hesitation. "We do not socialize in the same circles, but circles overlap." The reality was that Dali wasn't even a cocktail party acquaintance. The only truth to his recollection was that they were in a group show in 1932, and may have nodded in passing. It was a long time ago.

He excused himself and left Hertzberg's. His predicament was that he didn't want to sell the watch. Neither its pedigree as an authentic Dali Zodiac nor its cash value meant anything to him. It remained the one physical possession that linked him to Sara. Every purchase she made was done only after careful deliberation. She wasn't like Margaret Manheim, a wily negotiator snapping up fine works before an artist became famous, or Leonor Fini, who grew up poor and whose avocation was acquiring fine things on the sly. He didn't know how Sara acquired the watch and didn't care. He needed the money, but he wasn't ready to part with it.

He continued to the post office and waited for his friend's window to become available. Francisco Orozco greeted Cosimo with a wholehearted grin. An unusually large bouquet of flowers sat on a table behind him.

"Mr. Cano. I have very good news for you," he said.

"Do I have mail?" he asked.

"Yes, sir. I did the mail sort this morning. Good news, there are two letters for you."

Cosimo laughed. "Thank you. And, about those flowers behind you?"

"My fellow postal clerks gave them to me. I passed the bar and this morning I was sworn in as an officer of the court by Judge Carlos Cadena, one of my law professors. I am now an attorney." Francisco's grin could not be erased.

"Congratulations," said Cosimo. "Why are you still here?"

"Thank you, but I've only passed the bar, I don't have a job as an attorney. May the rest of your day be excellent. Next in line step up." He waved to the next person in the queue.

Cosimo stopped at one of the ornate Italian brass islands with glass tops and pens on chains and opened the letters. The first came from the French Consulate in Houston, Texas. The consul sympathized with his predicament and urged him to call between the hours of 10:00 a.m. and 2:00 p.m. to speak with their legal representative. The consulate might help him return to Paris. The letter ended that while it was not a normal function of the consul, they would attempt to forward a copy of his letter to Georges Bataille, Leonor Fini, and *L'Idiote Gallery*.

The second letter was from Charlotte, the concierge at *Rue Delambre* in Montparnasse. Leonor Fini was in North Africa making a film with John Huston and wouldn't return until September. Margaret Manheim had shuttered her museum for the summer and was in Switzerland with no phone number. Georges Bataille was hospitalized, seriously ill. The parrot was fine.

Cosimo thought about what the information meant. If all his options failed, there was an outside chance he could be stranded in Texas until September. There was no telling when Margaret would surface. More than likely she was seducing her latest acquisition before the artist became famous.

He called the French Consulate from the apartment building lobby. The quarters he fed into the slot were accompanied by a bright chime. The person he wanted to speak to was not in. The secretary, the woman who wrote the letter, advised him that the consulate could help him return to France. However, it could not help with regaining his property. If he wished to sue, it would be better if he stayed in Texas and hired a local attorney. She had the names of several attorneys which would require a substantial retainer. She added that attempting to sue from France could take a very long time.

"How long?" Cosimo asked.

"Seven to fifteen years," she replied. "If it is just the clothes you want, it's cheaper to replace them; and as for your money, prolonged litigation will make any recovery a loss."

Cosimo thanked the secretary and hung up the phone.

CHAPTER 27

Returning to the cabins, Cosimo knocked on Pito's door. Nothing around Pito's apartment had moved in some time. He hadn't returned from his aunt's final hours.

Cosimo had an idea for a project that he knew Pito would reject: trading painting the cabin for reduced or no rent. However, since Pito wasn't there to ask, it was worth giving the idea a try.

He walked around his cabin tapping on the walls with his cane. The lumber appeared solid and free of rot. On the negative side, where the paint had peeled, the exposed lumber had turned a paint-hungry ashy silver.

He found the paint closet. Suspecting the padlock could be broken like everything else around the cabins, he gave it a firm tug. It opened. Cans of useless paint were stacked everywhere. However, near the door were several two-gallon cans of white primer paint that appeared to be a recent purchase. Ladders, scrapers, spackling trowels, brushes, and an electric sander appeared to have been stored there recently.

He changed into his studio clothes, and using a hand scraper he took from the paint closet started on the window frames. The project may have been a better concept than a productive reality. After fifteen minutes his arms ached, and a blister formed on the side of his right thumb. He'd only done the bottom frame of the window, and not all that well.

At this rate the small shack would take weeks to prepare for painting. He returned to the paint closet and brought out the electric sander, dragging along an unspooled 25-foot extension cord. He'd heard of electric sanders, though he'd never used one. The design was intuitive. There was a handle, a metal enclosure for the motor, a two-inch wide band of coarse sandpaper, and an on/off toggle switch. Flipping the switch, the sander became a roaring, eight-pound struggling animal. Putting it to the window frame it crawled across the wood scraping and sanding at the same time. In less than a minute he'd sanded the side frame to primer-ready bare wood.

Cosimo didn't hear the white van that drove slowly into the driveway and stopped near him. He looked up when the van doors slammed and saw two men stalk in his direction.

"*Viejo, Que haces?*" They appeared angry. Cosimo stopped sanding.

He flicked the toggle switch off. "*Buenas tardes, señores. Que se ofrece?*"

"What the hell are you doing? And where the fuck is Pito? He told us we were supposed to paint and tile. Where is the bastard?" They spoke in Spanish.

"Pito's aunt died. He went to the funeral."

"He's been gone two weeks and we're left here with our dicks in our hands. We're sleeping in my truck, and you're using our sander."

"Are you the men from Monterey who did tile?"

The men could have been brothers; they had the same straight hair that lapped their ears. "You have any complaints about the work?"

"The work is fine. You could have cleaned up when you finished. You left a mess."

"Mess? We left things as they were because Pito sent us to Nuevo Laredo to buy more tile. Sonofabitch! How much is he paying you?"

"Nothing. Believe me. I thought I might be able to save on the rent by showing him that I know paint."

"No, señor! That is our job." The taller brother spoke up. "We've come to get paid and get our tools. Did you break into the paint closet?"

"No, the lock didn't work. None of the locks around here work."

The men looked surprised.

"We have his tile. He didn't front us enough, so I paid out of my own fucking pocket." The older brother leaned into Cosimo's face. Cosimo raised his hands.

"Hold on. Calm down. Listen. I cannot speak for Pito, but if he said he would pay you, I am certain he will. If these are your tools, I believe you."

"What is he paying you, old man," demanded the shorter man.

"We should get our tools and go."

"No, you don't want to do that."

"Why the hell not?"

"Look at me. Look at you. What are your names? I'm Cosimo Cano."

"Guillermo and Jose," answered the tall brother.

"We are both in a tight place. He owes you money, and I am low on funds. I believe we can help each other. Get your things and put them in cabin two. I know where the sheets and towels are kept. Take a shower. I have a place where you can get something to eat. And we can talk."

"What kind of shit is this? You say you are low on cash, but you're going to buy us lunch?"

"I have an arrangement. Believe me. I have no reason to lie."

"What about Pito? What's he going to say about this?"

"You should not be sleeping in your truck," said Cosimo. "Let yourselves in. You will not need a key."

Cosimo called the Little House Café from the pay phone in the lobby and asked Emma to feed the two men.

Reluctantly, the men went to the café and were fed without a question.

The meal and the showers calmed them considerably. Cosimo proposed how they could work together.

"Look, those are our tools," said Guillermo, the younger brother. "Especially the sander. We don't let anyone use the sander."

"Understood," said Cosimo. "The machine is too heavy for me, in any case. How much will you charge me to sand the cabin where I'm staying?"

"You're going to pay us?"

"A little, I mean Pito is the boss, and he's going to pay you to do the work anyway. It might take you two days with your sander. You will have your meals, and a place to sleep and bathe."

"The Pito we know is a cheap son-of-a-bitch. You're very generous with his money."

"I'm only paying you so you can go to a movie, or have a beer. What do you say. Ten dollars and sand my cabin?"

"What if Pito shows up and he says no."

135

"You will still have the ten dollars and your work to do. He trusted you with money to go buy him more tile; he is cheap, but I do not think he is a crook."

"Okay. We sand the cabin and that's all," said Jose, the older brother.

"Sanding and ready for primer. Well, maybe one more thing. Your ladders. I promise I won't break them."

Guillermo and Jose were from Sabinas Hidalgo, a town on the highway to Monterey. Officially, they were natural-born US citizens who were raised in Mexico and consequently spoke limited English. They carried small laminated copies of their birth certificates to show authorities when stopped.

The electric sander was a marvelous machine, cutting the sanding time from days to a matter of hours. The first coat of primer disappeared into the desiccated lumber. Residents of the nearby apartments stood by, amused by the crazy guest painting the cabin.

Twenty dollars and change bought four gallons of white paint and several quart cans of blue, yellow, red, and black.

Cosimo did his performance at the Little House Café in the morning and painted the cabin until dusk. On the third day, Emma brought him a bite to hold him until breakfast. He devoured the taco, gratefully. On the fourth day, Emma arrived with a tray with a full dinner. Setting it on the porch railing, she removed the towel keeping the food warm, revealing a pork stew with squash and kernels of sweet corn, flour tortillas, and a glass of iced tea.

"Emma, this is unbelievable. You could serve it to a king, and he would be humbled."

"You're hungry," she said. "*Don* Cosimo, do you think my sister is a good woman?"

Cosimo's heart leaped. "Why would you ask that? You both are very kind and generous people. You have brought me a feast."

"This month Graciela paid on the mortgage for the first time, on time," Emma said. "And we already have the money to make the next month's payment, as well."

"I am pleased to hear that."

"What would you think if you two had dinner together on Sunday evening, get to know each other better?"

It dawned on him that the food he was eating, the iced tea he drank, and the laundry they did for him amounted to an accounting. Emma was an intermediary representing one party in an age-old custom: a diplomatic exploration for a possible marriage.

He chewed slowly, giving him time to think. He drank tea to clear his mouth.

"Graciela is not only a good woman. She is generous, intelligent, a treasure. You, Emma, what are you, fifty? If I were looking, and I am *not*—you would be who I would chose. But I am not looking. Can you understand?"

Emma's eyes moistened. The corners of her mouth turned downward. "I'm fifty-eight. I can't have children, but my sister can."

"*Doña* Emma," Cosimo implored, delicately. "I am seventy. I am not going to start a family at this point in my life. I lost a dear lover seven weeks ago, and I am not ready for a replacement. I am stranded in this city because I came to live with her. That is my predicament. I don't want to burden you with any of this. I am trying to return to my life in France. Until then, I want to treat people fairly, and I want the same in return. You and your sister have been wonderful."

Emma pressed her hands against her thighs. She stood, wiping tears from her face. "Why are you painting this place? It's not yours. Pito won't care or pay you."

"I don't expect pay. It's what I do. This was a magnificent meal. I will understand if this is my last."

Stepping off the porch, Emma looked over the paint job. "Is it going to be white?" she asked.

"No, it has taken three coats of primer to seal the wood. It may take one more. You'll see. I'm mixing the colors myself."

The following evening, as he cleaned his brushes and put away the painting tools, Emma brought out his supper and a pitcher of iced tea. They went inside the cabin where she closed the shades.

"*Señora*, what about your neighbors?"

"Mister, get your mind out of the gutter." She stepped out and returned a few moments later with a curtain rod and a hammer. Tucked under her arm was a grocery bag. She opened it and took out a set of curtains made from the flour sack fabric of yellow ducklings swimming in a blue pond.

Cosimo blew her a kiss. "*Dona Emma, que perfecto y geñioso.*" He sat on the bed and opened his food as she swiftly measured and installed the rod. She moved with the same efficiency she had in the kitchen.

"Do you have children?" he asked. "And what about Graciela? I know nothing of your families."

She threaded the curtains on the rod and hung them "We have many relatives, around here, in Chicago, Montebello, California, *primos, primas, abuelas, tia abuelas.* Our parents passed on. I was married for a few years, had the one son. Marriages end. What can I say? My ex found another woman he liked better than me. My son joined the Navy when he was seventeen, retired after twenty years, and lives in California. He's divorced, too. Every Christmas he brings my grandson to visit. I don't know what's happening. In my parents' time, no one got divorced. They may have poisoned each other, but we never heard about it. There were many widows, though."

"It is a worldwide phenomenon." They laughed.

"Gracie was married to a young man who died in Korea. It broke her heart. We've lived together ever since. We ran the restaurant for the old owner, before it became ours."

"Thank you," said Cosimo. "Everyone has a journey. Thank you for telling me yours."

"We have a hot plate we're not using. I'd gladly loan it to you. And I have bottles of Ron Rico rum, vodka, Kahlua, and Drambuie my son brought home duty free from the navy. Graciela and I don't drink."

"That's very nice. I have a little money today; I'll buy the rum."

"Graciela won't hear of it. I'll bring them over tomorrow. Maybe you can use the rum to clean your brushes. It's one hundred and fifty proof," she laughed.

"I can use the hot plate, thank you," he said.

In the next several days, he painted the cabin exterior cherry pink; with a dark blue-green trim for the window frames and door frame. The door he painted a jacaranda violet-purple.

He found a rake and cleaned the area around his cabin, dismantled the unsightly fire pit made of cinder blocks and stones that Pito told him he could use to warm up his beans. He hauled the pieces and the grill to the trash and filled in the hole. As May became June, people came outside to sit in the shade of the three pecan trees and spend time with friends and neighbors near the inimitably painted cabin.

CHAPTER 28

The Saturday morning bus from Fort Sam Houston brought in the military moms, their children, and enlisted men to the library. Maddie stood outside near the main entrance holding a sign for "Book Buddies."

Shirley Childress, the five-and-a-half-year-old African American child who had filled out her own application form, accompanied by her aunt, ran up to Maddie.

"So nice to see you. Shirley? Am I right?" asked Maddie.

"Yes, but my friends call me Weegee."

"Can I be your friend and call you Weegee?"

Weegee nodded.

"You're going to enjoy the movie. The line has already started by the queue rope inside."

"Is there a book about Peter Pan?" asked Weegee.

"Oh, yes. There's an entire shelf with Barrie's books."

Three young soldiers eyed Maddie as they took the stairs to the entrance. Maddie could tell from their loose fitting uniforms and lack of stripes on their sleeves that they were still in basic training.

One of the soldiers took off his cap and bowed. "Be my date tonight, you delicious—"

"Watch it, boys!" Maddie interrupted. "Keep it civil. There are children here. If you're here to use the library, we have people standing by to help you." She pointed to Oscar and Richard standing inside the library doors. "Those two fellows will direct you wherever you need to go."

She gave Oscar and Richard a wink as she herded the mommies and children into the building. She glanced in the direction of the art and music department.

Oscar's eyes went to her sandal-clad feet and bare legs. "What . . .?"

"I didn't have time to go home and change." She ran ahead putting the moms and kids between her and the art and music department.

She waved her sign. "Line up here. We have five minutes before we start for the screening room."

"I'd like to see *Peter Pan*," grumbled Richard.

"Why would you want to see a silly Disney movie?"

Richard leaned closer. "Because I smoked a joint under the Presa Street Bridge. A silly movie would be a cool way to ride the high."

"Shush, man. Are you crazy?"

Doctor Samuels entered the lobby in his tweed sport jacket, striped shirt, and bow tie. He caught the eye of the three and motioned for them to join him at the front desk. "Over here, I need a word."

"Company, at ease." Maddie called. "Everyone wait! Stay." She scanned the room and darted across the lobby to join Dr. Samuels.

"I want to meet with the three of you in special collections room at 2:00 p.m."

"What's this about?" asked Oscar.

Richard rolled his eyes, lifted his hand as if he were about to make a point, and said nothing.

"I'll tell you then," answered Samuels. "Two p.m." he repeated, and walked away.

Returning to the foot of the stairs, Maddie glanced back at Oscar and Richard. Was this going to be their last day?

Maddie smiled through it all. "Okay, Book Buddies. Forward, march."

The second floor screening room filled with kids, moms, and several enlisted men. For a moment it appeared no one would sit next to Weegee and her aunt. Maddie grabbed one of the soldiers by the arm and sat him next to her.

"You look a little young for this movie," she said to the soldier. "Weegee here will explain it to you if it goes over your head." The audience laughed.

Oscar was the first to arrive at special collections. The door had been recently refitted with a stout lock and handle. A portion of raw wood remained exposed where the previous handle had been wider. Opening the door, Oscar saw Dr. Samuels facing a bank of filing cabinets. He turned long enough to acknowledge his entrance.

"Please have a seat." Samuels worked in his blue and white striped shirt with his sleeves rolled up. His tweed jacket hung on the back of a chair by the conference table.

"Is there some way I can help?" asked Oscar.

"There will be. For the moment, relax. I'm trying to determine how much work will be involved."

Samuels's response implied Oscar wasn't going to be fired. He unconsciously breathed more slowly. Two walls of the room had built-in walnut bookcases filled with what he assumed were rare books. Dr. Samuels moved from the tall filing cabinets to a wide cabinet with shallow drawers where flat artwork was stored.

He put on a pair of white cotton gloves and began sifting through the dozens of loose papers that had apparently been tossed in the drawer. Some pages had become dog-eared and wrinkled. He picked up a page by holding it with the tips of his gloved fingers and placed it on top of the filing cabinet.

Richard entered and plunked down next to Oscar, who shook his head, disapproving that Richard had shown up for work stoned.

Richard raised his arms as in surrender. "Yah, I'm walking and working. What do you want?"

Samuels ignored them.

Several minutes later Maddie entered, surprised when everyone turned toward her. "Sorry. There were a lot of people wanting to talk after the movie."

"It's all right. Have a seat. I'll be right with you." Samuels turned his back to them and continued sorting through the drawer.

Maddie mouthed, "What the hell is going on?" Oscar shrugged and indicated with his hands that they weren't in trouble.

Samuels turned with an armful of loose pages, carried them to the conference table, and placed them before them.

"Here's what I have," he said. He saw that they knew these were the censored images Ruthann Medlin had told them about.

"I've identified a number of books censored by the library. I found just short of thirty examples, but there're more. I want you to locate the books this artwork was taken from, and using the best restoration techniques we know, we will return the pages where they belong. Ilene Fischer will instruct you on the materials and procedures we have for doing that."

Samuels sorted through four Ruben's nudes, an El Greco crucifixion, and even *Nude Descending a Staircase.*

Maddie chuckled at the sight of the Marcel Duchamp painting. "What's that doing there?"

"According to the Decency Council, the painting insinuates sexuality which becomes a sin created in the mind. I'm told that suggestion for sin is worse than outright nudity." He removed the cotton gloves and ran his fingers through his gray hair.

"Why doesn't the library buy new books?" asked Oscar. "Aren't these coffee table editions?"

"You're right. Many of these are popular imprints. Until we have the budget to buy new, we will have to make do. However, here's the reason we're here. A number of these books are irreplaceable. Those will be handled differently. We don't want them damaged more than they already are. I'm asking you to do this beyond your regular hours—for pay, of course. You may come in when you have time to do this work—which will probably take weeks. You will report to the new head librarian, Ilene Fischer. She will oversee your work, book by book, page by page. Is this something you'd be willing to do?"

"Hell, yes," Maddie replied immediately.

"I'm in," Richard added quickly.

"Me, too," said Oscar.

"It's 2:30. Take a break, and when you're through, I want you to collect these titles and bring them here. So far, I've identified these books as needing restoration. They happen to be in all departments." He handed them lists.

Oscar's list was for books in art and music. Knowing that Ruthann Medlin took her break at 2:30, rather than taking his own break he hurried to the Art and Music Department, commandeered a book cart, and hustled through the aisles pulling the volumes from the shelves. When he'd gathered the books, he slipped the list into his back pocket, cleared the door, crossed the lobby casually, turned the corner, and hustled down the hall to the only elevator in the building. He pressed the button. The elevator cables popped and creaked as it came to a stop. Through the small glass window, he saw Ruthann pulling open the accordion gate.

Oscar had no place to go. The elevator door slid open. Blinking and in panic, he backed the cart into the elevator.

Ruthann saw the art books and shot a look at Oscar. "Where are you going with those?"

"Dr. Samuels asked me to take them to special collections."

"And why would he want you to do that?"

"I don't know," he lied. "Dr. Samuels asked me to."

"What's he planning to do with them?"

"Miss Medlin, you should ask him."

Ruthann joined him in the elevator, closed the accordion gate and stabbed the third floor button with her index finger. The elevator creaked and popped in ascent.

"Are you afraid of me?" Ruthann asked Oscar. "You should be."

"I need this job," he replied without looking at her.

Ruthann said nothing. Oscar felt if he were to spit, his hot saliva would freeze before it hit the floor.

The elevator opened and Ruthann sprang ahead of Oscar and his book cart.

By the time Oscar reached the special collections room the door was shut and locked, as well. He could hear Ruthann shouting through the door.

"You little twerp. This is the work of the Decency Council. You *will* put these books out again. That's the way it works here."

"Ruthann, that's not the way it works. The Decency Council has no authority here other than your saying it does."

"There's precedent. The council has established standards since 1955."

"Standards? There's nothing in our library charter, or in our contract with the city for a Decency Council. We're going to run the library like it should be run. Books are for the public. As long as you're here, I was going to meet with you today. I've appointed Ilene Fischer as head librarian."

"That afraid-of her-shadow shriveled chicken?"

"Stop that, Ruthann. She has a master's degree in library science. I'll ask you to respect her credentials."

"I know the Dewey decimal system. I ran this place from 1958 until you got here eighteen months ago. I've been here since 1936. I have *seniority*. I should be named head librarian."

"Knowing the Dewey decimal system is not the only skill required to run a library. This isn't a private domain where you or I can dictate standards. I have responsibilities far beyond the accession of books."

"And what about the moral standards of the community?"

"What qualifies you to be that arbiter?"

"My good standing in this town."

"Your uncle has chosen to remain hands-off to my decisions so long as I am director."

"We'll see about that! Do you think my uncle is the power around here? He's not!"

"Ruthann, stop threatening. My decision to choose Ilene Fischer over you has many considerations. Besides your lack of credentials, which played a big part in my decision, a couple of days ago the board completed an audit of the library's collection. You saw that we have a new lock on the door?"

"What does that have to do with me?"

"The audit was your uncle's idea; he wanted to make sure he knew what we owned. If he had to fire me, he'd know that I didn't walk away with the silverware."

"Bully for you. We don't have any silverware."

"What the audit turned up was that while you were acting head librarian several valuable new donations were destroyed, and a rare book worth fifteen hundred dollars was removed from the special collections—and is nowhere to be found."

"You know, books go missing every day," Ruthann huffed.

"Not from special collections. You accepted a gift of the five-volume *Five Centuries of Art* series. And one of the *Masters of the Twentieth Century* printed in 1920. Do you know what those six books in good condition are valued today?"

"Those arty books from Amsterdam? They came in with many other books. How was I supposed to know they were special?"

"That's my point. I would have known; Ilene Fischer would have known; you didn't know. Ignorance is not a crime, though it should be. The books had an appraised value of between three and five thousand dollars! You and the Decency Council mutilated them, and they're now worth next to nothing. Not a crime, but it is negligence. Like putting an 1885 first edition of Mark Twain's *A Connecticut Yankee in King Arthur's Court* out for loan next to the *New York Times* bestsellers—which you did, and the book hasn't been seen since."

"It was a new book."

"It was described by the donor as a mint condition, un-circulated seventy-five-year old first edition, and it's gone."

"If it's about the money, I'll write you a check."

"Ruthann, it's not about the money. You're not going to be the head librarian."

Out in the hallway Maddie and Richard arrived with their book carts. Oscar signaled for quiet and held his breath waiting for another exchange from the locked room.

The lock snapped and the door opened.

"You . . . you . . . This isn't over. Not by a long shot." Ruthann stepped into the hallway, her face red and eyes swollen. She froze when she faced Maddie, Oscar, and Richard.

"Young lady you're on disciplinary notice for being out of dress code." She looked at Oscar. "And as for you, you weasel, you wiggled yourself out of my hands into the reference department, and now you're kowtowing to the director."

"Don't say anything more, Ruthann," said Samuels. "As of this moment, you are no longer in charge of the pages. You choose, either go home, or return to your department, posthaste."

Ruthann smoldered, turned and strode past the pages, tripping on Richard's book cart. Her eyes flashed angrily. "You did that on purpose."

"I didn't do anything," mumbled Richard.

"Ruthann, posthaste," demanded Samuels.

Ruthann limped down the hall. Several steps short of the elevator her ankle faltered. She put one hand on the wall to steady herself.

"Damn, that's going to cost me," Samuels said loud enough for the three to hear. "Come in." He picked up his sport jacket and slipped it on. He straightened his bow tie in the reflection of a glass cabinet door. "In spite of what you may have just witnessed, we will proceed. Have a seat, or look around if you wish. Ilene Fischer will be here in a few minutes to begin with your instructions."

Dr. Samuels left the room. They sat silently for a moment.

Richard stood. "There's got to be some cool stuff in here." He drifted out of earshot.

Oscar shifted and asked, "Where were you last night that you didn't have time to go home and change clothes?"

Maddie shook her head. "Jealous?"

CHAPTER 29

Three weeks after he'd left for his aunt's bedside, Pedro "Pito" Vasquez returned to the Buena Vista Cabins at the wheel of a sun-bleached blue 1948 Chevrolet coupe.

Stopping in front of Cosimo's freshly painted multi-colored cabin, Pito opened the driver's side door and took two steps in the direction of the cabin.

He threw his arms in the air, *"Que chingaos!"*

A car door slammed behind him, and a woman with shoulder length salt and pepper hair and in a skirt too tight across her hips stepped up behind him.

"What's the matter, honey?" She stood a few inches taller than Pito. The lines on her face made her ten years older, and a smile revealed incisors and canine teeth rimmed in gold.

"Look! What the son of a bitch has done!" Pito waved at the cabin.

"Is this the motel you own?" she asked.

"Yes, and it's a goddamn mess."

"The painter should have finished all the units before you returned."

"What?"

"You only have one unit ready for customers. Why didn't he do the other five? Don't pay him until he agrees to finish the job."

"Stay here. I'm going to have a talk with him."

The woman returned to the car, lit a cigarette, and sat in the passenger's seat with the door open and her legs outside the car.

Pito pounded on the door, expecting it to open as it had before. He pounded harder, and before a third try, he heard a lock click and the door opened.

"What the fuck have you done to me?" Pito stepped back from the porch. "Are you some kind of a mentally crazy type of guy trying to take over my property?" he demanded.

"Pito, I tried to contact you. The two men from Monterey are in Cabin 2."

"Oh, shit. I forgot all about them."

"They're almost finished with the work. I've been feeding them and waiting for you to come back."

"How much is this going to cost?" grunted Pito.

"You will pay them what you promised. They were sleeping in their van, so I told them to move in. What happened to you? How could you forget?"

"I met a woman. What about your cabin? How much will that cost me?"

"What I've done won't cost you a cent." Cosimo saw the woman sitting in the car and waved for her to join them inside. Cosimo took Pito by the arm and brought him into the room. "You have this all wrong, Pito! I'm not after your property. This is all on me."

Pito entered, openmouthed. He took in a powder-blue wall, a sea-foam green wall, a pale rose wall, and behind him the door, wall and ceiling were white, creating an envelope of color. There was more! Curtains with a duckling design, a bistro table with two chairs of unknown origin, an antique chifforobe that didn't belong, a wind-up alarm clock on the bedside table, and a vivid *Jalisco* serape as a bedspread. On the walls were two drawings of the fox and the sour grapes, and the grasshopper and the ant, artfully mounted with art board.

"You've certainly turned this into a cozy little place. You even have a hot plate!"

"Everything is on loan. As soon as I can leave the country it all goes back to the kind people who let me borrow them."

The woman entered and reacted to the Caribbean colors. "Whooo!" She turned to admire the room, her cigarette hand inches from her lips. "Honey, this is like the place with the roller coaster, Playland Park."

"This is my friend, Hermina," said Pito.

"We're engaged! Call me Henny," she said, her head tilting slightly to keep the smoke from her eyes.

She smiled through her gold teeth and touched Pito's shoulder affectionately. Cosimo calculated she had once been passably pretty, long ago.

"Can I offer you a cup of tea? How about you, Pito?" He reached into the chifforobe for two cups and saucers, placing them on the wrought iron bistro table. "Please sit."

Henny backed into one of the chairs and removed a saucer from under its cup and flicked her cigarette ash. "Pito, is that what they call you?" she asked.

"He doesn't have to call me Pito. It's just a nickname," Pito protested.

Cosimo noted Pito's discomfort. "Henny, I apologize. I can't serve tea. I'm on my way out and I just noticed the clock. I have to be someplace before four-thirty. No time to boil water for tea. I'm going to make a change in our refreshments. One shot of Ron Rico rum for everyone and then I have to go. How about that?"

"A man after my own heart." Delighted, Henny winked at Pito.

"We drink to this man's heart, Pedro Vasquez, affectionately called 'Pito' by his friends."

Pito shook his head.

Cosimo brought out an unopened bottle of Ron Rico 151 rum, broke the seal and poured a fair amount into two teacups.

"I didn't mean to surprise you with the paint job, Pito." He handed a cup to Henny. "To tell the truth, I needed to keep working with my hands, otherwise I was certain to go crazy." He handed Pito his cup.

"Crazy is an understatement. But paint, I meant white paint," said Pito. "What's wrong with white paint?"

"I'm sorry. I wanted your permission, but you didn't leave an address or a phone number." Cosimo motioned toward the apartment building. "Honestly, honestly, I asked everyone around here if they knew where you were."

"I like it. It's cheerful," Henny said, sipping the rum.

Pedro took a deep draw.

"Be careful—" warned Cosimo.

Pito's uncontrollable coughing cut Cosimo off.

"*Hijole!*" Recovering, Pito rasped, "That's powerful . . . eh, stuff, where . . . where'd you get this?"

"Emma Vasquez's son brought it home duty free. She gave it to me for helping at the café."

"You helped at the café?"

Henny drained her teacup and held it up. "Ummm, so good. Tiny sips, Pito."

"Call me Pete or Pedro," he replied.

Cosimo refilled her cup and presented the bottle of Ron Rico to Pito.

"Take it. It's a gift. I have to get to the post office before it closes," he said. "We can settle the paint job when I return. We'll work this out. Take a look at what the men from Monterey have done. You are lucky. They are very good workers." Cosimo turned toward Henny. "A pleasure to meet you."

"Very pleased to meet you, too." Henny downed the refill and handed him the empty cup.

Cosimo retrieved his hat, cane, and satchel, ushered them out, and locked the door with a key.

He nodded toward the old building. "Did you know a locksmith lives in the apartments? This won't cost you, either. I have the master key. I'll give it to you when I return."

CHAPTER 30

eaving Pito and Henny, Cosimo took the bus to Walgreen's Drug Store on Navarro Street. From there he walked to Alamo Plaza, passing soldiers in clusters of two or three. They didn't feel threatening. Unarmed, their hair shorn, faces scrubbed, they appeared too young to buy alcohol, and too broke to do anything other than wander the unfamiliar city.

Arriving at the post office before five, Cosimo planned to blend in with the late day crush. As long as he was in the queue, the clerks would help him. He waited for Francisco Orozco's window to become free, allowing people behind him to go ahead.

Two men in dark suits came directly toward him. He fought an impulse to walk briskly away. He knew that would be a bad idea. He smiled, nodded. One of the men stopped about ten feet away while the second approached and said in a lowered voice. "Will you please step away from the line." Their faces were granite, revealing neither warmth nor malice.

Cosimo took several steps and looked back towards the queue. Francisco's window had become available.

"I'm next," he said.

"Can we see your passport?" Cosimo didn't see who asked, he was looking toward the post office window.

He handed the men his French passport.

"We'd like for you to come upstairs. We have a few questions," the man closest to him said.

"I'm expecting mail. Can I have my passport?" Cosimo urged. "I'm next."

The agents held out their credentials "I'm agent Marvin Sinclair, and this is agent Isaac Potter. We'll hold on to your passport for a few minutes. This is a courtesy request." The man closest to him held out his arm pointing in the direction of the interior hallway. This was not a request.

The last woman in the queue completed her transactions and turned away from the window. Francisco pointed at his watch. It was after five o'clock. He reluctantly put out a placard, "Closed."

"I was next," Cosimo complained. "Did you think I would run away if I had a head start? I have an arthritic knee."

"The mail will still be here in the morning," replied Sinclair.

Cosimo shrugged and walked in the direction they pointed. He may not have been in handcuffs, but the men positioned themselves so he had nowhere to go but forward. Sinclair had the look of rawboned peasants he'd seen in France, and Potter had the smooth face of an English university student. He estimated their ages to be in their late twenties or early thirties, and except for the slightly different ties, one striped the other plain, their dark suits and shoes were exactly the same. At the very least, these men were not the flag-waving Cubans he'd been avoiding.

They led him down the long post office hall, past banks of brass post office boxes, past the ornate Italian brass islands with glass tops with pens on chains. He counted six matching Italian chandeliers hung approximately every nine meters.

At the end of the hall, they unlocked an unremarkable service door with a key, which opened to an elevator that took them to the third floor. This wasn't the customs and immigration office.

Agent Potter opened the elevator door, as Sinclair stood behind him. The décor was utilitarian government issue. Sinclair continued to an inner hallway where he reached into a darkened room and snapped on the light. The florescent fixture buzzed momentarily, then diminished into a hum. The only object on the tired pea-green walls was an electric clock with the power cord snaking down to the plug near the floor. The well-worn wooden conference table and equally dinged chairs didn't hint of anything but tedium.

"How long will I be here?" asked Cosimo, as politely as he could muster.

"Do you need to be someplace?" Agent Sinclair asked, as if he were really concerned.

"Not exactly, but I have a routine to my day."

Agent Potter left the room and Sinclair took a seat across the table from Cosimo. He had an agreeable personal manner and wore a wedding ring.

"When can I return to my lodgings?"

"About that, what is your current address?" Sinclair folded back pages from a yellow note pad to a clean page.

"Number 4, Buena Vista Cabins, 1361 Buena Vista Street. Now, when can I leave?"

Sinclair added the address to his notes. "I don't know how long you'll be here. I only work at this hotel."

"I thought this was the FBI?"

Sinclair laughed. "You're correct, this is the Federal Bureau of Investigation, and we've been looking for you."

"Looking for me?"

"Yes, you weren't at the YMCA."

"Doesn't your office talk to the other government offices in the building, as in the post office downstairs? My records are with the immigration people on the second floor." He opened his satchel. "Here's my Cuban passport, I have copies of all my papers."

"You have two passports?"

"Yes, I was born in Cuba, and I became a citizen of France in 1918."

"Since you've been in the country have you attempted to distribute books or pamphlets?

"Why would I do that?"

Sinclair looked pained. "Can you answer the question?"

"The answer is no."

"Did you bring any books, pamphlets, correspondence, or diaries into this country?"

"To that, the answer is yes, but they're not in my possession."

"Where are they?"

"In possession of the Hunter family and their lawyers."

"Why aren't they in your possession?"

"You need to speak with Mr. Ernest Carmichael in the immigration office. Call him, please. He can tell you my story. I have his card here." He handed him Carmichael's business card.

Sinclair stepped out of the room and returned several minutes later. "Your friend Carmichael has left for the day. We left a message. Give me a brief version so I know the story as well."

"I didn't bring any books into the country myself, because they were shipped separately. They are my notebooks and diaries. I came to the US to live with my companion, Sara Hunter. My intention was to relocate here as a permanent resident. Before I arrived, my good friend Sara Hunter, maybe you heard, died in an automobile accident. Since then, Sara's family has not allowed me to access my possessions for some unknown reason. They are also not releasing forty-five thousand dollars Sara Hunter was holding for me. I have a business card for the Hunter family attorney, if you wish to speak to him."

"What's in the diaries?"

"My diaries? You want to know about my life as written to myself? I assure you there's nothing there to interest you. Fifty years of entries could prove embarrassing personally."

"Embarrassing? About your politics?"

"No, the reason is personal thoughts about life and people can be embarrassing. I started writing them when I was twenty-five. I have no politics."

"Everyone has politics," Sinclair said, half-chuckling.

"I am an artist. I have opinions. There's a difference."

"Creative people have been known to be political. Writers are the most political, don't you think? And you keep diaries," Sinclair said.

Cosimo shook his head, and put his hands on the table. "Agent Sinclair, did I pronounce your name correctly?"

"Yes."

"By tomorrow morning I will be cleared of any sinister suspicions. My status will be clarified, and I will soon retrieve my possessions and return to France. Let us get this done. First, I'd like to ask you a personal question, if I may."

"Perhaps, later. You're an artist. What kind? What genre?"

"Oil on canvas. Drawings. Etchings. My style is figurative, realistic. To a layman, that means when I paint a person, the finished art looks like a person. Anyone can drip paint on a canvas, or put a goat in a tire. Critics say I paint what's seen, to reveal what is unseen. These same critics have given it a name, figurative surrealism. Do I have any idea what that means? *Absolutely not.* I've had exhibits in New York, Paris, Moscow, London, and Rome."

"Moscow? Why did you show in Russia?"

"Because I was invited. The Russian politicians, like you Americans, know little to nothing about art. In an attempt to show how open-minded they had become, they allowed a show of decadent Western art to exhibit at the Pushkin Museum, which was attended by thousands and thousands of Russians." Cosimo laughed at his own story. "The embarrassed Russian politicians assured us that their own exhibits were equally well attended. Of course, one cannot lie about attending mass on Sunday, if someone is counting noses."

Amused, agent Sinclair warmed up to the short man. "I have no reason to doubt your story. I did read of Miss Hunter's death. That made the newspapers."

"How much longer will this take?"

"Yes. I have to follow up on your information with immigration and with the embassy in France. We Telex. We'll check you out with them and then you can be on your way."

Cosimo pointed to the clock. "You realize it is nearly 5:30 p.m. here? That makes it 2:30 a.m. in France, and the embassy does not open until ten."

"I've been informed of that. However, someone is there twenty-four hours." Sinclair opened the door to leave the room.

"Apparently you've never been to Paris," said Cosimo. He pushed his satchel, cane, and hat aside, crossed his arms on the conference table and lay his head down.

"Don't get too comfortable. You'll have another interview."

"What more?"

"Just relax. We are cooperating with the Defense Department,"

He took a bathroom break and came to regret eating a candy bar supplied from a vending machine. Three hours later, the door to the conference room opened and the Cuban he'd been avoiding, the one from the Alamo Plaza, entered, accompanied by hefty, mustachioed muscle.

The Cuban stood straight-backed with cheeks slightly swollen and pink from sunburn. His blue eyes studied Cosimo.

Cosimo assumed this man was an elite son of a well-connected family. His hair had been rendered lifeless with a stiffening wax. Sitting down, he dropped a file folder and a pack of cigarettes on the table.

"Did you know the United States ended diplomatic relations with Cuba in January?"

"We introduce ourselves, first. My name is Cosimo Infante Cano. Who are you? And you?" he said to the hefty man.

The men stared back. "I am Major Efrain Yñiego y Remedios, and this is my driver, Ernesto Pasos." His polished European/Latin accent informed Cosimo that the Major spent his student years in the United Kingdom.

"Yes, I've known of the diplomatic break, from the American perspective," Cosimo replied. "Are the cigarettes a threat or a bribe? I don't smoke."

"What do you mean by an American perspective?" asked the Major, putting the cigarettes back in his shirt pocket.

"What I've read comes from the *New York Times*, the *Austin American*, the *Express-News*, the *San Antonio Light*, and the *Christian Science Monitor*. The story is the same in all the journals. It is the American version," replied Cosimo. "I have not found recent issues of the *Guardian*, *Le Monde*, or *Der Spiegel*."

"Do you consider the invasion news American propaganda?"

"What else should it be called? It's the American version. You undoubtedly considered yours a noble cause. Cubans and Europeans might have another opinion. Tell me, where you were born?"

"Santiago del Mar."

"I went to school with Eduardo Yñiego from Santiago del Mar. By your pale skin and blue eyes, he could be your grandfather."

"My great uncle."

"What do you want with me?" Cosimo asked.

"Someone pointed you out as being born in Cuba. Is that correct? And you arrived in March?"

"And you called me out in the plaza. And your man here was the driver, if I am correct."

"Why didn't you cheer for Cuban liberation? Do you not love Cuba?" pressed the major.

"The question should be, 'Do you love Cuba?'" countered Cosimo.

The major's face flushed red. "Who did you meet with when you arrived in San Antonio?"

"Lawyers, the immigration department, business contacts, some people around where I reside."

"I'll need the names of those people. All of them."

"They're neighbors. Some of them don't speak Spanish."

"I still want their names."

"Since this is not a court of law, you cannot compel me to reveal casual acquaintances."

"That can be arranged. What does the 26th of July Movement mean to you?"

"Major, *that* is a ridiculous question. I have lived in France full time for the last nine years and part time for over fifteen years. Cuban politics have nothing to do with me. I used my French passport to enter the United States. Every day I search for news from inside Cuba, and do you know what I find in American periodicals?"

"What?"

"Nothing!"

"Did you know that my uncle Eduardo Yñiego was executed when they confiscated his land?"

"No, I did not know that. My condolences. What were the circumstances?"

"How about here in the United States, do you know Rocio Clemente or Felipi Sanchez de Sonja?"

"I have no idea who they are. Do they live here?" Cosimo replied, patiently.

"They seem to know you."

"That is strange. Tell me about them. Perhaps that will help me recall, though I am certain I have not met them."

"You met them at the Immigration Office."

"At INS? That is absurd. I did not meet any men at Immigration Office."

"Then, how did they know you pretended to be a French citizen, then admitted you were born in Cuba."

"Because I am a French citizen, and have been since 1918. I have two passports. Young man, are you accusing me of something? I care about my birth country. What happens there is important to me."

"Though you don't care enough to live there."

"Asked by someone educated in England and in the service of the United States. Forgive my comparison, but you are like your uncle. *Piel blanco y ojos azules como los reyes Borbones.*"

"You son-of-a-bitch."

"You are the descendant of semi-royalty. Tell me, within your class can anyone exercise their right to live wherever they desire? If I am a French citizen, how can you find cause for suspicion?"

"Many of the rebels have found refuge in France. It's a hotbed of intrigue."

"As it has been for as long as there has been a France."

"And you show up, a Cuban arriving from Paris to San Antonio. Of course, that makes you suspicious. Someone betrayed the brigade, and for some reason you've been very hard to find."

Cosimo spoke down to the major as if he were talking to an insolent servant. He hoped his act was keeping the major off balance.

"Tasked with finding a traitor in your midst, you are grasping to make yourself into a hero. I am not a scapegoat. Call immigration tomorrow, speak to Ernest Carmichael, he will tell you why I'm here in this city. I have not been hiding. Because my financial situation is dire, I am forced to live as a monk. You have no experience with poverty."

The door opened and Agent Sinclair motioned for the major to step out of the room. "You asked for fifteen minutes. Your time is up."

The major picked up his file folder and stood. "Now that I found you, I will get the names of those people." The mustachioed man never said a word and exited last.

Sinclair lingered at the door. Once the major and his driver had cleared the hall he asked, "Can I get you anything? Need a toilet break? A cup of water?"

Cosimo shook his head. He didn't want to owe these sons-of-bitches even a thank you. The door closed and he lay his head on the table.

At 12:45 a.m. Sinclair returned. "Here is your passport. You're clear. You're free to go."

"It's after midnight. The buses are no longer in service."

"I'll drive you to your digs when I get off."

"When is that?"

"6:00 a.m."

Cosimo gathered his belongings. "Thank you for the offer. I will leave now."

"I'll have to unlock the exit. We go this way." From the private elevator, they crossed the darkened post office lobby. Sinclair unlocked a side exit.

Cosimo paused before leaving. "By letting me go now, that means my story has been validated and we will probably never see each other again."

Sinclair shrugged, "Probably not."

"Here's my personal question, are your ancestors French from St. Clair, between Toulouse and Bordeaux?"

"My great grandfather was French. I don't know from where. Why?"

"You should travel to St. Clair. Your cheeks, chin, and nose were forged there."

"I'm one-hundred percent American," boasted Sinclair.

"That you are." Cosimo stepped into the warm night.

At 1:00 a.m., a peculiar silence enveloped the city. In the distance, the motor of an unseen auto echoed off the buildings, then faded and disappeared. Cosimo took a deep breath of the warm humid night air and descended the stairs to the street. His arthritic knee was going to be a problem.

He should have been pleased to be free of the inquisitors. Cosimo felt no sympathy for the major, who'd become ensnared by his own conspiracy. He had seen his kind before. No matter the outcome of any war, they were a resilient breed.

By the time Cosimo arrived at his cabin, Emma and Gabriela were rising for work. Emma, seeing him, waved for him to approach the window.

"Where have you been? Look at the time," Emma said in low voice.

"I'll explain later. I have to lie down."

"You sleep. Should I tell the people you won't be in today?"

"Yes, please do. I'll be in tomorrow."

He unlocked his door and looked in the direction of Pito's apartment. The lights were out. He put away his hat, cane, and satchel, limped the last few steps to his bed, and sat. His knee throbbed.

CHAPTER 31

Cosimo awoke to banging on his door. He lifted a corner of the curtain hoping it wasn't the Cuban. It was Pito, standing hands on his hips, looking dour. "Wait a moment, Pito." He called out. "I was asleep."

"Yeah, get up. It's ten o'clock. Yeah, take your time. You only fucked up my life."

Cosimo put on his pants, slipped on his shirt and opened the door. He motioned for Pito to enter.

"I did what?"

"You've fucked up my life."

"My heartfelt apologies. All it will take is a can of primer, and with two coats of white, you'll have your cabin the way you want it."

"*Cabron*, the people want all the cabins painted like this. You, son of a bitch, you said I'd be paying you one day."

"Pito, no, no, no. That was a joke. I may have to stay a few weeks longer than I anticipated. I was thinking if I can improve the value of your property, you would let me stay here gratis—for now. I will pay you every cent in due time."

"*Cabron*, you want to stay here free? People have been asking when they can have a turn staying here. They're willing to pay twelve dollars a night!"

"They can stay here after I leave. Until then, I would like to talk about a trade. The men from Monterey finished the tile work. You gave them money to buy tiles, you said you would pay them. They did the work, they finished, and cleaned up. And now they are available to paint all the cabins. And I know how to produce these colors. You can't buy them from Dutch Boy paints or anywhere else. I mix them myself."

"Do it. Paint them. The cabins are not my problem. It's the rum you gave me. Shit man, Henny drank most of the bottle. Right now she's in my bed snoring and farting like a pig." Pito's eyes welled with tears. "I thought she was a good woman. My aunt loved her."

"She is still a good woman."

"Shit man! Why me? Now I'm wondering if Henny took up with me because my aunt left me the car and a little money. I was happy and now I don't know."

"Stop that kind of thinking. Was she cruel to you? Did she hurt you or malign you?"

"No. She got drunk."

"When she was drunk did she curse you, hit you?"

"No, but . . . "

"The alcohol is used for daiquiris. Do not blame Henny. Pito, the rum was intended as an apology for not getting your permission to paint. I had no intention of doing anything that would cause you misfortune. For that, I am deeply sorry. How can I start to make this right?"

"Don't call me Pito."

CHAPTER 32

Maddie and Oscar hovered over a book they were repairing. Oscar held a half-inch stub of the page with the edge of a metal ruler. Maddie precisely aligned the loose page to the stub, then carefully reattached the page to the book using a thin strip of a library-grade transparent mending tape. They ended the repair with their heads close together.

"Can I kiss you?" Oscar whispered.

"Not here," Maddie said. She sat back and put another page in position. They repeated the ritual again.

Richard entered and looked over their shoulders.

"Hey guys."

"Shush. Put on some gloves. You'll be the finger man," said Maddie.

He slipped on the cotton glove, and wiggled his fingers toward the repair job.

"Stop it. You know what to do." Maddie frowned. "Will you focus, please."

Maddie stretched the mending tape across the cut.

Oscar pushed down on the ruler.

Richard held up his right hand. "Which finger?"

"Shush, pay attention. Touch lightly an inch from each end and then once in the middle. Don't press too hard in case we have to reposition."

Richard's long slender musician's fingers ably ran across the mend. Maddie leaned back. "This is stressful. It's easier with three people."

"We've done ten of these before you came. I have to give my fingers a break." Oscar flexed his hand.

"I have news," said Maddie. "I have an audition with the Stella Adler Studio."

"That's great! When are you going?" Oscar sorted through the loose pages.

"In September. I talked to my dad. I've saved bus fare, and he's willing to pay board at a women's hotel. If I get accepted, I don't know how I'll live. I'll wash dishes and scrub floors if I have to."

"Oscar, what will you be doing in the fall?" Richard asked.

"I've transferred to the University of Texas. I might have a job, but I have to be there to apply. I'm leaning toward showing up and hoping for the best. What about you?"

"I'm supposed to be at the Curtis Institute in September. I auditioned last fall when they came to town recruiting. I've received a partial scholarship," said Richard.

"Shiiit," Maddie shrieked. She hugged Richard. "Why didn't you tell us sooner? You jerk! That's fantastic news."

"It's not enough. My mom's a clerk-typist at Kelly Field, and she's barely hanging on as it is. I've got a younger brother, too. Even with a scholarship, there's rent, meals, and bus fare to Pennsylvania. And it's not for composition; it's for my piano skills."

"Yes, but once you're there, who knows what can happen? You have to accept," said Maddie.

"I don't want to think about it. Let's get back to work," mumbled Richard.

Oscar handed over the missing page. "Page thirty-eight is up. This one is special for Maddie, *Nude Descending a Staircase*." The famous painting dominated the page, and a small photo of Marcel Duchamp fit in the lower right hand corner. "I've seen pictures of this painting before, but not like this," said Oscar.

"If we're going to stop to admire each page, we'll never get out of here," said Maddie.

Maddie clipped the loose page in place. Oscar held the book open using the metal ruler, as Maddie stretched the mending tape. Richard's finger came in at the precise moment to set the tape.

Maddie smiled. "We're in sync." She turned the page to a painting they'd never seen before. A grimy-faced, war-damaged British World War I soldier grinned mischievously, his helmet slightly askew, his uniform soiled, his teeth crooked, stained. He held a ripe yellow and red pear in his mud-encrusted hand as if it were gold or a hand grenade. At first glance the image looked like a photograph. A small black and white photo identified the artist as Cosimo Infante Cano, Cuban and French citizen. The caption read, "*Soldier With Pear,* 1919, oil on canvas, 51 cm x 61 cm."

"That's him!" exclaimed Oscar.

"That can't be him," said Maddie.

"Well," Oscar said, tentatively. "But that's his name."

"Fucking impossible," grunted Richard. "What's a famous artist like that doing in San Antonio?"

"It looks like him. His hair is white now. Look at that nose!" Oscar pointed out.

"That's forty . . ." Richard closed his eyes. "Forty-two years ago."

"Can we do this page and talk about it after?" coaxed Maddie.

They finished the page and stared silently at the image of the soldier and the photo of Cosimo.

"Did you read this?" Richard held up a slip of paper. "A note inside the cover says the book sold for two hundred dollars in 1921."

"It's beautifully printed," said Oscar.

"Yes, but two hundred bucks in 1921!"

"I'm not convinced it's him. But *Je-zuz,* this painting makes me want to cry." Maddie's voice cracked.

"It's him," said Oscar.

"I almost missed something," Maddie said, surprised. "As realistic as he looks, the background is not a trench, it's a patched theatrical curtain. Is it life, or is it theatre?"

Richard touched his forehead. "My eye was drawn from the soldier's eyes, to his hands. The dark lines of the curtain are invisible, but once you see them, you can't un-see them. And your eye pulls back to see the entire image."

"I want to see the painting he did for the Armory show." Maddie leafed through the loose pages. "Do we have that?"

"I haven't seen it," said Oscar.

Outside in the hallway the sound of the elevator door opened and closed. They expected Doctor Samuels or Ilene Fischer. Instead, a well-dressed woman in her eighties with a crown of styled gray hair entered the room. Her steely blue eyes stared at the three hovering over the open book.

"What's going on here?" she insisted.

Oscar closed the book. "We're assigned here."

"You must be the barefooted dancer, and these must be the other two clowns Samuels hired."

"I beg your pardon. Can we help you? This is the special collections," said Maddie.

"Don't talk to me like I'm a slack-jawed yokel. I'm here to shut you down."

"Should we call security?" Richard looked at Maddie and Oscar.

"You're an idiot," the woman said. "The library doesn't have security, though it should. We wouldn't have to put up with the likes of you." She took a step toward them to see the book they were working on.

The sound of the stairwell door opening with a bang was followed by hurried footsteps. Dr. Samuels and Virgil, the custodian, opened the door. Samuels entered the room first.

"Mrs. Forester, what a surprise. Guys, this is Eula Forester, and Mrs. Forester, these—"

"I want these people fired," she interrupted, her eyes glistening.

Samuels put up his hands defensively. "Mrs. Forester, please. We're not firing anyone. Please come to my office. I've called your grandson, the mayor. He's on his way. We'll talk this out."

"I'm not going anywhere."

"As a board member emeritus and one of our largest benefactors, you're always welcome here. Let's leave these young people to their work and come to my office."

"My grandson either does what I want, or he can kiss his chances for reelection goodbye."

Samuels leaned close to her ear, "Mrs. Forester, this is neither the time, nor the place." He touched her shoulder in the direction of the door.

"Don't you dare push me!" Eula Forester stared at the director.

"I'm suggesting we proceed to my office," offered Samuels.

"The mayor will hear of this. You can't treat my Ruthann like trash. She's the heart of this library."

"Mrs. Forester. Let's go to my office and discuss what are confidential matters."

"What's he doing here?" Mrs. Forester pointed at Virgil.

"Mister Harper is a member of the staff as well. It's his duty to let me know if we have dignitaries such as yourself visiting our collections."

"We will see how long he'll be around."

"Mrs. Forester. Let's go to my office and let's have that meeting with the mayor."

Eula recoiled as if she expected a swat. "Don't strike me again, or I'll call the police."

"Ma'am, the director did not hit you," said Richard, looking to Maddie and Oscar as witnesses.

"Stay out of this, Mr. Krabb," Samuels quickly advised.

Too late. Eula focused on Richard. "You little shit. No wonder Ruthann considers all of you a nest of craven snakes."

Eula Forester stalked out of special collections. She was done with this place and these people. She didn't look back.

Samuels hurried to catch up with Mrs. Forester at the elevator.

CHAPTER 33

Mayor Morris Forester paced in the director's office, waiting for his grandmother and the director. He stopped at the window with a view of the cypress trees along the river, the Presa Street Bridge, and the parking lot where his Buick Electra blocked the delivery area. He turned the instant he heard the door open.

"Gran! You should have called me." He gave her an obligatory hug. "I can only stay a moment. You look very well. Is it that diet you've told me about?"

"Stop your ass kissing. I'm here to find out why your blood relative Ruthann Medlin is being crucified for stating her opinions."

"Crucified? There's nothing like that going on." The mayor looked at Dr. Samuels.

"Sit down, Mrs. Forester." He waited until Eula and the mayor were seated before he took his place behind the desk. "Ruthann is a long-term employee of the library. I can't talk personnel matters without her permission."

"I'm her grandmother, and Morris here is the board president. We can discuss Ruthann."

"I cannot and will not."

"Samuels, you are new to the city, and maybe you'd like to stay on a while?" asked Mrs. Forester.

"G . . . Ga . . . Gran?" stammered Forester softly.

"I've been here almost two years," said Samuels. "As I would never presume to call you by your first name, I expect to be addressed by my honorific of doctor. And I do not take well to threats."

"Aren't you the tender flower?" She turned to her grandson. "*Mister* Mayor, do I have the power to have him replaced?" Eula said.

"Gran, please."

Virgil knocked on the door and signaled for the mayor's attention. "Mayor Forester, your car is blocking the parking area, and a delivery van needs to leave."

"Can they wait?"

"They're on the clock."

"Here, take my keys and move my car." The mayor reached in his pocket.

"Mayor Forester, Mister Harper cannot move your car. We have no indemnity insurance, so . . . "

"He can move my car," Forester said, waving the keys.

"The board, and you included, voted against insuring personal vehicles."

Morris slammed his fist on Samuel's desk. "Piss me off, why don't ya! Gran, don't make threats, please." Virgil held the door open for the mayor, and followed him into the hall.

Hearing the hall door shut, Samuels asked, "Would you like a cup of tea, or can I offer you a cherry brandy."

He opened a drawer in his desk and brought out a tall paper-wrapped bottle.

"Are you trying to bribe me?"

"This is an American cherry brandy, aged twelve years, made by my family in Wisconsin. It has won five gold medals. Would you like to sample it?"

"You're not the first to try to seduce me with alcohol."

"Mrs. Forester, my intentions are honorable." He poured three small glasses and handed one to Eula.

"You're an impudent creature. Who are you?" She accepted the drink and held it to the light as if searching for shards of glass.

"How do you mean?" asked Samuels.

"You're not afraid of Morris, or me. That means either you're a trust fund brat or a fool."

"I'll leave that for you to ponder," he said returning to the desk. "Mrs. Forester, I am trying to turn this library into something this city deserves. You have a beautiful building here."

"And my endowment pays the salaries of everyone."

"As I addressed the board, at one time your endowment was the backbone of this institution. Not anymore. Times have changed. This beautiful building is capable of more services to the community. I've brought in grants so we can buy new books and hire staff to handle our increase in patrons."

She stared at him long enough to make him squirm. "Your family connections will do you little good here."

"I'm not counting on them." He took a taste of the brandy and put it down. "At least, now, we're speaking the same language."

"Things will go as I say, or there will be changes." She drank the cherry brandy in one swallow and held up the glass. "Not bad, for beer brewers."

After several minutes of awkward silence, Mayor Forester returned. "What do you have here?" He picked up the glass of cherry brandy and took a sniff.

"Mayor Forester . . . Morris, there's alcohol in the room. What are you going to do about it?"

"Gran, please." Her glare caused him to put down the glass. "Damn it to hell."

"We're Baptists!" she announced.

"Gran, we're Episcopalian. All right, already!" Forester sighed. "Doctor Samuels, the city has a policy of no alcohol on city property."

"There's nothing in the library charter. Send me a copy of the policy and I'll post it in the appropriate place."

"Look, Samuels, to you this is a library. To many, it's jobs for the political party in power."

"Not anymore. Look at the contracts. We must hire on merit. You signed off on that."

Eula stomped her foot. "This isn't getting us anywhere. What about Ruthann? Morris, what do you know?"

"I still can't discuss Ruthann Medlin," Samuels said.

"Gran, Ruthann damaged some books but it was with good intentions. It was while she was acting head librarian. Since the library hadn't purchased new books in several years, she took some new donations and put them out for the public."

"What's wrong with that?"

"Gran, they were rare books."

"How rare?

"Maybe two or three hundred dollars each?"

Dr. Samuels shook his head. "Three- to five-thousand-dollar total damage."

"For lord's sake, what were they, Gutenberg bibles?"

"No, they were donations from the Ellison and Harlen estates, one-of-a-kind rare books."

"Is that everything?" asked Eula.

Forester rose hastily to his feet.

"Gran, let me take care of this. I have a meeting with the Chamber of Commerce. I can't stay. I will take care of this later."

"You can't fire her," Eula snapped.

"I can't discuss this," said Samuels.

"I have a meeting with the city council at three. Do you need a ride back to the house?" the mayor offered.

"Don't rush me."

"Gran, there's nothing you can do here."

"Fire the insolent brats who have been making fun of Ruthann behind her back."

"I can't discuss that, either," said Samuels.

"Gran, I have to go."

Mayor Forester eyed the glass of brandy on the desk, took it, and downed it.

As Eula turned to leave, she fired her parting shot. "You can't fire her, and she needs to be treated with proper respect."

"Thank you for coming, Mrs. Forester. I'll give your comments due consideration. Good day, Mayor. We'll speak soon."

Eula glowered at Samuels. "Good day!"

At the elevator Eula clutched her grandson's lapel. "Fire the son of a bitch."

"Gran, people can hear." He lowered his voice. "We can't fire him. He's done nothing wrong. He's smart. He has a contract, and it will cost us if we let him go."

"Ruthann's a twit." Eula Forester said. "You're supposed to take care of her. What else has she done?"

"I've tried to keep her in line. God, I've tried." Morris glanced around making certain no one was within earshot. He continued in a lowered voice. "What Samuels can't talk about is that Ruthann organized two other librarians to not serve the coloreds. If she doesn't stop, he can fire her."

The elevator rattled to the floor. The mayor opened the accordion gate and the door.

"Morris, buy out his contract. I don't like him. Give him a good recommendation and send him on his way. Let's get back to running the library the old way."

"Gran, you can't make that decision, you're no longer board president. He's raising money like no one else can." He closed the door and pushed the button for the first floor.

"Ruthann told me the opening day was madness. The nigras were rude and bossy. She said a circus midget passed herself off as a child."

"Gran, you gotta stop paying attention to every snivel from Ruthann. It's not true. I received a letter from Pastor Horner of the Mount Zion African Methodist Episcopal congregation commenting on the friendly atmosphere on the first day of integration. Those are voters, Gran."

"We have plenty of white folks who think opening the library to the coloreds is surrender. And I agree with them." The elevator stopped. She stepped back for her grandson to open the door.

"Gran, one ignorant move from Ruthann and we could have pickets and television cameras. And that's something we don't want."

CHAPTER 34

On hearing the elevator door open, Maddie, Oscar, and Richard paused their production line.

Dr. Samuels entered the room and waved for them to continue. "Finish what you're doing, and take a break." He waited until they finished the mend.

"May I have a look?" He leaned over the table.

Oscar opened to the last page they'd replaced.

Samuels examined the mending, and turned to the previous repairs. "Nice work guys. It's a darn shame you have to do this."

The three expected worse.

"Take a seat," Samuels said, dragging a chair to the table and sitting. "I want to apologize for the interruption by the mayor's grandmother. That was entirely inappropriate." Samuels half shrugged and rolled his eyes. "She's living in another time."

They laughed uneasily.

"I want you to know that your jobs are safe. Ilene Fischer will be your boss. Of course, I don't know how long I'll be employed," he added with a gloomy chuckle. "There are better things for you out in the world. You'll see. For the time being, this is the best San Antonio can offer students like yourselves."

"Doctor Samuels? Are you leaving?" asked Maddie. "Should we be looking for another job?"

"We didn't expect this. I need the job. I think we all do," said Oscar.

"I know your jobs are on your minds. Obviously, my attempt at self-deprecating humor failed. I'm not leaving. I was making light of an embarrassing situation." He stood and pushed away from the table, returned the chair to the wall. "Again, I apologize for the situation you were put in. It will never happen again. And don't go looking for another job. I need you here." He took out his wallet and placed three ten-dollar bills on the table.

"Sir, you don't have to . . ." said Maddie.

"Take off early, have dinner on me, and leave a good tip," said Samuels.

"Thank you," said Richard, taking one of the tens.

Samuels nodded goodbye and left the room.

"Ten dollars!" said Oscar. "I'm saving that."

"Oscar, please. Let's eat at the Mexican Manhattan," implored Maddie. "I'm sick of Vienna sausages and saltines. I need a real meal."

"We can do it," said Richard. "Dinner's a dollar and a quarter, fifteen cent tip, and for forty cents we can split a pitcher at Elroy's. And for a dime more we can have frosted glasses. That's two dollars, and we will still have eight dollars."

At Elroy's tavern, Elroy set a pitcher of beer and three frosted glasses at the front table. The odor of cigarettes and stale beer was less offensive on a full stomach.

Maddie looked out the window. The setting sun rimmed the roof of the Missouri Pacific train station across the street. The center dome with the bronze statue of an Indian caught the last rays and shimmered, almost lifelike.

"Samuels blew me away," Richard said, pouring the three glasses.

"I think he was offering encouragement," said Maddie.

"I thought there was something ominous about the whole thing," said Oscar. "I don't think he was joking about being uncertain about his own future."

"There he goes again. Ominous?" Richard held up his beer glass. "I'll drink to 'ominous.'"

"I agree with Oscar," said Maddie. "I think he was feeling bad about something."

"Otherwise, why give us thirty bucks?" Oscar raised his glass.

"He's bribing us to stick around," said Richard.

"Exactly, and all bets are off if he goes," Oscar groaned.

"We should share our windfall with that guy." Richard pointed out the window. In the nearly spent daylight, he could see Cosimo approaching.

"That's him!" yelled Oscar.

Maddie scrambled to her feet and ran out the door, stopping Cosimo and inviting him to join them inside.

Cosimo stumbled, confused. Was this a mugging? He squinted and looked into the window where Oscar and Richard gestured.

As he entered the tavern, the tobacco-stained reproduction of the "Battle of the Little Big Horn" caught his attention.

"One more," Maddie motioned to Elroy.

Before they were introduced, Cosimo pointed at the battle scene hanging above the bar.

"The image makes the native people look like merciless savages. Weren't the Indians only protecting what was theirs?" He sat by the window and accepted a frosted glass of beer. "If the battle had been won by the men in the blue uniforms," Cosimo continued, "would there be a painting of soldiers scavenging through the Indian corpses for trophies? That is what happens after a battle."

Maddie let Cosimo's question hang in the air and squeezed in next to him. "We know who you are."

"How so?" he replied.

Oscar took out a folded paper from his shirt pocket. "You are, Cosimo Infante Cano, born in Havana and living in Paris.

"You know that from the library," said Cosimo.

"You painted the *Soldier with Pear* in 1919," said Maddie.

A smile spread across his face. "Is that why you were following me?"

"Actually, no," said Oscar. "We thought you were interesting before we knew you were famous."

Cosimo laughed.

"We found a painting and a photograph of you taken about 1921, in *Masters of the Twentieth Century*," said Maddie.

"And you recognized me from that? That was over forty years ago. When I discovered the book in your library my heart beat faster. Then I saw how the beautiful book had been mutilated."

"We were assigned to restore it and saw the missing page and your photograph," said Maddie.

"She said the pages had been destroyed, and perhaps they should have been incinerated. The book has been a curse to many, certainly the publisher. It was supposed to be the first in a series of books on Modernist painters. The publisher printed fifty or so copies. That is why I was surprised to see this extremely rare book here on a library shelf in this city. The book was a financial disaster. It was ridiculously expensive and many artists not included in the first volume refused to be part of any future publications. Until today its legacy has been one of bitterness and envy." He looked at the students. "Who made the connection that it was me?"

"We all did," said Oscar. "This is Maddie, Richard, and I'm Oscar."

"It was Oscar here who convinced us it was you," Maddie said.

"It's a pleasure to meet my pursuers. I've seen you all at the library where that mad woman is in charge of public morals."

"It's true," laughed Maddie. "Does that make us guilty by association? We only work there. We don't set policy."

"You are students?"

"Yes. And we agree. The woman is mad," said Oscar.

"So, I am not alone in my opinion," Cosimo chuckled.

"Nope, she's a certifiable booby," said Richard.

Cosimo roared.

"I have something for you," said Oscar.

"And what is that?" replied Cosimo, drinking his beer.

"The address for Leonor Fini."

"You what?"

"It took a while, but I finally found a review of one of her productions, which had an interview with her at her home. It gave a street and intersection location, and then with a map of Paris I was able to get a domicile address. I left a copy of the address at the reference desk, but I also hoped I might run into you." Oscar opened his wallet and handed Cosimo a slip of paper.

"That's remarkable!" Cosimo sputtered. "However, she's in Africa making a film."

"Then send it airmail and request forwarding," said Maddie. "I've done that when friends move and all I have is the old address. It costs a couple of dollars more. It's worked twice, and I've done it four times."

Cosimo motioned for Maddie to clear the way so he could stand.

"Thank you for the beer. I am profoundly grateful. Thank you. I must go."

"Don't go, not yet. You hardly touched your beer. You must tell us what you're doing here," said Maddie.

"That's too long a story for tonight. You will have to wait." He took a drink from the frosted glass. "If you are free between 9:30 and 11:00 a.m., come by the Little House Café on South Flores. It is across the street from the Courthouse. Come hungry. Your first breakfast there will be on me."

"You're inviting us to breakfast?" asked Maddie, standing so he could leave.

"I am. Monday through Friday." He drained the rest of the beer in one long swig.

Maddie gave Cosimo a hug. "We'll come."

"I am very grateful," he said. "You don't know how important this address is to me."

He bowed goodbye. "I have urgent business."

"Did that really happen?" asked Maddie, as Cosimo disappeared from sight.

"I don't know. Let's save some cash to cover breakfast, just in case," said Oscar.

CHAPTER 35

Meyer returned the Salvador Dali watch to Hertzberg's window display at 8:45 every working morning. Wearing a duster apron with sleeves to protect his dark salesman's attire, he refreshed the flowers, adjusted displays, removed dead insects with long-handled tweezers, and vacuumed away their flaky remains with a slender hose. At nine-thirty, a half-hour before the store opened, the displays would be flawless.

After his session at the Little House Café, on an unseasonably hot day even for Texas in June, Cosimo crossed Houston Street expecting to see his watch in the window. Panic flooded his chest as he neared. The watch wasn't holding the prime spot. He hurried the length of displays. It wasn't anywhere. He hurried to the entrance, gritted his teeth, and pushed past the door.

Meyer immediately pointed Cosimo toward Allen Goodman, the store manager, at the back of the shop. Goodman took two steps in his direction and motioned for him to come in. Goodman and Meyer's somber expressions and the clerks' curious faces only heightened his alarm.

"Where's my watch?" he demanded.

"Please have a seat, I have something to show you." Goodman went to his desk and retrieved a letter. "This is intended for you."

Cosimo glanced at the store employees staring back at him stone-faced, like witnesses to a train wreck.

Goodman handed him the letter. "One of our competitors has apparently given an estimate value of the watch to the Hunter family, and their attorney has found a receipt for its purchase in Sara Hunter's files. They claim they own the watch."

"Mister Goodman. Where is my watch, now?" Cosimo asked firmly.

"In our vault."

Cosimo closed his eyes and broke into a laugh. "That's great news," he beamed.

"How's that great news? They want the watch," Goodman replied.

"Of course, they want the watch."

"You need to take it off our hands," Goodman implored.

"Now that you and others have established its value, I do not have a safe place to keep it. I would like it to remain in your vault, for the time being."

"The watch is unequivocally yours. It is dedicated to you, inscribed in gold. It was in your possession when you brought it in. That will stand in court."

"Precisely. Please, for two more weeks. Put the watch on display and pay me one last time."

"If I have to pay for a lawyer, Hertzberg's owner won't like it. A judge can grant a writ of possession, and we have to turn over the watch to the sheriff."

"What happens then?"

"The sheriff will hold on to it until the real owner can be determined."

"It says you have thirty days to comply. I am only asking for two weeks. The receipt they found by itself does not make the watch theirs. Mr. Goodman, do not spend money on lawyers. This is almost over."

He waited until Meyer brought the watch from the vault and returned it to the window. Outside Hertzberg's, San Antonio's asphalt streets had softened to the point where women were forced to walk on their toes to keep the tips of their high heels from sinking into the tar.

Cosimo went directly to the post office where he waited his turn to see Francisco Orozco. The day's hundred-and-two-degree heat and humidity were relieved in seconds by the federal building's air conditioning. He could feel the perspiration evaporating from his forehead. For the first time since his encounter with the FBI and the Cuban military officer, he appreciated the benefits of the federal building.

Francisco Orozco had shaved his moustache and had a noticeably close hair trim. Cosimo assumed he was looking for a new job.

"Francisco, please send this letter air mail to France, and put on extra stamps to have it forwarded. And, I have your first case. Meet me at the public library when you get off work."

"I don't know if I'm ready," Francisco admitted. "I passed the bar, but I wasn't the top score."

"Didn't you tell me night school law school graduates on average take the test three times?"

"That's the average,"

"How many times did you take the test?"

"Once."

"That is better than average. You passed the examination, and you are licensed to practice law. You are ready. I want you to prepare a demand."

"A lawsuit? I don't have access to a law library. My fifteen-year-old Smith Corona has seen its last typewriter ribbon, and I don't have business cards. I'm not ready."

"You won't need business cards. That's why we go to the library and use the typewriters there. Francisco, I need this done."

The San Antonio Public Library's legal collection was a nook in the reference department funded by deceased ex-mayor and populist attorney Maury Maverick Sr., for non-attorneys and students needing access to typewriters.

"Here is what I want you to read." Cosimo retrieved the letter from his courier bag.

Francisco twisted his lips.

"Are you going to be sick?" Cosimo asked.

"Ah . . . This is the biggest law firm in the city, and maybe the state."

"Does that intimidate you?"

"No more than a fly is afraid of a fly swatter."

"You are not a fly."

"I'm more of a gnat."

"You have gotten your hair cut, shaved your moustache, and are wearing a tie. You look handsome. Now you need to start acting like an attorney."

"What does this letter mean to you?" asked Francisco.

"It means to me that they have gone through her files and found a receipt for my expensive watch, and they want it."

"Will you give up the watch?"

"Never! Definitely not! It's mine. I have had it for nine years. The Hertzberg store took photographs of the watch. I have photographs that show an inscription to me."

"What do you want to do?"

"If they have a receipt for the watch as they claim, they must have gone through her papers. Now that we know they have the papers, can I have a look at those same papers?"

"Yes. We have to petition the court and tell them bank records and business receipts are what you want to inspect. You have to tell the judge why you want this access. There's a filing fee. Then we have to serve them with a legal notice. There's a fee for the process server, which has to be cash. The next step is called discovery. Who are we suing?"

"The Estate of Sara Hunter, as represented by the lawyers who wrote this letter.

"What will you sue for?"

"I want to demand they return my two trunks and three paintings. I want them to show me her bank records. She accepted a check from me for forty-five thousand dollars, and I know she kept the receipt."

"Their claim that they have a receipt opens a legal door for you. I gotta let you know, though, they have attorneys that can drag this out hoping you'll die before you see a judgment."

"I am not waiting for a judgment, I want access to her letters and bank records. I can prove where my money is. I am counting on the fact the family *can* afford to drag this out. I want them to know I am serious. And because I know what rich people are like, they do not want to see legal bills pilling up for something that's not making them a cent. They will settle because I am asking for only what is mine."

"Mister Cano, we have to do things a certain way. Before you file a suit, there are other considerations. The process is intended to give all sides time to prepare. It's an adversarial system. They can stall by submitting continuance after continuance. What I suggest for now, and what I can help you do, is write them a letter."

"No, not a letter. A letter has no teeth. My dear friend Sara Hunter said, 'If you have a good case, and you are asking for less than a million, sue the bastards! They have too much to hide and do not want to go to court.'" Cosimo smiled. "I am more of a nuisance than a threat."

"They sent a letter; you send a letter. The moment you file a lawsuit, the knives come out on their side. They'll want to know what kind of damages you'll be looking for. You could ask for a bundle of money."

"A letter will only bog things down. I want them to comply."

Francisco smiled apologetically, "Here is what I suggest. They will respond faster to a letter than a lawsuit. It shows you're serious, and it will state how you intend to proceed if they don't comply. You'll have their first response in a few days, instead of months. What will you use as an address? You can't use general delivery."

"A letter!" Cosimo leaned back and opened his hands. "My address is the rental on Buena Vista Street. How much money will this cost me? I have about a hundred and twenty dollars."

"Save it for now," said Francisco. "If it comes to a lawsuit, you'll need to come up with more than that. Come back tomorrow. I want to talk to a few friends who may have some experience with Bluhorn & Carnahan."

CHAPTER 36

During the heat wave, the massive concrete San Antonio Public Library remained cooler in the morning. By afternoon, however, patrons entering the building brought with them an aura of heat. The air around the card catalogs and carrels in the reference department became steamy.

Ruthann sat at the front desk, fanning herself with a *Newsweek* magazine. Virgil backed a cart out of the elevator with two six-foot pedestal fans. He hefted one fan by the pole, placed it near the card catalog section, and plugged it into a nearby socket.

"Everybody hold down your stuff. I'm turning on the fan." He flipped the switch behind the motor. A high school girl's notes took flight.

A red-faced elderly man in a porkpie hat shuffled in from the street, took off the hat and mopped his brow and the wisps of hair on his head with a yellowed handkerchief. Seeing the fans, his hands searched for a spot where he felt the strongest airflow. He unbuttoned his shirt exposing his pinkish belly and gray chest hairs. He held out his arms to feel the rush of air in his armpits.

Ruthann leaped from behind the front desk. "Will you button your shirt? This is a library, you filthy man! Get out." She pointed toward the exit.

The man lingered as long as he could, rebuttoning his shirt.

"It's going to be one of those days," she griped. Ruthann considered working the front desk beneath her, though she knew why Dr. Samuels had sent out a directive ordering everyone, even librarians, to take a turn at meeting the public. It was a test. If she or the two librarians who were disobeying the board's policy refused service to anyone, Dr. Samuels wanted it to happen in front of everyone. At that point they could be fired for violating library policy.

At the half-hour, Maddie replaced Ruthann at the front desk. Ruthann stared at Maddie's clothes even though she could no longer comment on her appearance. Maddie's attire irritatingly complied with the dress code.

Five-year-old Weegee and her aunt Connie Childress entered the library. They set their belongings on a table in the children's department.

"I'll be in the mystery section. I won't be more than a couple of minutes, so find your book and I'll meet you at the front desk," said her aunt. "If you can't find what you want, ask the librarian."

Weegee's Mary Jane shoes clicked as she disappeared between the aisles looking for fiction books. Her socks and the ribbon in her hair matched her pale yellow dress with blue trim.

"It's not here," she called over her shoulder. Her aunt had gone. Weegee skipped toward Jane Jenkins, the children's librarian.

"I can't find a book, *The Yearling*," she said smiling.

Jenkins stared back.

"It's not on the shelf," Weegee continued.

Jane Jenkins looked about, expecting Maddie to field the request, then recalled that Maddie had front desk duty and wasn't coming. She picked up the phone and dialed the three numbers for the art and music department.

"Ruthann, I'm all alone." She covered her mouth with her hand and whispered. "*The coloreds are here, what do I do?*"

Jane Jenkins hung up the phone. "Someone will be here to help you," she said, opening her calendar and pretending to read imaginary notes.

Ruthann entered the room and saw Weegee standing by Jane Jenkins.

"You are not fooling anyone," chastised Ruthann.

"Ma'am?" Weegee replied.

"You're a circus freak, fooling people so they think you're a child."

"No, ma'am." Weegee backed away, startled.

"You must be. No one fills out an application at five years old."

"What do you mean?"

"What book are you looking for?"

"*The Yearling.*"

"That's not a children's book. It's in the literature department."

"I thought it would be here." Weegee was near tears.

"Why do you think you can read *The Yearling*?"

"My auntie says it's a good book."

"What's the author's name?"

"Marjorie something, I don't remember."

"You don't. Well, you should. How old are you?"

"Five and a half." Weegee's lower lip trembled.

"You've fooled everyone, but you're not fooling me," pressed Ruthann.

Virgil was spinning a pedestal fan on its round iron base when he saw huge tears leap from Weegee eyes. He rushed to her side and put his arms around her.

"What's going on?" Virgil demanded of Ruthann.

"This midget is checking out books that tell me that she's not five years old."

"This midget . . ." Virgil cleared his throat. "This child is my great niece, and she is five years old." He caressed Weegee's shoulders. "I'm here."

"That's impossible," replied Ruthann.

"Miss Medlin, you have made this child cry." Virgil looked up at Ruthann. "She's a happy, bright child and doesn't cry easily."

"How can a five-year-old read a book intended for adults?"

"Because she can." Virgil caressed the child's curls. "It's going to be okay. I'll help you get your book." Weegee continued to sob.

Maddie stood at the door to the children's department as Weegee's aunt rushed past. "What's happening?" Connie demanded. Virgil stood, allowing her to comfort the child.

As Weegee's crying subsided, an occasional sob shook her little body. She clung to her aunt, staring warily at Ruthann.

Dr. Samuels entered. "Miss Parker, will you hold down the children's section, and Virgil, please take the front desk until I have someone replace you."

Virgil hurried to the front desk where a line of patrons had formed.

Connie led Weegee away to the literature department.

After the child had left the room, Samuels pointed to Jane Jenkins and Ruthann. "You two, come to my office."

Ruthann passed the front desk and saw Virgil checking out books as though he'd done it before.

Jane Jenkins and Ruthann took chairs next to each other in Dr. Samuels's office. They waited several minutes before speaking.

"Will I be fired?" Jane asked, fearfully.

"What do you mean?" hissed Ruthann. "We're in this together. I'm not going to get fired."

"Yes, that's good for you. I can't make my car payments and rent without this job."

"You said you supported me," shot Ruthann.

"Two years ago! When your grandmother was president of the board, and you were acting head librarian."

"We have to stick together. My uncle is still president of the board, and Gran still has a lot of sway over his actions."

Dr. Samuels entered with his sport jacket over his arm. He removed a wooden hanger from a hat rack and hung up his coat.

Without acknowledging them, he opened the window overlooking the parking lot and returned to his desk.

Jane Jenkins, a thin woman whose fingers were stained from chain smoking, fidgeted in her chair.

"That was a travesty," Samuels said sitting down. "I'm hoping no one informs the press."

Ruthann attempted to speak. "Nothing that—"

Samuels shot his hand in the air and stopped her. "Ruthann, please wait out in the hall. I'll speak with you next," he said.

Ruthann stared at Samuels, then at Jane, before she stepped from the room.

Samuels turned to the children's librarian. "Miss Jenkins, did you refuse to serve patrons asking for assistance?"

"No, no, I asked for help from Ruthann."

"That is, you, a librarian with a bachelor's degree in library science, had to ask Ruthann Medlin, who has no such degree, how to do your job? Is that correct?"

"No, well . . . yes, sir," she offered meekly.

"And, do you wish to remain here as a librarian?"

"Yes, sir."

"Have you read the board's decisions regarding the expanded racial policy?"

"Yes, sir."

"When faced with a situation like you saw today, what will you do?"

"Follow the board's policies."

"I'm glad we understand ourselves. I'm putting you on notice. For now, you still have your job. Return to your post, and ask Miss Parker to return to her schedule. You may leave, now."

Jane Jenkins backed toward the door, nearly genuflecting with gratitude. "Thank you," she mouthed as she closed the door.

Ruthann re-entered, her face white with anger.

"Ruthann, what was all that about down there? Why did you make a five-year-old child cry?"

"I made a mistake. I thought the colored people were trying to make fun of us by passing off a midget as a child."

"Make fun of us. Why would they do that?"

"I, and many of us here, thought they would do just that."

"That's absurd."

"Worse things have happened," argued Ruthann.

"The precocious five-year-old, Shirley, is the daughter of a medical doctor stationed at Brooks Army Medical Center. She happens to be Mr. Virgil Harper's great niece."

"I have to say right here and now that I don't think Virgil is qualified to take on front desk duties."

"Ruthann, that's not your call, is it? Did you know he's a retired veteran and has an associate of arts degree from San Antonio College? At one time, he worked as a page at the George Washington Carver Branch Library? Next year, he graduates with a bachelor's degree in library science. He'll likely run one of our branch libraries."

"That's hard to believe. They all lie."

Samuels sighed. "Ruthann? You—"

"What? You're going to make a federal case out of a little mistake, aren't you?"

Samuels shook his head. "You don't have a reflective bone in your body, do you?"

"I have no idea what that means. Are you going to fire me?"

"Not exactly. I'm going to suspend you—with pay. I want you to go home."

"You can't suspend me without a vote from the board," she spat back.

"I have the authority to remove you from meeting the public, and one of my options is to send you home until the board has a chance to meet. That's approximately the same thing."

"I made a small mistake."

"Big, small, you can't rationalize yourself out of this. There are witnesses as to why you were called to the children's department to begin with. What happened after that, you have failed to explain."

"You can't fire me, and you know it." Ruthann stood.

"Leave the door open. Go home. I will inform you when you can return, if the board approves."

CHAPTER 37

Cosimo stood near the entrance to Hertzberg's, waiting for Meyers to join him.

"I'm glad to talk with you," said Meyers. "Where would you like to walk?"

"Just down the street by the river. I have something to ask you." Cosimo carried his portfolio of drawings.

Cosimo and Meyers descended the stairs to the river level. The deep shade from the cypress trees and the evaporation from the water made the temperature at least fifteen degrees cooler than at street level. Cosimo placed his portfolio on a stone bench, undid the ribbon ties, and opened it.

"My, oh my . . . These are astonishing. This? Is this what you do?"

"I also paint, but this is what I do here with what resources I have. My question is, can your Leica camera shoot high-contrast, fine-grain, black and white negatives of them?"

"What do you mean by high contrast?"

"I mean, I want the lines to remain sharp and dark as they are, and I want the paper color to disappear."

"I'll have to do a few tests, but yes, I can keep the lines as sharp as they are, and the white of the paper will disappear. They'll be like a high-quality transparency."

"That's what I want. What would that cost me? I have a reason for doing this."

"Mr. Cano, I'll do it because I can. This is a great opportunity to study your work."

"There is one more thing. The reason I wanted to meet you out here is because I want to keep this confidential."

"These are beautiful drawings. Why the secrecy?"

"I assure you, everything is legitimate. I consider these works of art, and like a proof for a piece of jewelry, I need discretion in the handling. When I am done, you can tell the world. Until then, please, mum. You will be remunerated."

"Because these are so fine, I agree," said Meyers.

Near closing time, Cosimo hurried to the post office. He caught Francisco's eye, and his friend held up his hand indicating for Cosimo to join the queue. As his turn came, he approached the window.

Francisco smiled. "You have two fat envelopes and one letter." He stepped away from the window. Returning, he said, "I hope it's good news. You'll need to sign as recipient."

Cosimo signed. The correspondence came from Banque Swisse, the *L'Idiote* Art Gallery, and one from Charlotte, the concierge.

"My future could change with these letters, or they could mean nothing. There is a possibility I could owe them all money!"

"I'll meet you at the library as soon as I'm off the clock," Francisco said, glancing at the queue. It was after 5:00 p.m., and a line of customers waited.

Cosimo found an overstuffed chair in the library's reading room and opened the concierge's letter first. Proust the parrot was fine. Charlotte needed more money, and she would be leaving her post at the *pension* at the end of the year.

That wasn't good news, but it wasn't a catastrophe. She mentioned nothing about Leonor Fini.

Banque Swisse had two photographic copies of the check he'd given to Sara Hunter. One copy was for him, and the second copy sealed with Banque Swisse's official stamp, was for the representatives of the Sara Hunter estate.

The envelope from the *L'Idiote* Art Gallery was a disappointment. Inside was his own letter. A note scribbled on the back read, "We are out of business and the owner is in the madhouse." Cosimo laughed, though it wasn't funny. The owner was an old friend. At least someone had the courtesy of letting him know that contact was gone.

"This is good," said Francisco, after having read the letter from Banque Swisse. "This strengthens your case that they have your property, and they have Sara's files."

Over the next two days Ilene Fischer watched Francisco use the small legal collection and type a letter with two fingers. She heard Francisco read the letter out loud to Cosimo, who asked for clarification on several points. Once they'd read through the letter the second time, Cosimo gave his approval.

"This has to be sent special delivery," advised Francisco.

Seeing that they were about finished, Ilene offered, "If there's any help you need, I type fifty words a minute with no errors, or hardly any. I've typed letters for Mr. Cano in French."

"She's a bargain at ten times the price, and she's the reason we are here," said Cosimo. "I'm paying."

"I won't charge. This is a worthy cause," said Ilene.

"That would help a lot. As you saw, I'm quite slow," said Francisco.

Francisco had been a regular patron of the library and recognized Ilene from previous visits. Ilene pretended the young man she'd seen many times was an intriguing total stranger.

Ilene went over the pages with Francisco. She sat at the typewriter, combined a top page, two onionskin pages with fresh carbons, and typed the letter in less than five minutes.

"I'll take it from here," said Francisco to Cosimo. "The letter will be at Bluhorn & Carnahan by tomorrow afternoon."

"Should I sign the letter?" asked Cosimo.

"No, I'll do that and use my post office box as my business address."

"Thank you, so much. We will talk in a few days." Cosimo shook Francisco's hand and thanked Ilene for her help.

"You're an attorney?" Ilene asked Francisco, removing the carbon papers from between the copies.

"Yes, I passed the bar in May."

"Was that your first try at the bar exam?" she asked.

"Yes," he replied modestly.

"Congratulations! I know several lawyers, and none passed it the first time. Is this your first case?"

"I suppose. I'm helping the old man. I don't know why."

"I know why." She handed him the carbon copies. "I think he's real."

Francisco wanted to ask her how she thought Cosimo was real but replied instead, "I think he's real, too."

CHAPTER 38

The lights were out at Elroy's Bar.

Richard tried the door. Oscar peered through the window where they usually sat. Inside a bare bulb illuminated the hallway near the toilets.

Maddie knocked on the glass, and after a beat, Elroy poked his head out from the hallway. "Go away. I've been shut down," he shouted.

"What?" Maddie shouted back.

Elroy stepped into the hall light. Seeing Maddie, he took several steps closer. "It's Eunice, right?"

"Eunice Roebeck, that's right."

"I can serve you but not them," he said motioning toward Oscar and Richard. "Come back in two weeks, I'm shut 'til then."

Elroy returned to the hallway and disappeared.

"Why does he remember your fake name from looking at your ID one time, and he can't remember our names? We're 'them' and you're 'Eunice,'" kidded Richard.

"Get over it. You men are so predictable."

"How's that?" challenged Richard.

"When a man looks at a woman, it's face, tits, and tail. Am I right, Oscar?"

"Not necessarily in that order, but guilty."

"I don't," protested Richard. "That's categorically not true."

"Yes, well, you're a category apart," said Maddie.

"And what's that?" pressed Richard.

"Richard, if you don't know, I can't tell you," answered Maddie.

"You can dish it out, but you can't take it," Oscar razzed.

"You guys are ganging up on me. Not fair," grunted Richard.

"Richard, forget about it." Maddie turned away from the window. "Let's go find our artist friend."

"I'm game," said Oscar.

"We know approximately where he lives. We'll figure it out from there. Are you with me?" She gave Richard a nudge.

"Why not?" he said, looking grumpy.

They had seen Cosimo last at the corner of Buena Vista and Medina Streets. Buena Vista's business area had once thrived. Now, amateurishly lettered signs for used furniture, upholstery, and a radio and TV repair shop were painted on the cinderblock walls.

The scent of blooming wisteria perfumed the street. Two three-story apartment buildings were separated by a sixty-foot trellis and a driveway. At seven o'clock in the evening, flashing televisions could be seen in rooms on the first floor. Traffic moved both ways on Buena Vista Street.

"We've got nothing," groused Richard. "Let's say we call this off. We can sit by the river and share a joint."

Laughter coming from beyond the trellis drew them toward the voices and the discovery of the shotgun cabins. One stood out, painted a striking pink with green trim, and in the fading light, what looked like a violet door.

"That's gotta be it!" declared Maddie.

The laughter came from the doorway to the apartments where Cosimo stood with Graciela and Emma Vasquez. Seeing Maddie, Oscar, and Richard standing at the entrance to the patio, Cosimo grandly waved them in.

"Graciela and Emma, these are my friends from the library."

They nodded hello.

Cosimo turned to his Little House friends. "Good night. I'll be there at 9:30."

He approached. "How did you find me?"

"It wasn't hard," said Maddie, nodding towards the vividly painted cabin.

"Would you like to see the inside?" Cosimo asked, walking towards his cabin.

"Sure." Maddie glanced toward Richard and Oscar. They could hardly believe their luck.

Cosimo unlocked the violet door and stepped back. "Please. Look around."

Maddie took Oscar's hand and entered first. Richard followed a few steps behind.

"Far out!" Maddie let go of Oscar's hand, and turned a full circle. "The room! The colors."

"Did you draw these?" Oscar said, looking at the Aesop's fable drawings on the wall.

"Whoa!" Richard reacted to the walls and the ceiling.

"Are these originals?" asked Oscar.

"In a word, yes. They are not unique. It's a trick I learned as a young man."

"A trick? Must be a magic trick," said Maddie, stepping closer to the artwork. "These are ink, with colored pencils."

"Correct."

"Why is it a trick? They're stunning," Maddie looked closer.

"I'll tell you about the drawings. First, please, sit down." He pointed to two chairs by the bistro table, the bed, and two other chairs. "Plant yourselves anyplace you want and I will hydrate you, as my old lover used to say."

Oscar and Maddie took the bistro table, and Richard pulled over a chair to join them.

"I have Stolichnaya vodka and Kahlua. I don't have ice, but these make a black Russian. Mind you, Soviet vodka acquired duty free could make communists out of you."

"I wouldn't like that," said Maddie. "Maybe, just a little socialist since Kahlua is a coffee liqueur."

"I'll have one." Oscar held up his hand.

"Better red than dead. Make mine a double, please," said Richard.

"There's no rush. The bottles are here. Help yourself."

Cosimo took out glasses similar to those used at the Little House Café.

He handed out the black Russians and returned to the question Maddie had asked.

"About my drawing trick. In 1908, I matriculated at the École des Beaux-Arts. I had paid for my voyage from Cuba and paid the stipend the school required. I had letters from the local officials that said I was from a proper family. What I hadn't told my parents was that I had made no plans for food and lodging. I don't know what I thought. It was not like Havana, where I had an aunt and friends. It only occurred to me on the boat ride that I had no idea where I was going to eat or sleep. That's how badly I wanted to be in Paris."

He held up his glass, "*Salud.*"

"*Salud,*" they responded.

"Artists with paintings to sell set up on the street level overlooking the River Seine. I had nothing to sell. I was going to starve if I didn't invent some way to make a living." Cosimo took a drink from his black Russian and recalled a memory from long ago.

"What did you do?" Maddie asked.

"I had a little money. And I went through that in four days. I slept under a bridge for a few nights, telling people I was there to draw the sunrise. On other nights I slept in doorways. With my last *sou*, I purchased a book of Aesop's fables from a man more desperate than I, and it saved my life. The stories in the book were parables. I created an illustration for each Aesop story, and then I would reproduce it in front of the buyer for a *sou*. If you wanted an inscription that was two *sous*, a matte three *sous*."

"Like practicing an instrument," Richard said.

"Yes. Once I had done the same drawing often enough, it's like calligraphy. It becomes a second-nature skill—or a trick to someone uninitiated."

"How much could one *sou* buy?" asked Oscar.

"In 1908, it bought a dried herring. For three *sous*, add a piece of bread and a glass of beer. That may not sound appetizing, but it fed me. On the good days I would sell five or six illustrations. Which meant not only meals, but a bed and a pitcher of water to bathe with. In half a year I earned enough to rent a *pension* of my own. I could have written home for money, and my mother would have come and dragged me back to Cuba."

"You must've been painting all that time," said Maddie. "How did you get into the Armory Show in 1913? You were twenty-two years old?"

"I didn't plan it. I was very young and naïve. There was a show in the art district, and a man named Walt Kuhn selected several of my paintings for consideration for a show in New York. I did not think much about it. The art world lives on schemes that never transpire."

Cosimo glanced at their glasses to see who needed a refill. Only Richard held out his glass.

"The show turned out to be real. I don't know who made the decision. My fortunes changed; that is the truth. Only one painting was in the show, but all three sold. I had enough money to travel to New York for the opening at the Armory show."

"Did you meet Picasso, Matisse, Cézanne, Duchamp, Magritte?" asked Richard.

"Not Cézanne; he died before I arrived in France. At one time or another, I've met them all. Truthfully, I didn't socialize, not like they did. Henri Matisse was a real gentleman, though."

"So you didn't have picnics where you dressed in dark suits and women took off their clothes?" asked Richard.

"As in *Le Déjeuner Sur L'herbe* by Edouard Manet? On many occasions I still see nude women. It's one of the benefits of being an artist." He laughed. "If paintings of naked bodies drive your librarian lady mad, *L'Origine du Monde* by Gustave Courbet would put her into an asylum."

"*The Origin of the World.* I don't know that painting," said Maddie.

"If you get to France, go to the d'Orsay Museum. It's a work every boy should see."

"What about girls?" asked Maddie.

"There's nothing you girls haven't already seen. And if you haven't, all you need is a mirror."

"Oh!" Maddie yelped.

"Yes, down there," said Cosimo. "And the anatomy is beautifully executed. Courbet is one of my favorite painters."

Richard spilled his drink, laughing.

"I'll get that." Cosimo tossed a washcloth on the floor and wiped the splashes with his foot.

"What about the painting in the book, *Soldier with Pear*, 1919?" asked Oscar.

"I find it haunting," said Maddie.

Cosimo underhanded the wash cloth into a basket "The image haunted me as well. I had to paint it to get it out of my head."

"How did you imagine that man?" Maddie asked.

"In 1916, my life as an artist took a detour. I served in the war, first as an ambulance driver, then as a hospital orderly. Some agency had brought in fresh pears from a nearby village, and I saw this wretched soldier dressed in pajamas holding the fruit. He may have been safe and far from the front lines, but his mind was still out in the trenches shattered by what he'd seen."

"It makes me want to cry," said Maddie.

"It was intended to evoke a response."

"You paint him in a grimy uniform in front of a theatrical curtain." said Maddie.

He shrugged. "Because when all the *sturm und drang* is done, war is nothing more than a pretext for theft. Flags wave and speeches are made about how their sacrifice will never be forgotten. But, they are forgotten. That broken soldier and the millions of dead and wounded remain the detritus of someone's profits."

"That's bleak," said Richard.

"That's war," replied Cosimo. "That's what it is, clear and simple."

"What brings you here? To this city?" Maddie asked.

"That's too long a story."

"We have time," said Oscar.

"Let's refresh drinks all around." Cosimo stood. "This is strong stuff."

Cosimo refilled his own glass as well as Richard's. Maddie and Oscar were still working on their first.

He gave them a shortened account of his friend Sara Hunter and of his time in San Antonio.

"Sara was the second love of my life, or better said, the third love of my life. I had been married before and had a child, a little boy."

"I had seen death. I conveyed wounded men back to the medical areas, and too many times the men died on the way." He breathed deeply. "I met Lili, a Spanish nurse, at a field hospital in October 1917. She and I decided from the first day we were in love. I may be 163 centimeters tall, but I was quite dashing. We were transferred to different hospitals and I thought I would never see her again. As luck would have it, we were transferred again to the same hospital in Bray."

"Was that when you painted *Soldier With Pear*?" asked Maddie.

"I started it before the Armistice, but didn't finish it until later. My photograph for that book was taken two years later. Lili was a nurse, could have been a surgeon if the medical schools had allowed her to enroll. Beautiful, too, so I didn't just love her for her brain. We married and had baby Hector. They both gave me so much happiness. My heart still aches and it's been years."

198

"In 1920, the year before that book was published, the Spanish Flu destroyed our lives. I had seen too much death. I thought I had become desensitized, then death visited me personally. As skilled as Lili was as a nurse, she could not save our baby Hector . . . and then she could not save herself." He paused and closed his eyes until he felt in control of his heartache.

"My mind went cold for six years. I painted colors, color wheels, color tests, color portraits. Yes, I painted portraits of color. *I introduce you to Yellow!* It was as though I was trying to fathom what reality was made of. I became obsessed with Heisenberg's Uncertainty Principle. Not that I understood the physics. The building blocks of our reality are particles, and at the same time they are energy. They are real, and they are there and then they are not there." He laughed.

"The electromagnetic spectrum, the periodic table of the elements, the chromatic scale, the audio frequencies, these are the truths that make our world. Do they exist? They must. I can knock on this table. I hear it, see it, feel it. It's there. Our reality is created every instant, woven from electrons, protons, neutrons, and whatever else exists in the cosmic loom."

Cosimo stopped himself, looked pensively into his cocktail. "I don't usually drink this kind of alcohol. Wine is my drink."

"You're a poet, Mr. Cano," said Oscar.

"Hardly. I like thinking out loud. Have you seen the motion picture *Room at the Top?*"

"I have," answered Maddie.

"The actress, Simone Signoret, was an acquaintance of Sara's. She was beautiful in the film, though in 1948 when I first spent time with her, she may have been the most beautiful woman in the world. You remind me of her," he said to Maddie.

"That's very kind. I don't believe a word of it."

Oscar chortled, "Now who's fishing for compliments. He only said you may be one of the most beautiful women in the world. Isn't that enough?"

"Did you know any of the ex-pats, the American lost generation?" asked Richard.

"Briefly, Hemingway in France, during the war, and later in Spain. He loved the bullfights. For him it was man versus the primal self. I never cared for that kind of primitive ritual. The bull never has a chance."

Richard helped himself to another black Russian.

"I have a good story you might like to hear. My friend Leonor Fini worked with John Huston on a film in Rome. She swore the man was addicted to gambling. He'd bet on anything. If he saw two birds sitting on a telephone wire, Huston would take out his roll of cash. 'Twenty bucks says the one on the right goes first.'"

Oscar looked at his watch. "Guys, it's almost ten o'clock."

Maddie and Richard ignored him.

"Huston had the entire crew taking his bets. The producer finally ran onto the set screaming, 'Get back to work!' The joke was that Huston and the crew were betting how long it would take him to appear. Leonor also worked with Cocteau."

"Excuse me. We won't make our buses," warned Oscar.

"I'm not ready for this to end," said Maddie.

"I don't want to leave," protested Richard.

"If we don't make the buses, we've got a long, long walk."

Maddie took the lead and came to her feet.

Oscar nudged Richard's shoe. "Come on, let's go."

Richard huffed, annoyed.

"We're honored that you invited us in. Thank you," said Maddie.

Cosimo looked at his three guests. "One thing is different today. I have never spoken about my wife and son as I did tonight."

"I felt privileged to hear your stories. Thank you." Maddie embraced Cosimo.

Richard leaned back. "I want to hear about Cocteau."

"My new friends, we will have other days to visit. I have a suggestion. How would you like to stay here?" Cosimo offered.

"What?" asked Richard.

"Not here in this room, but there are two refurbished cabins, with new mattresses, clean sheets. They're not painted like this, but they are ready for occupancy." He opened the door and looked toward Pito's apartment. "The light is still on. I will be right back."

On returning, he waved for them to step outdoors. "Let us take a look at the rooms and see if they meet with your approval."

"I can't afford a room," said Oscar.

"Henny will be out here in a few minutes and put out towels and soap. If you leave the sheets and towels, it won't cost you anything," he added.

The two rooms were exactly the same, a double bed, new tile in the bathroom, and painted immaculately, azure blue.

Cosimo proudly turned on and off the water in the lavatory sinks.

"They were finished Tuesday. Curtains went up today. The workmen have not installed the toilet paper holders. You will find a roll on top of the toilet tank. There are no shower curtains so be careful not to get water on the floor. I am sure you can figure it out."

"Thank you," said Oscar. "It's better than where I live now."

"Here are the two keys. In my day, one double bed would have been considered deluxe accommodations. Three of us would have slept comfortably."

He expected a comment; none came.

"Seventy-five years ago, these simple cabins would have served as the summer cabins for aristocrats. I'm going back to my room, now. As long as my light is on, you are welcome to visit. In the morning, I will take all of you to breakfast."

"Thank you," said Maddie. "This is more than enough."

"I have not had many good days since I have been in this city. Other events this week and your visit made this different. Thank you for that." Cosimo left them standing on the porch.

"Boys take cabin two, girl takes cabin one," suggested Richard.

"Oscar will you bunk with me?" Maddie asked. She put her arm over Oscar's shoulder.

"Hey, I don't want to sleep alone, either," protested Richard.

"Are you kidding? I choose Maddie," said Oscar.

Richard kicked the door. "Well, you guys go to hell." He stepped off the porch.

"Richard, don't go off like that." Maddie stepped down and put her arms around him. "You know why," she whispered in his ear.

"It's not what you think," Richard whispered back.

"I know, I know, it's not what I think. Do you have a joint you could spare? I'll pay you Friday."

"You've got a lot of nerve. Fuck you." He drew out an envelope from his shirt pocket and handed her a joint,

"Here. It will cost you a buck. I'm going back to hear the rest of the Cocteau story."

Maddie kissed his cheek.

"See you later," called Oscar.

CHAPTER 39

enny arrived in a bathrobe and slippers, carrying towels and bars of soap.

"Hi, guys. This is nice, huh? The old man knows his colors. He told you we don't have shower curtains, right?"

Maddie nodded.

"You kids going to be all right?"

"Yes, I think so," said Maddie.

"Is the other fellow using the second cabin?"

"Yes," said Maddie, taking the room's towels and a bar of Coco Castile soap.

"Then, I'll just put his towels in his place. Good night."

Maddie closed the door. She put the towels on the bed, opened her purse, found a matchbook, and glanced around for an ashtray. She found glasses in the bathroom and brought one to the bed. She offered the matchbook and joint to Oscar.

"Uh . . . sure." He sat next to her.

She pressed the joint into his fingers.

"I've never lit a marijuana joint before."

"Give me that." She took back the joint. "Tell me the truth. Does it bother you that I'm not a virgin?"

"What?"

She put the entire joint in her mouth and slightly dampened the paper. She put it to her lips, struck a match, inhaled twice, and handed it to Oscar.

"Does it bother me that you are not a virgin?" He took a hit. "No. No," he said, his voice squeaky from holding his breath. He exhaled. "You drive me crazy. You make the rules. I play by them. No, I don't mind that you have more experience than I."

They passed the joint back and forth several times.

"Technically, I may be a virgin," said Oscar. "In my heart I have loved many times. It is what boys do. You're not Donna Matranga, my previous ideal. I never kissed her. I did slow dance with her once. She was taller, smelled of Ivory soap, and wanted to lead. I stepped on her feet. She was an athlete; you're a dancer. Your body, like hers, is extremely firm."

"I'm not your virginal Donna."

"No. And I don't mix you up. You actually have boobs. Donna had bumps, like three-quarter inch rosebuds I saw through a sweaty t-shirt."

"Am I buzzed, or what? That's funny."

"Funny? More likely pathetic for my thinking about it."

"Do you still want to kiss me?" she asked, putting the joint aside.

Oscar kissed her. He wanted her lips. He kissed them. Her eyes stared back into him. He made them close by kissing. He kissed her nose, lips, eyebrows, and chin. His tongue slipped into her mouth and touched her tongue. His hand slid across her belly into her panties. Her legs parted just enough to welcome him.

Her panties slipped down her legs. She tugged at his trousers, and he lifted his hips enough to slide the pants down to his ankles and drop to the floor. His underwear went with them.

Maddie sat up, reached for her purse, dug through, and brought out an object she hid from him. She opened her hand and presented to him a condom, laughing as if she'd pulled a practical joke.

Oscar reacted, hurt and perplexed.

"Are you pouting? Did I hurt your feelings?" She patted his cheek.

"Are you making fun of me?"

"No." She glanced at his rigid penis. "You guys forget the boy scout motto is 'be prepared.'"

"Wait. I didn't get up this morning thinking I'm going to get lucky tonight, better pack condoms." He was right, and she didn't appreciate what it implied.

"Give me that," she said and took the condom from his hand. She'd never seen an uncircumcised penis before; that was a bit of a surprise. The condom rolled down effortlessly. She kissed him.

Oscar, wanting to make the moment last, kissed her lips, her cheeks, and her eyes. His erection wasn't going away.

Maddie moved her body under his, never separating from a kiss. He was in her, as deep as he could be in her, sucked in, surrounded, absorbed, alive.

With his next kiss he exhaled his breath into her mouth, and once he sensed her lungs were full, he began to gently inhale. He did this twice before their lips parted to refresh oxygen. As they began to kiss again, she felt light-headed. In that moment, a flash of something resembling bliss swept over her. She shuddered. His penis was there, and his kiss was there, she felt her flesh glowing. The phenomenon happened again, then again. She lost control and repeated, "Oh no, oh no, oh no . . ."

Oscar paused his penetrations to look into her eyes. She felt petrified, as if he knew every secret she kept.

"No, no . . . You can't do that . . ." She slapped him and pushed him away.

"What the hell? What did I do?" He sat back, stunned.

"You can't own me." Her body shivered.

"I don't own—"

"How did you do it?"

"Do what?"

"It must have been the pot. You looked at me as if you owned me. I hate you for that."

"I looked at you? I did. I did look at you. I was admiring how beautiful you are. I don't want you to hate me."

"Oh, shit . . . You're going to be nice. I HATE you." She put her head on his chest. He felt her slender shoulders trembling.

"You're crying. *Jesus Christ*, Maddie? What the hell? Did you hate making love with me that much?"

"No . . . no . . . and yes . . ." She kept her face turned away.

"Then, why did you do it?"

"I wanted to be close to you. And I thought I could own you," her voice broke.

"Is that some weird sex thing? You can't own me."

"I can't now. You stole that from me."

"Stole what? What did I do that was so bad?"

"The orgasm."

"You had an orgasm?"

"As if you couldn't tell?"

He sat on the edge of the bed.

"Maddie, I don't understand. My brain is telling me *run*. Get as far away from you as possible. If you want to hate me, there's nothing I can do about it. This was a mistake."

He kneeled and found his shoes, gathered his pants.

"Stop." She reached out and put her arms around him from behind, pulling him back into bed. "Don't go. I wanted to be close to you because I like you," she said behind his back. "You've been nothing but nice to me. I liked it. It made me feel safe. I like you."

Oscar tried to turn around and she tightened her grip on him. "Why did you slap me? It didn't hurt but it took me by surprise."

"Men want sex quick, like I'm an appliance that gets them off. After sex they want to know if it was good for me. When I say, no, they look disappointed. That's when I own them."

"You're too much for me, Maddie. I don't treat you like an appliance. Except right now, you're a toaster and you're sparking and scaring me."

Maddie laughed, and held firm so he couldn't turn.

"Let me go," said Oscar trying to break from her arms.

"No, I'm not letting you go." She hugged him harder. "I'm sorry I slapped you. It scared me."

A hard knock at the door startled them. Oscar found his pants and hopped to the door as he slipped them on. He inched back the curtain to see. Outside, Cosimo rocked anxiously.

He glanced over to Maddie, who pulled the sheet over her. Oscar opened the door.

"Mister Cano, is everything all right?"

"Your friend left, and I do not mean for his domicile." Cosimo appeared concerned.

"Where did he go?" Maddie stood behind Oscar with the sheet wrapped around her like a toga.

"He said he was going to Travis Park to get, excuse me, 'sucked and fucked.' He was very drunk. I do not think that is a good idea."

"It means someone's going to hurt him." Maddie quickly gathered her clothes and ran into the bathroom.

CHAPTER 40

Cosimo knocked at Pito's door.

Henny answered. "Señor Cano, what is it now?" She filled out pink baby-doll pajamas. Seeing Oscar approaching, she closed the door to a quarter of an inch.

"It's late," she said through the closed door. "Come back in the—"

"Pito? Don Pito? I mean, Don Pedro, I have to speak to you," Cosimo spoke over Henny's objections.

She stepped back. A naked Pito came to the door, pulling on Henny's bathrobe.

"So it's Don Pedro, now. You're a *chingon* pain in the ass. What do you want?" Pito protested.

"We have a young man in danger."

"Is he here threatening anyone?"

"No, he is gone. He is drunk and is going to get himself assaulted."

"If he's here, call the police. If he's not, why should I care? Tonight, the kids are your responsibility."

"What is your car worth?"

"Whadayamean?" Pito spoke so quickly it took Cosimo a second to decipher.

"What is the value of your car? According to insurance?"

"I think two-fifty, maybe three hundred," he ventured. "It's not insured."

"I will advance you one hundred dollars for the use of your car right this moment. If I return the car to you in the same shape, you keep twenty-five."

"Let's see the money?" Pito demanded.

"I have it here," he separated four twenty-dollar bills, a ten and two fives. You keep twenty-five, and refund the rest to me when I return the car."

Pito snapped the money from Cosimo's hand.

"Henny, give me the car keys."

Cosimo took the keys and held them up for Oscar and Maddie.

"I can't drive a stick shift." Maddie admitted.

Oscar took the keys. "It's an oldy, all right."

"Travis Park isn't that far away. Richard could already be there. We'll go, Mr. Cano. You've done enough. We'll be back," said Maddie.

"Let us find your young man." Cosimo climbed into the back seat.

Oscar turned the key and a rapid clicking noise surprised him, he shut down the starter, looked at his companions, and shrugged. He rattled the key and tried a second time. The engine turned over and died. He gave the gas pedal one push, rattled the key, and tried again. The engine started. He put the car in reverse, backed out and turned east onto Buena Vista Street.

"How'd you do that?" Maddie asked, surprised.

"What? Start the car? I don't know."

Travis Park occupied an entire city block surrounded by two- and three-story office buildings on two sides, an Episcopal church, a parking lot, and on the opposing corner the Mariners Bar with a small neon sign of a fouled anchor. Bordering the entire south side of the park was the impressive seven-story St. Anthony Hotel. Its elegant arched windows on the first floor looked out on well-maintained shrubs and deciduous oak trees. Maddie and Cosimo scanned the area as Oscar circled the park.

"I don't see him," said Maddie.

Oscar slowed and stopped the car near the church across the street from the park. "I don't see anything, either."

"Why is this place important?" asked Cosimo.

"It has a reputation for homosexual trysts," said Maddie.

"I've passed by here in the daytime. People eat their lunches in the shade of these handsome trees," said Cosimo.

"It would give them pause if they knew what took place on those benches at night," said Maddie. "I've heard the Chamber of Commerce has every piece of litter removed and the trashcans emptied at 6:00 a.m. They erase any trace of nighttime indiscretions."

Cosimo laughed.

"How do you know that?" Oscar wondered.

"Come on! Everybody knows that, and I've only lived here for two years."

Across the park, a taxi dropped off a guest at the St. Anthony Hotel. All other traffic had destinations. They passed and were gone.

The neon sign at the Mariners Bar went dark. Half a dozen men exited and after goodbyes, four walked in the direction of the parking lot. Two men crossed the street into the park.

"Where is the danger?" asked Cosimo.

An older model pick-up truck turned on to Travis Street and cruised slowly as if looking for someone.

"That's the danger. I don't see Richard," said Maddie.

The driver of the pick-up truck focused on the park and didn't see Maddie and Oscar ducking down in the Chevy. Cosimo didn't attempt to hide. He knew the darkness kept his secret as long as he didn't move.

Seventy-five yards away Richard appeared and sat on a bench. Moments later a man from the bar approached him, appearing to ask for directions.

"There he is. Let's get him," urged Maddie.

Oscar rattled the key and turned the ignition. The starter motor turned over and over, and nothing. He smelled gasoline. "I've flooded the carburetor. Shit!"

The stranger and Richard lingered in conversation while the pickup truck made a U-turn and braked a short distance away. A blond man vaulted out of the bed of the pickup holding an ax handle. The rangy driver also exited, dragging a baseball bat. The stranger talking to Richard bolted. Cut off by the driver, the stranger fell to his knees and shielded his head with his arms. Richard scrambled out of sight and into the night, chased by the man from the truck bed.

Oscar sprang out of the Chevy, screaming in an attempt to foil the assault. "Stop! Call the police! Call the police! Stop!"

Oscar confronted the thug only to be struck on the back. Oscar went down.

Cosimo came close behind. "Stop immediately! Why are you doing this?"

"Because they're fags!" Unlike the blond who constantly shot jittery glances toward the surrounding streets, this man's eyes were steady as he sized up Cosimo. The victim he'd beaten crab-walked away and when far enough, scrambled for the shadows.

Cosimo stepped between Oscar and the driver. "You would hit an old man?"

"You're damned straight I'd hit an old queer like you," said the man.

The blond in pursuit of Richard returned to back up his cohort. Oscar recognized him as Toby, the driver of the yellow Corvette who terrorized Maddie at the library. Toby saw Maddie approaching and hid his face with his hand.

"Bobby Lee, it's time to split. Let's go, quick," Toby spit out.

Cosimo whacked Bobby Lee across a knee with his cane.

Hopping on one leg, Bobby Lee managed to grab the cane away from Cosimo and with both hands tried to break it on the pavement. The cane didn't break. Instead, it sprung away from his grasp. Bobby Lee collapsed.

Cosimo retrieved the cane and struck hard against Bobby Lee's kidneys. Bobby Lee curled into a fetal position, moaning. Toby came closer, reaching out to help Bobby Lee to his feet.

"This man is not going anywhere," Cosimo growled, holding the cane over his head like a samurai sword.

The injured stranger staggered back into the light, holding his head. Rivulets of blood streamed down his white shirt.

Bobby Lee cowered, expecting another blow. "Help me," he bellowed at Toby. He rolled over on his belly and reached out. "Take my fucking arm, damn it. Get me out of here."

Police sirens echoed in the distance.

"You better run," Maddie called to Toby. "Fucking frat asshole!"

Panicked, Toby sprinted toward the pick-up. The engine started, tires squealed. "You mother-fucker, get back here," howled Bobby Lee.

"All of you need to leave," a voice came from behind everyone. It was Dr. Samuels.

Samuels helped Oscar to his feet. "Are you all right?"

"Yeah," said Oscar.

"Doctor Samuels, what are you doing here?" asked Maddie.

"I live in the St. Anthony. No time to talk. Get going. Get your friend and get out of here." He looked to Cosimo. "None of you were ever here."

"What happens to him?" Maddie indicated Bobby Lee. "And the man bleeding over there?" The stranger sitting on the bench, pressed a bloodied handkerchief to his head.

"I'll find out when the police get here. The injured fellow may have to go to an emergency room. Find your friend and go."

Bobby Lee managed to get to his feet and stumbled toward the opposite end of the park.

Maddie shouted, "Richard! Come on!" Richard, hair in his eyes, clothing disheveled, hobbled in their direction. She met him halfway and hurried his walk.

"Let me help you," Oscar reached out to assist Cosimo.

Cosimo gestured to Oscar. "Get to the car. Calm yourself."

Oscar returned to the car and slid behind the wheel. He reached for the ignition, and realized his hands were shaking uncontrollably.

Maddie opened the passenger side door and saw Oscar staring at his hands. "Are you okay?"

Oscar gripped the steering wheel. "I'm okay."

Richard opened the street-side back door, then stopped. Edging his way to the rear of the car he vomited. He wiped his mouth on his shirt sleeve. He came around the car and climbed in behind the driver, leaving the street side door open for Cosimo.

Maddie, Oscar, and Richard watched anxiously as Cosimo took an eternity to limp the last thirty yards. He closed the car door and settled into the back seat with a sigh. His knee was killing him.

The car started on the first try. Oscar shifted to first gear and lurched away from the curb.

Maddie leaned over the seat. "Are you all right?" she asked Richard.

Richard nodded. "He didn't hit me. I was doing the limbo like crazy. Mr. Cano, I'm sorry. I didn't mean for anything like this to happen." He shook his head. "I'm sorry."

Cosimo closed his eyes. "Young man, this is life. We all learned something. You learned you have friends who are willing to risk their safety for you. And I learned that I can no longer serve hard alcohol to Americans. You people have no sense of moderation."

CHAPTER 41

osimo knocked at cabin number one's door at 8:30 in the morning. After a moment Oscar pulled back the curtain and waved with half-closed eyes. He opened the door. Cosimo stepped in to see Richard asleep, a space for Oscar on the bed, and Maddie staring at him sleepily.

"It's 8:30. If you are ready by 9:15, we will walk to the breakfast place where I have a commitment. You are my guests." Cosimo turned and stepped off the porch, limping significantly more than yesterday.

Oscar closed the door to the bathroom and peed. He splashed water in his face and brushed his teeth with his finger. Something about him smelled musky. He sniffed his hands, the back of his hands, arms and armpits. This wasn't his scent. He tore away the paper wrapping on the Coco Castile soap, turned on the shower enough to thoroughly wet his torso, and lathered his hands, arms, armpits, penis and testicles with the strongly scented soap. After, he dried himself, the musky scent was less, but still there.

He opened the door. Maddie, in bra and panties, pushed him out of the bathroom and closed the door. He heard the tinkle of her morning pee, a pause before the flush. She opened the door. "Are you going to take a shower?" she asked.

"I did, and guess what? I smell of you."

"What do you mean?

"I mean, I smell like your . . . vag—" he whispered.

"That's disgusting. Take another shower!"

"Your scent won't wash off."

"That's impossible. You used a rubber."

"I don't know. But I kind of like it." Oscar touched her chin, and she leaned forward for a kiss.

"We should wake him." Maddie said, pulling back mid-kiss.

"He looks comatose," Oscar whispered.

"I'm awake," moaned Richard. "And I heard everything."

Oscar sighed.

"How do you feel?" asked Maddie.

"Truthfully, last night was more humiliating than this hangover, and I'm feeling pretty fucking miserable now. I could sleep until tomorrow."

"Take a shower." Maddie took his arm and pulled him out of bed. "We've been invited to breakfast. And, after what our host has done for us, we're obliged."

As Richard passed, Oscar tossed him the towel. "I only used it on my face."

"Hey, I know better, and there's no shower curtain."

"Yeah, be careful. Don't get water on the floor."

Richard closed the bathroom door.

Maddie watched Oscar find his clothes. "Gawd, you've got every right to be so full of yourself, but you still don't own me."

"Maddie, if I owned a car, I couldn't maintain it. How can I possibly own you?" he said, pulling on his pants.

"Last night, not the part about us . . . after. You were out there. You made me feel proud. You have every right to strut like a rooster."

Oscar sat on the bed and pulled on his socks. "Rooster? Proud? I felt like the most stupid human on the planet. I'm lucky I didn't end up at the Robert B. Green emergency room. Mister Cano saved me."

"You got us there in that clunker in time to find Richard. You jumped out of the car, shouting like a madman to save your friend from ending up with a cracked skull. You *saved* Richard, before the redneck smacked you."

"I drove a clunky old car and got hit by a thug. No big deal."

"Well, if you can't accept a compliment, fuck you." Maddie shoved him.

Oscar ran his fingers through his hair, while checking himself out in the mirror.

"Look at you." She laughed. "You so fucking think you own me."

"Maddie, cut it out." He turned and stared at her.

"You're right. I'm teasing you. I thought you could take it. I like you."

"I never pulled on a pretty girl's pigtails because I liked her. Most girls aren't like you. They don't carry condoms. If they have sex with you, it's a big deal. And if she gets pregnant, you're expected to marry her."

"Okay, okay, you made your point."

Richard stepped out of the bathroom entirely naked. "Ready! Where's the line for coffee?" His pinkish white skin and penis glistened. "I need a cigarette."

"And my, aren't you the pretty one?" Maddie teased.

"You know, Richard, nine out of ten men who have tried camels still prefer women." Oscar laughed.

"Oh, you son of a bitch." Richard snapped. "You think you can rag on me? I'll kick your ass—"

"Richard, get dressed," interrupted Maddie. "He saved your pretty *ass* last night, and don't you forget it."

Maddie picked up a clean towel she'd saved for herself. "I'm taking a shower. I'll be out in five."

CHAPTER 42

A round of applause greeted Cosimo as he pushed open the door of the Little House Café. Maddie, Oscar, and Richard grinned, embarrassed that the customers stared at them.

Graciela, standing behind the cash register, handed them menus and pointed to a table that had been reserved for them.

The regulars to the drawing sessions dragged chairs to form a semicircle. John and Colleen, who met here weeks before, now held hands.

Emma set out the paper, pens, brushes, and inks in the manner of a theatrical stage dresser. Cosimo's table now featured an improvised easel made from a three-quarter-inch-thick rectangle of corrugated cardboard and napkin holders.

Emma approached to take their orders.

"Order whatever you want," said Cosimo to the three. "I recommend the flour tortilla tacos, potato and egg, beef, pork, *frijol* . . . the lot."

"*Dos tacos de res, gracias.*" Oscar ordered first.

"One potato and egg," ordered Maddie.

"I'll have the *rez*, like he said," said Richard, pointing to Oscar.

"*Tacos de res*," Emma said. "Thank you."

Emma returned with their plates.

"How do you eat this?" Richard asked, holding up a taco.

"You start at one end and eat until you get to the other end," Emma chortled.

"You have to pinch the opposite end so the filling doesn't fall out," Oscar added.

"Oh, oh, oh, this is so good," Maddie spoke with her mouth full. "I want one every day for the rest of my life."

Cosimo pointed to Colleen. "What story did you read last?"

"The one I read was short, the crow and the pitcher of water." she answered, glancing at her companion, John.

Cosimo located two ashtrays, filled one with water, and placed it next to the easel. Cosimo flipped over a Little House menu and secured it to the cardboard with paper tape. He dipped the pen in ink and drew a small oval on the paper, quickly followed by two larger and wider ovals, forming balloons floating on the white paper. In what appeared to be an accident, he smeared one of the larger ovals with the heel of his hand.

John motioned to Colleen, nodding quizzically toward the artist. Was the smeared ink a gross mistake?

She shrugged.

What followed were a series of long wavy lines, squiggles, and dots.

Richard said, "I see it."

Maddie cocked her head. "I don't."

Cosimo poured ink into the dry ashtray, then brought out an artist's paint brush, something the customers had not seen him use before. He dipped it in the ink and filled the spaces defined by the longer lines, forming the body of the crow. The squiggles became feet. The small circle he'd drawn first became the crow's eye, and one of the ovals became the lip of a transparent glass pitcher.

The drawing came together quickly. The crow held a pebble in its beak, head cocked to see how many more pebbles it would require to put the water within reach. The smeared ink became the distorted reflection of the crow on the glass. With his colored pencils he added a dot of red at the edge of the crow's eye.

The onlookers applauded.

"Very cool," said Richard.

"I don't see how that's not a unique work of art. I want to own one," said Maddie.

Hearing Maddie, the customers' applause echoed their own desire to own one of these special works.

"The expression on the crow's face is . . . what . . . delightful!" gushed Colleen.

While everyone had been focused on the performance, Major Efrain Yñiego y Remedios, the Cuban US Army officer, now dressed in a black suit like the FBI agents, entered the café and stood, arms crossed, behind the customers. His sullen, mustachioed driver, also in a suit, stood near the door.

Cosimo recognized him. "You are looking official today," Cosimo said across the room. "This is not what you are looking for."

Everyone in the café turned.

Major Remedios announced to the room. "How many of you know this man is a communist? He's spreading propaganda about the failed liberation of Cuba."

The word "communist" startled the group. Sensing a confrontation, many of the customers stood and backed away.

"Colleen, I forgot to file a couple of reports," John excused himself. "Sorry, I have to run." By twos and threes most of the customers deserted the café.

"You've accomplished what you set out to do," Cosimo admitted to the major. "The vilest name you can call an American is *communist*. It is the plague word of the twentieth century. You might as well have shouted 'leprosy' to illiterate medieval peasants. You have come to hurt me, but you have only hurt the people near me. And here is the point that eludes me. You do not give a damn who you hurt."

"These paintings look like communist propaganda," he said to what remained of the crowd and the Little House staff.

"That's ridiculous," Colleen spoke up. "These are drawings from a book of Aesop's Fables. I borrowed it from the public library. Mister Cano never says a word about politics."

"You don't understand. He's a communist."

"Repeat it as much as you want," said Cosimo. "You have failed. I am not a communist, nor am I the traitor you are looking for. This is a harmless morning exercise. I do not get compensated. I pay my way in-kind. Did those English schools tell you about 'in-kind,' meaning to barter or trade? Are you against free enterprise?"

Emma stood nearby, seething. "And you, Buster," she called to the Major. "You're not going anywhere. You owe us $35.20 in unpaid tabs for the folks who walked out." Emma waved the unpaid checks in his face. "You did this. Pay up. And I expect a 10% gratuity."

"Get out of my face." Remedios slapped the unpaid checks out of Emma's hands.

Cosimo stood, angry. "You idiot! *Eres Mierda*! You are not worthy of cleaning this woman's shoes. Mind you, Major Remedios, these people are as ignorant of your cause as I am. You have failed to justify your investigation. You are a fool."

"Go to hell," the Major blurted.

Emma stood inside the door, grasping the driver's sleeve. The driver muscled her out of his way. Major Remedios and his driver backed out the door.

"Emma! Leave him. Let him go," called Cosimo. He held on to the edge of the table and lowered himself to the chair. His face turned ashen, and his body tumbled from the chair to the floor.

Emma rushed to his side. His head came to rest on her lap.

Cosimo motioned for Oscar to come closer. He closed his eyes and his head fell back.

Graciela took down a business card pinned behind the cash register, and dialed the number. Witnesses stood, shocked and silent.

CHAPTER 43

Ruthann Medlin sat outside of Dr. Samuels's office, a crumpled tissue twisting in her fingers. Samuels opened the door and motioned
for her to enter. Already in the room were the new head librarian, Ilene
Fischer, and the mayor, Ruthann's uncle, Morris Forester.

"Do you want someone to represent you?" asked Samuels.

"Do I need it? I mean, my uncle the mayor is here."

"Ruthie, we're here to get past this and move on," said Morris Forester.

"He represents the board," said Samuels. "It's up to you if you need
extra representation. Miss Fischer, as head librarian, is here because this
is a personnel matter. She's here as your supervisor. As far as the library
and the board are concerned, this is a confidential hearing regarding your
behavior and your future employment. Have a seat, Ruthann. Let's talk."

"Yes, let's talk. I saw the three insolent brats strutting around downstairs."

"Ruthann, they work here," said Samuels.

"What are you going to do about their insolence?" Ruthann said.

"That information is not available to the public, or you."

"I'm their supervisor. She gets to be in here." She jabbed her finger at
Ilene Fischer.

"Need I remind you, you are no longer page supervisor," said Samuels.

"Ruthie, watch your temper. That's what got you here to begin with," said Forester.

"What are you going to do with me?" Ruthann stared eye to eye with Samuels, as if she knew the answer.

"What do you think we should do with you?" Samuels replied.

"I think I should continue as I am. I will do better with the coloreds. I will apologize to the board."

"Ruthann, this isn't about apologies any more. You are not a trained librarian. The books you destroyed can be chalked up to ignorance. You honestly didn't know what those books were worth. The other demerits on your record have to do with you. You were insubordinate a number of times, made derogatory statements, organized colleagues against the board-approved policies on integration day, and on at least two occasions were uncivil to black patrons, including a child, because you thought her race and size were a prank, and you made her cry."

"That's why I will apologize. I made a mistake. Ilene Fischer participated. Why isn't she being disciplined?"

"I'll speak for myself," said Ilene. "I froze. I was scared and a coward. I apologized to Dr. Samuels that day."

"There's a double standard here. If I had apologized early on, it would be all right, then." Ruthann countered.

"We're not here about Miss Fischer. We're here about you," said Samuels. "Apologies have nothing to do with this. Ruthann, your opinion of fairness doesn't matter. The board approved a policy for all of us to follow. Do you understand that?"

Ruthann didn't answer.

Morris Forester stood and approached Ruthann. "Ruthie, sweetie, you know I care about you. I have a solution that you'll go for. You know the Navarro Branch on South Flores Street. You'd be head librarian, with a full-time aide and two part-time pages."

"Weren't you going to shut down Navarro Branch for lack of patrons?"

"No, no." Morris Forester looked at Samuels and Ilene for support. "On the contrary, we're seeing increased patronage and a real opportunity to improve service in that community. The more patrons, the more staff we can provide. Ilene Fischer will be in charge of all the branch libraries." The mayor motioned to Ilene. "Help me out here."

"Most of your patrons will be children from the local schools. The records show that as the older residents moved away and passed on, the new residents have families. There's been an increase in library users. There are so many ways to reach out and bring in new patrons. I can provide you with a lot of support, more children's books."

"Isn't that a new Meskin . . . I mean, Spanish part of town. I'd be there all alone."

Ilene looked to Samuels for permission to continue. "You'll never be alone. The policy on staffing is that there must always be two employees present in order to open. If there is only one, the library remains closed until there are two. Yes, as the older white residents have moved away, Mexican American families have moved in, and that's good for the library."

"What if I don't accept?" Ruthann said, as if she were thinking out loud.

Samuels grimaced. "Considering your attitude toward the demographic of the Navarro Branch, I should take the proposal off the table. Ruthann, this is the plan approved by the board. It's not what I wanted. However, it's a compromise I can live with, just barely. That's the offer. You either accept, or resign."

"Resign? No, Gran said I'd keep my job if I apologized." Ruthann came to her feet.

"Ruthann, you are keeping your job, just not here in this building," said Samuels.

Ruthann's face reddened. "No, no, no, no. No!" Flecks of spittle appeared on the corners of her mouth.

"Ruthann, I had to beg this man to keep you," Forester pleaded. "This is a respectable opportunity. Take it. You'll be the head librarian,"

"I'm not apologizing. You want me to grovel? I won't." She dropped the wadded tissue in her hand on the floor and went to the door. "This isn't over."

CHAPTER 44

Built in 1917, the Robert B. Green Hospital's waiting rooms were inadequate for 1961. Families waiting to see a relative or hear from a doctor gathered in the hallways and spilled out on a small lawn near the visitor's entrance. Emma Vasquez paced just inside the main door.

Francisco Orozco approached. "Are you Emma?"

Looking at his new navy-blue wool serge suit, black shoes, and spanking new briefcase, Emma said, "And you must be the lawyer?"

"I am. Call me Francisco."

"They won't let me see him because I'm not a relative."

"I'll see what I can do. Hang tight a sec."

He went to the front desk, put his briefcase on the counter. "Where can I find my client?" he asked the receptionist. He paused to read from a three-by-five index card. "Mister Cosimo Infante Cano." He handed her the card. "He was brought in this morning about 11:00 a.m." He handed her his new business card, which sealed the deal.

The receptionist picked up the phone. "Cano, Cosimo Infante, came in this morning at eleven or so. Thank you." She turned to Francisco. "He's in the cardiac ward on the fifth floor, room 564."

"Thank you," he said and turned from the desk, motioning furtively with his hand for Emma to join him.

"What did you do?" she asked.

"I'm his lawyer, and you're here to translate."

"What? Don't you speak Spanish?"

"If anyone asks, make something up. You're his American relative. You're my nurse medical adviser. You're his neighbor and his only acquaintance. Don't worry about it. We're in."

Exiting the elevator to the fifth floor, they entered a maze of hallways created by multiple renovations and additions. They found the room and walked in quietly. Cosimo looked wan, his unkempt hair splayed out across the pillow and stuck to his cheek. He opened his eyes the moment he sensed someone standing next to the bed.

"Francisco and Emma." He spoke between breaths. "So pleased to see you."

"Are you all right?" asked Emma, patting his hand.

"I'm fine. My heart rate was the problem." He pushed the hair from his face. "Palpitations, the doctor says. I passed out."

"What did they do for you?" asked Francisco.

"They gave me digitalis to slow my heart," he said, sounding like a doctor. "I'll go off the medication as soon as I can prove to them my heart is normal again."

"Cosimo, you've been driving yourself like a man half your age. With the painting and renovation of the cabins, and you were out with those kids last night," said Emma. "You need to slow down."

"I will slow down. I am well," he assured Emma. Turning to Francisco, "When that man pushed Emma out of the way at the café, I became infuriated. That is what caused this."

"Yes, well." Emma laughed. "I won't be picking any more fights." She caressed his cheek.

"And you," he asked Francisco. "What have you to tell me about Bluhorn & Carnahan?"

"Maybe we should wait until your heart rate is normal."

"The digitalis has slowed my heart rate to fifty-five beats a minute. I need bad news to get me up to normal."

"Are you sure? Let me call a nurse in here first." Francisco took several steps toward the hall.

Cosimo sat up. "Come back here and get it over with!"

Francisco opened his briefcase and handed Cosimo a letter. "It's from Bluhorn & Carnahan, henceforth referred to as the adversary. The

Hunter family believes you have taken advantage of a lonely spinster for your own benefit. They say they would welcome a lawsuit to expose your avaricious ambitions, and they want the gold watch."

"The watch? I expected some resistance, but this is greed." He held up the letter. "What about our request to review the documents?"

"I cannot discuss information in front of Mrs. Vasquez, without your permission."

"You mean Emma? You have my permission." Cosimo looked at Emma. "She's the only reason I'm alive and well today. What about the documents, Sara's papers?"

"They've raised the drawbridge. They're going to fight all the way. At least that's what they're saying. They expect us to sue. Cosimo, even if I file, it will take months before we see anything."

"I am not asking for anything from those goddamned people, other than what is mine."

"They're acting confidently," added Francisco. Which means they're either certain they're going to dominate, or they don't have crap and it's all bluster."

"Which do you think it is?" asked Cosimo.

"There's only one way to find out. I can file the petition tomorrow."

Cosimo took in Francisco's new suit. "Look at you. You look ready to go to court. File that lawsuit for me, please. But, after that, I want to pay you what I owe you. You've been very generous. I don't want you to waste any more of your time."

"Cosimo, I took the case on contingency. I have a steady job. We'll weather it together. You're my first official case, and I'm taking your advice. If I'm going to be an attorney, I better start acting like one. I do have some good news. You've received another letter."

"A letter?" Cosimo's eyes widened.

Francisco brought the envelope out of his briefcase.

Cosimo held out both hands and accepted the letter as if it were a gift.

"It's from Leonor Fini." He laughed, and looked at Francisco. "Do you have a knife? You should have given this to me first."

"You asked about Bluhorn & Carnahan." Francisco shrugged. "I don't have a knife."

Emma reached into her purse and handed him a metal nail file.

"It's in French. It says she's sorry to hear about Sara. She was lucky to receive the letter at all because she, Kot, and the Count were in the

South making a film. She has two husbands and many lovers," he said as an aside to Emma. "She is mortified by my troubles and sent my letter and the name of the Hunters' San Antonio attorney to Margaret, who is in Switzerland and will return to Venice . . . umm . . . last week." He put down Fini's letter. "That's great news."

"Who's this Margaret?" asked Emma.

"Margaret Manheim owns a gallery on the Grand Canal in Venice. She owns two of my paintings. I'm saved."

"And the Leonor, with all the lovers? Who is she?" asked Emma, ready to hear a lot more.

"An artist and good friend of Sara. Leonor . . . Yes, Leonor. She's a very clever woman, works in the theatre and cinema, designs handbags and such for the fashion houses, and specializes in portraits of artists."

Emma raised an eyebrow. "Has she done one of you?"

"Yes."

"Were you one of the . . . you know?" asked Emma.

"No, not me," he lied. "My relationship with Leonor has been through Sara, who did English translations for her productions."

"How can they help?" asked Emma. "They can't do anything from Europe."

"They know I am in trouble, that is all that matters." He laid his head back on the pillow and closed his eyes.

"Cosimo, I hope you're right. On the legal front it's been a bad day. Let's hope they'll cut you loose tomorrow." Francisco laughed. "Listen to me. I sound like one of my law professors, a criminal defense attorney. 'Ah s'pect they'll cut my client loose in the mornin','" he mimicked in a Texan drawl.

Cosimo laughed. Sara would have mimicked the same accent.

As Francisco and Emma exited Robert B. Green Hospital, the 7:00 p.m. evening shift change was in progress. They paused on the lawn. Twilight revealed fewer people waiting to visit patients.

"What do you think?" asked Emma. "Can this woman in Europe help?"

"They could send him money so he could return, but that doesn't resolve his situation with the Hunter family. I asked him why he didn't accept the offer from the French Consulate in Houston. They could at least get him back to France. He said he's not leaving the US without his money and his things. He's the real deal, stranded here without money," said Francisco. "He has a good case, but the family can drag out the legal process with continuances until he's gone and we're in rocking chairs."

"I see something in him," said Emma. "People expect him to drown, but he won't let it happen."

"He's not so tough today," said Francisco.

"He could make good money letting Graciela sell the drawings. He'd get twenty-five or thirty dollars each, and sell many."

"I asked him the same thing. He won't allow it."

"What do you think they're worth?" Emma asked.

"I'm not an art expert," replied Francisco. "They're worth nothing until someone wants to buy one. He's broke. My expectations are that he may have to settle for less than he should. The family and their lawyers are going to try to starve him, to make him go away."

"He's not a stray cat!"

"These are very powerful attorneys. They add up the numbers. That's how they make decisions."

CHAPTER 45

Dr. Samuels opened the door to the library's main entrance and stepped out on the landing. Climbing the stairs were Virgil, the custodian, and his great-niece, the five-and-a-half-year-old Weegee Childress. Virgil wore a suit and tie.

"Thank you for bringing her," Samuels said to Virgil. "Looks like we might be in for some rain."

"Yes, it's quite overcast and getting breezy," said Weegee.

"I'd like to invite you to my office. I have refreshments. Will you join me?" Near the arched windows in Samuels's office, a small table and three chairs were set with teacups, saucers, silverware, and cloth napkins for the guests. A tea service waited nearby.

"I hope you don't mind. I took the liberty of putting on a pot of peppermint tea."

"I like peppermint. Thank you," Weegee replied.

"Please, sit down." Samuels took charge of serving.

Weegee sat, changed her mind, and stood. "Dr. Samuels, may I look out the window?" she asked.

"Certainly, there's a small step stool that might give you a better vantage." Samuels took her hand and steadied her on the two-step library stool.

"I thought you might see the river from here," she said, disappointed.

"I know. The parking lot and the retaining wall block the river view. We can see those fine trees and the very sturdy truss bridge, though."

"I like bridges," said Weegee stepping down from the stool. "That one looks as if it were made with an Erector Set."

"That's true. A truss bridge is a special kind of structure. The triangular units cause the weight of the bridge to be distributed in a clever way, so it won't collapse," said Samuels as he prepared to pour tea. "Mr. Harper, would you like tea, or would you rather have milk?"

"I'd like tea, thank you."

"This is very pretty china," commented Weegee.

"This whole service of tea pot and dishes has been in my family for at least eighty-five years. Can you imagine? Nobody wanted them, so I made them mine."

"As well you should," she said stirring her tea.

Weegee's reply sounded so adult Samuels had to laugh.

"I have lemon cake, my favorite. I hope you like it, too." He set out the lemon cake on the matching dishes.

Weegee squinted her eyes, "Uncle Virgil, did you tell him I like peppermint tea and lemon cake?"

Virgil lifted his hands in helpless surrender.

Samuels waved away Virgil's concession. "I confess. I asked your uncle what you like. It happens that I like the same things."

After pouring his own tea, he joined them at the table.

"The reason I invited you here is because I want you to know that this library belongs to all of us who love books. Treat it as if it belongs to you."

Weegee smiled shyly.

"Is this an easy job?" she asked.

"You mean, being director? It's not a physical job like a carpenter or a brick mason, but it takes time and thought. See that stack of papers on my desk? Those are proposals that other libraries have submitted to the Smithsonian Institution. I have to read all of those and make a decision if the applicants are deserving of getting grant money, and if they can do what they say they want to do."

"And you alone decide?

"No, I'm one of ten people reading the same proposals. That's what makes it fair. No one person can exert undue influence. Let's enjoy our lemon cake, and I'll tell you what happened to that view of the river." Samuels continued, "The original plans for the library called for an attractive patio with a high wrought-iron fence as one might find in New York City, a pleasant place outdoors with trees and benches, a place to enjoy books with a view of the river. The architect called it a 'phrontistery,' a place for study and meditation. But, guess what? People had cars, and deliveries were made in trucks. So, the phrontistery became a parking lot and loading dock." Weegee's concentration appeared focused entirely on the lemon cake. "Did she hear any of that?" Samuels asked Virgil.

"You'd be surprised," said Virgil.

"This cake is *so* good," cooed Weegee. "What did you say?"

"I said, thank you for being five years old."

"Five and a half."

After finishing tea, Samuels stood to clear away the tea service. Out the window he saw a taxi entered the parking lot. Eula Forester, the mayor's grandmother, stepped out of the cab and fished through her purse for change to pay the driver. The wind stirred the cypress trees.

"I think we're in for a squall," Samuels said half to himself. He glanced at his guests. "It appears I have new business I must contend with. I want to thank you, Weegee and Mr. Harper, for coming for tea. I hope we can do it again."

"Thank you," said Weegee. "I'm sorry they didn't make a patio, but the cars and trucks need a place, too."

"So true," said Samuels, shaking his head in admiration.

He didn't hurry his guests, even though he knew two storms were approaching.

He walked Weegee and her uncle to the lobby as Eula Forester came in from the rear entrance.

"Mrs. Forester, to what do I owe this pleasure? Please wait by the front desk a moment. I'm just saying goodbye to Shirley 'Weegee,' Childress, and her uncle, Virgil Harper."

Eula marched right up to them and stared at the child. "Is this the little girl that . . ."

"Weegee," Samuels cut off Eula, "is a new patron to our library, and she's an avid reader. Weegee, this is Mrs. Eula Forester, the mayor's grandmother and a patron of the library."

Weegee nodded politely. "Very pleased to meet you."

Eula paused. "Yes, it's a pleasure to meet you." She said nothing to Virgil, recognizing him as the custodian.

"Ask Weegee something, Mrs. Forester. You'll find her very interesting." Samuels didn't say another word, leaving Eula to fill the silence.

"What do you want to be when you grow up?" asked Eula.

"An adult." Weegee laughed at her own joke.

"I mean, as a job, a career," Eula said, a trifle peeved.

"Study economics, because my daddy says if you understand economics you'll understand how the world works. My momma says he's joking. I want to find out for myself."

"Do you even know what economics means? That's a ridic—"

Samuels cleared his throat loud enough to cut Eula off again. "Excuse me. Something is caught in my throat," he said, continuing to clear his throat, only not so loudly.

"What would you do with a degree in economics?" asked Eula.

"Become a college professor, or I could be mayor, or a library director."

Samuels and Virgil suppressed their laughter.

Aware she had lost the exchange with a child, Eula turned to Samuels. "I want to see you in your office, right now."

"My office is open. Head on up, I'll join you in a moment. If you'll excuse me, I'm saying goodbye to my new friend."

He walked Weegee and Virgil to the entrance, shook hands, and opened the door for them. As he crossed the lobby, he headed for the reference department. He pulled Ilene Fischer aside and whispered urgently. "Call Mayor Forester and tell him that his grandmother is here. Then, wait by the phone. I'm going to call you to my office when I'm ready."

Eula stood by the tea setting, noting three cups and saucers, dessert plates, and forks. "You're having tea parties with *nigra* children?" she said as Samuels entered the room.

"Mrs. Forester, yes, that was the child Ruthann made cry. You've arrived without an appointment. How can I help you?"

"The uppity little twerp thinks she could be mayor. Not in my lifetime!"

"Considering you're eighty-two, and she's five and a half, it's quite likely you'll never see her become mayor."

Eula shot him an icy glare.

"I have a good idea why you're here." He went to the window and watched Weegee and Virgil crossing the Presa Street Bridge. Weegee paused and stood on the bottom frame of the railing to look down at the water. Raindrops began ticking on the window. Weegee and Virgil hustled away. The sound of thunder rumbled in the distance.

"Did you apologize to the child's family for Ruthann?" asked Eula.

"Good lord, never." Samuels turned to her. "Ruthann's opinions have nothing to do with the library. She spoke for herself."

Eula lowered herself into the armchair across from Samuels desk. Comfortably settled, she went right for him. "Let me grab this chicken by the neck and give it a spin," she warmed up.

Samuels laughed. "That's colorful." He began putting the dishes and silverware on a tray.

"You were named as a witness in an altercation in Travis Park," she said, lifting her chin to see his reaction.

"That happened, yes. Do you read police reports?"

"The ones the mayor gets to see. And you were out just taking a walk at ten minutes after midnight in that same neighborhood."

"I have a room at the St. Anthony Hotel. What do you make of it?" He wiped off the table and moved it to the wall.

"The man arrested claims he was assaulted by a gang of homosexuals."

"If he wants to make that claim, perhaps it's true. I didn't see it. When I came on the scene, he was holding an ax handle, and the other man had to be hospitalized with head injuries. Are you drawing any conclusions?"

"Conclusions aren't required in your contract. The appearance of impropriety will do. A pouf incident, in a pouf place of assignation, after midnight . . . pouf."

"That's irritatingly British." He picked up the tray of dishes and took them to a storeroom.

"Will you stop moving about?" she called after him. "You're not being respectful."

"You are here without an appointment, and I have things to do." He reentered his office and went to his desk.

"I'm here on a peace mission," she said. "Let's put everything back the way it was before the incident with the *nigra* girl, and all of this will be forgotten."

"You go for the jugular and call it a peace mission. I anticipated you might do something like this." He retrieved a file folder from his desk, removed a page, and handed it to her.

"What is this?" Eula felt around in her purse for a pair of glasses and read the first paragraph. "You're resigning?"

"Did you expect I'd cave like your fawning relatives? I don't want to resign, but you're willing to blackmail me so your malicious, incompetent granddaughter can keep her job. I can't allow that."

"Blackmail is a loaded word."

"No, that's exactly what this is. If your intention is to get rid of me, you'll succeed. However, for the good of the library, Ruthann is gone. After she rejected the board's offer, replacements for the art and music department and the Navarro Branch Library have been approved and hired."

"That can be undone!"

"You forget you're blackmailing *me*, not the library. I don't enjoy being disrespectful; however, this is no longer your playground. Your endowment was beneficial in 1950. Today the endowment covers only a tiny part of overhead."

"You're being extremely rude."

"I'll resign rather than become the butt of jokes and lurid innuendo."

"That settles it for me. Glad to see you go." Eula put away her glasses.

"Here's the phone. Call your grandson. The library's budget is part of the city budget. Every cent and every staff person is accounted for. We have grants that take the library several years into the future. Your grandson is currently mayor, but there's an entire city council appreciative that we bring library services to their districts. We have a bookmobile that goes to the Lincoln Projects, and to the newer McCreliss developments on the Southside. We have a collection of documentary films people can check out. All of this has come about in the last two years. People use these services. They count on them. You can't undo it."

"And you would leave all that? What a martyr."

"I can't have a sword of Damocles hanging over my head. Once you make an accusation about my private life, it stays in people's minds. Whatever I do in life, innuendo will be my epitaph."

"It doesn't have to be like that, you fool."

"Mrs. Forester, you've resorted to blackmail. Only a fool would trust you."

Out in the parking lot a car horn beeped short bursts over and over. Samuels looked out the window. Mayor Forester stood outside of his yellow Buick honking his horn and looking toward Samuels's window. The rain had increased to a steady downpour.

Samuels waved for the mayor to come up. Forester made a dash for the sheltered loading dock.

"What imbecile is making a racket out there?" grumbled Eula.

"It's your grandson, the mayor."

"Well, bring out the cherry brandy, and let's have a tea party."

"Mrs. Forester, this is not an appropriate time."

They heard a loading dock door slam, feet running upstairs, footfalls coming to the door. The mayor in shirtsleeves charged in, his shirt dappled with raindrops.

"Gran, you said you weren't going to come here."

"Ruthann reminded me I'm still a member of the board in an oversight position."

"Gran, Ruthann is wrong. You are an emeritus board member. That means you're welcome to come to meetings, and in certain situations the board might even ask for your advice. This is not one of those occasions. And you no longer have a vote on the board."

"You are my vote on the board!"

"Gran, it's not like before. You do not have a say in proceedings anymore because you retired. *Re-tired.*"

Eula stared at her grandson.

"Gran, what have you done?"

After a moment, Eula waved toward Samuels. "I reminded *Doctor* Samuels that his contract has a morality clause, and he has told me he's going to resign."

"Noooo . . . Gran, he can't resign. We lose too much if he leaves. He's the administrator for most of the programs and grants he's brought in. If he goes, the city loses money."

"If it keeps the *nigras* out, and Ruthann keeps her job, what's the loss?"

"Gran, *nothing* is going to change. The city has settled the lawsuit with the NAACP, and Ruthann turned down the position the board offered her. I begged her to take it."

"He's a limp wrist, hanging out at Travis Park after midnight."

"He's just another citizen and a witness to an assault."

"What was he doing out *there* at that time of night?"

"Your brother, Kenneth, and his friend Steven, do you want me to talk about them?"

"Don't you dare say anything against Kenneth! He and Steven are confirmed bachelors."

"Doctor Samuels, I apologize for my grandmother. Will you do me a big favor and leave the room for two minutes?" He held up two fingers. "Please, all this will get resolved. You may have written a letter of resignation, but the board won't accept it. Please, give me two minutes."

Samuels left the room without a word. Outside the rain pelted the window. A flash of light was followed in an instant by a loud thunderclap.

"Morris, the man is rude and disrespectful. I don't care who he is," complained Eula.

"Gran, listen to me. Kenneth and Steven are homosexuals. Kenneth spent six months at state hospital for the criminally insane. Remember why?"

"I don't want to hear gossip. He had a nervous breakdown," she replied angrily. "*Everyone* knows that."

"He was arrested for sucking a teenager's dick in the bathroom of the Texas Theater. He could have gone to jail. Our money got him into the state hospital, instead."

"Stop it! I don't want to hear trash like that. It's not *true*. He had a nervous breakdown."

"Believe what you want. It wasn't the first time he was caught. It was the first time Kenneth was arrested. Doctor Samuels has done nothing wrong. If he leaves tomorrow, every major library and museum would kill to have him. He likes it here. I was tough on him at first, and you know the man keeps his word. Ruthann has lied, gone behind my back, and abused our name to shame us. She caused a disturbance at the critical moment when our administration and the library could have been embarrassed in front of the entire city. She's gotten you involved in something that is none of your concern. You said it yourself, she's a twit."

"I'm trying to take care of family, which is more than I see you doing."

"Gran, have you forgotten? Running the city and selling contracts used to be our business. Things have changed. After we built this library, it became a cash sinkhole. That's why Samuels is our political golden goose. He brings in money and expands circulation and fulfills community needs. General McMullen, from the San Antonio's military command, has said that if we don't integrate, there are plenty of US cities that would love to host a military base. And we have five!"

"We still have the votes."

"No we don't. The Mexicans are making friendly noises; the blacks have dropped their lawsuit; and Catholics, Protestants, Jews, and Chinese are fine with us. We're the reform party."

"We can't have a known homosexual running the public library," she said acidly.

Samuels knocked, then opened the door. "There's a car here for Mrs. Forester." He didn't enter and closed the door.

"You better go, Gran. It's raining hard."

"Do I have any influence at all?" pleaded Eula.

"Sure you do, Gran, just not over this."

CHAPTER 46

Outside of Samuels's office window, the thunderstorm whipped the cypress trees into a dance. Rain pelted hard against the glass.

Pencil in hand, Samuels sat at his desk reading grant proposals.

Mayor Forester reentered the office and went directly to the window. "Do you think my car will be all right? I see marble-sized hail mixed with the rain."

Samuels assumed the question was rhetorical. "Did your grandmother get off all right?"

"Yes, her nurse is driving her. What is it they say? 'If you don't like the weather in Texas, wait thirty minutes.'"

"That's a fallacy." Samuels put down the manuscript, removed his reading glasses, picked up the phone, and pushed one button. "I'm ready for you now." He hung up. "Rain squalls were predicted for today. The Mexicans call this kind of cloudburst, *un brazo de lluvia*, an arm of rain. Out on the plains, it appears to sweep like an arm bringing winds, lightning, rain, and hail, then it passes."

"Do you have a shot of that brandy?" asked Forester.

"After your admonition, I removed it from the premises."

"Damn it to hell, you don't have to take me so goddamn literally. I'm very sorry about Gran. She used to be one of the sharpest ladies in town."

"She hasn't lost her edge."

"Ruthann is gone, fine. So, what's the story? What are you going to do?"

"These are proposals the Smithsonian has sent me to review. They've offered me a job as a program officer, and I've decided to accept it."

"No, you can't do that. Gran is going on a long vacation to our place on Padre Island. Ruthann? With Gran's influence and a check, she will be appointed to the board of directors of the Texas State Historical Society, and she will act as their librarian. Once a year the society has a banquet recognizing the remaining original Daughters of the Texas Revolution. She can't do any harm from there." He waved his arms, "Forget about Ruthann. As board president I've backed all your actions."

Samuels thought. "And I cleaned up Ruthann's mess, and the library is no longer a financial embarrassment to the city. And how long do you think it will be before Ruthann or your grandmother share their gossip about me?"

"I can't keep them under my thumb all day long. What the hell were you doing out there at midnight in Travis Park?"

"I don't need to explain."

"It only makes you look compromised. The good thing is no charges are being filed. This will disappear from the radar."

"Except for your grandmother and Ruthann."

"Gran is too smart to talk. And no one pays attention to Ruthann." Samuels shook his head and looked out the window.

"Okay, so you leave us, what happens to all the grants?"

A knock at the door brought Samuels to his feet.

"One moment." Samuels went to the door. "I've invited Miss Fischer here to answer your question."

"Thank you for coming," He motioned for Ilene Fischer to enter and take a seat.

"My, look at that rain," remarked Ilene. "Mayor, good to see you. Is everything all right? What's this question I'm supposed to answer?"

"Good to see you, too, Miss Fischer," said Forester. "Doctor Samuels has me on tenterhooks about our future."

"Our future?" Ilene looked at Samuels.

"Miss Fischer, I'm submitting my resignation as director of the San Antonio Public Library."

"That's a joke! Right?" Ilene exclaimed. "Doctor Samuels, you're making a world of difference here. Mayor, tell him he can't go?"

"I've done the best I can," said Forester.

"Ilene, I'd like for you to take over administration of the grants. I'm giving thirty days' notice. I'll be here to train you, and you will do some travel to meet people at the Ford Foundation and other organizations that give the library grant money."

"Travel, we have no budget for travel," responded the mayor.

"That's very kind, Dr. Samuels, except I've never written a grant."

"Ilene, I've read your narratives and seen your budgets. Compared to other possible applicants, you're way ahead. I assure you if you keep that standard of effort on the grant proposals, you'll do well."

"This is sudden. It's flattering that you think I could do even a small part of your job. I'll have to think about it. I had no idea you were looking to move on." Ilene's eyes teared.

"Life throws us a curve sometimes," Samuels said.

"A big goddamn curve, pardon my French," said Forester. "The rain is letting up a bit. I better get back to my office before they give the city away."

Samuels escorted Fischer and Forester to his office door.

"Take your time, Ilene. I'm here if you want to talk," said Samuels.

"Sir, you're a big picture person," said Ilene. "I'm someone who lives in the details. I like that."

"We'll speak in the morning," said Forester.

Samuels shut the door behind them, paused, then locked it. In the storeroom, he opened a cabinet and brought out the bottle of cherry brandy. He filled a teacup and downed it in one long swallow. He lowered himself to the floor and put his head in his hands.

CHAPTER 47

Wearing new white pajamas with blue pinstripes, Cosimo sorted through a stack of drawings spread on the bed. He selected one and placed it on his cardboard easel on the bistro table. After giving it thoughtful concentration, he either signed the drawing in pencil in his distinctive calligraphy, identified the Aesop tale, and added the year, 1961, or he ripped the drawing to pieces and tossed it on the floor. On the bed were a stack of duplicates, too good to discard. To those he added "2 of 2" after the name of the drawing. He carefully arranged the master drawings in a cardboard portfolio with precut sheets of glassine between each. The duplicates he rolled and placed each into its own mailing tube. He wrote the drawing's name on a label, moistened the adhesive side, and applied it to the tube, then sealed the tube with metal caps on the ends.

Emma knocked on the window, then entered with a tray of tacos and a glass of tea.

"*Santa Maria y Jesus*!" she screamed at seeing the torn drawings on the floor. "Why are you tearing up these drawings when people would pay good money for them?"

"Leave them," he said.

"You're the one who needs money," said Emma. "Why don't *you* sell? You could make four or five hundred dollars."

"I will not do that." He removed the easel from the table to make room for the meal.

"I don't understand." She put down the tray.

"I have my reasons." Still standing, he took a hungry bite of taco.

"Sit down. You're supposed to be resting." She scooped up the paper scraps from the floor and dropped them in the trash.

Cosimo backed onto the bed. "I rested. Now I have to work." He touched Emma's hand. "I pray you are not losing business because of the communist nonsense."

"Business is fine." She pulled up a chair and sat across from him. "Walk-ins slow up between 9:30 and 11:00, but not like before. You were right to have Gracie change the menu."

Cosimo finished the taco and went for the second.

She held out her hand to slow him. "Not so fast, you'll choke."

"I am hungry." He took a drink of iced tea.

"Where did you find all these tubes, and what are you doing with the drawings?"

"Francisco got them from the federal building. The government office that sells maps sells the tubes, too. I have many people to thank. I am giving several drawings to you and Graciela. I have a notebook where I will keep the information on each piece and who has it. These are originals. I did more than one drawing of the same story until I got what I wanted. These are the best. They are slightly different but I cannot use both. I have one condition. Hang them in the café, or keep them in a clean dry place, but do not sell them."

"There's nothing wrong with your appetite. So, okay, we won't sell. You didn't have to tear up all those drawings. I thought all were good."

"The ones I destroyed were among my first. I got better, and had better ideas as I drew more." Cosimo pushed his hair away from his face.

"Would you like me to cut your hair?" Emma leaned around to look at the back of his head. His hair hung below his shoulders.

"Yes, I would appreciate that. In France no one would notice. Here, it is a curiosity." He finished the taco and wiped his fingers and lips with a napkin. "And thank you for the pajamas."

A knock on the door brought Emma to her feet. Maddie, Oscar, and Richard stood on the porch.

"Hello. We're here to see how Mr. Cano is doing." Maddie leaned into the room.

"*Seguro,*" called out Cosimo.

"Cosimo, I have to get back to the café," Emma said, gathering up the tray.

He drained the glass of tea. "Do you have the car?" he asked, handing her the glass.

"Did you think I flew here with hot tacos? Yes, I have the car."

"Can you give us all a ride? I have business that needs my attention."

"You're supposed to be resting."

"As I said before, I rested. These young students can help me. Here." He handed three tubes to Richard and two apiece to Oscar and Maddie. "Give me five minutes to dress."

"We came by to see how you were doing. We don't intend—" said Maddie.

"I am doing just fine. Wait out on the porch."

They shuffled out the door and stood outside.

"I have to be at work in an hour," said Maddie.

"If he gets us to the courthouse in a car, we save twenty minutes," Richard replied.

Fifteen minutes later they walked into the Little House Café. Cosimo pointed to three seats at the counter and beckoned for the mailing tubes with his fingers.

"Emma, please give them whatever they want." He sat at a nearby table and sorted the tubes by name.

"What can I get you?" asked Emma.

"Your menu says you'll make a taco out of anything," grinned Richard, as if he had found a flaw in the menu. "I want a fried chicken taco."

Emma picked up tongs, opened the warmer, selected a chicken leg and put it on a flour tortilla. "Here you go, smarty pants, a fried chicken taco." She placed it on a dish in front of him.

"What if I had ordered a meat loaf taco?"

"Same thing, but only on Wednesdays." Emma's eyes sparkled when she laughed.

"She got you," teased Oscar.

"Okay, okay, I'll take two beef tacos," Richard ordered. "And I'll have that chicken leg, too."

Oscar gave a wistful glance at the list of taco selections. "My dream is to come here with ten dollars and say, 'Start at the top of the menu and keep them coming.'"

"You can't eat ten tacos. What if I bring them to you one at a time until you say stop?"

"You can do that?" Oscar asked, feeling guilty for abusing Cosimo's hospitality.

"Watch me." Emma penciled plus ten in the check pad. She glanced at Maddie.

"I want two potato and egg tacos. And can you please make them to go?" Maddie said.

Cosimo invited them to join him at the table. "Before your food arrives, I want to speak with you. Thank you for being curious about me," said Cosimo. "I had moments when I questioned my own identity. You found me. For that, I want you to have this." He handed each a tube. "The drawings are duplicates. I selected one for the show, and the twin belongs to you. Here is the bargain. Do not sell them. If you have not heard from me after one year, you can do whatever you wish, though I recommend keeping them for at least ten years."

"What? We didn't—" said Maddie.

"I have a notebook here. Take one page and make it yours. I need an address where I can always write to you, and include the name of the drawing I have given you."

"What else do you want us to do?" Maddie said, picking up the pen.

"Add a note, or not."

Emma arrived with their orders.

Richard was the last to fill in his information. Cosimo reviewed their entries, placed the book in his courier bag, and bound together the four remaining tubes with rubber bands.

"You have your drawings. You have signed my book. Your food is here. There's more I need to tell you, but I am late. Be sure to check in with the cabin where I'm staying. I will leave you my address with the owner if I do not see you again." He donned his Panama, picked up his cane, and exited the café.

"How does he pay for this?" Maddie asked Emma.

"We owe him money." She held up the green order pad. "He takes payment in meals."

"Where's he going?" asked Richard. "He just had a heart attack."

"Cosimo claims he didn't have a heart attack," Emma replied.

"Still, he shouldn't be out and about," said Maddie. "He looks frail."

"He may be putting his affairs in order," said Oscar.

"Don't say that!" Maddie cried.

Emma shook her head. "I'm afraid I thought the same thing."

The bells on the door jingled as more customers entered.

"I have to go," said Emma.

"*Jeezus,* if he dies, our drawings could be worth hundreds of dollars," Richard said.

"That's enough." Maddie stood. She picked up a brown bag with her tacos to go and placed a quarter on the table. "Remember to leave a tip."

At Hertzberg's, Cosimo was met by smiles and hellos from the clerks. Meyer half ran across the room to greet him. "I have your negatives," he whispered, before anyone else neared. "Everything came out just as you wanted. I hope you like them."

Two clerks, seeing Cosimo, hurried over.

"Mister Cano, I heard you were hospitalized. How are you?" Meyer raised his voice.

"Much better. Perhaps too much excitement, but that's done with. I am on my feet and ready to dance." He did a shuffle with his feet and held his cane like Fred Astaire.

The sales clerks laughed.

"So good to hear," said Meyer.

"Is Mr. Goodman in?"

"He's in his office. He definitely needs to see you."

Meyer led the way to Goodman's office. The sales clerks trailed behind, glancing at one another as to who would remain on duty near the store's entrance.

Goodman rose quickly. "Mister Cano, how are you?"

"Much better. No need to make a fuss. I want to give you both a token of my appreciation for all your help." He handed them their mailing tubes.

"What's this?" Goodman asked.

Goodman and Meyer immediately popped the end caps off the tubes.

"A work of art on the back of a menu!" Goodman laughed. "*The Wolf and the Crane.*"

"Thank you. It's delightful," Meyer said with a wink. "*The Fox and the Crow*, a real work of art. I didn't know you were also a penman."

"Please do not project any meaning into these as it may relate to you. The gifts come with one restriction. Do not sell for at least a year."

Goodman grinned. "Sell? This is going up on my wall."

"Thank you. This is not the version for children," said Meyer, clearly moved. "You can see the fox's ribs poking out above the narrow haunches, while the crow is sleek and well fed."

Goodman rolled his drawing and returned it to the mailing tube. "We have to talk. The marshal is looking for you with a court order to hand over the watch."

"Yes, the watch," echoed Meyer. "Do you have your passport with you?"

"Of course," replied Cosimo.

"We have a temporary solution, which takes us off the hook regarding liability and protects you," said Goodman.

"We better go right away. I'll explain later," urged Meyer.

Goodman opened the standing safe and returned with a metal strong box. He retrieved the Dali Zodiac timepiece and placed it in a briefcase. "I will hold it until we get to the bank. The marshal asked me for your address. I didn't give it to him, but, well, he's out there somewhere looking to serve you."

"I have a safety deposit box at the Alamo National Bank," Meyer explained. "We will meet you there in ten minutes, and we'll put the safety deposit box in your name."

"Is this the best way? The law offices of Bluhorn & Carnahan are in the same building."

"The marshal is likely over on Buena Vista Street. He won't be looking for you right under their noses in the same building with the law firm. This way even if they are able to serve you, you won't have the timepiece on you, and you're not obligated to tell them where it is."

"Is this necessary?"

"If you are served with a writ of possession, and they know the watch is here, they can come and take it. We can't stop them," said Goodman.

Cosimo, Goodman, and Meyer walked separately into the Alamo National Bank and convened in privacy at a table outside the safe-deposit vault. The entire exchange took place in less than a half hour, and out of the public's view. Cosimo went into the vault by himself. Before he placed the watch in the safe-deposit box, he took a last look.

"I'm winding you a couple of turns to hold you until I get back." The sun's eyes rolled back in pleasure.

Cosimo slipped the safety deposit box key into his wallet and placed it in the courier bag. He rejoined Goodman and Meyer. Goodman took a receipt form from his coat pocket and had Cosimo sign. The watch had been officially returned.

"This is so cloak and dagger," Cosimo said.

"The watch is now safe, and you can retrieve it any time you want," replied Goodman. They left the bank separately, Goodman first.

Meyer handed Cosimo an envelope. "I shot two exposures of each drawing using Kodak's fine-grain film. I hope they're what you want."

"If they are as good as the photos of my watch, they are more than satisfactory."

They staggered their departures from the bank building, exiting through different doors. Cosimo had two remaining mailing tubes and proceeded east on Market Street to the library.

Richard sat at the front desk as Cosimo entered.

"Is the library director in?" Cosimo asked.

"I don't think so. Hold on." He pushed the button for the head librarian. "Miss Fischer, is Doctor Samuels in?. . . No? Cosimo Cano, the artist, is here to see him."

"Is Miss Fischer available?"

"He wants to know if he can meet with you? Sure." He hung up the phone. "You know where it is, go on back. Thank you for the artwork, and thank you for breakfast. On the money I earn, I don't eat like that very often."

Ilene stood to greet him and directed him to the reference desk. "How can I help you, Mister Cano?"

"I am not here to ask a question. I would like to have a conversation," said Cosimo.

Ilene stared back quizzically. "Please come to the accessions room. We can sit and talk."

"I only need a few minutes. I don't want to impose."

Ilene motioned for Oscar to come over. "Hold down the reference desk, please."

Oscar pushed the book cart behind the counter and took a seat at the reference desk.

"This is my workplace." Ilene sat at her desk, surrounded by the Dewey decimal system dictionaries and the inks and pens she used to write the catalog numbers on the spines of books. "I like it here…" She glanced around. "I fear losing it."

"Why would you lose it?"

"Doctor Samuels is leaving, and I've been asked to take over the administration of the grants. It's fulltime."

"Where is he going?"

"He's been offered a position at the Smithsonian. It's a staff position. He belongs here, or someplace where he can run a library."

"Was this sudden?" he asked.

"Yes, very sudden. We found out yesterday."

"I am sorry to hear that. He is a personable young man. However, the reason I am here is that I have a gift for you. It is humble and from my heart, in gratitude for your assistance." He handed her a mailing tube.

As she removed the metal cap, the drawing slipped out. She caught it and spread the artwork out on her worktable.

"Oh, it's magical. The mouse and the lion!" She laughed.

"Please, do not see yourself in the fable. This is my personal exercise in interpreting the story. Take away from that what you will. I would like that you enjoy it."

"Enjoy it? I love it! Thank you. I don't know what to say. Can I pay you for it?

"No! It is a gift."

"Yes, but I know you're in need of money. I'd like to help."

"You already did."

"Any help I gave I would have done for anyone."

"The gift is not for the time you spent. It is for your enthusiasm while you were doing it." He explained how the gift came with conditions, then had her add name and address to the notebook.

It was the worst time of the day to be out on San Antonio streets. The sun was relentless, and the Buena Vista Cabins were a mile and a half away. Cosimo's stomach ached and he felt lightheaded as he approached the cabins. The humid air stung with the acrid scent of burnt pinto beans. He glanced toward the Vasquez sisters' windows, and as expected, they were still at work. No one was out in the August heat.

Pito took a step out of his apartment and called Cosimo over. He dressed better since Henny moved in with him. He wore his starched shirt unbuttoned, exposing a fresh white undershirt. His khaki pants had a neat crease.

Inside Pito's darkened apartment an evaporative cooling fan roared in the front window. A soap opera flashed on the television.

"I am glad you're here," said Cosimo, taking off his hat and dabbing his brow with a red bandana.

"Come in. You look like you could use a glass of tea," called Henny.

"Thank you, I can use a glass of water if it is not too much to ask."

Henny turned off the TV and went into the kitchen.

Pito leaned close. "Cosimo, there was a marshal here to give you some papers. He waited most of the afternoon. He wanted to look through your cabin. I wouldn't let him. He asked if we knew you had a fancy watch."

"Thank you for not allowing him to enter."

"He'll be back."

"I am tired, but before I go, I want to give you something."

"Hey, you've given me plenty of headaches." Pito laughed. "And your units are renting out every night. Sometimes, two or three times."

"That's not true," said Henny, handing Cosimo a glass of water. "Only once a night. Come in and stand by the fan." The evaporative cooler aimed its stream of air toward the center of the room.

"I want to give you a gift." He handed Pito a mailing tube. Henny turned on the light and stood behind Pito to see what Cosimo brought.

"What's this, a menu from Little House. You're buying me dinner?"

"Pedrito, there's a painting on the other side." Henny said.

"An original pen and ink drawing," said Cosimo.

"Of what?" Pito turned the paper over. "What's this, a bird putting rocks in a jar?"

"An Aesop's fable, of the crow and the pitcher of water. Whatever you do, do not sell it until you hear from me."

"If somebody offers me ten bucks for it, I'm taking it. Though I don't think anybody would want a painting of a crow."

Henny put her arms around Cosimo and kissed him on the cheek. "It's a beautiful painting. Thank you. He's not going to sell it."

In that instant, Cosimo saw Henny as she was long ago before she drank too much cola and men lied to her, an awkward bright child brought up in poverty.

"It's modern art, like Picasso," said Henny, stepping back from the hug.

"What do you know about this Picasso? Is he an old boyfriend?"

"You're so wrong! Picasso was an artist who died a long time ago," Henny countered.

"Actually, Picasso is still alive, and I accept the compliment," said Cosimo before he was drowned out.

"So, does Picasso come around when I'm not here?" Pito said, only half joking.

"What are you talking about? He's famous. I thought you had to be dead to be famous."

"If he's famous why haven't I heard of him?" argued Pito.

"Excuse me," interrupted Cosimo. "Pedro, stop. Picasso is about as famous as an artist can become. I do not paint like him, but that is not important. Henny has accurately defined a period of art where I belong. For that, she is correct."

"You see?" Henny said, putting her hands on her hips.

"Henny has never met Picasso. I've only seen him three or four times myself; we are not friends."

"What are we supposed to do with this?" Pito allowed the drawing to curl back into the shape of the tube.

"Save it, hang it in your house. It is a token of my appreciation for your kindness."

"Thank you. You still have to pay the rent." Pito grinned.

Cosimo closed the door to his cabin and put his courier bag on the table, his hat and cane next to it. He sat on the bed. It had been an exhausting day. He kicked off his counterfeit Hushpuppy shoes and fell asleep before he could undo his belt.

CHAPTER 48

At seven the following morning, a black Lincoln Continental blocked the driveway to the Buena Vista address. The driver, a lean man in a black suit, exited the limo and curled a pair of aviator sunglasses onto his ears. Walking to Cosimo's cabin, he assessed the working class surroundings. This was not the type of neighborhood where he usually picked up clients. He stepped onto Cosimo's porch and knocked on the violet door.

Cosimo opened the door. "If you are the officer with the warrant, I do not have the watch."

"Sir, I'm here from Bluhorn & Carnahan. I've been asked to pick you up for an important meeting. I'll wait until you're dressed."

"You are not the marshal?"

"No, sir. I'm not the law. I'm just a driver. Your presence is requested, and I'm here to drive you there."

"What time is it?"

"It's after 7:00 a.m. If you need to bathe, I'll wait. Your presence is requested as soon as possible."

Francisco Orozco was similarly awakened and summoned to the offices at Bluhorn & Carnahan. On an entirely different floor from the one Cosimo had visited before, a red-headed young man escorted them into a well-appointed conference room with polished walnut paneling, a gleaming conference table, fine leather swivel chairs, and a wet bar. Guns and large photos of hunting kills dominated the décor.

Estes Bluhorn entered. "Mister Cano, Mister Orozco, I know we've gotten you up early. We have refreshments, and there's an executive kitchen on the floor. They can make you an omelet, pancakes, almost anything you want—even *way-vos ran-cher-ohs*, if you want. There's a menu on the service table. The men's room is across the hall. There're towels, even complimentary shaving gear, if you need."

He opened a cabinet and switched on the wet bar's backlight, giving the premium brands of spirits an inviting glow. A coffee pot and a Lalique crystal serving tray with cinnamon-scented bear claws waited on the service table, along with matching cups and saucers, a variety of glasses for different types of alcoholic beverages, and a carved-glass bucket with ice.

As Bluhorn turned his back to pour himself coffee, Francisco and Cosimo shared a glance. *What the hell is going on?*

"These bear claws are from Joske's Bakery, without a doubt the best in town," said Bluhorn, taking a bite of the pastry. "Please help yourself to anything."

"Why are we here?" asked Francisco.

"Yes, what is different this morning?" seconded Cosimo.

"We are complying with a request to communicate with you. The technician is setting it up now. At this point there is nothing else I can say. The reason for getting you up early is that the exact time for an international connection is unpredictable."

"International connection?" asked Francisco.

"The set-up could take five minutes or an hour, and we couldn't begin until you were here. This is a big deal and it's costing a load of dough. They're patching phone connections through European countries, using the transatlantic cable to Nova Scotia, then from Canada to here."

Francisco poured a cup of coffee and placed a bear claw on a dish. "Can I get you something?" he asked Cosimo, who shook his head.

When Bluhorn stepped out of the room, Cosimo whispered. "I do not want anything from these bastards besides my things."

After a half hour, the young red-headed associate and a technician brought in a telephone and amplifier. After a series of squeals and buzzing noises, the technician motioned for Cosimo to sit in a designated chair at the conference table. He could hear test voices coming from the speaker. The technician held his hand up for silence. "Hush, please." He pointed to Cosimo.

Over the speaker he heard the thin, filtered voice of his friend Margaret Manheim. "Cosimo, *caro*, are you all right? Can you hear me?"

"Yes, I hear you. It's comforting to hear your voice."

"How many people are there?" she asked.

"Five," Cosimo replied.

"Is there anyone there who speaks French?"

"Who speaks French?" asked Francisco. All except for Cosimo said no.

"In that case we speak in French. My god, this is awful. I can hardly hear you. I'm shouting as if I were in La Scala's basement trying to be heard in the highest balcony." She took a breath. "Caro, how are you? Don't answer, no time. My heart is broken at Sara's loss. She was so dear to me. Listen, Cosimo, there are a couple of things you need to know. Don't talk. Put on your best poker face. Sara left a will, and apparently since you didn't ask about it, the family didn't bother to tell you. How have they treated you?"

"Not well, except for today." he replied, smiling at the curious faces staring at him.

"Have your lawyer ask them for Sara's will. I'm fronting this phone call and the car. Sara's lawyers are going to make sure I get paid back . . . for everything. Stick it to them, and enjoy it all, my dear. Shouting like this is driving me crazy. Listen, Sara and I used the same law firm in London. Their New York office will be in touch momentarily. You must come see me in Venice. I'm expecting you will have something to show me. We should talk about a show. Did you hear anything I said?"

"Yes, I heard you," he half shouted.

"*Addio!*" The phone went silent.

Cosimo turned to Bluhorn. "I would like privacy with my attorney."

"Is this room secure?" asked Francisco.

Bluhorn nodded. "I'll clear the room for you."

"Thank you," said Francisco.

Bluhorn held the door open as the technician gathered his amplifier and phone and withdrew. Hearing the door close, Francisco huddled with Cosimo.

"Let's keep our voices low. What did she say?" he whispered.

"Sara left a will," Cosimo replied.

"Oh, shit!" Francisco said loud enough to be heard in the hall.

"You are supposed to ask the family lawyers for one. Sara's firm has lawyers in New York, they will call."

A knock at the door prompted Francisco to come to his feet. "Oh shit," he said again.

"Do you think they know?" Cosimo nodded toward the hall.

"If they don't know, they suspect. Otherwise we wouldn't have the likes of this."

Bluhorn knocked and entered, "It's New York for you," he said, walking toward the wet bar. "It's patched through a line over here." He took a phone from the counter, with a cord long enough to reach the conference table.

"I'll leave you to it," Bluhorn said and left the room.

"Francisco Orozco here." He paused to listen. "Yes, one moment, please." He handed Cosimo the phone.

"*Bueno* . . . Cosimo Infante Cano. Where was I born? In Ciego de Avila, Cuba . . . in 1893 . . . He has been very helpful to me and has advised me how to proceed to recover my things. I have asked him to represent me. He has prepared letters on my behalf." He handed the phone back to Francisco.

Francisco listened.

"I passed the bar in May, 1961. . . St. Mary's University Law School. It's here in San Antonio . . . I took the case *pro bono* because Mister Cano was in need of help. I have filed a suit requesting access to Miss Sara Hunter's records, and they have gotten a judge to grant them a writ of possession for the return of a watch Sara Hunter gave to Mister Cano. I think they look on us as very small fry."

He glanced at Cosimo for assurance that everything he said was correct. Cosimo nodded.

"One moment, please." Francisco reached in his briefcase, found a notepad and pen, and sat at the table. "Go ahead. I'm ready." He made notes as he listened. At the end, he said, "I can do that. That would be acceptable. Yes, thank you." He returned the phone to the cradle.

"Cosimo, what would you like?" said Francisco, bringing his notes.

"You know what I want. I want what is mine. That is all."

"What if they were supposed to pay your living expenses, first class, from the day you arrived?"

"That is something Sara would do."

"There's more. What if she provided an allowance of fifty thousand dollars a year for life, for you and Proust, a parrot, I presume. There should have been a copy of the will in her personal documents. The reason the transatlantic phone call took place at all was because Miss Manheim became incensed at your treatment."

"What should we do now?"

"I need to tell you. Solomon, Solomon & Sachs are going to pay me to represent you. They don't like that I'm a complete rookie. They've never heard of St. Mary's University. I'm going to be more like the tip of a legal finger. I'm not complaining. They want the family to pay for the indignities you have had to endure."

"I do not want revenge. All I want to do is to return to France with what belongs to me."

"There's a lot more coming to you." Francisco opened the conference room door and called for Bluhorn to enter.

Bluhorn took his time, finishing a conversation with a secretary, going to the wet bar, and pouring himself three fingers of Johnny Walker Black Label. He let himself drop into one of the leather swivel chairs, lit a cigarette, and picked a tobacco thread from his tongue, disposing of it in an ashtray. He took a deep swallow of scotch. "I've been up since 3:00 a.m. setting up this phone call. I'm ordering something to eat." He picked up the phone. "Consuelo, send me a club sandwich, you know how I like 'em." Bluhorn hung up the phone. "Strange that Solomon, Solomon & Sachs arranged for that call, price no object, and only this morning at 3:00 a.m. did I learn they represent you."

"I have been hired by Solomon, Solomon & Sachs to represent Mister Cosimo Infante Cano," said Francisco. "I've been instructed to ask for a copy of Miss Sara Hunter's will. It was supposed to be in her personal papers."

"We do not have one," said Bluhorn.

"Then the New York offices of Solomon, Solomon & Sachs is sending one by telex. It could take as much as a half-hour before they send it."

The red-headed associate knocked, opened the door, and rolled in a cart with three bankers' boxes.

Bluhorn picked up a box and shoved it on the table.

"These are Miss Sara Hunter's personal and business files in three boxes. The family has agreed for you to look at them," said Bluhorn.

"Stay as long as you need. Somebody's here around the clock. It's going to be a long day. I recommend you have something to eat."

"Only if it's understood we are not doing anything *quid pro quo*," said Francisco.

"Professional courtesy, son." Bluhorn held up his glass of Johnny Walker. "We know when we're outclassed. At this moment, I can only disclose that Bluhorn & Carnahan did not advise Mr. Cano of a will, because we had no knowledge of one. And I doubt you'll find one here."

The phone rang, Bluhorn answered. "The telex?" he asked. "I'll be in my office."

Bluhorn left his glass of scotch on the table.

"Do you want something to eat?" asked Francisco.

"Normally, I would want nothing from these bastards. Today, find the most expensive item in their kitchen and have them make it for me."

Francisco perused the menu. "They have an aged tenderloin for twenty-two dollars. Jesus, that better be good. I may have one myself."

"Order that for me," said Cosimo.

Bluhorn returned after they'd finished their meal.

He sat at the conference table and rediscovered his scotch.

"I was ready to relax when this turned into a tornado. The telex came through, and we're making photographic copies." He took a drink. "Today, in broad strokes it looks like this. The Hunter family has agreed to turn over everything to Mr. Cano: his forty-five thousand dollars, his paintings, his luggage, and they give up any claim to a Salvador Dali Zodiac watch."

"When will this take place?" asked Francisco.

"Soon, today if possible."

"We assume you've had a quick glance at the document," said Francisco.

"We have. They will pay for a suite at the St. Anthony retroactively from the time of his arrival. They'll pay for Mr. Cano's return trip to France first class. He will also receive a retroactive stipend of fifty dollars a day for meals. They're considering a figure to offer Mr. Cano for his inconvenience. We're still drawing this up, and I would like for both of you to return tomorrow morning after the family has finalized the details."

"Inconvenience? Mr. Cano has been living like a pauper in a shack on the other side of the tracks," countered Francisco. "The family has gotten you to file a writ of possession to have him return a watch given to him by Sara Hunter in 1952. By not living in a manner he is accustomed to, his health has become seriously compromised. He was hospitalized only six days ago."

"Hold on," said Bluhorn. "Let's wait until tomorrow morning to start negotiations. We're making a copy of the will for you and Mr. Cano. I think you're going to find the family very generous."

"Considering someone pulled the will from her documents," countered Francisco.

"If, and I'm not saying they did, if the family did find a will and didn't tell us, we were blindsided, Mr. Cano. When would you like to leave for France?"

"As soon as I have my things."

"Bluhorn & Carnahan will do everything to expedite your departure. I personally apologize for my dismissive attitude at our previous meeting. At the time, I was speaking for the family and not for myself or the firm. The car is at your disposal until you leave the city. And I'm working on getting your things to you today, if possible."

Outside of the Alamo National Bank Building, Cosimo and Francisco strolled in the direction of the river. They continued to the Presa Street Bridge, and stopped in the middle, turning to the river view.

"This is the only place that connects me to Sara," said Cosimo.

"You have a better connection now. She's taking care of you from the other side."

"Besides the money, what does any of this mean?" wondered Cosimo.

"What's going on is that they *may* have taken the will out of her files and not informed you of your rights. That is fraud, a serious felony. They're giving you everything you want, and more, so you will go away without raising a stink."

"Can they be counted on to do that?"

"That's where Solomon, Solomon & Sachs comes in. A portion of Sara's money will be set aside to pay for your yearly stipend. The Solomon firm will be the minders of the account and will take a fee, naturally, until such time as you die, then the money reverts to the Hunter estate. Let's hope you live to a hundred and fifty, because everyone but the Hunter family will make money from that account."

They turned from the bridge and walked back in the direction of the bank.

"I'll be going back to go through the boxes," said Francisco. "I'll see you in the morning. They said about ten o'clock."

The limousine appeared apparently out of nowhere. The driver exited and held the door open for Cosimo.

CHAPTER 49

Returning to Buena Vista Street, the limo drove into the yard, stopping in front of the cabin. The driver opened the door for Cosimo. Immediately, whispering neighbors gathered in the shade of the apartment building, with Pito and Henny joining in on the speculation.

"I'm on call, and at your service. Here's my phone number." The driver handed him a business card.

"I won't need anything else today. Pick me up at nine in the morning, thank you. I will be ready."

Before Cosimo could open his door, Pito and Henny caught up with him on the porch.

"Cosimo, what's going on?" blurted Pito. "Yesterday, a marshal stakes out your place with a warrant, and today a limo is driving you around like a movie star."

Henny's eyes asked exactly the same question, as did a half dozen neighbors, gathered nearby.

"I had business dealings."

"Yes, but the big *pinche* car? What about that?"

"If things had gone the way they were supposed to when I arrived in this city, I would not have a car and driver. Because things went badly, now I have them."

"That makes no sense." Pito shook his head.

"That is the best I can explain."

"You're not going to jail for stealing a watch?" asked Henny.

"Is that what people are saying? That I am a *thief?*" He laughed, glancing at the inquisitive faces looking in his direction. "No, I am not going to jail."

"Then what?" urged Pito.

"I have reconnected with my friends, and I am returning to France."

"Wonderful. That's great news for you." Henny gave Cosimo a hug.

"You sure like hugging this old man," growled Pito.

"Pito, you are a lucky man," said Cosimo.

"I liked it when you called me Don Pedro."

Cosimo put his hand on Pito's shoulder.

"Pito, I envied the boys with names like Jose. People would call them Pepe. An Eduardo became Lalo; Arturo became Tutti. I have always been Cosimo, like the early Renaissance tyrant." He yawned unexpectedly. "Excuse me, I need to rest."

Cosimo closed the door to the cabin.

"You're my Pedrito. How's that?" said Henny, kissing Pito on the cheek.

"I think he's been drinking. I've never seen him so happy," said Pito.

Walking back to their apartment, Henny and Pito were circled by neighbors.

At 3:00 p.m. a furniture van entered the patio, and the red-headed associate who had been part of the international phone call exited the van and knocked on Cosimo's door.

"Mister Cano, my name is Franklin McCome. I'm an associate at Bluhorn & Carnahan, and we're here with two trunks. If you can make a cursory examination of the trunks, we can leave them with you. Your signature only confirms you have accepted the trunks into your possession. The Hunter family states they have not opened the chests and have no idea of the contents."

"Any one of dozens of trunk keys can open these," chuckled Cosimo.

"If there is anything missing, you must let us know," said McCome.

The number of curious neighbors doubled under the pecan trees, daring to stand even closer.

Cosimo had the keys to the trunks in his courier bag. The contents had shifted, though essentially the contents appeared arranged as Sara had packed them.

"Everything appears to be here. I will look more carefully tonight."

"You're expected at the office at 10:00 a.m. If everything goes smoothly, you'll be able to fly out of here by Friday. That's three and a half days. Mr. Bluhorn mentioned you were anxious to return to France. I need your signature." He handed Cosimo a clipboard with the property release.

Cosimo signed.

"A professional packer and expediter will meet with you tomorrow afternoon. If you need luggage, we have an arrangement with Joske's Department Store to send travel collections. Should I schedule your flight?"

"Tell Mister Bluhorn that I will make that decision tomorrow."

McCome and the driver carried the trunks into the cabin.

"Is there anything else we can do for you?" asked McCome.

Cosimo waved him off. "No, I will see you tomorrow. Thank you."

Emma arrived as McCome was exiting. She carried a supper tray and a folded brown paper bag.

"You're early," said Cosimo.

"I came as soon as I could get away. Should I be here?" Emma asked.

"This is where you belong. They are the strangers," said Cosimo, holding the door open for her.

"I came by last night. You were asleep. I didn't have the heart to wake you. This morning I got a call at the café that you were taken away. What's going on? Everyone is talking about the fancy car, and now these deliveries."

"First, tell me, are the people out there still saying I stole a watch?"

"They're saying you're planning to buy the property. You're going to make this a fancy hotel."

"That is rich!" Cosimo laughed.

"Don't laugh at us."

"I am not laughing at you. I am delighted by ambitions I did not consider."

Emma set the dinner tray on the bistro table.

"Is it true you're returning to France?"

"Yes."

"When?"

"In a few days."

"Why so sudden?"

"You know I was only here until I reclaimed my possessions. It was simply a matter of time."

She pushed the supper tray in his direction.

"I'll cut your hair after you eat if you want me to."

"I had a big meal earlier. I would like for you to cut my hair."

Emma opened the brown paper bag and brought out a barber's cloth, scissors, and a comb. She wrapped the cloth around his chest and fastened it with a safety pin behind his neck. "Why can't you stay here?" she asked.

"This is not my home."

She wet his hair with a damp cloth, then combed it back, over and over until it glistened. She found his profile, prominent nose, high cheekbones and strong chin alluring for an old man. She set the comb aside, gathered the ends of his hair with two fingers and began trimming.

"What happens to me?" asked Emma, standing behind him.

He tried to look at her without moving his head. "Emma! You are a biblical heroine. You fed me when I was hungry; you clothed me when I was almost naked; you raised my spirits. How can I repay you?"

For the next ten minutes Emma silently measured and cut hair. She put aside the scissors and began combing the hair back faster and harder.

"What are you doing?" Cosimo stopped her.

"I don't want you to go."

"Don't uproot my hair. I would like to keep it." He looked into Emma's eyes. "Come visit me in Paris. Bring your son and grandson," he urged.

Several minutes passed as Emma finished the haircut and removed the barber's cloth.

"When do I have time for a vacation, or the money?" Emma put away the scissors, and folded the cloth. She wouldn't meet his eyes.

"When you have a successful business, anything can happen," encouraged Cosimo. "Tell me when you want to visit, and I will take care of the rest."

The following morning at seven two photographers and a newspaper reporter knocked on the violet door. The instant Cosimo answered, they began snapping photos. He slammed the door shut.

"Sir, sir, sir—Please, we're here from the *San Antonio Light.*"

"And I'm from the McNay Art Institute." The McNay photographer slipped his business card under the door.

"No photos until I come out," Cosimo said through the closed door.

The limo arrived, and the driver waited by the passenger side door for Cosimo to emerge.

Cosimo made the photographers and reporter wait until the morning sun shone on the brightly-painted cabin. He stepped outside, a Mayan figure in a bespoke Italian suit, and his favorite Joan Miro tie. He posed on the porch, leaning on his cane.

Curious neighbors came out from the surrounding apartments. The photographers followed Cosimo, shooting as he put a mailing tube under his arm, locked the cabin, and waited for the driver to open the car door.

The photographers were loving it. Cosimo knew how bizarre this must have appeared to the neighbors.

"Take me to the library and park right in front," he told the limo driver.

Jane Jenkins, the children's librarian, saw the limo stop in front of the library. The driver opened the door for the strange little man who appeared in the city about the time Ruthann's troubles began. Except, he wasn't poor. He was dressed in tailored clothes and traveled in a chauffeured limo. His cane was no longer a crutch, but an accessory.

Cosimo went directly to the stairs leading to the director's office. Ilene Fischer intercepted him before he could knock on Dr. Samuels's door.

"Mister Cano, you look so distinguished."

"Thank you. I'm here to see Doctor Samuels."

"Just a moment. Let me look in on him."

Before she could check the door, Samuels stepped out of his office. "Absolutely, I can see Mister Cano." He pointed at Cosimo's suit. "Brioni, Rome."

"Very good. You recognize the cut."

"Come in, what can I do for you?"

"I am here to give the library a gift." He handed Samuels a mailing tube.

"A gift? Shall I look at it now?"

"If you wish."

Samuels read the caption. "That's . . . that's beautiful pen work. *The Ass Carrying an Image*, I don't recall the fable."

"The story goes that there was once a donkey that carried a heavy religious icon on his back. As he went from town to town, people bowed in respect and brought food and water to him. After a time, the donkey tired of carrying such a heavy load. He decided that if food and water came to him, why should he move at all? As much as the people urged him to continue his task, the donkey stubbornly refused to take another step. The icon was taken away and given to a jackass that proudly pranced away. Several hours passed, the donkey became hungry and thirsty, and nothing came. The next day, famished, the donkey begged for food, but everywhere he went he was scorned, stoned, and ultimately driven from the country."

"Am I the ass?" Samuels looked at the artist with mock suspicion.

"Not in the least. Some people don't know their burden is their life." Cosimo said.

"I can intuit a resonance." Samuels laughed.

Cosimo gathered his courier bag and cane. "I understand you may be resigning," he said, standing to leave.

"I'm still weighing the options. I'm not sure of the fallout of . . ." He shrugged.

"Fallout? Certainly nothing worse than what you have imagined for yourself. I am not here about anything other than to say thank you," said Cosimo.

"For what?"

"Thank you for allowing me to use your library. My rescue was planned and executed from here with the assistance of Miss Fischer and the students. Thank you."

"It's a resource for the people."

"Listen to you, a humanist. Why leave this place?"

Samuels shook his head, glumly.

"You Americans! Do you like it here?" Cosimo asked.

"Yes, I do."

"I will be leaving your town in a few days. And those students will be gone in a few weeks. They respect you. There will be no fallout."

At the offices of Bluhorn & Carnahan, Francisco waited for Cosimo by the elevators and pulled him aside.

"According to the lawyers, the family is sticking to their story that there was no will in Sara's files." Francisco presented to Cosimo two letters from Soloman, Solomon & Sachs. "However, one letter confirms an appointment to write a will; a second one a month later states the will was ready for her signature."

"Yes, she said she was going to London to take care of business. What are the dates?"

"December 1960 and January 1961. The family has agreed to comply with all parts of the will without question. They're offering you fifty thousand dollars for your trouble."

"I'll accept it," said Cosimo.

"You could squeeze for a lot more," counseled Francisco.

"I can't have Sara back. Otherwise, I have what I want."

That afternoon, Joske's Department Store sent several choices of luggage. Cosimo met with the planner, began packing and preparing to ship his crates separately.

With the assistance of Henny and Pito, Cosimo returned or gave away the furniture to new owners.

"Are you really famous?" asked Henny.

"No, I am not. To tell you the truth, the limousine was kind of a vengeful practical joke."

"That's one helluva joke," said Pito.

CHAPTER 50

n August, between the end of summer classes and the beginning of the fall semester, apartments became available near campus. Maddie learned that the second floor of a two-story Victorian on West Craig Street was paid through the end of August. It didn't take much to persuade Oscar and Richard to leave their month-to-month rentals and move in with her for free.

The old house had only recently come back on the rental market and retained the spotless patina of the previous longtime resident. The doors had transoms and the rooms had ceilings thirteen feet high. There were two fair-sized bedrooms, and for some unknown reason, a tiny kitchen.

When Richard arrived, Maddie had already staked claim to the larger bedroom with a stained glass window over the bed. Her belongings, watches, jewelry, knick-knacks, were spread out on the mattress. "I can't take all this stuff to New York," she grumbled to Richard. "Every piece means something to me, but it's too much."

Richard looked out the window at the copper roof of the porch below. "This is something else. How do you learn about these places? No one ever offered me anything like this for free."

"Come on. Sometime, somewhere, someone gave you something free," retorted Maddie.

"Yeah, when I was six, the Santa Claus at Woolworth's gave me a lollypop, once, only once. This place, on the other hand?" He cocked his right eyebrow, implying nefarious doings.

"You can be a prick, you know? I love you for that, and it pisses me off. So what are you going to do about your *free* scholarship to Curtis Institute?" Maddie needled.

"Stab me in the heart, why don't you." Richard realized he shouldn't have teased her.

"Well?" she persisted.

"I can't accept the scholarship. It's not enough. I can't afford it. Mom can't afford it."

"You have to take it. Richard, there's got to be a way."

"I've tried. I've saved some, but . . . " Richard's eyes lost focus. "I volunteered for the draft. I leave August 31."

"No! That's nuts. You can't do that." Maddie grabbed his shoulders and shook him.

"Too late. I've done it. It's two years, and when I get out, I'll have the GI Bill." His eyes teared.

"No, no . . ." Maddie wrapped her arms around Richard. He resisted.

"I d-didn't get the recommendation for composition. I wanted it bad," he stammered.

"You wanted it *badly*," she corrected.

He chuckled, but tears welled in his eyes.

"Hold me," she asked. "Come on, hug me back, please hold me." Richard finally put his arms around her. Maddie let the subject drop.

Perhaps proximity had something to do with a change in Maddie. She and Oscar inexplicably, rapturously fell in love. Without the pressure of exams and assignments, and only their work at the library, they had time to revel in their setting. The tiled bathroom was enormous by contemporary standards. The toilet and lavatory were from a long-bygone era. Their favorite fixture was the deep cast iron tub with clawed feet. Their shared nightly baths took over an hour. Richard kept a discrete distance, with the door to his bedroom closed.

By the time the Sunday, August 27 editions of the *San Antonio Light*

newspapers were being stacked on newsstands or thrown on the city's front lawns, Cosimo had departed San Antonio.

Richard knocked on Maddie and Oscar's bedroom door. "Get decent," he yelled, opening the door.

"Look!" He tossed the society pages of the *San Antonio Light* on the bed.

Maddie snatched up the paper. "Oscar, look."

Oscar peered over her shoulder. The headlines on the society page read: "FAMOUS ARTIST MAKES AN UNUSUAL STOP IN S.A.," "Creates Works of Art from Unusual Objects." A photo of Cosimo dressed in his Italian suit stared out at them, proud and defiant. There were two photos of the cabin, and one of Pito and Henny holding their Aesop drawing. A short article interviewed Pito about the cabins and Graciela about the menus.

"You did it. You recognized him," bragged Maddie.

"Well, it was all three of us," protested Oscar.

"Shut up, and take a compliment."

Richard pulled at Oscar's foot. "Let's go see the cabins."

Two groups of curious strangers explored the patio, taking photographs and peeking through the windows of the vibrantly colored cottage. Henny sold soft drinks from a metal tub filled with ice.

Pito saw the three and beckoned. "He left you a letter." He went back to his apartment to retrieve an envelope.

Oscar read the letter. "He made arrangements with Graciela at the Little House Café to feed us until we leave."

Oscar put down the letter. "We hardly did anything."

"Well, it must have felt like a lot to him," said Maddie.

For the next three days, they took their breakfasts and lunches at the Little House Café. Graciela and Emma were thrilled to see them, grinning as if they shared a private joke. When Oscar tried to pay, Emma shook her hand in his face.

"Don't even tip. He paid for this and more."

On Thursday the thirty-first, at 6:00 a.m., Maddie was the first to leave for New York. Oscar and Richard accompanied her to the Greyhound Bus station. In the waiting area, she handed Richard a small leather case.

"It's a World War I compass. It's brass and belonged to my grandfather. I want you to always know where you're going and how you can find me when you get back."

"I'm sorry, I didn't get you anything," said Richard.

She put her finger to his lips and hugged him. She pulled Oscar aside, out of the public's eye, and kissed him.

"I love you," said Oscar.

"You are my first real love," said Maddie, looking into his eyes.

"Do you mean you'll have others?"

"Stop it. You know what I mean."

"You're never coming back to San Antonio, are you?"

"Probably not. No matter what happens at the audition, I'm staying in New York."

"Will we ever see each other again?"

"Come see me in New York. I'll write."

Maddie reached in her purse and held up a journal. "This was my dad's. He never used it, so I thought you should have it. Write. Write to me. Write about me. Write."

On the inside cover she had inscribed, "I will always remember you, Love Maddie." She touched his cheek.

They held one another until she had to board. As the bus pulled out from under the Greyhound station's canopy, Maddie waved goodbye through the window. Richard stood behind Oscar and waved back.

"Well, that was maudlin." Richard said, as they walked away.

"Fuck you," replied Oscar.

"Yeah, I'm going to miss her, too."

Later that morning, Oscar accompanied Richard to the Armory off Alamo Street, where he joined several dozen young men waiting to be transported to Fort Hood for basic training. Richard noted that the Mexican American men gave their sons or brothers an *abrazo* as a goodbye.

"Is that all you're taking?" asked Oscar, pointing at the small bag with Richard's things.

"Yeah, well, it's all I'll need for a while." Richard handed Oscar a slip of paper. "It's my address for the next eight weeks."

"I'll send you mine as soon as I know what it is." They shook hands. "Don't get killed."

"I won't." Richard threw his arms around Oscar, and planted a kiss on his cheek. He stepped back. "It's what the Mexicans guys are doing," he said.

"Yeah, but we don't smooch." Oscar glanced about, wiping his cheek.

Oscar returned to the Victorian house. The rooms echoed hollow without his pals. He gathered up kitchen trash and shoved it into a brown grocery bag. He checked the bedrooms and closets. Richard left a few of his civilian clothes. Oscar decided to leave them; maybe someone could use them. He found a pair of Maddie's panties behind the bathtub. He recalled the exact moment those panties came off, but until that instant he'd forgotten about them. Now, dried and wadded, he tossed them into the grocery bag and carried out the trash. He laughed that the previous evening, when Maddie couldn't find that very pair of panties, she accused him of taking them as a souvenir. At the last moment he reached into the bag and retrieved them.

Carrying a small suitcase, Oscar caught three buses to the end of the line on the Austin Highway. Another quarter of a mile down the road, he found a spot where he could be seen from the roadway and stuck out his thumb.

CHAPTER 51

Paris, September 1961

Cosimo's taxi pulled up to the curb where Charlotte, the concierge, had reserved a spot. He stepped onto the sidewalk. *Rue Delambre* felt vaguely unfamiliar. The newsstand featured headlines about the United States sending forces to Indochina. The flower shop's autumn marigolds filled the air with the sharp aroma of funeral flowers. Spring and summer had passed. He felt deflated standing there without Sara.

Charlotte embraced him and directed the driver to put the luggage on a cart she had brought to the sidewalk. Charlotte pushed the cart into the lobby.

"I'm so sorry about Sara," Charlotte said. "We miss her. Naturally we missed you as well. Such a fine person. A shame." She began loading the luggage into the tiny cage of an elevator.

"I have two trunks coming separately," he said.

"I'll take care of them," replied Charlotte.

"I thought you were leaving us," said Cosimo.

"I was, but the lawyers for the American woman, Margaret, paid your lease and suddenly the owner could keep me."

"You squeeze into the lift with your luggage, and I'll take the stairs."

She gave Cosimo a push, pressed the button for the third floor, and closed the cage door.

Charlotte was waiting for him when the lift stopped. She held out her hand to keep him from tripping on the luggage. "I should be angry with you. The bird has not been friendly. He chews up books. He doesn't eat them, just makes a mess."

"I apologize. I will make good on any damage."

"They were your books," she said, carrying the luggage to his room and handing him a new key.

"I clean the room daily. However, the parrot always leaves surprises."

"This is for you." He handed Charlotte a mailing tube.

"What's this?"

"A souvenir from America. Leave the luggage here. I will take it in myself."

"Thank you. It was kind of you to think of me. I have to warn you. The bird is insane. He sits there morosely and only eats when he's alone. Last month I felt sorry for him and reached out to stroke him. The cursed beast bit me! He's your bird. I am never going near him again. And, welcome back." She kissed his cheek.

Proust hadn't seen Cosimo since February. He began to rock back and forth.

"I am home," he said to Proust.

Proust turned his head so both eyes had a turn to observe him.

"I am alone. Sara . . ."

Proust instantly lifted his head. "Za?" His high pitched voice asked. "Zala?"

"Sara is not coming home. No more Zala. Remember Tito? The blue-green parakeet? You saw him die. We could not save him. That is what happened to Sara. I did not see it. Sara is not coming back. Sara and Tito are dead." More than the words, Cosimo's somber tone got the message across.

"Zala, Tito," Proust repeated. "Tito, Zala."

"Zala, Tito," Cosimo nodded.

"Zala, Zala." Proust lurched up and down, calling Zala over and over. He flew into the windows in attempts to escape. For nearly a half hour the bird landed on shelves and knocked down books and sent framed photographs shattering on the floor. Finally exhausted, Proust landed on the arm of the settee.

No one had wept for Sara, not until Proust demonstrated his grief. No one had shared Cosimo's loss. Sara's lawyers and relatives didn't cry. His Texas friends, as much as they expressed their sympathy, didn't know Sara. Even he had held his sentiments in check.

"I know we should never have gone. It was an enormous, tragic mistake." Cosimo touched Proust's neck and began to weep uncontrollably. He wept until there was nothing left to regret.

The tears drained him. Exhausted, he picked up Proust and returned him to his pedestal. He dragged in his luggage from the hall. He took out the Zodiac watch and placed it on the table next to him. The sun's eyes scanned the room, looking almost surprised, Cosimo thought. He stretched out on the settee.

"Proust?" he asked into the air.

"Como," replied the bird.

"Proust, Como is home. Where do I begin? We will have to plan a memorial. Invite her fans, friends, and collaborators. I have so much to tell you, Proust, all about my time in Ameri–ca." His voice trailed off. He fell asleep.

"Ameri–ca," repeated Proust.

EPILOGUE

In Texas, as Cosimo had predicted, several individuals endeavored to locate and purchase the Aesop drawings. The newspaper article made the hunt for the images comparable to the search for the Holy Grail. No one admitted to selling his or her drawings.

In March 1962, Cosimo, through his attorney Francisco Orozco, notified the recipients of Aesop drawings that a gallery in Venice, Italy, was preparing a show of his prints. The letter stated that their drawings were considered "duplicate masters" used to create the final printing plates. The gallery offered to pay $1,600 per drawing, and suggested that if they didn't sell now, the drawings should not sell to any other party for less.

Not all recipients took advantage of the offer. Who did and who didn't sell remained a secret, since the gallery considered the information proprietary. Meyer, who had made the fine-grain black-and-white negatives of the original drawings, was the sole San Antonian to travel to Venice for the show's opening.

Tall, leggy Margaret Manheim embraced Meyer and introduced him to a gaunt Alberto Giacometti and the magnetic actress Anna Magnani. For several minutes, Meyer would later recall, they spoke about Cosimo's drawings in English and his own role in producing the final prints. He spent five days with Cosimo in Paris, and lunched at *La Coupole* with the designer and artist, Leonor Fini, and her two "husbands," providing Meyer with a lifetime of stories.

Emma Vasquez paid for her son and grandson to accompany her to Paris in the summer of 1962. Manuel ("Manny"), a heavyset man with jowls and thinning hair, had lips that looked as if they were in a permanent pout. His son, eight-year-old Rudy, hardly spoke a word, but his eyes saw everything.

Cosimo took interest in the Kodak Brownie camera Manny carried everywhere. Manny explained the camera settings, and Cosimo took photos of them at the popular tourist sites. He gave them guided tours of Versailles and the Louvre. On a boat ride on the River Seine he showed them where he began his life as an artist.

As a special extravagance for Emma, he took them all shopping and purchased clothing so they could enter any fine Parisian restaurant. Outfitting Emma's son and grandson was easy enough. Interestingly, with Manny's pout and paunch, he could have passed for a bored blueblood.

Emma protested, "My body shape is not Parisian, and my feet are like huge yams."

She might have been right except that after four or five attempts they found one dress, elegant and understated, in gunmetal gray, that fit her perfectly.

She showed Manny the price tag. "What does that mean in dollars?"

He fished a money conversion card out of his breast pocket. "About four hundred dollars," he replied.

"It's too much," she whispered to Cosimo.

"You saved my life. It is my thank you. Ah, here are the shoes."

The shop clerk arrived with six boxes of shoes in her size.

"Apparently, the French recognize that women from the Mediterranean have feet in the shape of yams," he kidded.

Emma smacked him with her new clutch.

The two shop clerks hinted that Emma's hair and makeup might do with a touch, and the shop had the facilities that could do just that.

Emma reluctantly agreed to a session with a hairdresser and makeup artist. Her eyebrows were plucked and shaped, the fuzz on her upper lip was removed with a lotion that stung. She allowed the hairdresser to modestly shape her hair, not cut it drastically. When the results of the hair and makeup sessions were unveiled, her son and grandson stood in admiration.

"Mama, you're beautiful," said Manny.

"Yeah, Grandma, you're beautiful." echoed Rudy.

Cosimo gave Manny and Rudy an art lesson that afternoon. He had them do drawings of Emma while she posed stiffly in her new look. For the afternoon, she allowed herself to become Cosimo's creation. Manny snapped photos of his mom. Privately, when she caught a glimpse of herself in the mirror, she saw her old face staring back from behind a mask.

As much as she enjoyed the generosity and respect Cosimo showed to her family, by the time the days in Paris ended, something nagged at her. His friends, those who spoke English, didn't engage with her and her son beyond, "Where are you from in America?" and "How do you like Paris?"

Preparing to leave, she confessed to Cosimo, "Your friends are artists. My son works at the Kaiser plant in California, and I'm a cook in a diner. We're hicks."

"We are all hicks. Most people simply do not know it," confided Cosimo. "When I arrived in San Antonio, I was the hick. I knew nothing of you or how you lived. I met people living without pretense, only wanting to endure gracefully. Do you think Leonor's two husbands could survive as I did? They would throw themselves into the San Antonio River to drown in less than a meter of water."

She laughed with Cosimo.

"They're very clever. I wouldn't underestimate them. But the dress and the hair, it's not me. I feel like an imitation of the fancy women in the shops. Are you trying to make me into *her*?"

"Sara? No, absolutely not. You are not an imitation of anyone. I want you to be yourself. Consider the clothes and hair the native costume of Paris. The makeup will wash off. Your hair will grow back. You are healthy, funny, and quite comely—not like an ingénue but like a woman."

"Thank you," said Emma, holding back tears.

"Emma, if you do not like the dress, we will take it back."

"No sir," she guffawed. "I'm keeping that dress. If I never wear it again while I'm alive, I damn well want to be buried in it, and the shoes, too."

Cosimo kissed her.

Emma kept a scrapbook of her Paris trip. Whenever Rudy, her grandson, visited from California, he pored over the souvenirs and photos. There were three drawings of Emma. His own eight-year-old attempt, his father's not much better attempt, and Cosimo's, where his grandmother appeared as an elegant mid-century matron. "She was that beautiful; then she became my grandma," observed Rudy.

Cosimo occasionally sent postcards, which she included in the scrapbook. The last entry was the newspaper clipping of Cosimo's passing in 1977, at the age of eighty-six.

On the same page as the obit, there appeared a photo of a blue heron that had stopped the previous morning on the banks of the San Antonio River below the Presa Street Bridge. "Odd Bird," read the caption.

A dozen passers-by gathered on the bridge witnessed the five-foot tall bird step into the water, then freeze for a full minute. The heron's long neck flashed like a whip. The bird lifted its head from the water with a six-inch yellow perch in its long beak. With a flip of the head the fish slipped down its narrow throat. The heron caught a second perch, then returned to the bank, and for the next half-hour preened its gray-blue feathers.

With three beats of its powerful wings it became airborne. Flapping a few feet above the water, it followed the curve in the canal, flew over the next bridge, and rose above the cypress trees. It circled, regained its bearings, and continued its journey.

ACKNOWLEDGMENTS

I completed the first draft of *Odd Birds* while I was Writer-in-Residence at Texas State University, San Marcos, in the fall 2015. Dr. Jesús Frank de la Teja, director of the Center for the Study of the Southwest, provided me with a cabin in the woods, exquisite solitude, and white-tailed deer as neighbors.

Most of this book is a product of my imagination. Several of the secondary characters are based on an actual Surrealist circle of friends in Paris. The fictional characters of Cosimo and Sara are placed in that milieu. None of the events described took place.

The character of Mayor Morris Forester is fictional and does not represent either of the real San Antonio mayors, J. Edwin Kuykendall or Walter W. McAllister, whose terms bridged the period of the story. Eula Forester and Ruthann Medlin certainly never existed. Their opinions and attitudes were of the time.

Salvador Dali designed extraordinary jewelry and watches; however, the time piece described in this book is an invention.

There was an authentic Little House Café in San Antonio. Its proprietor was a charming woman named Gracie. I have appropriated her name and the café as an homage to the many fine meals that I and friends enjoyed there. The Little House made the best flour tortillas outside of my mother's kitchen. The back lives of the sisters, Graciela and Emma Vasquez, are complete fabrications. As far as I know, no artist ever made ink drawings of Aesop's fables at the café.

I have taken liberties with San Antonio history and some of the locales. The integration of the public library did not take place as depicted. I chose San Antonio as the setting because, half a century ago, I knew the city well. The story could have taken place in any city where there is a river walk, five military bases, and a war memorial in the center of town. Any resemblance to any person living or dead is coincidental.

I am profoundly grateful for the loving support and encouragement of my wife, Judith Schiffer Perez, who edited far too many drafts of the manuscript. I am indebted for the thoughtful notes from Steve Davis, Dan Bessie, Carlos Rene Perez, Adrienne Mayor, Jeanne Joe, Eleanor Burian-Mohr, Terry Shtob, Jennifer Turvey, and Carol Annette Perez. I gave every comment considerable reflection.